Lucky Secrets

by

B.T. Polcari

A Mauzzy & Me Mystery

Cover Art by *Lea Schizas*

The Wild Rose Press, Inc.
PO Box 708
Adams Basin, NY 14410-0708
Visit us at www.thewildrosepress.com

Publishing History
First Edition, 2025
Trade Paperback ISBN 978-1-5092-6142-0
Digital ISBN 978-1-5092-6143-7

A Mauzzy & Me Mystery
Published in the United States of America

Dedication

To my mother, Ida Lou Polcari. A force of nature who believed she could do anything. And then she went and did it. Repeatedly. I love you, Mom.

Author's Note

Since *Lucky Secrets* is all about solving puzzles and riddles, for readers interested in solving a special little puzzle, I have embedded a code key in the book that reveals a message from me to you, pulled from the first two books in the series: *Against My Better Judgment* and *Fire and Ice*. Once you finish reading *Lucky Secrets*, you will have all you need to discover the message. This is your first clue. Your second and final clue is: There are *eleven* prime numbers between one and *thirty-one*, but there are forty-six chapters in the book. Feel free to email me any requests for additional clues at bt@btpolcari.com.

Good luck and enjoy the book.

Main Cast of Characters

The Contestants

Karsh Azarian, financial asset manager and billion-dollar hedge fund manager

Jessica Doerr, mortgage lender specializing in refinancing services for seniors

Sara Donovan, University of Alabama business major and recognized amateur sleuth

Jimmy Dougal, real estate agent specializing in high-end luxury properties

Olivia Fantucci, attorney specializing in large class-action and personal injury lawsuits

Spencer Fernsby, founder/CEO of the telecom giant, CLATEL Communications

Burl "Scooter" Jablonsky, owner of five car dealerships, including two luxury franchises

Rodney "Rod" Toft, cryptocurrency exchange investor and technology venture capitalist

Frederick Volkov, highly successful financier, stock trader, and arbitrageur

Sara's Circle

Mauzzy, a miniature red dachshund, Sara's roommate, and her trusty (?) sidekick

Zoe Harp, Sara's best friend going back to the seventh grade

Matt Donovan, Sara's brilliant younger mathematician brother and only sibling

Sadie Majelski, Sara's mysterious octogenarian friend, part-time bouncer at Sunny Time's Stein Room, and supposedly linked to shadowy international syndicates and intelligence agencies

Melvin "Finn" Finnegan, former cop, proprietor of Finnegan & Associates, and Sara's boss

Bertram, aka "Bertie," Finn's loyal longhaired dapple dachshund

Having all the luck is not always a good thing.

Chapter One

The package

I recently overheard my golf-crazy dad go on and on about some of his golfing buddies insisting on taking something he disparagingly called a "mulligan" when they hit a crappy shot. Dad complained that allowing mulligans removed consequences for poor performance and decisions and hurt the integrity of the game. At the time, he seemed to make a good point, although I was only half listening. Why they call it a mulligan I haven't a clue other than it sounds better than admitting you're cheating. To me, it sounds delusional. It's a do-over. Plain and simple. Kinda like that big red button with the word "RESET" emblazoned in big white letters across its middle.

But today, as I considered the consequences of my latest questionable decisions, I could really use a mulligan. Or a reset button. Anything to reverse course before I end up...I can't even say it. Let's just say, the least of my fast-growing concerns is graduating. Breathing has jumped to the top of the very long list.

My name is Sara Donovan. I'm a third-year business student at the University of Alabama who, before my current situation, was hoping, more like praying, to graduate early this May to save my penny-pinching dad a year of out-of-state tuition.

Unfortunately for me, at the eleventh hour, the Universe decided to poke her skanky nose into my business to apparently force a life lesson down my throat. Yeah, she's given up on trying to teach me. This latest attempt is something about "things are never what they seem."

Fingers crossed I don't choke on it.

****

"And that was pretty much the week," I said with a sigh.

I was lounging on a couch in my crappy off-campus one-room cottage in an area of Tuscaloosa I called Sketchville. Because the place was—sketch. The last five minutes encompassed me giving my forever best friend, Zoe, a scintillating review of my just-completed spring break back home in Annapolis.

"Sara Donovan, that has got to be the most pitiful spring break ever," Zoe said from the floor beside her boyfriend, Matt, their feet up on the scarred coffee table. "Even for you."

Matt, a freshman at 'Bama but practically a junior with all his advanced-placement and dual-enrollment credits, was my only sibling. He ended up living with me because he made a last-minute decision to enroll and all the university housing was filled. Dad called it a knee-jerk reaction when Matt walked away from a full math scholarship at a prestigious New England university to attend school here. Just to be with Zoe. Although 'Bama was ecstatic to have him and pulled out all the stops to make him happy, including matching his full scholarship, they couldn't free up any campus housing. And even though Dad loved Zoe like a daughter, he made it crystal clear he wasn't springing for off-campus housing after Matt walked away from

2

the "opportunity of a lifetime" to be with her. So, he's been sleeping on my ratty couch. Not exactly how I envisioned my last year at 'Bama. But he was my brother.

"Glad I stuck around here for that conference on algebraic geometry," Matt said. "Sounds like I had a lot more fun than you, Sara."

Zoe groaned. "Only to a brainiac."

"Yeah, Mom wasn't happy about it," I said. "She missed her—"

A series of knocks on the front door about busted the thing down. Granted, my cottage was not the most sturdily-built structure, although it had a very cool loft. Okay, the place was barely a step up from cardboard, but still, whoever was at the door clearly had an overinflated ego. Or a misplaced sense of authority. Or…authority? The authorities?

Crap.

Cops.

Bang. Bang. *Bang.*

Mauzzy, my adorable yet occasionally vindictive and always devious miniature red dachshund, leaped from his dark-purple child's recliner and scurried to the door. He placed his front paws up on the door and let loose a torrent of ferocious warnings. At least, they were ferocious to him. To the obnoxious cop on the other side of the door, doubtful.

"You gonna get that or wait for it to fall in?" Zoe asked.

I stood but made no move toward the door. "What if it's, you know, the cops?"

In a flash, Zoe's petite wiry body bounced in front of me like she was on a pogo stick, normally stunning green eyes giving me the business. I never understood how eyes so mesmerizing could instantly turn into lethal weapons of scorn and fury. Or worse. Even the emerald-green streaks in her tousled black hair glowed with disapproval. "The *cops?* What'd you *really* do last week in Annapolis?"

"Nothing. Honest. Like I said, hung out with—"

Bang. Bang. Bang.

Mauzzy's barking went a pitch higher and shifted into double-time.

A male voice called out from beyond the accosted door and over the frantic warnings of my in-house security. "Hello? Sara Donovan? I can hear you in there. Hello?"

Of course the dude can hear me. My cottage is barely waterproof, let alone soundproof.

I stepped to the door, hushed Mauzzy, pushed aside purple fabric tacked over a narrow side window, and peeked out. On the front deck stood a bearded man wearing a dark-blue jacket with an orange-and-yellow logo and matching ballcap. Could be a delivery guy, although I hadn't ordered anything in weeks. He studied a clipboard, a thin shipping box tucked under an arm.

"Can I help you?" I shouted.

He angled his head toward the side window. "You Sara Donovan?"

I eyed him. He seemed legit. Especially for this neighborhood. Nobody trying to break in around here would be dumb enough to use a courier uniform as their cover because couriers rarely ventured into Sketchville. Without a partner. Unarmed.

"I am."

"Need to see some ID."

"Why? You a cop?"

The unfazed man held up the box. "Need you to sign for this."

"I didn't order anything."

The courier leaned back to check the house number, then the box, and shrugged. "Got the right address." He tapped a shipping document on the box. "And says here this is for Sara Donovan. So…"

He held out the box for me to see. It had my name and address but I didn't recognize the shipper, Creighton Winston PLC.

"Hang on," I said, digging my driver's license out from my purse on the foyer table and slapping it up against the window.

The courier peered at the driver's license, then at me, then at the license, then back at me. "Might could be you."

"It's me."

"Not the best picture, huh?"

I winced. "That was four years ago."

He threw me a not-buying-it face, but held up the package again and gave it a little wiggle.

I cracked open the door, making sure to block an agitated but silent Mauzzy from slipping past.

"And I had just finished my road test," I added, for some reason feeling the need to defend my indefensible God-awful photo. I really wanted to explain that the sadistic examiner ended the test with parallel parking and I was driving Mom's SUV, but clearly, my jury already reached its verdict.

"Sure." The courier stuck the box and a pen through the narrow opening. "Sign at the bottom.

Original is for me."

I grabbed the box, signed, snapped off the bill of lading's top page, and passed it and the pen back to the courier.

He took both, added the paper to a stack on the clipboard, and smiled. "Thanks. Have a nice day."

"You, too," I said, closing the door.

I returned to the couch, followed closely by a very interested Mauzzy and Zoe. Matt remained on the floor but was now sitting, fully attentive. I tore back a tab to open the box and pulled out an ivory-colored letter envelope with my name in gold-embossed lettering, a regular-sized manila envelope, the kind with a metal clasp, and a ring-sized red-velveted jewelry box. I placed the three items on the weathered coffee table and dropped the shipping box to the floor.

Zoe leaned over Mauzzy, who was burrowed between us on the couch, and reached for the jewelry box. "What'd Grant do, send you a marriage proposal via courier? That'd fit the jerk."

I snapped it away from her outstretched hand. "Of course not. And he's not a jerk."

"Says you," Zoe replied.

I gave her an exaggerated smile before examining the letter envelope. It was sealed and had no other markings on it besides my name in fancy lettering. The manila envelope was unclasped but sealed. On the front, *For Sara Donovan's Eyes Only* was printed in bold red on a plain white label.

Matt scooched up to the table, peering at the contents of the box. "Who sent you the package?"

I picked up the box and read the bill of lading. "Creighton Winston PLC."

"PLC?" Zoe asked.

"A limited-liability company owned and operated by people of the same profession," Matt replied. "Lawyers, accountants, doctors, something like that."

A tingling erupted in my chest and shot out toward my arms and legs, my stomach going into a freefall. "Lawyers?"

"That's my bet," Matt said.

Mauzzy whined, jumped off the couch, and in three quick steps launched up onto the child recliner. He spun and contemplated me, his disappointment palpable. Seconds passed before he let out one judgmental yip, then laid his head on the recliner's arm and sighed. The little fella knew what was coming. He's been through this impending disaster a few times.

Zoe pulled back with arms crossed, her eyes searching mine. "Now, why would lawyers be chasing after you?"

I swallowed. "How the heck should I know?"

"Yeah, this is fast shaping up to be another Sara Donovan"—Zoe motioned with air quotes—"situation."

My head dropped. Eyes closed. An all-too-familiar feeling crawling up my spine.

"One way to find out," Matt said.

I opened my eyes. The bill of lading stared back at me. "Hey, this says the package is insured."

"If it's insured, the sender definitely knows Sara Donovan," Zoe said with a chuckle.

"Ha, ha. Very funny," I said.

"How much?" Matt asked.

I glanced down at the document, then back up. "Fifty thousand dollars."

"What?" Zoe exclaimed. "Fifty G's?"

I handed her the box. "See for yourself."

Zoe read the bill of lading and tossed the box to the floor. "C'mon, open it all up. I say it's in the jewelry box."

I picked up the letter envelope, flipped it over, and examined it closely.

"What are you waiting for?" Zoe cried. "Tear it open."

With my eyes trained on the envelope, I said, "Just making sure it's not a bomb."

Mauzzy flipped around, his butt facing us, and buried his head into the corner of the recliner's cushion. A muffled tortured whine floated through the air.

Zoe groaned. "*Bomb?* Who'd wanna bomb you?"

"Can't be too careful," I said. "Dad says complacency will get you killed."

"Yeah, and he also says you're your own worst enemy," Zoe countered.

Zoe spent last summer interning at the NSA where Dad works, meaning they had plenty of time carpooling to chat. About me. And my—tendencies.

I closed an eye and flinched as my finger tore open the envelope. With an exhale, I extracted two pieces of paper.

"Hey, we're all in one piece," Zoe cheered.

Ignoring the sarcastic sprite, I read the first page. It was on letterhead embossed with Creighton Winston PLC and a Birmingham address in the same fancy gold lettering as on the envelope.

Dear Miss Donovan,

Congratulations. You have been selected to participate in a very special two-week contest that could drastically change your life for the better. An orientation meeting shall be held in two days on 14 March at two o'clock in the afternoon. Should you choose to participate, attendance at this meeting is mandatory. You are to bring both envelopes with you. Since winning the contest shall require an extraordinary level of resourcefulness and acumen, you are allowed to bring one associate to the meeting. Once designated as your associate, this is the only person who may assist you during the contest. Upon conclusion of the meeting, should your associate choose not to participate, no replacement shall be allowed. Moreover, should for any reason *during the contest your associate is no longer able to or decides to no longer participate, there shall be no replacement. Prior to this meeting, you and your associate, if any, must sign non-disclosure agreements (NDAs) at the above office, after which you shall be given the address of the meeting. As a gesture of good faith, the item in the jewelry box is yours to keep, regardless if you decide to participate. A certificate of grading and authentication is attached for your records.*

Best regards,

Creighton P. Winston, Esquire

I let the letter drop to the couch and scanned the certificate. "I…um…This says…" My throat went dry as a buzzing filled my head. "I've been…"

"You okay?" Zoe asked. "Speechless isn't your thing."

"I've been invited to some big contest, and they gave me a three-carat diamond as a gesture of good faith. This says it's worth fifty-thousand." The certificate slipped from my hand and floated to the couch. "Why does it have to be another diamond?"

9

Zoe's eyes widened. "And that's a bad thing, how?"

"You know why. That Star of Midnight created some big problems for me last summer."

Zoe snatched the papers off the couch. "Yeah, but it all ended well." She glanced down. "Holy crap. Is this legit?"

I shrugged. "It says I can keep the diamond regardless."

Zoe put up a cautionary finger while handing the papers to Matt. "*If* it's a real diamond."

My brother read through both pages twice before setting them on the coffee table and going on his phone. "There's a website for Creighton Winston PLC and it has a pic of a building with matching signage. Appears to be a real firm. Same with the grading institute on the certificate."

Zoe popped off the couch, her arms flying straight up. "Who gives away an expensive diamond? This thing reeks."

A pensive look crossed Matt's face. "Somebody who *really* wants my sister in their contest."

My freefalling stomach hit rock bottom and began churning out acid as the perspiration machine cranked up. "Like…who?"

"I'd start with someone who has money," Matt said.

"The only people I know who have serious money are…you two," I said, the last words trailing off.

"What money?" Zoe growled. "That reward money from the museum is locked away in trusts until we're twenty-five." She pointed an accusing finger at me. "Thanks to your brilliant suggestion."

Last summer, Zoe, Matt, and I solved a mystery that resulted in an unexpected financial windfall for the Carlton Museum. The Board of Directors were so grateful, they paid each of us a five-hundred-thousand-dollar reward with the proviso that the reward money not be publicized.

"We all agreed it was a good idea," I fired back. "You'll thank me later when—"

Matt stuck a hand out like a traffic cop. "Stop. Let's focus on the current matter." He turned to me. "Open the jewelry box."

I shot Zoe one last look, then picked up the red box and flipped open the lid. Inside, a single loose diamond flashed a kaleidoscope of brilliant colors as the light bounced off it. "It's beautiful," I breathed.

Zoe bent down and examined the sparkling stone, sucking in a breath. "Sure looks like the real deal."

"Whoa," Matt uttered, his eyes fixed on the box.

"Sara, what're you gonna do?" Zoe asked, the concern in her voice doubling as an apology for our last exchange. We could never stay mad at each other for longer than a hot minute.

What *was* I going to do? Out of the blue, someone sends me a fifty-thousand-dollar diamond to keep and invites me to a contest that could drastically change my life for the good? Dad was always saying if something sounded too good to be true, it usually was. And this certainly sounded too good to be true. It could be a trap, luring me to what, I didn't know. But a trap nonetheless. My eye caught the refracted light from the diamond. It was alive. Shimmering. Fiery. Real.

I breathed in deeply and exhaled slowly. In that moment of serenity, I made a snap decision. Even though my snap decisions rarely ended well, the diamond was speaking to me. And I liked what it was saying.

I closed my eyes, envisioned the firing squad bringing its guns to bear on me, and looked up at Zoe. "I'm going to do it." A beat. "And I want you to come with me."

Zoe exploded. "What? Are you out of your *effing* mind?"

Despite the heat searing my chest, I remained calm. "I need to see this through. You with me?"

"No. Fricking. Way."

"Zo, if we win, our lives will be changed forever."

"Uh-uh. There's no 'we,' sister," Zoe insisted. "I like my life just fine as it is. You're on your own."

"C'mon, we're a team. Since seventh grade."

Although Zoe was a Tuscaloosa local, her family moved to Annapolis for five years when she was in the seventh grade, which was where we met. We've been the best of friends ever since, despite being complete opposites. I was just under six feet tall. She was barely five feet. I had long dirty-blonde hair. Hers was black, above the shoulder, and constantly sporting streaks of ever-changing colors. I avoided confrontation like the plague, always polite, and considerate of people and their feelings. Calling Zoe feisty didn't do the pixie justice, and she didn't care whose grill she got up into or who she pissed off. Like I said. Opposites.

Zoe held my gaze, let out a huff, and appealed to Matt. "What do you think?"

He screwed up his pale narrow face. "I think you should go. At least see what's said during the meeting."

I stuck a finger out at Zoe. "If you agree to go, you

can't bail on me later. Remember the rule. No replacements are allowed."

She put her hands on her hips and stuck her head out. "You sure have a way of winning people over."

"You in?" I asked.

Zoe blew out. "I'm gonna regret it later, but yeah, I'm in." She pointed to the manila envelope on the couch. "What's in that?"

I picked it up, tore open the top, and slid out a stack of eight-by-ten photographs. The top photo knocked the wind out of me, shoulders sagging, head throbbing. My chest tightened, a knot forming deep within, making breathing difficult. A chill unlike any other spread from the pit of my stomach until it consumed me.

"Sara, you okay?" Zoe asked.

I shook my head and tapped the top photo. "This is…This is me. From…a couple years ago." I paused in a futile attempt to gather myself. "In my car. In a— church parking lot."

Zoe's eyes bugged out. "You mean when you ditched that tummy-tightener thing?"

I briefly closed my eyes and nodded. "When I went commando to that charity auction at the Dauphin."

Zoe sat next to me and stared at the photo. "Holy sh…"

With great effort, I placed the horrific pic on the couch, my gaze settling on the next in the stack. It was also of me, crouching behind a rack of clothes, talking into my phone. I recognized it immediately. I was on a surveillance op.

At Flossie's Fashions.

In Tuscaloosa.

I was terrified to continue going through the photos, but I pressed on. The third was a night shot, although it appeared like day with all the blinding spotlights on me. In handcuffs. Being led to an Alabama state police cruiser. The fourth was of me in front of a museum display case full of diamonds and rubies. To be specific, in the Gem and Minerals Hall of the Carlton Museum. Staring at the Star of Midnight. In the fifth, I was walking Mauzzy alongside a creek. Piney Branch Creek. In Washington, D.C.

My mouth fell open when I got to the sixth. Staring back at me was an open laptop on my desk in Annapolis. In the background, Mauzzy lay on my bed gorging himself on dog treats. The seventh, Matt and Zoe were pushing through the doors of an immense hall with a gleaming white floor, on their way outside to a parking lot. With a book stuffed down the back of each of their shorts. From Arcadia.

These were photos cataloging the last two years of my life. During challenging times. When I was dealing with—situations—Life had thrown at me, in cahoots with the Universe.

I gave Zoe a sideways look. It was the first time she'd ever appeared stunned. She took the photo and held it up for Matt to see, whose face went from natural pale to ashen.

"Zo?" he croaked.

She returned his plea with a slight headshake. "Dunno."

The last two photos were nothing like the first seven. As I pored over them, my body pressed into the couch, an absolute surreal heaviness weighing me down. Time slowed as synapses fired like a never-ending string of firecrackers. I had no idea where or when these pics were taken, but the implication was chilling. One was of a safe-deposit box signature card, with my signature on it, and several dates when I accessed box seventy-seven. The "date rented" was during my second semester at 'Bama. The final photo was of the box with it opened. Inside it were several cut and uncut emeralds, a gold bar, and—an ancient Egyptian gold funerary mask.

At the bottom of the nine photos was a typed note on plain white paper. As I read it, the influx of competing emotions was unlike anything I've ever experienced. Anxiety. Fear. Terror. Anger. And, resolve.

As you can see, my dear, I have been watching you. Closely. For some time, now. And my goodness, you have quite an interesting safe-deposit box. I strongly recommend you participate in my little contest. This is just a taste of what I can do.

Speak of this to no one.

Or else.

Chapter Two

Mrs. Majelski?

I showed the note to Zoe and Matt. "Already showed you the pics, so might as well show you the note, too. Just keep this to yourselves."

"Like, who am I gonna tell?" Zoe said.

"Still," I replied. "We don't know who this person is, so until we do, it stays with us."

Zoe picked up the note, studied it, then jumped up and spun to face me. "I know exactly who the eff this is."

I crossed my arms and leaned back. "Who?"

"You're not gonna like it."

"Try me."

Zoe exchanged a glance with Matt, then focused on me, her gaze unwavering. I was sitting, and she was standing, yet we were practically at eye level. "Mrs. Majelski."

The mysterious octogenarian's name being thrown out caught me off guard. Although I guess I should have expected it from Zoe. She never trusted the enigmatic white-haired geriatric. We met at the gym in Tuscaloosa a few years back and ever since...she's been watching out for me. Could she be behind this? I pushed the absurd thought out of my head. It was something I couldn't fathom. Just, no way. In fact, she always seemed to show up when I needed help, even though each time, I didn't realize it in the moment. But, somehow, she knew. And she helped. She was never antagonistic or threatening to me, like the note with the photos. Never. Not once.

I shook my head. "Impossible. That sweet old lady has been getting me out of trouble, not creating it."

"That's what she wants you to think," Zoe said, her tone hard. "Think about it. Ever since you arrived in Tuscaloosa, every time things went sideways in your life, who popped up?" She eyed me. "Majelski."

I stood and pushed past Zoe, only stopping at the door to peer out the side window. No activity in the parking lot. Nobody crouching behind the front deck. Nothing. All quiet in Sketchville. For now.

I turned but stayed by the door. "You're wrong. You're just wrong. Grant even said I was the granddaughter she never had. He recommended her to the FBI as a possible consultant."

Grant was an up-and-coming agent for Homeland Security. We met a couple of years ago in Tuscaloosa when he was working on a case and ever since have been trying to figure out if "we" were something worth pursuing.

Zoe's eyes bugged out. "*Grant?* I thought you ended it. You know I don't trust him."

"I'm well aware."

Zoe let out a little sardonic laugh. "You still believe that BS he told you about Majelski? Sara, consider the source."

"You're wrong about him, too."

"Don't believe me. Look at the evidence. Other than those last two photos, all the others were taken of you either here or in D.C. or Annapolis. Only two people I know of, other than me, have been around you both here and up there during the time those photographs were taken. Grant. And Majelski."

I crossed the room, in four steps, and sat in a folding chair at the card table doubling as my kitchen table and crafting workspace. Three feet away from the table stretched my crappy galley kitchen with crooked cabinet doors, dripping faucet, and partially-burned dishtowels. Plus, three fire extinguishers, two of which were fully extinguished and therefore useless.

Reluctantly, I had to admit, Zoe had a point. Over the past two years, only Grant and Mrs. Majelski were with me both in Tuscaloosa and the D.C. area. In fact, she even showed up in North Carolina when we went to investigate at Arcadia. Was it possible?

Zoe pulled me out of my thoughts. "I warned you back in Annapolis they were working together. That they were hiding something. Remember? It all fits."

"I remember."

"Hey, I just noticed something." She shot around the coffee table and shoved the note in my face. "Read it again. Carefully."

I took the note and read it. Nothing jumped out at me so I went back and took it word by word. And then I saw it. A single word. Innocuous by itself. But it might as well have been a picture of Mrs. Sadie Majelski.

"See it?" Zoe asked.

"Dear," I said quietly.

Zoe beamed, triumph splashed across her face. "Believe me now?"

Mrs. Majelski referred to everybody as "dear," and the word punctuated her speech. She seemed to use it reflexively, like most people used the word "um." In fact, I never met anybody who came close to her use of the word. And now it stared at me from a note with an implicit threat directed at me. This was spiraling out of control.

I pushed up from the chair, careful not to collapse the table. "I need to talk with Finn."

"About what?" Zoe asked.

"To get his take on what's going on."

Matt spoke up. "Sara, is that a good idea? You just said we were keeping this thing to ourselves."

"I trust him. And I won't tell him about the photos or note. I just wanna get his thoughts on this supposed contest."

Zoe followed me to the door. "Yeah, your judgment of people is questionable. In fact, it sucks. I'm going with you."

I took a look outside, then faced Zoe. "Not sure that's such a good idea. He's—different."

"I don't give a crap." She pointed to the couch. "There are shots of Matt and me in that stack of glossies. I'm going."

"I'm not going to show him any of those."

"Don't care."

I scrunched my face up. "I really don't think—"

She stuck a finger out at me. "Who turned you onto this Finn guy? Told you he was 'looking for somebody just like you,' I believe were her words?"

I thought back to August when, after two years of unofficially taking down perps and making a name for myself with law enforcement, for the most part, a relatively decent one, I decided to be a private investigator when I graduated. After that momentous decision, I was realistic and recognized that to make it in the rough-and-tumble PI world after graduation, I needed to learn real investigative techniques from a seasoned professional. With that goal in mind, I asked Mrs. Majelski if she had any recommendations. After all, she seemed plugged into all things law enforcement. Seemed like a good idea at the time. She mentioned this ex-cop Finn Finnegan was looking for an office/research assistant. I checked online, found a job posting by Finnegan and Associates, and applied. Ten minutes later, I received a notification of a job offer. No interview required. I jumped at the chance. Turns out, I was the only applicant. My predecessor lasted one month.

I pressed my lips tight. "Mrs. Majelski."

"Exactly," Zoe said. "And now you think this is a good idea to take this thing to him?"

I threw my hands up. "Who else can I go to?"

"Certainly not Grant," she huffed.

"I don't know about 'certainly'—"

"Trust me—*certainly*. He's a fed. Enough said."

"Well, Finn has given me no reason not to trust him."

"What a relief," Zoe shot back.

"I'm talking with him tomorrow at work."

"And I'm gonna be there when you do. Besides, I wanna finally meet the dude whose wife cleaned him out and took off with her hairdresser."

Chapter Three

The illustrious Melvin "Finn" Finnegan

Across the cramped office on a neglected barren wall of the private investigation firm, Finnegan and Associates, hung an old round clock with a white face and black hands, the time showing one o'clock. I had only been there one hour and was again questioning why I applied for this job last semester, which seemed like eons ago but was really only seven months, five days, and one hour.

Not that I was counting.

I spent the first two hours of every workday by myself while Finn was off with Bertie drinking his lunch, presumably trying to forget his ex-wife. On my first day way back on the fifth of August, I enthusiastically reported to work. I was stoked, ready to assist the unrenowned yet Majelski-recommended, and sorta sober, Melvin "Finn" Finnegan, with taking down perps, crooks, and degenerates. Instead, I spent that day and most of the last seven months digging up dirt on two-timing husbands, boyfriends, and insurance fraudsters, and tracking down the last location on the Internet for delinquent debtors and the occasional bond jumper. Truth be told, the only time I spent out of the office was walking from my car to the dang building and then back again for the trip home to Sketchville.

But working the streets on a high-profile case? Any case?

Not a chance.

A typical weekday for me consisted of business and criminology classes in the morning, then grabbing a quick lunch of fifty-cent noodles and a cola before jumping in my traumatized hatchback more the color of gray primer than its original black and flying up I-59 to one of the more questionable areas of Birmingham for a scintillating five hours as a part-time receptionist and researcher for Finn. And if that wasn't enough to light up my life each and every fricking day, my drive home was a daily battle-royale with crazed Birmingham commuters reminding this soon-to-be college graduate, *hopefully*, that I was no match for their unparalleled skill at breaking every traffic law in the book while exhibiting quite the fluency in sign language.

The office door burst open and in strode Finn, an athletically-built ruggedly good-looking man a couple of inches taller than me, putting him at six-foot-two. He wore sagging jeans, scuffed black cowboy boots, and a tucked-in red plaid shirt, a portion of which peeked out from a good-sized hole just above a rear pocket. Graying brown hair was pulled back tight in a ponytail and scruffy sideburns wandered down to his jawline. A goatee that cropped up once every two or three weeks when he decided to shave was lost today in a scraggly salt-and-pepper beard. Bertie, a cute longhaired dapple dachshund with one blue and one brown eye, dutifully trailed behind him.

"What are you doing back so early?" I asked.

"Your text said you wanted to chat. Cut it short, just for you," Finn grumbled as he nimbly dodged the front corner of my desk and moved behind a way-too-close desk that faced the door and sat perpendicular to mine. He dropped his wide frame into a desk chair that habitually tilted to the right, sending the thing rocking so hard he startled and grabbed the desk's edge before it could dump him backward. Bertie padded behind the desk and took his customary nap spot in a gray, fluffy bed at Finn's feet. "Only a two-beer lunch. Any calls."

Every day when Finn returned from his two-hour lunch at Frenchie's Bar and Grille, that was always the first question. And for the past seven months, my answer never changed. "No, sir. All quiet."

"Dadgum it."

"Well, I appreciate you cutting lunch short."

"Hmm," he grunted. "What's on your mind?"

"I need to wait until my friend, Zoe, gets here. Said she wanted to meet you."

"Yeah?" He whipped around and reached for a near-depleted bottle of bourbon sitting next to a half-full bottle of whiskey on a battered filing cabinet. With hand mid-air, he paused before spinning back to face me. The bottle and its companion remained on the cabinet. Untouched. For now. "She cute?"

"Finn, she's my age. So gross. And very."

He flashed a crooked grin with his hands up, palms out. "Just curious."

The intercom on my desk buzzed. I held down the button and spoke into the box. "Finnegan and Associates. Can I help you?"

"Hey, skank," came Zoe's voice from the box. "Let me in."

I shot Finn a pained look, who replied with an indifferent shrug. "The door buzzer is broken. I'll be right down."

"Well, make it quick. This area is worse than where you live."

As I came from around the desk, Finn apparently reconsidered his earlier decision because he grabbed the bourbon, poured a quick drink in a filthy glass tumbler, and knocked it back in one gulp. "Aaahhh." He slammed the glass down on the desk. "Go fetch your cute friend."

"Behave. And be nice."

"Of course. I'm nice to everyone."

"Yeah. Right."

"You don't count. You're my employee." A beat. "For now." He finished with a sly smile.

I thought about flicking the bird, but instead gave him a sickeningly sweet smile and headed for the door. Exiting the office, I carefully descended four flights of stairs, avoiding all handrails, to a grimy lobby with cracked green linoleum flooring and walls straight from a seedy public bathroom, phone numbers offering all kinds of disgusting things scrawled all over the place. Despite the increased risk of a fall, I refused to use the handrails because I didn't carry enough hand sanitizer to offset whatever was breeding on them. To top it off, the lobby smelled like a high school gym right after a boys' PE class. Not the most professional first impression for potential clients. Right in Zoe's wheelhouse, and I'm sure I'll hear about it.

Outside the front door's cracked glass, Zoe stood in a vestibule that held eight brass mailboxes, a black intercom button beneath each. With her back to the inner door, full attention focused on the jungle outside, she didn't notice me.

I tugged the door open and stuck my head out. "Hey. Zo."

Zoe startled, then spun toward me. "Damn, you scared the living hell outta me. Who in their right mind would venture *here* to see a dude who lost his wife to her hairdresser?"

"You'd be surprised." I fully opened the door and stepped back, motioning for her to enter. "Finn's waiting upstairs."

She entered and wrinkled her cute little nose. "What's that smell?"

I closed the door and let out a short laugh. "Who knows. With this building, it could be anything."

Zoe looked around the lobby as she stepped over to the elevators before turning to face me. "Is this guy really that good, because"—another glance around—"it sure doesn't appear like he's raking it in."

"Don't let the place fool you. He's the best. And not just because Mrs. Majelski said so."

"Majelski," Zoe spat. "You're not helping the dude's case." She sniffed. "Neither is this building."

I walked past her to the door leading to the stairs. "Yeah, those elevators don't work."

"What a surprise."

We made the climb to the fifth floor. At the summit, I was huffing and puffing. Zoe wasn't close to being out of breath.

"Why…Why aren't…you breathing hard?" I asked. "We just…climbed four flights."

She smiled mischievously. "I run. Daily. You don't."

I clasped my hands behind my head and sucked in deep. "Gonna start soon."

She chuckled. "Girl, who you think you're talking to? Running is so not your jam. Bend over and put your hands on your knees."

"What?"

"You'll recover faster. Go on. Hands on knees."

I did as she said and took a deep breath. Angling my head up at her, I said, "Hey, you're right. I can breathe easier."

"If you'd taken more than a quarter of PE back in high school, you'd know what to do."

I straightened and opened the door to the fifth floor. "If I'd done that, I wouldn't be alive today."

"Valid point."

Zoe followed me down the short corridor with buzzing half-lit fluorescent bulbs. I stopped in front of a door with a frosted window, *Finnegan and Associates* stenciled in black on the glass. "Just like the lobby, don't be thrown by Finn's appearance. Or demeanor. He really is the best."

Zoe's eyes widened. "It just keeps getting better and better."

"Trust me, he's the right one to talk to about all this," I said, opening the door and entering the office. I scooped up the gold-embossed envelope and jewelry box off my desk, extending an arm toward Finn's desk. "Zoe, this is Melvin Finnegan."

I couldn't help myself. He absolutely despised his first name. Blamed his mother for it. So, every chance I got, I poked the bear. With glee.

Finn stood and came out from behind his dented metal desk with chipped chrome legs. With a rare warm smile, he extended a hand toward Zoe, who was taking in the crappy office. "Hey, there. Folks just call me

Finn." He shot me a disparaging look.

She took his hand and shook it in one confident motion. "Zoe Harp."

"Pull up a chair," he said, gesturing toward two blue plastic chairs in front of the desk.

Zoe and I each took a seat.

Finn returned to the wobbly chair and folded his meaty hands on the desk. "Have any trouble finding the place?"

Zoe shook her head. "Just parking."

He raised a cautioning hand. "Hey, hey, just so you know, we don't validate."

She gave him a sideways look.

"He's joking," I said dryly.

"I was going to say," she said. "Like, the building has no parking to validate."

Finn laughed hard. "Right?"

An uneasy smile crossed Zoe's face. "Um, right. Hey, can I ask a question?"

"Sure," Finn replied. "Fire away."

She glanced around the room. "There are only two desks in here. And I know one is Sara's. Like, who are your associates?"

He grinned at me, then Zoe, a glint in his eye.

I cringed. *Oh, God, Finn. Don't say it.*

Hooking a thumb over his shoulder, he said, "Jack and Jim."

My shoulders sagged.

Zoe's gaze tracked past Finn to the bottles of booze, then over to me. I gave her a nervous smile.

"We go *way* back," Finn said, not knowing when to keep his mouth shut.

Typical guy.

Zoe continued to look at me, her face saying it all. I closed my eyes and gave her a brief headshake.

My idiot boss, yet excellent private investigator, swiped a hand through the air. "Ah, c'mon now, I was just kidding around." Addressing me, he asked in a serious tone, "What can I help you with?"

I explained to him about receiving the package but left out the manila envelope with the photos and unnerving note.

He put a hand out. "That the envelope?"

I handed it to him along with the jewelry box. "Yep."

Finn looked at the front. "Fancy. Someone's sparing no expense." He pulled out the Creighton Winston letter and the diamond certificate, reading both twice. Then he opened the jewelry box, the diamond just as resplendent as it was yesterday. "Nice rock."

"You think it's real?" I asked.

"Dunno, but that paper says it is." He pulled open a drawer, rummaged through it for a few seconds, and pulled out a jeweler's loupe. I knew what the gizmo was called on account of my eventful summer at the Carlton Museum with the Star of Midnight. "Let's take a look." He bent close to the diamond, peered through the loupe from several different angles, then rechecked the certificate. "Gotta say, this baby's real."

"How can you tell?" I asked.

He flashed a playful smile. "Trust me. I can."

"Just because you have a jeweler's loupe doesn't make you an expert," I countered.

Finn held up his hands in mock surrender. "There's a serial number lasered into it."

"And it matches the certificate?" Zoe asked.

"Sure does." Finn pushed his office phone into the center of the desk. "One last thing to check." He picked up the certificate, hit the speaker button, and punched in a phone number from the document.

"Good afternoon. The International Institute of Gems." The male voice was full of itself, beyond haughty.

"Yeah, this is Melvin"—his eyes shot me a warning—"Finnegan. I have a diamond with a grading certificate from your institute. Can you confirm if the IIG examined this stone?"

"Certainly. Serial number?"

Finn read him the number from the certificate.

"One moment."

The man put us on hold, soft jazz music flowing from the phone. Zoe rolled her head toward me and put a finger gun to it. Finn reached down behind the desk, a jangle and low moan rising from Bertie. And the sax just kept on playing. Unmercifully.

Eventually, thankfully, the man came back on the phone. "Yes, sir, I can confirm we examined the stone, inscribed it with the serial number you noted, and issued the certificate. Anything else I can help you with today?"

"Can you tell me who sent the stone?"

"I cannot. I am sure you can understand. But it was one of eight we received together two months ago for grading and certification."

Finn diverted his attention from us to the phone. "Really? Eight? Together?"

"Correct."

He leaned toward the phone, as if it were a person and he was emphasizing a point. "Stolen?"

A huff of indignation came through the speaker. "Sir, please, we simply do not grade stolen gems."

"I'm sure, but how you reckon—"

"There were no reports of stolen diamonds matching the ones we received." A pause. "Is there anything else?"

"Nah, I appreciate your—"

The line went dead.

"—time." Finn grabbed his computer's keyboard, thick fingers soon flying over the keys, round brown eyes hooded by unruly eyebrows studying the monitor. A mouse click, more typing, reading, another click, and more typing. He studied the monitor before pushing the keyboard away and addressing us. "A quick check don't show any reported jewel heists, burglaries, or the like, goin' back six months 'round here." He picked up his cell, tapping and swiping as he spoke. "Lemme just check with an FBI buddy of mine over at the field office…Hey, Jack. How's it going? Uh-huh. Yeah, not too bad. Surviving, I reckon. Krystal? Nah, she was good riddance, for sure. Hey, I've got a question, y'all…"

As Finn talked, I squeezed my eyes shut, praying he didn't mention my name. Suffice it to say, there were a couple of agents over there that were a part of my not-always-upstanding history with law enforcement. Including one named Jack. Not that I was ever officially arrested. But, yeah, they probably would not be too thrilled to hear my name. Ever.

Finn tapped off and set the phone on the desk. "They got nothing either. Looks like you got yourself a legit clean diamond." He read the letter again, his eyes narrowing. "Huh."

That didn't sound good. I edged forward in the chair. "What?"

"Just 'huh.' Nothing else." He folded the letter and certificate, stuffed both back into the envelope, and slid it and the jewelry box across the desk to me. "Anything else in that package besides these?"

I took the items. "Nope. That's about it."

A whine rose from beneath the desk. I peeked under it. Bertie lay there, head hanging off the bed, paws covering his eyes.

Finn glanced down, then up at me. Head cocked. Eyes fixed. "You sure 'bout that?"

That damn Bertie. Finn loved that dog. I loved that dog. Everybody loved that dog. He was the only thing Finn wanted from the divorce because Bertie alerted him to his ex-wife's cheating. With her hairdresser. Although not all the time, Bertie possessed the uncanny ability to sense when somebody was lying or being deceitful. And now he was ratting me out. He could've been a dappled longhaired Mauzzy.

I straightened, my throat tightening. "I am."

Finn leaned forward, the chair squeaking in protest. "Yeah, you should know better than trying to sneak one by 'ole Bertram here. Or me." He pointed to the envelope I found myself clutching. "Says in that letter there you're s'posed to bring two envelopes to that meeting. You only brung one here." His eyebrows raised.

I swallowed, attempting to clear my throat, but it was like I guzzled a glass of sand. "Um, yeah, about that." I exchanged a glance with Zoe, whose eyes implored me to come clean with the man. *Or else* resonated in my head from the note. "So, um, there *is* a second envelope, but…Yeah, I can't tell you about it."

Zoe groaned. "It's full of—"

"*Yet*," I hissed at my best friend. "I can't tell him *yet*."

The little narc glared at me but kept her mouth shut.

Finn smiled without humor as he sized me up and I fought every urge to look away. After several seconds of contemplation, he said, "Yeah, not gonna pry. You know where to find me."

A wave of relief washed over me. I needed to get the conversation off that envelope before Zoe thought better of her reluctant seething silence. "Finn, you think I should go to this meeting?"

He leaned back, the chair gently tilting to the right. "Setting aside this mysterious second envelope, what's your concern?"

"I mean, well, we have to sign NDAs in order to go. What if this is about illegal activity?"

Zoe broke in. "Seriously, *now* you're exercising caution. You won't tell him about that frigging envelope of…" She caught herself, regathered, and continued. "But you're all worried about illegal crap going down at this meeting?"

Finn raised an eyebrow at me.

"Ignore her," I said. "So, what do you think?"

"An NDA can't keep you from reporting a crime to the cops," he replied.

"You sure?" I asked.

"Pretty sure."

"That's not reassuring."

He shrugged. "Best I got. Not a legal hound."

Zoe typed into her phone, studied it, then showed it

to me. "He's right."

I read the page she pulled up confirming Finn's statement. "Okay. So, I should go?"

Finn eyed me warily. "Up to you. Apparently, I don't know the whole story. Can't make a recommendation without all the facts, ya know?"

He was right. But I also couldn't tell him all the facts. Not yet, although I knew at some point Finn needed to get involved if I had any chance of tracking down the blackmailer and confronting him.

I considered the contest and the note's implications. If it ran more than a few days, there was also the little detail of missing classes. Including the GPA-killing, soul-sucking, dream-crushing, GBA480, which I needed to pass to graduate this semester. Unfortunately, someone was out there threatening to destroy me if I didn't participate. And those photos tell me he's serious, that he's invested considerable time and resources into his scheme. Whatever it might be. In the big picture, failing a class and delaying graduation was nothing compared to what could happen if I refused to participate. A blackmailer possessed intimate knowledge of me and my life for the last two years. And perhaps, longer. Not to mention what he might know about my family. There really were no options available, no decision to be wrestled with, no choice to be made. If participating cost me graduating this year, so be it. Dad would understand. Eventually. Maybe.

I blew out. "I'm going to go."

"Just so you know, I can't go with you," Finn said. "Starting up a big case."

That got a short laugh out of me. "Your idea of a big case is a hot twenty-something looking for the goods to divorce her sugar-daddy husband."

He wagged a finger at me. "Careful now. Them cases pay the bills, including your paycheck. And this one ain't like them. Gonna take some real detecting on this one."

"Um…Crap…I didn't mean to—"

With a wave of the hand, he said, "Nah, don't worry 'bout it. That'd be a nice case, too. Who you gonna take?"

"Me," Zoe groused.

Finn chuckled. "Don't sound like you're too happy 'bout that, either."

"I'm not. If you knew Sara like I know her, you'd understand."

A knowing smile crossed his craggy face. "I have a pretty good notion 'bout her." He turned to me. "A real good notion."

Chapter Four

El Sueño

The following day, I blew off morning classes to get some high-priority research done for Finn on his latest "big case" before Zoe and I headed off to sign the NDAs and attend the meeting. After blasting me over my latest "questionable academic decision," she agreed to meet me at the office at twelve-thirty so we could go together to the Creighton Winston PLC office and then on to the big meeting. Grudgingly, she also agreed I would drive since I knew Birmingham much better than she did. And "grudgingly" is being nice. Way nice.

Finn was leaning up against his desk, a risky move considering its condition, sipping on an Irish coffee, his lunch delayed pending my departure. He stuck around to make sure my research covered everything he needed, and to be there for any last-minute questions before the meeting. Gone was the scraggly beard, replaced by a groomed goatee making its biweekly appearance. The ever-loyal Bertie lounged at his feet.

He motioned toward his desk with the coffee mug. "Figure out why my computer didn't start?"

"I did."

His face lit up. "See, told ya, you're a techy."

"The power strip was turned off," I deadpanned.

"But yet you figured it out," he crowed.

"I've told you too many times to count, you're in a *whole* lotta trouble if you have to rely on me to fix your computer."

Finn took a sip of his special coffee. "From where I'm standing, you're doing just fine."

"Well, you're playing with IT fire. That's all I'm saying."

"Ain't worried."

"You've been warned. Again."

He shrugged me off. "Still, ain't worried. I'm a good judge of talent."

"Obviously. You hired me."

Zoe's ringtone chimed from my phone. "Hey, Zo, you downstairs?"

"I'm out front. Hurry up before I get carjacked."

"I'll be right down." I tapped off and grabbed my purse. "Wish me luck."

Finn pushed up off the desk and pointed at me with the coffee mug. "I know it's gonna be difficult for you, but my recommendation, say as little as possible." He finished with a big grin, revealing a small gap between his front teeth.

"Ha-ha. Very funny."

"Just remember it." Finn angled his head toward me, index finger out. "And you best keep me briefed."

I gave a thumbs-up, shot out the door, and headed for the foul stairwell. With its four flights of stairs and petri-dish handrails. Zoe waited for me in a little red sedan parked in front of the building. As I stepped toward the curb, I caught a glimpse of a black jacked-up pickup with massive bull bars idling in a parking lot down the street, the deepthroated engine rumbling its impatience to get moving. Although several blocks away, a head of snow-white hair poking above the truck's steering wheel screamed at me.

While I recognize jacked-up pickups in Alabama were not unusual, there was only one person I've ever known to routinely drive one who sported white hair and could barely see over the wheel.

It had to be her.

Mrs. Majelski.

Was I imagining it, or was the octogenarian oddity really shadowing me? Yet again. And if so, why this time? Was she the person behind the package and the beyond unsettling photos, like Zoe thought? I knew what my feisty best friend would say, so I made the snap decision to keep quiet about Majelski watching us. For now.

I jumped in Zoe's car and directed her to where I was parked. In the side mirror, the pickup slipped out of the parking lot and eased down the street, keeping a block between us. We switched cars and headed for the offices of Creighton Winston PLC, the truck staying with us. Thirty minutes later, we were barreling out of town to a place called El Sueño with copies of our signed NDAs in hand, the pickup still hanging in the background. In the legal documents, we agreed not to disclose to anybody what was to be discussed in today's meeting and any details regarding the ensuing contest, even after its conclusion, "in perpetuity." In other words, we were to keep our yaps shut about this whole thing. Forever. Easier said than done for me. Yeah, I took a *deep* breath before I signed that thing.

Zoe clung to the handhold above the door as my little hatchback shot down the entrance ramp toward I-459. "That paralegal was fast. Like your effing driving.

Slow down, girl."

I checked for oncoming cars and zipped across traffic to the outside lane, a blaring horn or three registering their unnecessary complaints. "She was rushing us out because the place we're going to is an hour outside town."

"Well, the way you're going, we'll get there with thirty minutes to spare. Slow the eff down."

"Better than being thirty minutes late."

"Debatable."

Forty-five minutes later we pulled into a wide entranceway of light and dark-brown pavers, stopping in front of closed black iron gates attached to heavy stone posts. I could no longer see the pickup, but I knew the old lady was out there, somewhere.

Watching.

Stone lions sat atop each gate post, staring down on all visitors. Matching black fencing extended away from each post, enclosing far-reaching grounds, broken up periodically by smaller stone posts. The gates were eight feet high and about ten feet wide. On top of each, swirling metal embellishments angled two feet upward, meeting at the center of the drive. Off in the distance was a sprawling mansion with terracotta-clay tile roofing, sandstone-colored walls, arched windows and doors, soaring spires, and a towering three-story turret. The place looked like a fancy Spanish villa. Or extravagant castle.

"Wow," I said. "This is somebody's home? Like, someone actually lives here?"

"Maybe, but it sure isn't a home. Looks more like a castle."

"A ritzy castle."

I lowered the window and punched a code given to me by the paralegal into a keypad at the edge of the driveway. The gates slowly opened inward. I eased the panting car past the stone sentries and down a paver drive to a parking area holding one white and three black luxury sedans, two oversized black SUVs, and a red exotic-looking two-seat sportscar. Dominating the center of the parking area, a three-tiered stone fountain rose from a round water basin, the sides matching the mansion's walls. Brilliant red flowers extended three feet out from the bottom of the basin in all directions.

"Flowers seem excessive," I said. "Especially for March."

"Not for this place," Zoe replied in amazement. "I bet they got their own greenhouse."

I parked my junky little car next to one of the self-important sedans, the contrast and message all too obvious. My chest tightened as I got out of the car, breaths coming in short snatches. This meeting could go any number of ways. And most ended badly. For me.

"You remember the envelopes?" Zoe asked.

I raised an oversized purse, my response fighting its way out of a dry throat. "Uh-huh."

We hurried toward the mansion and as we approached, a heavy wooden door with an off-center four-paned window slowly swung open. In the doorframe stood a slim man of maybe sixty with perfectly-trimmed short gray hair and a pale complexion begging for a hint of color. He wore a black suit, gray vest, and crisp white shirt with gold cufflinks and a black tie. The man stood a good four to five inches shorter than me, putting him at no more than five-foot-eight.

Standing ramrod straight, the man bowed his head slightly. "Miss Donovan, we've been expecting you. Percy Pembarton, at your service."

My head jerked back. "You know my name?"

"Of course, madam." He gestured to the diminutive Zoe. "But I do not know this young lady."

"Mr. Pembarton, this is my friend from school, Zoe Harp."

The man raised his pointy chin and considered Zoe, then me. "Madam, please call me Percy." He stepped to the side and beckoned for us to enter. "Welcome to El Sueño."

I followed Zoe past Percy and stepped into an entrance rivaling Oliver Carlton's historic Arcadia estate, a place I discovered last summer when I worked for the Carlton Museum in D.C. Beneath a domed ceiling and acting like giant welcoming arms, twin curved staircases with polished wood handrails swept up along each side of the entrance to an open walkway looking back down on hardwood floors and a cream-colored circular rug. In the center of the rug, a round wooden table held a vase of elegant white lilies.

"Everybody is waiting in the music room," Percy said, leading us to the far side of the entrance toward a wide-arched opening.

"We're the last ones here?" an incredulous Zoe asked, a not-so-subtle swipe at my driving.

"It would appear so, madam," Percy replied, his tone as clipped and proper as his gait.

Off to the side of the archway stood an incredibly large man in a black suit with a buzz cut and flat expression. His height and bulk would dwarf most high-end refrigerators. But what caught my attention, an obvious bulge beneath his jacket. He pointed to a small table holding a wicker basket. "All phones and electronic devices go there. Gonna also need to search your bag and her backpack."

A thousand pinpricks attacked my skin. In my head, I wasn't surprised there was an armed guard here, considering the whole situation. But my body wasn't in step with my head, as it screamed, *Why is there an armed guard here?*

With my head ringing, we did as directed. A drop of perspiration meandered toward the small of my back. Followed by another. The gunman rummaged through my purse and Zoe's backpack, his face remaining expressionless. He pulled out my pepper spray and held it up. "You can get this back after the meeting, along with your phones." Setting our bags on the table beside the basket, he said, "Arms out to the side, please."

"Excuse me?" I asked.

"Need to pat you down."

I took a step back. "Why? We already signed your NDAs. We're not gonna—"

The Refrigerator took a step toward me. He was so—big. And even more intimidating. "Ma'am, just doin' my job. Boss's orders. No pat down, no entrance. Your choice."

Percy clicked his tongue. "Madam, I suggest you do as the gentleman says."

Zoe and I slowly raised our arms. I squeezed my eyes shut as thick hands deftly roved all over my person.

"Turn around, please."

Hands slid down my back, shirt sticking to me,

gently over my butt, and down the back of my legs, ending with a brief grab at both ankles. For a big man, he had a surprisingly gentle touch. Finished with me, he moved to Zoe and repeated the process.

"Hey, easy there," she snapped, blazing green eyes looking over her shoulder at the apparent perv. "That's all me, buddy."

He said nothing, finished the pat down, and gestured to the inner room.

We retrieved our bags from the table, and with a fluttery feeling roiling my stomach, walked past the stoic sentry into a room so grand and amazing, it fully supported the exterior's excess. The focal point of the incredible space with rich deep-red carved wall panels, cream hues, and gold accents was a huge circular opening in the twenty-foot-high ceiling. A tiered crystal chandelier hung through the yawning opening, the top third of the glittering feature stretching up into a second floor with a gold decorative railing and floor-to-ceiling glass panes matching the back wall of the music room. Set beneath the chandelier on a circular rug of browns and golds were four sofas facing each other over the long sides of a low-slung rectangular table, all filled with men and women at least twenty to thirty years older than us, although there were several easily in their sixties or seventies. On one of the short sides of the table sat two pairs of armchairs, of which two were vacant. In one of the chairs slumped a dumpy dude in his thirties with frizzy black hair, cargo shorts, and well-worn flip-flops. In another, a gorgeous man in his early-forties with classic good looks. Olive skin, wavy black hair, vibrant blue eyes set off beautifully by the dark hair, high cheekbones, tightly-trimmed beard. The man looked mmmm-mmmm good.

Zoe and I sat in the two vacant armchairs.

Percy appeared at the open end of the sofas and chairs, directly opposite Zoe and me. "Ladies and gentlemen, everybody is now here. Mr. Winston will be addressing you promptly at two. Please remain seated until then. Thank you." With a curt nod, he departed through the arched opening.

The good-looking man stood, smoothing a deep-blue sports jacket with light-blue crisscrossing lines. "Well, if we have a little time to kill..." He strode to the most magnificent piece in the room, not counting the god-like man himself, a marbled turquoise-colored grand piano with gold trim on the edges and feet. It was truly a unique instrument.

A sheet of music sat on the piano's music stand. The man studied it briefly. "Ah, yes, this is a wonderfully devilish piece, challenging for even the most accomplished pianist." He glanced back at the group, his blue eyes absolutely electric. "Let's see how I do."

The man sat, took a theatric pause, exhaled, then ripped off a wildly-fast performance. Fingers flew over the keys with left-hand flourishes, the right dancing and wiggling among the black keys, his torso and head dramatically bobbing and dipping with emphasis. He never once took his eyes off the keys, the sheet music but a prop for the performance. Two minutes later, he finished with a crisp crescendo on the lower keys. After several seconds of stunned silence, the group erupted in applause, including me and Zoe.

That is, everybody except one man. Even sitting down, I could tell he was tall. He had styled dark-brown hair and matching goatee, amazing brown eyes that seemed to have eyeliner, and a brooding look.

The pianist stood, faced us, and took a deep bow.

The brooding man spoke up. "A good effort, for sure. However, the execution is not entirely your fault. Chopin's 'Etude in C Sharp Minor Opus Ten, Number Four' is considered one of the most difficult piano pieces to master."

Not put off by the man's snobbish attitude, the pianist's smile was easy. Relaxed. "I haven't played that piece in fifteen years, back when my fingers were nimbler."

"And it showed," the man taunted.

Sitting on one of the sofas, a fully bald, bearded man with a healthy belly and broad shoulders slapped his thigh. "Well, shoot, buddy, don't know how them fingers coulda been any nimbler. You did more than tickle them ivories, that's fer sure."

The pianist nodded his appreciation. "Why thank you, Mr....?"

"Burl Jablonsky," the bald man blurted. "But y'all can call me Scooter."

"The car magnate?" the pianist asked.

Scooter's face smiled with pride. "Yes, sir. Got five dealerships all 'round Birmingham. After that there concert, I can get you a damn fine deal. Your name is?"

"Thank you...Scooter. I'm fine on the automobile front. The name is Jimmy Dougal."

What a shame such a beautiful human being had such a *dreadful* name. Like Finn, he should blame his parents. With his looks, the man deserved a dazzling name with a foreign flourish. Like Antonio Cappucci. Or Francois Le Mans. Not Jimmy Dougal.

Scooter grinned. "Well, Jimmy, you just lemme know if you change your mind."

"Certainly." Jimmy turned to a black stand beside the piano holding a striking deep-reddish-brown violin. He picked up the gleaming instrument and bow, gave it a once-over, then raised it to his chin. "Let's see how I do with this fabulous piece of art." A torrent of notes tore through the air as the bow sawed at the strings, left fingers a frenzy of movement. His body leaned back and forth as the pitch and intensity rose and fell, the violin following suit. A minute later, he finished with a series of rapid plinks on the strings and a deep bow.

This time the group went wild. Except for the same one man. He remained unimpressed.

Jimmy raised the violin and bow. "Thank you, thank you. That was the thoroughly brilliant, 'Flight of the Bumblebee,' by Nikolai Rimsky-Korsakov as part of the opera, *The Tale of Tsar Saltan*. He wrote it in 1899 to celebrate the one-hundredth anniversary of the birth of the eminent Russian author, Alexander Pushkin." As the composer's name rolled off his tongue, the pronunciation sounded thoroughly Russian.

"You some kinda mae-estro or something?" Scooter asked, eyes widened.

"As a matter of—"

A sharp-toned voice cut through the air from the arched entranceway. "He may be, but that violin is off-limits to *everybody* but the owner of El Sueño. Do not touch it again."

Standing just inside the room, a white-haired man wearing wire-framed glasses and an expensive-looking dark-blue suit had an arm extended toward Jimmy. Dominating the wrist, a heavy gold watch.

Jimmy carefully placed the violin back on its stand and put a hand to his chest. "My apologies, sir. I would gladly purchase this exquisite instrument from the owner."

The man approached the group as Jimmy Dougal returned to his seat. "It is not for sale. And if it was, I highly doubt you can afford it. The violin you were violating is an extremely valuable and rare one."

The unimpressed man spoke up. "Undoubtedly a Strad. I'm guessing fifteen million or more." Pomposity flowed from his mouth and being.

Jimmy angled toward the uppity man. "Sir?"

"It could be *The Lady Blunt* or *The DaVinci*. I would have to examine it. However, it is definitely a Stradivarius. It has the unique varnish used by Antonio Stradivari and the sound is superior. There is such a caliber, a resonance, of the higher notes that it transports the listener to an unearthly place where time stands still. The unmistakable sound of angels leaves the—"

"Thank you, Mr. Azarian, for your critique," the white-haired man said, his voice raised. His piercing black eyes tore into the arrogant man. "However, I am on a tight schedule, so let us begin."

Chapter Five

The meeting

The white-haired man, holding a blue folder, addressed everybody from the same open end of the seating arrangement as Percy had ten minutes earlier. "Thank you for coming. I am Creighton Winston, attorney for the contest's founder, whose name shall remain confidential. However, rest assured, this person is a generous philanthropist, scholar, and respected citizen." The attorney's gaze traveled along the occupied sofas and chairs. "Has everybody brought their envelopes per the instructions?"

Some nodded their assent, others held up letter and manila envelopes, all looking daggers at the man. I pulled my envelopes out and held them up.

"Very good," Winston said. "Full disclosure, my firm only prepared the invitation. The founder provided me with the sealed envelopes to go with each specific invite. Only you and the founder know the contents of your second envelope."

That statement confirmed the so-called founder was the blackmailer. And assuming he owned El Sueño, he was also extremely wealthy. It made sense. With wealth comes power. I studied the attorney. The man oozed money. Could he be the person behind all this? Was he just pretending to be the founder's attorney and in fact, I was staring at my blackmailer?

A smallish middle-aged woman with toned arms and perfect makeup raised a manila envelope like the one I received. Small dark-brown eyes that appeared even smaller behind oversized black-framed glasses glared at the attorney. "Are you telling me you had nothing to do with this sordid envelope and the despicable allegations it contains?"

"That is correct, Ms. Fantucci. All I know is, the founder believed some of you might have needed a little—push—to attend this meeting. And hence, your second envelopes."

"More like a swift kick in the britches," Scooter complained.

Mumbles and grumbles rolled through the room.

Winston forced a smile. "The founder imparted to me that every contestant was personally selected because each of you has a secret that absolutely must remain—a secret. Especially from law enforcement." He glanced at me and raised an eyebrow. "Since the winner of the contest will become fabulously wealthy, it would seem, everyone is here because of a potentially—*lucky secret.*"

Zoe's head whipped toward me. With eyes wide, she mouthed *law enforcement*. I threw her a little headshake, even as my body exploded in tingles. I have no such secrets—anymore. I think. A picture popped in my head of the open safe-deposit box with the gold artifact, gold bar, and emeralds. With my name on the signature card. Somebody obviously manufactured a secret for me. But why? And is it the same for all the contestants? Were they also blackmailed into coming for something they didn't do? Or were they...

The attorney opened the blue folder. "Before reading the contest rules, I would like to briefly introduce the contestants, all of whom are based in the greater-Birmingham area, and their associates, if any." He nodded in my direction. "With the exception of Miss Donovan, who is from Annapolis but goes to school in Tuscaloosa. When I say your name, please raise your hand." His attention focused on the man who saw himself superior to all in the room. "Mr. Karsh Azarian."

The pompous violin expert flicked a hand.

Winston nodded toward the man. "Mr. Azarian, who is here on his own, is a former collegiate basketball player at an academically-elite university and financial asset manager with an enviable record of providing returns that consistently beat the market by a surprising margin." He paused. "And apparently, he's also a Stradivarius aficionado."

Azarian glowered but said nothing.

"Ms. Jessica Doerr," Winston said, looking at a platinum-bottle-blonde unsuccessfully trying to appear in her fifties. She briefly raised her hand. Next to her sat a withered woman easily in her eighties. "Ms. Doerr, who is here with her mother, Virginia Byrd, is a mortgage banker with her own agency, specializing in refinancing services for the senior community." He looked to the flip-flops dude slumped in one of the chairs. "Mr. Rodney Toft."

"I go by Rod," the frizzy-haired man stressed.

"Very well," Winston replied. "Mr. Toft, who brought his girlfriend, Ashley Tennison, is a cryptocurrency exchange investor and trader as well as a technology venture capitalist. His recent meteoric rise with regards to wealth generation has been the talk of the financial world." He motioned to the seething lady who had spoken up earlier. With a fake smile, he said, "Everyone met Ms. Olivia Fantucci, who is an attorney with her own firm specializing in large class-action lawsuits and personal injury. People either love her or hate her."

The lady returned the attorney's plastic smile with a death stare, thin lips pressed tight, eyes mere slits. Menacing.

Winston's smile broadened, lingering on Fantucci for a second or two. "Ms. Fantucci's associate is her friend, Marissa Chevalier." He turned to a trim grandfatherly-looking man with short, white hair, a receding hairline, and a hooked nose. Sitting next to him was an elegantly-understated woman with an air of quiet wealth and privilege. "Mr. Spencer Fernsby."

The man half-stood and threw a little wave and nod before sitting again.

"Mr. Fernsby, who is here with his wife of forty-eight years, Kathleen Fernsby, is the founder, CEO, and majority shareholder of the telecom giant, CLATEL Communications. In a mere five years, Mr. Fernsby has overseen the growth of CLATEL from a mid-sized regional provider to a national behemoth and stock-market darling." Winston gestured to the gorgeous musician. "You also have met Mr. James Dougal, who, like Mr. Azarian, is here on his own. He is a real estate agent with his own agency specializing in high-end luxury properties."

Dougal stood and bowed, a glittery smile on his face. "If you're looking to buy or sell, call—"

"*Mr. Dougal*," Winston interjected, "this is neither

the time nor place for personal aggrandizement or"—he gave him the snootiest of looks—"advertising."

Jimmy's heartwarming smile vanished. Putting up a hand, he said, "My apologies," and quickly sat.

Like he did earlier with Fantucci, Winston's gaze lingered on Jimmy before addressing the car salesman. "Mr. Burl Jablonsky is the owner of four car dealerships—"

"Five," Scooter said.

"Excuse me, five car dealerships including—"

"Just opened the fifth last month. Probably why you don't have it in that there file."

Winston eyed the beaming Jablonsky. "Yes, of course, you did. Mr. Jablonsky is the owner of *five* car dealerships including *two* luxury franchises. Correct, Mr. Jablonsky?"

The car man gave a thumbs-up. "Yes, sir. And like I said, y'all can call me Scooter. Got the nickname way back when I bought a scooter franchise and my baby brother here, Billy—"

Winston broke in. "Thank you, Mr. Jablonsky, but you can regale everyone with your colorful life stories over the next two weeks during dinner, which I will be getting to momentarily. Mr. Jablonsky's brother, William Jablonsky, is his associate." He extended an arm toward a dull-looking man in a plain black suit with a long, narrow face, pallid skin, and slicked-down silver hair combed to the side. "Now here we have Mr. Frederick Volkov, an immensely successful financier, stock trader, and arbitrageur. And as all can see, Mr. Volkov's associate is his brother, Ivan Volkov."

The dour Frederick Volkov sat motionless, heavy-lidded gray eyes focused on Winston with a burning intensity contrary to his persona. Next to him sat a carbon copy of the man, less the white-hot glare. His identical twin. And I mean—identical. Right down to the suits they wore.

Winston turned to me. "And last but certainly not least, we have Miss Sara Donovan, a business student at the University of Alabama and a nationally-recognized amateur sleuth. With her is Miss Donovan's friend, Miss Zoe Harp."

I gave a half-wave, my ears burning.

Winston consulted the folder in his hand. "Miss Donovan is the only contestant under twenty-one, although she will be celebrating a birthday tomorrow." His gaze settled on me. "Which happens to be the Ides of March."

Scooter jumped up. "Hey, y'all, you know what they say,"—he jabbed a stubby finger at me—"beware the Ides of March."

"Please be seated, Mr. Jablonsky," Winston scolded, "and refrain from any further outbursts."

The man sat, his bearded face crimson, a vein pulsing in his temple.

Karsh Azarian sized me up, his brow furrowing. "All very interesting. Amateur sleuth, hmm? We will have to keep a close eye on that one."

Winston put his hands out. "That will be enough. Now, I am required to read you the contest rules, a copy of which will be in each of your El Sueño welcome packets. These rules are ironclad. Once you agree today to enter the contest, any breach of any rule, no matter how small, shall be grounds for immediate disqualification and forfeiture of your diamond. Failure to turn over the diamond will result in swift legal action." He paused to allow his gaze to travel around the room. "And worse. Understood?"

Not a single word was uttered. Not a single head nodded. No movement. No nothing. Just total silence.

Percy entered the room wheeling a gold tea cart with a stack of folders on the top shelf, followed by the paralegal we met at the law firm's offices. Percy parked the cart to the side and behind Winston, then quietly exited. The paralegal stood beside the cart, arms lowered, hands clasped.

Winston glanced back at the cart and the paralegal. "Very good," he said, turning back to face the group. "Now the rules. Please note, these are in addition to those stipulated in the invitation regarding the use of an associate. *One.* This is an all-or-nothing contest. There shall be only one winner. The winning prize shall be a minimum of five hundred million U.S. dollars, cash, payable within three weeks of the contest's conclusion."

An irritated Winston looked up as multiple conversations, whispers, and murmuring broke out.

Five hundred million dollars to the winner? I couldn't believe what I just heard. A sharp kick to my foot told me Zoe couldn't either. I snuck a peek at her. The girl's slitted eyes and set jaw said she was going to let me have it with both barrels, hopefully alone after the meeting concluded. Just not now. Please, God?

Winston held up a hand. "*Please.* I must get through these rules." He waited for the group to quiet, then resumed reading from the folder.

"*Two.* Contestants may form alliances at any time, but only one per team, and they shall decide among themselves how to split the prize should they win. So that appropriate adjustments can be made within the contest, an alliance must be duly registered with me via the proper paperwork and once made, it cannot be reversed or changed. Should a contestant in a registered alliance leave the contest for any reason, including death, the remaining contestant in that alliance may continue participating but shall not be permitted to form another alliance. Throughout the contest's duration, Percy shall have the requisite blank forms. A duly registered alliance will be considered one contestant.

"*Three*. Use of the Internet is allowed, but no outside help shall be allowed other than from a contestant's chosen associate, if any.

"*Four*. The contest shall last one fortnight less one day and end the evening of March twenty-eighth at seven o'clock, which is a Wednesday. If there is no winner at that time, at my sole discretion I will enact remedies to ensure a winner is determined.

"*Five*. The contest shall be comprised of seven levels and take place entirely upon the grounds of El Sueño. As such, contestants and their associates shall be required to stay each weeknight at the mansion. To ensure a successful conclusion, the contest shall be suspended on both weekends to allow staff to assess progress and make any necessary adjustments. All contest participants must depart El Sueño by noon each Saturday and may not return before eight o'clock Sunday evening. A secure suite with full amenities shall be provided to each contestant with sleeping accommodations for two. Participants may leave the premises during the day but must return in time to attend each weeknight's *mandatory* dinner which shall be *served* at seven o'clock sharp in the grand dining room. At a minimum, business casual. A brief reception for mingling and cocktails shall precede the dinner service. Failure to appear by the commencement of the dinner service shall result in disqualification. Dinner shall *not* be served the last night. Breakfasts and lunches shall be available in the secondary dining room but attendance shall not be mandatory. All room and board costs at El Sueño shall be borne by the founder. Final check-out shall be no later than noon on March twenty-ninth.

"*Six*. The east wing is strictly off-limits as it is the El Sueño owner's private chambers. Anybody caught attempting to defeat the lock and gain entrance shall be disqualified from the contest and prosecuted for criminal trespassing."

The east wing? I made a mental note to check it out. If the founder, aka my blackmailer, owns El Sueño, there might be clues to his identity behind those locked doors.

"*Seven*. With my assistance, the winner shall establish an unfunded joint trust with me in the Cook Islands in which we are dual signatories on the account. Also, with my assistance, the winner shall establish an unfunded sole trust in the Cook Islands in the winner's name. A standing dual authorization with the joint trust shall authorize all monies coming into the trust be transferred as follows: fifty percent to the aforementioned winner's sole trust; forty-nine percent to the founder's Cook Islands sole trust; and one percent to my law firm's trust in the Cook Islands.

"*Eight*. Any situation arising during the contest not addressed herein shall be resolved by Creighton Winston PLC in consultation with the founder with no recourse available to any contestant. All decisions shall be final."

Winston closed the folder and looked up. "Upon conclusion of this meeting, all contestants may go home to pack a bag and return to check in today but if not, you must be back no later than three o'clock tomorrow afternoon. If you are not checked in by Percy by that time, your contest is over. You may keep the diamond but the NDAs and rules regarding total silence will still apply. Now having heard the rules, no questions shall be honored." He extended an arm toward the paralegal. "Mrs. Sanchez has an acknowledgement of the rules and a release for each of you to sign signifying your entry into the contest."

Olivia Fantucci, the lawyer who earlier challenged Creighton Winston, stood. She couldn't have been more than five-two, but the woman obviously worked out. Not only were her arms toned, her body was tiny, tight, and taut. She could be Zoe in thirty years. "Now hold on, Mr. Winston. Why must the winner give the founder money *back* from the winnings? That sounds highly suspicious."

Frederick Volkov stood. "Who's funding this contest?"

"This all does sound rather odd," Jimmy Dougal said from one of the sofas, a leg casually crossed over the other.

"Dude, can I get my money in crypto?" Rod Toft asked, still slumped in his chair.

Despite the onslaught, Winston kept his cool and fired off answers. "Although my earlier stipulation stated no questions shall be honored, I will entertain these questions only. No crypto. Winnings shall be remitted in U.S. dollars. I am not at liberty to speak about the source of funding, just know it is legitimate. Giving the founder forty-nine percent is non-negotiable and not to be questioned. No laws will be broken by your participation in the contest." He again extended his arm toward Mrs. Sanchez. "Please."

Olivia Fantucci huffed, grabbed her handbag from the floor, and stuffed her envelopes into it. "I'm taking my diamond and leaving. This sounds beyond fishy."

Creighton Winston clucked his tongue and stuck out a hand. "Very well. Your envelopes, Ms. Fantucci."

The lawyer drew back. "Excuse me?"

He smiled politely. "You may certainly choose not to participate in the contest, but you must turn over your envelopes to me. *Both* of your envelopes." He flipped a hand at her. "Of course, you may keep the diamond and the grading certificate."

Fantucci stared into her handbag.

Winston curled his lip as he again extended a hand. "The envelopes, Ms. Fantucci?"

She bristled, nostrils flaring, face darkening. The livid lawyer looked away, then up at Winston. "I'm in," she spat.

With a hollow smile, he said, "Good luck."

Chapter Six

Check-in

The next afternoon, Zoe and I were back in my hatchback rocketing along I-459 around Birmingham toward El Sueño. We were running just a tad late because I had both a Homicide and a Fraud-Risk Management class in the morning, the latter of which was also known as the insidious GBA480. And no way I could blow either off today because I needed to talk with my professors about getting the notes or lecture slides for any classes I missed. Kinda important. Although, I was only going to miss four classes per course, which was nothing. I skipped way more than that each semester. But still, the responsible thing to do was make advance arrangements with my professors, even if it included telling a little white lie about a family emergency. Poor, poor Gee-ma. Plus, I lost time packing for El Sueño. That ended up being two large stuffed suitcases for me, plus Mauzzy's travel bag full of Mauzzy-gear, food, and treats.

With minimal grousing, other than from the churlish Olivia Fantucci, everybody at yesterday's meeting signed up for the contest. Zoe and I were the last to sign the rules acknowledgement and waiver because it took my best work to convince her we had to enter. That and my reminding her of those compromising photographs, even though the last couple were faked. We had to find out who was behind it, meaning we had to uncover the identity of the mysterious founder. There was no choice but to partici—

Whoooooosh.

A fancy red sports car roared by us on the right, top down, black frizzy hair blowing in wild protest. Rod Toft, hiding behind dark wraparound sunglasses, threw us a wave and a smirk as the racing machine blew by and cut in front of us, forcing me to hit the brakes, the haggard hatchback swerving to the left. Hard.

"*Hey!*" Zoe's right hand grabbed for something, anything, while the left returned Toft's obnoxious wave with a vigorous middle-finger salute.

I fought to regain control of the overmatched little hatchback, yanking it off the shoulder and back into the lane.

Seconds passed, Zoe's chin resting on her chest. She took several deep breaths before opening her eyes and looking at me. "How can that effing guy be the talk of the financial world? Dude looks like a pothead."

"Beats me. Is he even thirty?"

"If even. But he sure drives like you."

With the car back under control, I punched it, slamming Zoe's head back into the headrest. After all, we were late. I looked over at my petrified partner. "What'd you tell your parents about being away?"

Since Zoe lived with her parents, and was a terrible liar, I needed to make sure she didn't tell them what was going on. Between being warned in the note to stay quiet and the NDAs threatening immediate and severe legal action for any confidentiality breach, it would be disastrous if the people behind the contest found out we told anyone. Since I lived eight hundred miles from home, I didn't have to tell my parents anything, and Matt was staying at my place and could cover for me if something happened to come up. But Zoe? She was the wildest of wildcards.

The poor girl had a death grip on the handhold above the door, head pressed hard into the seat. Through clenched teeth, she spit out an answer. "I'm…renting a room…for a few weeks…from a friend to…oh my, God…" A deep breath. "To get prepared for living on my own after graduation."

I stared at her. "Seriously? That's the best you could come up with?"

"*Eyes on the road,*" Zoe screamed.

I tapped the brakes and veered onto the left shoulder to avoid clipping a pickup truck. "What'd they say?"

No answer, head up against her upraised arm, eyes closed. She blew out. "Why'd I let you drive?"

I maneuvered the car back into the lane behind the oblivious pickup truck. "Zo, what'd they say?"

Head still tucked in her arm, hand gripped tight above, she opened her eyes and took me in. "*What?* We almost wrecked. Get your priorities straight."

"Pssh. I've had way worse. And this is really important. What'd they say?"

Zoe let out a pained moan, followed by several seconds of silence. "They supported me."

"Wow. With that feeble story?"

"Mom came in while I was packing. Caught me off guard."

"Should've thought about it ahead of time."

Zoe glared at me as she hung from the handhold. "Sorry I'm not an accomplished liar like you."

"I'm not a liar."

"Okay, I'm not skilled at deceiving my parents like you are."

"It's called deception by omission."

"*Oh, my God.*" Zoe slammed her feet into the floorboards as I attempted to get around the lagging pickup truck but had to abruptly abort, a car moving up fast on the right blocking my move. Another sharp exhale, more seconds of silence, her head hanging. "I told you to pack yesterday," she said quietly.

"We'll make it."

"*Not if we end up smeared over the highway.*"

Finally, I cut around the dawdling pickup that so didn't belong in the hammer lane, a horn blaring as the hatchback zipped back into the left lane.

Zoe's other hand grabbed for the handhold. "Cripes, girl. This isn't D.C."

A motorcycle blew by us on the right and cut in front.

"Both hands on the wheel," I shouted at the fast-disappearing bike. "Ten and two, mister."

Zoe glanced over at me and shook her head, hands white-knuckling it on the handhold. "Unbelievable."

"Thanks. I get it from me."

"Our exit's right there," Zoe cried.

"On it."

"Oh, my God," she wailed. "Just go to the next—"

I checked over my shoulder. Relatively clear. The hatchback cut across two lanes, catching a bit of the shoulder in front of a crash barrier, fortunately just missing it, and shot onto the exit ramp. I hammered the brakes to keep us from ending up in an imposing ditch on the right side of the ramp, then punched it to regain speed, the hatchback fishtailing as it fought to comply.

Zoe buried her face in her outstretched arms. "Holy—"

A muffled yelp came from the milk crate in the backseat where Mauzzy was buried under a pile of pink blankets featuring powder-blue doggie bones. I had no clue what he was complaining about. He was used to my driving. He knew we always arrived safely. Such a drama queen.

The car straightened out, roared around the ramp, and hurtled onto the road leading to El Sueño.

"See, I had it," I said.

A muffled groan came from the passenger seat.

I checked the dash clock, then crushed the accelerator. "We got less than forty minutes. Gonna be a little tight."

Another groan from Zoe, higher pitched this time, followed by a whine from the backseat. No faith.

For the next half hour or so, we raced in silence, except for the occasional gasp, shriek, moan, or whine. At the gates, I punched in the code and as they opened, slammed the accelerator to the floor.

"Yikes," Zoe shrieked.

The hatchback fit through the ever-widening opening and sailed across the pavers, only coming to a screeching skidding halt in the parking area directly outside the walk leading to the mansion's front door.

I jumped out and yanked open the back door to leash up Mauzzy.

Zoe, still clinging to the handhold, exhaled hard and looked back at me. "Aren't you gonna park?"

"No time. We got one minute."

Zoe sighed, pushed open her door and fell out, hugging the side of the hatchback like a drunk staggering along a wall.

I picked up Mauzzy and ran toward the front door, calling over my shoulder, "We'll get the luggage later."

"Go ahead. I'll catch up."

Just like last time, the thick arched door swung open as I approached. Percy stood there, envelope in hand, chin in the air. He checked his watch and huffed. "Madam, it is three o'clock. You have not checked in. The rules state—"

"I'm here, aren't I?"

"Indeed, you are, but I haven't checked you in yet."

I snatched the envelope out of his hand. "This my room info?"

"Yes, but—"

"Then consider me checked in. What time you got?"

He looked at his watch. "One minute past."

From my arms, a low guttural growl came from Mauzzy.

"Well, you said it was three when you opened the door, so that's the same as checked in."

With an eye on Mauz, he said, "I suppose."

Zoe came up behind us. "Hey, Percy."

He nodded toward her. "Miss Harp."

I took a step forward but Percy slid sideways and blocked me. With a frown at Mauzzy, he set his jaw. "I'm sorry, madam, but no dogs allowed."

Mauzzy leered at the man, his growl increasing in volume.

I rested a hand on my riled roommate's head in a hopeless attempt at quieting him. "But he has to come with me."

An amused look came over the butler's face. "And why is that?"

"Because...um...he's...my emotional support dog. Yeah, so, kinda need him."

Mauzzy glared up at me.

Percy gave him the once-over. "I see no identification that it's such an animal."

With a series of sharp barks, Mauzzy's head whipped around toward Percy, ending with a threatening growl.

The butler took a quick step back, his eyes on the provoked pup. "For what purpose do you require this animal?"

"Already told you, emotional support," I said, winging it. "And I don't recommend calling him that?"

"Excuse me? It is an animal, is it not?"

More growling.

I scrunched my face up. "Yeah, not to him. *Really* best not go there."

Percy considered Mauzzy. "I see. Do you have documentation certifying its working dog bona fides?"

Zoe showed Percy her phone. "She's not required to provide proof, and he doesn't have to wear any identification."

Percy Pembarton took the phone, studied it, and handed it back to Zoe. He took out his own phone and placed a call. "Yes, Mr. Winston. Miss Donovan is at the front door with what she claims is her emotional support"—his gaze cut to a glaring Mauzzy—"dog. It is wearing no identifying vest and she refuses to provide any documentation." He listened dispassionately, nodding his head once, his attention shifting between Mauzzy and me. "I see. Understood. Thank you, sir." He tapped off. "The dog is allowed. *However*, it shall not be permitted in any of the dining rooms. Understood?"

"Understood," I said.

The butler nodded once, stepped back, and gestured with an arm to enter. "Welcome back to El Sueño."

As we passed into the elegant entrance with the domed ceiling and sweeping twin staircases, Percy's disapproving look at Mauzzy said anything but welcome, and Mauzzy's identical look at me said anything but gratitude.

Percy closed the door and faced us, posture perfect. "In your envelope is a map of the mansion that also identifies your suite's location, and a seven-digit combination to the door. For your own security, it is recommended you memorize the combination rather than carry it around on your person. The dinner service shall commence at seven o'clock, sharp. Are there any questions?"

"Who owns El Sueño?" I asked.

"That should be of no concern to you."

"But do you know?" I pressed.

The butler raised his chin and sniffed. "Are there any *pertinent* questions, Miss Donovan?"

I considered the emotionless man. His face gave nothing away. An absolute dead-end. "Are jeans acceptable for business casual?"

His lips curved upward in a tight, forced smile. "No jeans or shorts, nor skirts or dresses above fingertip

65

length."

"Fingertip length?" I asked.

He put his arms straight at his side, wriggled his fingers, and gave me a pinched smile. "Anything else?"

My cheeks burned. "No, sir, that's it."

"Very well. Should you require anything before dinner, just ring me. My card is on the desk in your suite."

Percy tipped his head, spun about, and marched off, leaving us alone in the entrance.

I scanned the space. "You know, for security purposes, I sure hope they have cameras. For every other moment…I pray they don't."

"Oh, I'm sure over the next two weeks some security people are gonna be *thoroughly* entertained by you."

I threw her an exaggerated smile. "Ha. Ha."

My phone chimed. "Hey, Grant." I watched Zoe do a slow burn as Grant talked. "Uh-huh. Awesome, that'll be great. Uh, can't do dinner Friday. But I'm good Saturday. Sure, I can do lunch. Abuela's Casa? Great. I'll see you then."

I tapped off.

"He's coming down this weekend?" Zoe fumed.

"He's in Montgomery through the weekend. He'll pop up to Tuscaloosa on Saturday. Says he's gotta talk to me. In person."

"What the…didn't you just see him on break?"

"He said something big happened earlier in the week that we need to discuss."

"I bet. He's up to—"

"Zo, he's in the area. Said we need to talk. It's a good thing because we need to figure out where we're going."

She crossed her arms and stuck her neck out. "I can tell you *exactly* where it should be—"

"He's a good guy."

Zoe held my gaze, then gestured to the envelope in my hand. "Speaking of, where we going?"

I opened it, studied the map, and five minutes later we entered a small suite. The living room, decorated in a southwestern motif with colorful wall art and throw rugs, was furnished with a brown leather couch, a red fabric chair with no arms, a red oak chair with a brown leather seat and back, a long black credenza upon which sat a flat-screen, and a matching writing desk with lamp and phone. A low-slung square glass coffee table filled the space between the chairs and couch.

Zoe disappeared into the bedroom and quickly returned. "Thank God they got two beds in there. I was so not looking forward to sharing one with you."

Mauzzy worked his way around the room, sniffing up a storm, several times retracing his steps like he discovered something, only to resume his investigation with a snort.

Zoe dropped onto the couch. "For such an impressive mansion with all that space out there, they really skimped on the guest quarters. This place is pretty small."

I poked my head into the bedroom to take a quick look. "Dad always said you never want your houseguests too comfortable or else they'll never leave."

"Sounds like him."

I went to sit in the red armless chair and about flipped out of it. "Whoa, this thing's on a swivel or something."

Zoe howled. "You think?" she said between belly laughs.

I gingerly maneuvered myself out of the precarious chair and stepped over to the desk, Zoe's laughter subsiding to a few giggles, followed by a big exhale. On the desk was a leather portfolio, like an information guide, the kind you find in fancy hotels listing all the amenities. Next to it sat a palm-sized light-blue camera. I examined the camera from all angles. It wasn't digital, having only a viewfinder, and was built of molded plastic with a slitted opening in its top. I brought it close to my—"*aaahhh*"—a flash of white light obliterated my world, followed by a mechanical whirring. The hand holding the camera dropped to my side.

Zoe lost it. "Looks like you got yourself a self-portrait." More laughter.

When my vision returned, sticking halfway out the top of the camera was a photograph. I pulled it out and looked at it. The image was blurred, which had me worried the flash did some serious damage to my rods and cones, but eventually, a shape emerged. Of my face. Super close to the lens. Uncomfortably close.

"How you look?" Zoe asked, struggling to contain herself.

I showed her, and she burst out laughing. Again. "Not sure why there's an instant camera in here," I said, cautiously setting the offensive camera back on the desk. I picked up the information guide and opened it. Inside was a single sheet of typed paper.

Welcome, Miss Donovan.

While you and Miss Harp are here, we want you to

enjoy your stay. Should you require anything at El Sueño, please reach out to Percy Pembarton, whom you met at check-in. His card is on the desk. El Sueño is not responsible for your valuables, but there is a small safe in the bedroom closet for your convenience. Below are some of the estate's amenities available to you:

—A wonderfully curated art gallery containing artifacts and artwork from all over the world, including from some of the most ancient civilizations. Even if you are not a history or art enthusiast, we strongly encourage you to visit the gallery.

—To move about the estate's grounds, you may use one of the golf carts parked outside the garage. Just return it at the end of the day so it can be charged for the next day. You are responsible for all transportation off the premises.

—Should you require use of a computer, printer, or copier, these are available in the office.

—For recreation, there is a game room, indoor/outdoor pool and hot tub, library, and the music room, of which you are familiar. Other than the piano, please refrain from playing the instruments in the music room.

And now, like a shot in the dark, when the new day begins, so does the game.

A final bit of advice: Remember, it is a long road. The key is, early on, don't get too high, or sink too low. Steady wins the race.

Good luck.

Chapter Seven

Dinner

"Good evening, ladies," Percy said as Zoe and I entered the grand dining room. He extended a white-gloved hand to a massive table with elegant place settings in the center of the room. Over the table, two crystal candelabra chandeliers hung from a magnificent white coffered ceiling. "Contestants dine at the main table. Their associates"—his arm motioned to a table extending from a far wall—"will dine there."

The main table had four dark-wood chairs with white-cushioned seats on each side, but it easily could have handled eight per side. Seven of the eight cushioned chairs were taken. On each end of the table was a patterned silver upholstered chair, one being empty. Enthroned in the other, the self-important Karsh Azarian. Naturally, the man would choose to sit at the head of the table. The associates' table was half the size with four chairs on each side matching the main table. Seated at the table were the associates introduced at yesterday's meeting.

Zoe gave me an overly-sweet smile, her eyes saying something entirely different, and headed for the smaller table.

I approached the empty chair at the main table between a debonair and tuxedoed Jimmy Dougal and a very-not-debonair Scooter Jablonsky in a powder-blue polyester jacket. "Good evening, everyone."

Jimmy shoved his chair back, jumped up, and pulled out my chair. "Good evening, Sara," he said smoothly, his lustrous blue eyes staring directly into mine, and on into my soul. "Allow me."

As I sat, he gently slid the chair in behind me. "Why, thank you, Jimmy."

"The pleasure is all mine," he said with a brilliant smile of perfect white teeth and deep dimples peeking out from above a trimmed beard. Retaking his seat, he leaned toward me and winked. "Happy birthday."

Instant heat radiated out from my chest, kicking my heart into overdrive. I couldn't believe this hottie-with-the-body remembered from yesterday it was my birthday today. "Thank you," I forced out from a fast-tightening throat. "That's...um...so sweet you remembered."

"But of course." Another wink.

Sitting directly across from me, the grandfatherly Spencer Fernsby smiled warmly. There was a gentleness to his face, kind blue-gray eyes welcoming me to the table to break bread with him. "Good evening, my dear. We were wondering if you were going to make it."

Karsh Azarian, elbow propped on the table, head cradled between thumb and forefinger, droned, "Thrilled you're here."

The prickly Olivia Fantucci took a sip from a martini. "Or not," she sneered.

Percy appeared behind me. "Miss Donovan, may I get you something to drink before the dinner service commences? Champagne, perhaps?"

Scooter leaned back, held up a half-empty drink glass over my shoulder, and wiggled it. "Hey, Percy, another bourbon, son."

"Of course, Mr. Jablonsky."

Jimmy glanced over his shoulder at Scooter's antics behind me but said nothing, turning back to me with raised eyebrows.

"And less water, more bourbon," Scooter added, his flushed checks sending the opposite message.

"Certainly," Percy replied. "Miss Donovan?"

I twisted around toward the butler. "It's my twenty-first birthday. Champagne sounds wonderful. Thank you."

Ignoring my birthday comment, he simply said, "Very good," before disappearing through a swinging door in the corner of the room beside a white-brick fireplace with a richly-carved mantle.

Jessica Doerr, the mortgage lady trying to turn back the clock chemically and surgically, gave me a realtor's smile. "I have a granddaughter who just turned twenty-one, too."

"Nice," I said, my insides quivering. This was fast becoming way too much about me.

From the end of the table to Karsh Azarian's right, Frederick Volkov raised a champagne flute, his heavy-lidded eyes and long face giving the appearance of complete disinterest. In a clear voice, he boomed, "Happy birthday."

Terrific.

Everybody at both tables raised a glass, except for Olivia Fantucci, who made it a point to quickly set hers down. "Happy birthday," the group chimed in unison, less one cold-eyed ambulance chaser.

"Thank you, everybody," I said, just as Percy placed a flute of bubbling golden elixir on the table in front of me. I raised my glass. "Cheers and good luck in the contest."

As glasses clinked and a smattering of "cheers" and "good lucks" bounced around the room, a wee, wiry woman wearing a white chef's jacket, classic toque, and simmering scowl entered the room through the swinging door and stood at the vacant end of our table. She straightened, but the lady didn't even reach Zoe's lack of height, which was saying something.

"My name is Barbara Doll, your chef," she announced, a sterile austerity in her tone, and attitude the opposite of her diminutive stature. "My staff and I will be preparing all your dinners at El Sueño. A menu for the following day's dinner will be left in your room each morning by housekeeping from which you can place your order. Failure to leave a completed order in your room by the turndown service will result in you being served whatever dish I have the most of, period. There will be no exceptions. We will always have—"

Karsh Azarian stood. The man was tall, at least six-five, with broad shoulders and a flat stomach. He wore pressed gray slacks, a button-down blue-checkered shirt with open collar, and a navy-blue blazer with bronze buttons. "I beg your pardon, Babs, but will fish always be on the menu? I don't eat anything but fish."

The tiny chef marched around the table to the giant of a man, and in a flash, whipped out a wooden spoon from somewhere within her jacket like a crazed ninja in a knife fight. Dark round eyes glared up at Azarian, who held his ground, despite the spoon being thrust up under his chin. "You *ever* call me that again, and I'll gut you like a fish," she snarled. "The name is Barbara, but you *will* refer to me as 'chef.' And if you had let me finish, we will always have a catch-of-the-day, a meat, and a fowl. Satisfied?"

With the back of his hand, the man eased the spoon aside as he stared straight down at the combative chef. "Yes…chef…and my apologies. It seems I jumped the gun, now, doesn't it."

As fast as it appeared, the spoon magically disappeared. If her cooking was as amazing as her sleight-of-hand, we were in for a treat over the next two weeks. And probably a diet over the following two months.

"So, it would seem," the chef replied, her jaw set. She turned back to our table. "As you just heard, we will have fish, meat, and fowl each evening, as well as assorted desserts prepared on-site by our baker. Any questions?"

Karsh Azarian slipped into his seat. Nobody breathed a word. Nobody moved a muscle.

"Good. Enjoy your meal," she snapped, before storming back through the swinging door.

"That was fun," quipped Jimmy Dougal, his smile, resplendent.

Jessica Doerr held a dramatic hand to her chest. "Goodness, she's in the service industry? That would never fly in my business."

A crafty smile came across Volkov's face. "The lady's a shark. She would be fantastic in arbitrage."

Fantucci took a sip from her martini, a glint in her eye. "She'd make a killer attorney."

Spencer Fernsby wrinkled into a kind grin and chuckled softly. "My human resources people would pack her off for sensitivity training." He paused. "And probably team communication and conflict resolution training, too. She'd be gone for months."

"I bet that little 'ole gal would be a barracuda selling cars," Scooter said, gulping down his drink. "She wouldn't let nobody get outta the dealership without a sale."

"I just hope she can cook," Jimmy said. "I'm famished."

Rod Toft looked up from his phone. "Anybody read the info sheet from your room? Like, dude, what does 'like a shot in the dark' mean?"

Jessica Doer's pale-blue eyes grew big. Beneath them, cracking pancake makeup was not doing its job with her dark bags. "Didn't even notice that, but what's up with the instant camera?"

An astonished Karsh Azarian looked down the table toward Doerr, then the crypto dude. "Why would any of us answer either of those questions? This is a contest."

"For a half billion dollars," Volkov emphasized.

"Just trying to read the room," an impassive Toft replied.

"For what purpose?" Azarian fired back.

Toft took a drink of water and leaned forward, his gaze traveling around the table. "I'm looking to form an alliance. Someone with a creative mind."

Doerr excitedly waved a hand. "I'd be interested."

The crypto trader wrinkled his nose with a brief headshake.

Her hand lowered, embarrassment stretched across her plastic face.

Azarian scoffed. "Preposterous. I don't need any

alliance." He flicked a contemptuous hand. "Especially not with the likes of any of you."

"Who said I was asking you," Toft countered. "Besides, I said someone with a *creative mind*. You're just a money manager. Dime a dozen."

Azarian's face turned shades of dark reds and purple, but he said nothing.

Frederick Volkov drained his champagne and raised a long skinny finger, exposing a thin pink-gold watch with wheels and gears visible against a deep-blue background. "Are you familiar with arbitrage?"

Toft nodded, imperceptible air currents nudging his wildly frizzy hair, a tight-lipped knowing smile on his face. "It takes vision. And timing."

Volkov's grin was wicked. "And creativity."

Toft raised his water glass. "A topic for further discussion." He considered the still-fuming Azarian and smiled pleasantly. "Of course, after dinner."

Chapter Eight

A shot in the dark

Back in our suite after dinner, which was delicious and fairly uneventful after the Azarian-Toft dustup, Mauzzy snored away on the couch while I sat at the desk going over the information sheet. Standing next to me, Zoe played with the instant camera.

"You think Rod is onto something, about this 'shot in the dark' thing?" I asked.

"I can't believe they put me at the kiddie table," Zoe groused. "It was like being at Nana's for Thanksgiving all over again. When I was like fricking ten."

I gave her a look. "Oh, my God, it wasn't a kiddie table. You had old people sitting with you."

"It was rude. Your table was big enough for everybody."

"You're too sensitive."

Zoe let out a mocking laugh. "Right. I'm the overly sensitive one."

I ignored her spot-on comment and got back to the topic at hand. "So, what do you think about this 'shot in the dark' thing? It's strange, isn't it?"

Zoe set the camera down and looked over my shoulder at the paper. "I guess. Depends on who wrote it. If it was that dull lawyer dude, Creighton what's-his-name, yeah, it would be strange. But if someone all about the drama wrote it,"—she nudged me—"like you, then it would be perfectly normal."

"Funny."

"Just saying."

I stared at the sentence, rolling it around in my head. *And now, like a shot in the dark, when the new day begins, so does the game.* There was something about it. "Zo, maybe the 'shot in the dark' line is a red herring to throw us off."

"You think?" she huffed. "That's because it doesn't make sense. Unless someone is going to take a potshot at us."

I turned in the chair to face her. "Nobody is getting sho...hey when does a new day begin?"

"Midnight."

I stuck my index finger out with a flourish. "Exactly. Something is happening tonight. At midnight."

Zoe grunted. "You're right about that. I'll be sleeping. And so will you."

"Not at midnight." I picked up my phone and set an alarm for eleven-fifty-five. "We're both gonna be up and ready."

"Ready for what? Mauzzy's snoring?"

Sweet Handsome raised his head off the couch, looking disoriented, before settling on Zoe. He let out a yip, and when he got Zoe's attention, stared her down. Mercilessly. One thing I learned years ago—never mess with his sleep. Ever. Because if you do, he *will* get even.

Zoe broke eye contact with Mauz. "He's making me nervous."

"You should be. The last time I crossed him. I mean, *really* crossed him. He peed on my head. In the middle of the night. So…"

Another sharp yip.

Zoe looked over her shoulder toward the couch. Mauzzy stared back, stone-faced, eyes unblinking. Point made, he laid back down and nestled into the cushion.

"Sheesh," Zoe said. "At least he can't jump up on my bed."

I chuckled. "Yeah, I wouldn't be so sure. He's crafty."

She ran a hand through her black hair, the light animating its emerald-green streaks as her fingers combed through the thick locks. "He wouldn't, would he?"

I shrugged. "With him, anything's possible."

She swallowed. "Crap."

"That's possible, too."

A wince. "He wouldn't."

"Probably not."

"Probably?"

I turned back to the desk and pored over the information sheet. "This says there's an art gallery here with artifacts from ancient civilizations." I spun around toward Zoe. "Bet they have Egyptian stuff."

My biggest hobby was all things ancient Egyptian. Although, a couple years back, that hobby ended up getting me into some serious hot water. Like boiling. It was touch and go, but eventually I was able to extricate myself from the situation. With Mauzzy's help. As usual.

Zoe let out a long sigh. "Let's pray they don't.

We're going to have enough drama."

I caught sight of the desk's clock. "Hey, it's past ten. We need to go to bed."

"Yeah, I suspect we've got a long day ahead, with it being the contest's first day."

"That, too."

Zoe eyed me, her normally stunning eyes two ice-cold green marbles. "We're not getting up at midnight. You're pulling a Sara Donovan again, reading way too much into something."

"Of course, we're not getting up at midnight. That's ridiculous."

Relief washed over her face that, even at this hour, was disgustingly cute. "You're finally starting to listen."

"We're getting up five minutes before midnight."

****

A sharp punch in the arm startled me awake. "What the…"

The room was bathed in light.

Zoe leaned over me, her face inches from mine. "Get up."

In the background, an electronic tone sang.

Mauzzy groaned as I shoved him to the side and sat up, my head in a fog, hand searching for the phone on the nightstand. "What time is it?"

She stood there, hands on hips, eyes letting me have it. "Almost midnight. That thing's been going on for at least three minutes. Shut it off."

I fumbled with the phone, eyes trying to come into focus, fingers trying to stay asleep. After a few failed attempts, I got the alarm stopped, tossed the phone on the bed, and stood. "We have a minute. Whaddya think's gonna happen?"

"Besides me going back to sleep in the next two minutes? Nothing."

I tramped to the door leading to the living room, legs fighting the command to wake up. "We should be out here."

Zoe followed me out into the living room and plopped onto the couch. "Doubtful."

I turned on the desk lamp, took a wide berth around the red chair, and dropped down next to her. Sitting in that gyrating red dervish at this hour, especially after just waking up, would be like trying to ride a mechanical bull, drunk.

Both our eyes were glued on the desk's clock. When it flipped over to midnight, we glanced around the room. Everything remained unchanged. No secret compartment revealed itself. The phone on the desk didn't ring. No knock at the door. Mauzzy's snoring continued from the bedroom.

How could I be wrong? "When the new day begins" is obviously midnight, which is when the contest starts. So, why has nothing happened? Zoe's all-too-frequent words from the past reverberated in my head: *You're usually right, but always wrong.* Her point being, my instincts were usually right about something going on or about to happen, but always wrong about who or what was behind it.

Emphasis on *always*.

I stood and walked to the front door, opened it, and poked my head out.

All quiet.

I closed the door and returned to the couch where Zoe sat. Arms crossed. Lips pursed. Breathing loudly through her nose. I've seen her like this way too many times, right before she—

"Why won't you ever fricking listen to me?"

—blows.

Her onslaught continued. "Nothing is out there, right? It's past effing midnight and we're sitting here staring at each other and nothing else. You hear me? *Nothing*. How many times do I have to warn you about reading too much into things?"

My head dropped. "I really thought the contest was starting at—"

"Midnight? Who starts a contest at midnight? I told you. I fricking told you." She popped up off the couch and whirled to face me. "If you want my help with this contest, you're gonna need to start listening to me. Deal?"

"Deal," I replied quietly.

She turned for the bedroom. "Good. Now let's go back to sleep."

I stood, stepped over to the desk, and snapped off the desk lamp. Outside the bedroom door, I hit the light switch that turned off the two floor lamps in the living room. But instead of the room going completely dark, there was an eerie glow. On the flat-screen.

10. 19. 40. 31. 48. 13. 39.

Vindication! I knew I was right. Victory was mine. For once.

I stuck my head in the bedroom. "Uh, Zo? You might wanna see this."

"Not getting outta bed," she called out.

"You will for this," I sang.

Zoe rolled over and glared at me. "For what?"

I pointed back into the living room. "That."

With an annoyed grunt, she climbed out of bed, stomped to the door, and looked to where I was pointing. At the flat-screen. "What the…" She cocked her head at me. "You do that?"

"Nope. Just appeared when I turned off the lights."

She turned back to the glowing flat-screen. "Huh."

I returned to the couch, navigating in the gloom past the red chair, and slowly lowered myself, eyes glued to the flat-screen. Zoe flopped down beside me. We sat for a good thirty seconds, staring in wonder at the shimmering bluish-green numbers.

"What do you think they mean?" Zoe asked in a hushed tone.

"Don't know," I murmured.

"Should we write 'em down in case they go away?" Her tone, dreamy. Spellbound. Hypnotized.

Like Zoe, I couldn't take my eyes off the screen. The numbers were mesmerizing. Floating in the dark. "Guess so."

She got up and drifted toward the desk, still gaping at the numbers.

I repeated the numbers out loud as Zoe rooted through the desk looking for pen and paper. She shoved the middle drawer closed, sat at the desk, and held a pen over a small hotel-type message pad. "Okay, call 'em out."

"Ten. Nineteen. Forty. Thir…*Crap.*"

"Ah, hell."

Like the room, the screen was black.

Sitting in the dark, staring ahead, I said under my breath, "Like a shot in the dark."

Chapter Nine

Was it six? Or seven?

Zoe snapped the desk light on. "Why'd you turn the TV off?"

"I didn't."

"You sit on the remote?"

"Nope. It's on the table."

Zoe darted to the flat-screen and inspected it, her hands running over the unit. "It's turned off." She turned to me, mouth open. "And the thing's cold."

"Then how'd the numbers appear? And why for only a few minutes?"

Zoe returned to the desk, sat, and spun to face me. "Beats me. Maybe someone likes playing dirty. You remember all the numbers?"

"And why no warning before they disappeared? I mean, how would we know—"

"*Sara.*"

"*What?*"

"Focus. Those numbers are important. How many were there? Seven?"

"Yeah, I think so. Maybe six. Although…They took up the whole screen. So, yeah, maybe seven."

Zoe wrote on the message pad. "Do you remember them? I know forty-eight was one because that's my dad's age."

I squeezed my eyes shut, trying to see the floating numbers. "Um, ten, nineteen—"

An exasperated Zoe cut in. "And forty. Yeah, I got those. Plus, forty-eight. What else? Thirty-what?"

"Thirty-one. Definitely. And…hmm…there was another thirty-something. Eight, maybe?"

"Got it. That's six. I swear there was another number in the teens. Eighteen?"

White spots danced in front of me, obliterating any numbers attempting to manifest themselves. I opened my eyes. "That's all I got."

Zoe read from the pad. "Okay, ten, nineteen, forty, forty-eight, thirty-one, thirty-eight, and I'll go with eighteen." She looked up. "What do they mean?"

I stuck my hand out. "Bring that over here. And the pen."

Zoe bopped over to the couch, handed me the pad and pen, and plopped down beside me. We studied the numbers in silence. Beneath Zoe's number set, I rewrote the numbers in sequential order.

10. 18. 19. 31. 38. 40. 48.

"I don't see any pattern," Zoe said. "You?"

"Nope. And nineteen and thirty-one are prime numbers, but the others aren't. So, no hidden set of numbers can be developed from their divisors."

Zoe leaned away from me, a look of astonishment on her face, although I'm going with admiration. "Look at you with the geeky math talk?"

I grinned. "A little of Dad and Matt rubbed off on me, I guess."

Zoe returned my smile before focusing back on the set of numbers. "Hey, look, nothing in the twenties. You think the answer is something by omission? Like your whole 'deception by omission' thing?"

Could that be it? If so, it would mean we were dealing with up to ten numbers instead of seven. That would make things even more complicated. Although, with a half billion dollars on the line, cracking this thing was not going to be easy. But nine numbers—

"Hang on..." I hesitated. "What if...Maybe we need to step back before drilling down into the numbers."

Zoe narrowed her eyes. "I'm not getting you. Step back how? Where?"

"Not where. Let's look at the numbers *in total*."

"Add them up?"

"No, although let's come back to that if I'm wrong." I handed her the pad. "How many numbers are there?"

"Seven."

"Maybe we first need to focus on what has seven numbers, and if we figure that out, then we can use the individual numbers. Somehow."

Zoe placed the pad on the couch between us and scratched her ear. "There are seven characters on a 'Bama license plate."

I did a doubletake. "Really?"

"Sadly, yeah." She sighed. "I need a life."

I gave it a quick think before shaking my head. "Uh-uh. That would mean multiple plates because 'Bama plates use letters, too. Plus, we're looking for seven double-digit numbers. Not seven single-digit ones. What else?"

"A phone number, without the area code?"

I cracked a smile. "Hello, all single digits."

She smacked her forehead. "Duh."

My eyes searched the room, looking for anything that could be tied back to seven numbers. "The door's combo lock has seven digits."

Zoe grinned. "Uh, all single ones."

I returned her playful smile with a sheepish one of my own. "Obvis."

"*I got it.*" Zoe snatched the notepad, launched off the couch, and headed for the bedroom. "There's one of those hotel safes in the closet."

I scrambled after her. "Yeah, but those use three or four single numbers. Not seven double-digit ones."

"Maybe it's a special safe," Zoe said over her shoulder. In the bedroom, she slid open a closet door, revealing a standard-sized hotel safe with an electronic lock built into a vertical set of cubbies. "Whoa. It's locked."

I tugged on the door. It didn't budge. "It's supposed to be open so we can set our own code. This has gotta be it."

"Let's try high to low." Zoe entered the numbers from the pad. Nothing. She reversed the sequence. Nothing. With a huff, she popped the safe with the heel of her hand. "I thought for sure this was it."

We stood there, staring into the closet. I took the pad from Zoe and considered each number, turning it around in my mind, before moving on to the next. The numbers on the TV had been shimmery, with the edges blurred. They weren't sharp, focused, crisp. They were just the opposite. Was it possible?

"Zo, try these." I read off the numbers, going high to low, except instead of thirty-eight, I substituted thirty-nine.

She punched in each, finishing with ten. The lock

mechanism made no noise.

"Nope," Zoe said.

I gave her the reverse sequence.

"Damn it," she growled, giving the safe another good smack. "Maybe it's not so special and this isn't it."

"It's locked for a reason. Try this." I read off the numbers, high to low, this time changing the eighteen to a thirteen.

After another unsuccessful try, Zoe shrieked, stepped back, turned sideways, and raised a menacing foot briefly toward the safe before setting it back down. If she could have kicked the crap out of the thing, she would have, but it was at her eye level. Instead, she pounded the stubborn safe with the side of her fist, then reversed the sequence without my prompt, having committed the numbers to memory. Still nothing. With a long exhale of frustration, she leaned up against the cubbies and eyed me. "Got any other great ideas?"

"Let's keep working the safe." I showed her the pad. "We know ten, nineteen, thirty-one, forty, and forty-eight are correct, because I read three of those off to you from the TV, I'm certain about thirty-one, and—"

"And I'm positive about forty-eight."

"Right. So, what if the other two, eighteen and thirty-eight, what if I was close but got one slightly wrong because the numbers were kinda wiggly on the screen? And since they were the last two, I hadn't fully focused on them before everything disappeared. Maybe one of those eights I thought I saw was really a three, or a nine?"

Zoe rattled her head. "I'm with you, I think." She

looked at the pad. "So, if you're right, then that eighteen would have to be thirteen since we already have nineteen."

"Right. That was the second number I called out before the TV went dark. Great catch."

She scrunched up her face. "We've been going on there being seven numbers. What if there are only six?"

"Then that would be awesome."

Zoe pulled her head back. "Awesome?"

"We already have five of the numbers. If it was a six-number combo, for the last number we just need to work our way up starting with the number one until the lock releases."

She turned back to the safe. "Brilliant. Let's get cracking."

I grabbed her arm. "Hang on. Before we invest time in that, let's finish out my theory. Let's say the eighteen is thirteen, and the thirty-eight is thirty-nine. Again, first go high to low."

Zoe punched in the numbers from the pad, making the suggested substitutions.

A whirring sound came from the safe as the locking mechanism disengaged.

We looked at each other, eyes wide, mouths open.

"Holy crap," Zoe uttered as she eased the door open.

We peered inside. It was empty, except for a slip of folded paper. I took the paper out, unfolded it, and read it.

Congratulations. We are just getting warmed up. But be careful with me, lest you get burned. Seek the person who believed in me over all the others.

Chapter Ten

Sun-dried tomatoes?

After cracking the safe's combination, we spent an hour trying to solve the riddle. But with the time nearing two in the morning, and both of us fighting to stay awake, we reluctantly agreed to get some sleep. In the morning, we consulted the mansion's map and found the secondary dining room where breakfast was being served. Mauzzy was peeved he couldn't go, until I filled his food bowl. Then I was dead to him.

This dining room was not nearly as impressive as the main one, but it still rivaled anything I had ever seen. The room was half the size, with a lighted tray ceiling encircled by recessed lighting above five four-seat tables arranged like pips on a game die. A single crystal chandelier hung over the center table, at which was seated Karsh Azarian by himself, sipping from a teacup, reading a newspaper. No surprise he positioned himself in the middle of everybody. Three of the other four tables were filled with contestants and their associates. At one, the financial genius Frederick Volkov with his spitting-image brother, Ivan, and the disheveled crypto trader Rod Toft, back in his cargoes and flip-flops, with his bookish girlfriend, Ashley Tennison. Volkov and Toft sitting together was not unexpected since last night at dinner, they seemed to bond over discussing a possible alliance. At another table sat the phony mortgage banker Jessica Doerr and Olivia Fantucci, whom Scooter Jablonsky admiringly referred to as a barracuda and Volkov likened to a shark. Not flattering descriptions, but for a personal injury lawyer, probably the highest compliments you could pay her. Also at the table was Jessica's elderly mother, Virginia Byrd, and Olivia's friend, Marissa Chevalier, who had an air about her exactly like Olivia's. Condescending snobbery. At a third table, the likable Spencer Fernsby sat with his tastefully-dressed wife, Kathleen, while the irrepressible car dealer, Scooter Jablonsky, talked up a storm with flailing hands and a torrent of words. As Scooter yammered on, his thick bald brother Billy encouraged him with the occasional "got that right" or "damn straight." And throughout Scooter's verbal disgorgement, the telecom CEO sat with a polite smile, throwing in the occasional head nod but saying nothing.

Zoe and I steered clear of the sullen Azarian and approached the table with the charming and smoking-hot Jimmy Dougal. "Good morning, mind if we sit here?" I asked, praying he said it was okay. I can't overstate the man's hotness.

Just like at dinner, he was up in a shot, sliding out a chair next to his own, his face all gleaming teeth and dimples. "I cannot think of a better way to start my Friday."

Zoe looked to the ceiling with a brief headshake as I moved to sit in the chair Jimmy held out for me, pulse quickening, body tingling. "Thank you."

We all sat, and a waiter took our order. I asked for black coffee and plain yogurt with sliced strawberries and granola. Petite little Zoe ordered three eggs over easy, bacon, hash browns, chicken-fried steak with buttermilk biscuits smothered in white sausage gravy, wheat toast with orange marmalade, and a large glass of orange juice. A typical meal for her. Volume. Jimmy ordered English breakfast tea, a plain bran muffin, and a fresh fruit bowl.

After the waiter left for the kitchen, Jimmy eyed Zoe with a disarming smile. "Somebody's hungry."

Scooter, whose table was next to ours, had stopped talking and was watching us. Closely. He called over to Zoe. "Y'all have a good night?"

She opened her mouth to reply but I beat her to it. "We were in bed by ten."

He chuckled and stroked his thick beard. "I bet you were. Y'all sort out that whole shot-in-the-dark thang? Or that picture camera?"

Fernsby gently set his coffee cup down. "That's enough, Scooter."

Jablonsky twisted around toward the CEO. "What? Just tryin' to smoke 'em out. Seeing if we can learn something."

The white-haired old man with the compassionate face forced a smile. "Remember what we discussed."

"But I was just—"

He softly patted the table several times. "I understand. Now is not the time."

"Dadgum it, sorry 'bout that."

Spencer put a finger to his lips.

Jessica Doerr's excited voice rose from the other outer table next to ours. "They couldn't figure it out."

Olivia Fantucci shushed her as she took a quick look around the room.

On the other side of Karsh Azarian's table, I caught a glimpse of a smirking Frederick Volkov. Even at breakfast, he wore the same outfit. Black suit. White dress shirt. Understated red-striped tie. Combined with his long face, heavy eyes, and waxen complexion, the somber man looked like a mortician. He said something to Rod Toft, who glanced over at Doerr's and Fantucci's table, a malevolent smile spreading across his wide fleshy face.

The waiter appeared with our tea and coffee, Zoe's juice, and cream and sugar. "Your orders will be right up."

"Thanks," Zoe said, grabbing her orange juice and taking a healthy slug.

Jimmy prepped his tea with a splash of cream and a spoon of sugar. Lifting the teacup with one hand and the saucer with the other, he raised the cup to his lips. With a knowing smile, he said, "Other than that Azarian fellow, it would seem everybody else has partnered up."

I slurped some piping-hot coffee. "You think so?"

He sipped his tea, setting the cup down on the saucer he still held with the other hand. "No doubt. That puts you and I at a competitive disadvantage with the rest." He motioned toward Zoe with his head. "And seeing how you have a lovely associate, and I have none, my disadvantage is extreme."

"You wanna team up?" I asked.

Zoe shot me an *are-you-nuts* look, but kept her mouth shut. For once.

Jimmy gazed back at me, his hypnotic blue eyes searching mine. "Perhaps. Let's give it a few days, shall we, and then reassess." Another sip of tea, his attention flickered to Zoe, then back to me. "I could be wrong over who has the biggest disadvantage."

Before Zoe could lay into the unsuspecting man, I quickly changed the subject, asking him, "Hey, who do you think the founder is?"

"I haven't the foggiest. Does it matter?"

I shrugged. "Guess not. You think it's the attorney?"

"Sure sounds like it matters," Jimmy said with a wide smile.

"Just curious, is all. You think he owns El Sueño? This place is amazing."

"Creighton Winston?" Jimmy asked.

"The founder," I replied.

Jimmy took a sip of tea, considered my question, then set the cup and saucer on the table. "I suppose it's possible, but it could also be leased for the contest." He chuckled lightly. "But I would love to have the listing if the owner ever decided to sell, that's for sure."

"I bet," Zoe said. "What would the commission be, a half mil?"

Jimmy raised an eyebrow. "At least."

I glanced around the room. Scooter was back to his incessant talking while Spencer Fernsby politely tolerated the jabbering with a soft smile. Volkov spoke with Toft in a hushed tone as he kept a sharp eye on the offensive Karsh Azarian, while the surly Olivia Fantucci and submissive Jessica Doerr ate their breakfast in stony silence. What dark secret, what compromising piece of information, forced each to the contest? Catching Karsh glaring at me, I turned back to our table and focused on Jimmy. His face was full of warmth and kindness, like Spencer. I couldn't imagine why either were involved in the contest. Maybe they were being blackmailed with manufactured evidence, too.

Jimmy stared back at me, his eyes smiling. "You still thinking about the founder?"

"Actually, I was wondering about your lucky secret."

"Excuse me?"

"You know, your lucky secret. Creighton Winston said we were all here because each has a lucky secret. So, what's yours?"

"Ah, right. Now if I told you, it wouldn't be a secret, would it?"

****

After breakfast, which Zoe devoured and left nothing on any of her plates, we returned to the suite to pick up Mauzzy before venturing out into the mansion on our quest to solve the riddle. Something told me we needed Sweet Handsome involved if we were going to win the contest.

I shoved the instant camera into my backpack, slung it over a shoulder, and hooked Mauzzy up to his retractable leash.

"Why you bringing that camera?" Zoe asked. "We got our phones."

"It's here for a reason."

A giggle. "Yeah, to take self-portraits."

I made a face at the snickering sprite. "So funny. When the time comes, we'll figure it out."

Zoe furrowed her brow. "You think Jimmy was talking about me, about that whole disadvantage thing?"

"What? No. He's just being careful. Can't blame

him. A lot of money is at stake."

"The dude looked right at me when he changed his mind over who had the biggest *disadvantage*."

"Man, who *are* you," I said. "We come to this place and suddenly you're all sensitive and stuff."

"Just making an observation."

"A wrong observation."

"Whatever." My unexpectedly fragile friend picked the riddle up from the coffee table. Next to it was the leather portfolio with the welcome sheet. We had been studying both before breakfast, but couldn't come up with anything. "This says, 'but be careful with me, lest you get burned.' Who, or what, can burn you?"

I moved toward the front door, Mauzzy in tow. "I dunno. A match?"

Zoe intercepted me at the door, jumping into my personal space to keep me from opening it. "C'mon. Think. This is your thing."

"Riddles?"

"No, you idiot. *Getting burned*."

"What the heck are you talking about?"

Zoe was ready to explode, her little body bouncing from foot to foot. "All you do is burn stuff, including yourself. So, it's simple. List off everything that's burned you." She stopped her aerobics to put out a cautioning hand. "But we don't have all day. Keep it to last month."

I grimaced. "Last month?"

She nodded.

"Let's see." I tucked the leash case under an arm and counted off on my fingers. "Curling iron. A fricking March sunburn last week out on Dad's boat. Who gets sunburned in March?"

"Only Sara Donovan," Zoe crowed. "Although, it was hot down here during Spring Break, too. 'Cept I just got tanned. Keep going."

"Okay, jalapeño in the eyes. Lemon juice, both in the eyes and in a nasty knife cut I got chopping onion. Stove, obvis. Multiple times. Steam from a microwaveable veggie bag. Air fryer. Coffee in the lap, but just twice. One small fire in the kitchen but—"

Zoe put up both hands. "*Enough. Got it.* We need to visit the kitchen." She pulled the El Sueño map from her back pocket and consulted it. "Okay, let's go see if we can get you burned."

With Sweet Handsome leading the way, we left the suite and headed for the grand dining room, which was attached to the kitchen. He didn't need any map. The little guy could sniff out food from Tennessee. In a double-baggie. Finding a kitchen in a sprawling mansion? Please.

We walked through the empty dining room and pushed open the swinging door by the fireplace leading into the kitchen.

Standing inside at a stainless-steel work table, Percy Pembarton and the chippy chef, Barbara Doll, were in an intense conversation.

The chef didn't have her wooden spoon, but from the looks of things, she was doing just fine without it. "You listen to me, Pembarton, it's *my* menu. *I* decide what's served. Nobody else." She jammed a forefinger at his chest, inches away from making contact. "You just make sure it's properly served."

"I understand, chef. However, a guest requested Tuscan—"

"I couldn't care less what someone requested," she

barked. "Sun-dried tomatoes flat-out stink, like a pair of old sneakers. And taste even worse."

"With all due respect, that is just your opinion. This guest is—"

The tiny lady arched her back, neck stretching up toward the relatively short butler, bony forefinger shifting from the man's chest to just under his chin. "In this kitchen, my *opinion* is *fact*. Case closed. Now, butt out."

Percy caught sight of Zoe and I just inside the door, listening. Then he saw Mauzzy, and his expression went from a polished smile to absolute disdain. He pointed emphatically to the door behind us. "Animals *are not* allowed in the kitchen."

Percy's insult elicited a low growl and fierce stare from Sweet Handsome.

After shooting a fierce look at Percy, the chef approached a miffed Mauzzy, knelt, and gave him some loving. "If it was my home kitchen, you could stay as long as you want."

Moaning and groaning in ecstasy, Mauzzy's head tilted up toward his newfound friend, making sure she got under the muzzle.

"What a good pup," she crooned. With a withering look over her shoulder at the butler, she continued, "Yes, I know, he's a butt. But he's right, we can't have you in the kitchen." She looked up at me with, oddly, a pleasant smile on her face. "What's his name?"

"Mauzzy."

"Hello, Mauzzy," she said, her fingers scratching under his chin. "I love wiener dogs. *Oh, yes, I do.*"

I cringed, waiting for Mauzzy to let her have it. He despised being called a wiener dog, and never disappointed when someone insulted him with the derogatory moniker. It was right up there with being called an animal. Instead, he laid down and rolled over, stubby legs straight up in the air, inviting her to partake in some belly rubs.

The chef complied, saying, "He's just adorable."

I bit my tongue and smiled graciously. "He has his moments."

With one last belly scratch, she stood and addressed us. "I'm so sorry but Mr. Pembarton is correct, you will have to leave the kitchen. However, I can cook little Mauzzy's dinners for you, if you'd like."

With the mention of dinner, Mauzzy flipped back over and sat at attention, his eyes trained on the loving Barbara Doll. Who would've thought the two crankiest people in the mansion, by far, would get along so well?

I waved her off. "Thank you for the offer, that's very generous. But I'll have to pass. While he loves people food,"—I fanned the air in front of my nose—"it doesn't love him. And I have to sleep with him."

Mauzzy angled his head up at me and scowled, not appreciating the airing of his dirty laundry.

She gave Sweet Handsome one last ear scratch, then stood, her laugh easygoing. "My Taffy is the same way. And she's a big girl. A bluetick coonhound. So, when she gets hold of food from the table, the results later are *really* bad."

Percy came up to us. "Please, Miss Donovan. You really must leave the kitchen."

"Of course," I said. "C'mon, Mauz."

The leash fed out as Zoe and I moved toward the door. But Mauzzy didn't move, hence said leash feeding out. I locked it and gave it a tug. "Let's go,

Handsome."

He refused to budge and gave the chef a pleading look, who cheerfully said, "Go on now, Mauzzy. I'll see you later."

Recognizing she was not coming to his rescue, he popped up and followed us out of the kitchen into the dining room.

"That's one tough chef," Zoe marveled.

"Big time, and I think she solved the riddle, too."

Zoe stopped and considered me. "What? I didn't hear anything."

"Sun-dried tomatoes," I exclaimed.

Her eyes narrowed. "You been burned by tomatoes? Seriously? Even for you, that's hard to believe."

"You were right. Back in the room. This riddle is so my thing."

She frowned. "Getting burned?"

"Close. Sunburned. Sun-dried."

"What the heck are you—"

"*Ra!*"

"Wow, that's some enthusiasm for sun-dried tomatoes."

"Not rah. RA!"

Zoe stared back blankly. "Girl, you losing it."

"Ra. The Sun God." I paused, excitement welling up in me. "From the ancient Egyptians. And Akhenaten, who became a *devout worshiper* of Aton, the sun's disc, over all the other gods. Just like the person in the riddle."

Zoe looked at me sideways. "That the same Aka dude you got all wrapped up with a couple years back? With the feds?"

I took a deep breath, refusing to let one very bad memory chill this moment of triumph. "One and the same. He was the tenth ruler of the Eighteenth Dynasty. Some scholars refer to him as—the Sun Pharoah."

She arched an eyebrow. "Meaning?"

"El Sueño has an art gallery. With artifacts from ancient civilizations. I'm willing to bet it has stuff from the ancient Egyptians. Including Akhenaten."

Chapter Eleven

The art gallery

It took fifteen minutes of wandering through endless hallways, spacious foyers, and multiple breezeways, but eventually we found an entire wing off the main structure housing the art gallery, a spectacular building with artifacts rivaling Birmingham's Dauphin Museum, a place I worked freshman year. Two twelve-foot-high paneled doors opened into an airy two-story space with soaring windows, a stone slab floor, white walls, and recessed lighting. On the far end, a staircase led to a mezzanine with a glass half-wall, beneath which was an expansive built-in wall unit holding statuettes, busts, bowls, and vases. Scattered throughout the space, pedestals held bronze and stone statues, colorful gold jewelry, funerary masks, and other ancient artifacts.

After a brief look around, Zoe and I stood in the middle of the first floor, surrounded by bygones of ancient civilizations including the Greeks, Romans, and to my surprise and overwhelming joy, all thirty-three pharaonic dynasties of the ancient Egyptians.

"What are we looking for?" Zoe asked.

"Anything related to the sun or Ra or Akhenaten."

"The sun I can do. You focus on all your Egyptian crap."

I unleashed Mauzzy and we all split up, wandering through the gallery, stopping occasionally to examine, or sniff, a particular item. In an alcove beneath the mezzanine, I came across a four-foot-high pedestal holding a pinkish gypsum bust of Akhenaten. The information card said it was discovered in the ancient city of Tel El-Amarna.

Also known as—the Sun City.

This had to be it.

With heart jittering, my hands wandered over and around the pedestal. The surface appeared smooth. No ridges, indentations, or grooves that could have been the edge of a hidden compartment, secret button, or latch release. With a deep breath, and quick prayer, I focused on the top of the pedestal and the irreplaceable bust, my fingers slowly probing along its base. If this thing toppled over onto the stone floor, I was going to need to win the contest just to afford paying back the El Sueño owner. But I found nothing. Again.

Stepping back from the pedestal, I took it in. There were only two places on it I hadn't physically examined. The bust itself, and the information card, which was enclosed in glass or plexiglass and at an angle for easier reading by patrons. A quick internal debate ended in the no-brainer decision to keep my unreliable hands off the priceless artifact and focus on the information card. I attempted to pick it up, but after a good tug, it seemed firmly attached to the pedestal's top. I gave it another tug. A twist. Then a jiggle and—the card flipped backward flat against the top. The pedestal's entire front panel slid to the right, scaring the bejesus out of me, revealing a three-foot-high safe.

"Zoe," I yelled. "Get over here."

From somewhere, her muffled voice reached back. "Where?"

"Main room. Under the mezzanine."

Footsteps pounded above me, then on the stairs. To my right, paws pitter-pattered, nails clicked and scratched, tags jingled, as Mauzzy tore around a corner and raced toward me, ears straight out, riding the wind. Both arrived at the same time, skidding to a halt in front of the opened pedestal.

Zoe crouched and peered at the safe. "Holy crap. This is just like the room safe. Only bigger."

A panting Sweet Handsome put his front paws up on the safe as if hugging the thing, head pressed sideways against the metal. I couldn't tell if he was catching his breath, licking the keypad, or listening to what was inside it. But he was up to something. Totally on brand.

Still bent down examining the safe, Zoe looked back at me. "You happen to bring the combo for the room safe?"

I pulled the small notepad out of my backpack and read the numbers off as Zoe worked the electronic keypad.

"That didn't work," she said. "Maybe for this one, it's low to high."

I read off the same numbers but reversed the sequence.

"Crap." She stood, gave the safe a quick kick, and faced me. "What now?"

"First, no kicking or hitting the safe," I said, eyeing the priceless artifact perched atop the pedestal. "Please?"

She stuck her head out, a cheeky smile on her face.

"Then give me the right combo."

"Let's assume it's still seven numbers, and still has a high-to-low sequence."

"You think it's a different combo and it's in here somewhere?"

I nodded. "Gotta be. Let's look around."

"Did you see any TVs or monitors that could display numbers, like in the room?"

"Nope. You?"

"Nah. How we gonna find a bunch of numbers in a place full of numbers?"

She had a point. There were hundreds of exhibits, all with placards containing dates, some with dynasty numbers, others with ages.

I screwed my face up. "Very slowly, I suspect. Don't know what else to say."

"Not helpful." Zoe examined the Akhenaten card. "Like, just on this one, there's the year 1912 when the thing was found. It's dated to around 1345 BC. The dude ruled for seventeen years during the first and second dynasties and may have been as old as forty when he died. If you split the years into two numbers each, right there you have eight numbers." She threw up her hands. "And that's not counting the different years when his tomb may have been discovered. For one fricking exhibit."

"I get it."

Zoe slowly turned around, shaking her head as she took in the daunting task.

"Wait, what'd you say?" I asked.

She looked back at me. "About what? All that Egyptian crap I just read?"

"Was the information card you read really for

Akhenaten?" Without waiting for an answer, I read the card, rubbed my eyes, and refocused on it.

Were my eyes fricking with me?

I leaned closer, squinting. "This is wrong."

Zoe let out a half-laugh. "You're telling me."

"No, that's not what I mean," I said, pointing to the card. "That's way wrong. It says Akhenaten ruled during the first and second dynasties, but everybody knows he ruled during the eighteenth."

"Pssh. Everyone knows that," Zoe scoffed.

Continuing to reread the information card, I said over my shoulder, "How could they get that so wrong? I mean, they got the duration right for his rule, but the dynasty number isn't even close. It's just *so* wrong, it doesn't make any sense." I turned back to Zoe. "And not that it matters, no pharaoh's rule spanned two dynasties, but this card says Akhenaten ruled during two dynasties."

"Totally agree. It doesn't matter. Nobody cares."

I pressed the point. "Don't you get it? This card is blatantly wrong."

"Only to you. You're the Egypt dork. Pretty sure nobody else would notice."

"You're probably right. Most wouldn't notice or care. And if someone wants to hide numbers…" I raced to another Egyptian exhibit, a set of limestone Canopic jars from the fourth dynasty, dated between 664 and 525 BC. "*Zo, this one's wrong, too.*"

She rushed over to me. "Yeah? How so?"

"Just like the Akhenaten bust, this card has the wrong dynasty. It says these jars are from the fourth dynasty, but if the dating is correct, then pretty sure the dynasty should be the twenty-sixth."

Zoe read the placard, then considered me, head tilted to the side. "You sure?"

I double-checked on my phone. "Yep, confirmed. Should be twenty-sixth."

"What if they made an innocent mistake and got the dating wrong, but the dynasty number is correct?"

I blew out. "Hadn't thought about that. But then you still have incorrect info, it's just the years and not the dynasty number."

Zoe studied me, her eyes narrowing. "You *certain* the dynasties are way wrong back on that bust?"

"Absolutely. Not even close. Akhenaten is my favorite pharaoh. By far."

She rubbed her chin, took in the room, and turned back to me, pointing to the jars. "It's not a coincidence we've found another dynasty is wrong. I think three of the numbers in the combo are four and…What were the first ones? For your boy back there?"

"The wrong dynasties?"

She nodded.

"First and second."

"Right. One and two. Okay, so let's assume there are four more incorrect dynasties listed somewhere in this place."

I started a note in my phone. "Then those plus one, two, and four are the combination numbers."

"Or, it's the other way around, and the *correct* dynasties of the incorrect ones are the numbers, meaning we need five more. So, keep track of both."

"Good point." I added to the note. "How we gonna do this?"

She pointed to herself. "*We* aren't doing this." Her index finger flipped around toward me. "*You* are.

You're the Egyptian nerd."

I threw her a thumbs-up and took off in search of the next Egyptian exhibit. I hustled from artifact to artifact to artifact, but after hours of bouncing around the first floor, all the Egyptian exhibits identifying dynasties correctly matched the noted time periods on the information cards. "This is hopeless," I complained.

"Keep going. I know we're onto something. You still got the whole upstairs to do."

And just like that, as if Zoe's never-ending confidence was the secret sauce we needed to crack this thing, the very next Egyptian exhibit listed an incorrect dynasty. "Bingo," I shouted. "This says forty-second dynasty, which is so obviously wrong. There is no forty-second dynasty."

"What should it be?"

"Let's see, Ramses II? Uh, hello. Nineteenth."

She briefly looked to the heavens with a headshake. "You sure?"

My mouth dropped open. "OMG, it's Ramses II. Aka Ramses the Great. Of course, I'm sure. Besides,"—I struck a pose, one hip out, hands on both, head stuck out—"the New Kingdom is my *jam*."

Another deprecating headshake at my expense. "Such a fricking dork."

With a triumphant grin, I typed forty-two into the phone note for the incorrect dynasties list, and nineteen for the correct one. "You're welcome."

A quizzical look came over her. "Hold up. You say there is *no* forty-second dynasty? You sure?"

"Positive. There are only thirty-three."

"Don't ask me why, call it a gut feeling, but I think it's the incorrect dynasties we want. I can see someone *maybe* typing the wrong dynasty, you know, like mixing them up, but not a non-existent one. And forty-two isn't even close to thirty-three."

"Works for me, but I'll still keep both lists." I bolted for another exhibit. "We need three more wrong dynasties."

With renewed energy, I tore through the rest of the first floor and most of the second, with Zoe and Mauzzy in my constant wake. After several more hours of testing my Egyptology knowledge, and with the help of searches on our phones, we had seven incorrect dynasties listed on exhibits.

Zoe ran for the stairs leading down to the first floor, the Akhenaten bust, and the safe within its pedestal. "Let's go crack a safe."

I chased after her, catching up at the safe, where both she and Mauzzy impatiently waited. "Man, you two are quick."

"Or you're not," she teased, crouching in front of the safe. "Give me the numbers, high to low."

I read from my phone note. "Forty-two. Thirty. Twenty-six. Twenty-five. Four. Two. And one."

"Nope. Give it to me low to high."

I did, but the result was the same. "It's gotta be something that makes sense, otherwise nobody will be able to get it."

"So high to low, and low to high didn't work," Zoe said slowly. "What about a combination of the two?"

"How do you mean?"

"Low to high to low. Starting with the one. And if that doesn't work, high to low to high."

I studied the numbers on my phone. "Zo, it could work."

She turned back to the safe. "It better work, because I'm out of ideas. And I can't kick it."

"Here we go. One. Two. Four. Forty-two. Thirty. Twenty-six. Twenty-five."

A whirring sounded, followed by a clunk.

Zoe looked up at me, all gleaming white teeth and twinkling green eyes. "Boom," she said softly, opening the safe's door.

I bent down, and with our heads side by side, we peered inside it.

"Huh? Is that…" I muttered.

We looked at each other, agape.

Zoe's eyes were two green dinner plates. "What the heck is *that* doing in there?"

Chapter Twelve

Another clue

Inside the pedestal's safe sat a polished orange sphere of some kind. I dropped my backpack, lifted the object out of the safe, and straightened. "This is heav...*Whoa.*"

I yanked my foot back, the bowling ball just missing as it bounced off the stone floor with a resounding *plunk*, followed by a second, and quickly a third, before rolling away. I took off after the offending orb as Zoe roared.

Catching a bowling ball that had a bouncing head start is not an easy task, but I chased it down, trapping it up against a wall. I *carefully* picked it up and returned to a sniggering Zoe and an indifferent Sweet Handsome.

"This has a seven on it." I turned the ball around so Zoe could see. "You think it means something?"

She didn't even look at it. "Yeah."

"*Really?*"

"It weighs seven pounds."

More laughter. And this time, a double-snort from an amused Mauzzy. And these were my best friends.

When I put the ball back in the safe, I removed a slip of paper from the top of a small stack of envelopes and read it.

"Crap."

"What's the matter? What's it say?" Zoe asked.

"Removal of the object and this paper from the safe are grounds for disqualification, including loss of my diamond." I threw the paper back in the safe like it was on fire and glanced around the room, looking for cameras. "You think they saw me?"

"Who?"

"I dunno. The lawyer guy. His people."

Zoe's eyes bugged out. "His people?"

"You know, security."

"Girl, you are so paranoid. And too literal. You gotta remove the paper to read it. What's in those envelopes?"

With another quick look around, I took out the envelopes and sorted through them. They were the same type of ivory-colored envelope that came with my package when this whole thing started four days ago. "They're sealed. Each one is addressed to a different team or person."

"Read 'em off."

"Frederick Volkov and Rodney Toft. Jessica Doerr and Olivia Fantucci. Burl Jablonsky and Spencer Fernsby. Karsh Azarian. Jimmy Dougal. And me."

"Cool. That means we're the first here. Open yours."

I replaced the other envelopes and tore open the one with my name in gold-embossed lettering and took out a slip of matching ivory paper with a single line of print. "It's another riddle. '*We can go round and round on this, but trust me, I hold one of civilization's oldest inventions.*'" I handed Zoe the riddle and envelope. "Any thoughts?"

She read the paper and looked up at me. "Yeah, someone is having a lot of fun effing with us."

"It's for a half billion dollars."

"Still."

"And why do we have to keep everything in the safe?" I asked. "Why can't we take the stuff with us?"

"You wanna lug around a frigging bowling ball?"

I pulled back. "No. It's just strange is all."

Zoe shrugged. "Probably gotta keep it all there for the others. I guess we're all hunting for the same crap."

"We're getting the same clues? In the same order?"

"Doubt it. Probably same clues, different order. They don't want us bumping into each other. That's how'd I do it."

"Makes sense." I dug into my backpack and pulled out the camera. "Bet that's why they gave us this. There's gonna be a bunch of objects we're supposed to photographically collect. Whoever finds them all and turns in the proof at the end of the contest, wins the money."

Zoe slipped the riddle into the envelope and handed it back to me. "Maybe. Gonna need to wait and see what else turns up. Seeing how today's the first day of a two-week contest, who knows what's coming."

"Any thoughts on some of the oldest inventions?"

"Fire?"

I frowned. "How's that an invention?"

"How's it not?"

"It's more of a discovery."

She flipped a hand. "Whatever. It could be a room with a fireplace. Or the kitchen. I saw a cook this morning using a gas range."

I took out my phone and did a search on the oldest

inventions. "Oh my gosh, it's like the art gallery all over again."

"How?"

I showed her the phone. "There are all kinds of super-old inventions. Stone tools date back millions of years. A hand axe was found in Ethiopia from over two million years ago. Bone tools a million years ago. Even agriculture is considered an invention."

"Yeah, well, we're out of time. We need to get going."

I took a picture of the bowling ball and closed the safe. After securing the camera, photograph, and my envelope in the backpack, I threw it over a shoulder and leashed up Mauzzy. "Let's get out of here before someone sees us."

"Or because it's almost time for dinner. We missed lunch and I'm starving."

Mauzzy looked up at me and yipped.

"Yes, Sweet Handsome. I know."

He smiled and with head held high, trotted for the entrance doors, happily leading the way back to the suite. And his long-awaited and, apparently, way past-due dinner.

We hurried through the connecting breezeway and were entering the main house when—

Mauzzy let out a high-pitched yelp.

—we ran into Jessica Doerr, Olivia Fantucci, and their associates, the doddering Virginia Byrd and snooty Marissa Chevalier.

"Oh," Doerr cried. The mortgage banker stepped back and reached down toward Mauzzy. "I'm so sorry. I didn't see the poor little thing."

Mauzzy danced away from her flailing hands

before setting his feet and eyeballing the woman. Hard.

Virginia put a bony hand to her chest. "Oh, goodness me. You stepped on it, Jessie."

"I didn't mean to, Mother." Jessica inched toward the indignant dachshund. "Ah, now, come here, sugar. It's okay. I have a little one, too."

"It's a dog," the short but extremely fit Fantucci said, her tone dripping with condescension.

"Barely," Marissa said with a huff.

"His name is Mauzzy," I said, "and he's perfect."

Doerr made another attempt to apologize to Sweet Handsome. "Oh, Mauzzy, come here. I'm so sorry I hurt you." She glanced up at me. "My little one is Dusty. He's a miniature poodle."

The lawyer sneered at her groveling partner, then turned and inched toward me, her dark beady eyes full of venom. A manicured finger sliced through the air at Mauzzy. "I don't care what its name is. *Why* is it here?"

I gulped. This lady was beyond fearless, and even more scary. "Um, he's my emotional support dog."

"That's a lie," she snapped. "Where is its vest?"

Zoe jumped into the space between me and Fantucci. "Give it a rest, lady. He's not required to wear one."

Jessica Doerr froze mid-reach for Mauzzy and stared over at Zoe, mortified. Virginia appeared to be in shock while Marissa's terrifying visage mirrored her friend's.

Fantucci didn't budge. In fact, she leaned in toward my personal protector. "I will do no such thing. It is not allowed and I shall take it up with Creighton Winston first thing in the morning."

Zoe took a step toward the woman, fists clenched.

"*Yeah?* Percy said he's cool with it."

"He's just the butler," she spat.

"Who runs the frigging place," Zoe shot back. "And who also cleared it with Winston."

A fluttery feeling attacked my insides. I've seen this before with Zoe and braced for a fight. And I mean, an actual fight. The girl did not tolerate bullies. At all. Especially when I was the target.

The personal injury lawyer recoiled, taking a step back. "We shall see."

"Knock yourself out, lady."

A shaken Jessica Doerr stood and addressed me. "Were you coming from the art gallery just now? That's our next—"

"Shut up, you fool," Fantucci barked.

The mortgage banker reddened. "See you at dinner."

"Sounds good," I said quickly before dashing down the hall and around the corner, Mauzzy's stubby legs working hard to keep up.

In the distance, Fantucci's shrill voice rose as she berated poor Jessica.

"Hold on, slow the eff down," Zoe called out. "You're going the wrong way. Our suite's the opposite direction."

I stopped and faced a visibly annoyed Zoe. "I wanted to check out the east wing real quick."

"We're gonna be late to dinner. Besides, the lawyer said it's locked, and if we go inside it, we're out of the contest."

"We're not going inside. Yet. I just wanna see if it's a simple door lock or something more sophisticated. You know, so we're prepared for later."

Zoe groaned. "Oh, my God, now you're suddenly an expert on locks? *And* we're busting in later?"

"I need to identify the founder, and that wing is the key."

"Only if the founder is the El Sueño owner. If he isn't, you'll be accusing an innocent person of blackmail."

"Who said I'd be accusing anybody?"

"Right, you've never done such a thing."

I ignored her snarky but accurate comment and headed down the hall. "C'mon, at the end of this, we hang a left and it should be right there."

I raced to the end of the hall, a grumbling Zoe following close behind. Rounding the corner, I came to a stop in front of two heavy wooden doors with intricate carvings on the center of each, and a keypad with a scanner mounted on the wall at eye level.

I tugged on one of the door handles. "Locked. And that's gotta be a retinal scanner. We'll never get in."

"What a surprise," Zoe said with a huff. She pointed to above the door. "Smile for the camera."

****

"Here you are, Miss Donovan," Percy Pembarton said, leaning in between me and Jimmy Dougal at the dining table and placing a glass of champagne in front of me. "And at your request, I discussed your emotional support dog situation with Ms. Fantucci and everything is straightened out."

I glanced across the table at the glowering lawyer, her flinty eyes trained on us. "She doesn't look too happy about it."

"Certainly not. But it's not her concern, either. Enjoy your meal."

117

After Percy left, Jimmy raised an eyebrow. "Trouble?"

"We had a little run-in today."

"Over?"

I explained what happened, but left out our quick visit to the east wing.

"She appears to be quite spicy, doesn't she," Jimmy murmured.

"Ha. If that's what you wanna call it. She's not a nice person."

He picked up his own champagne flute, held it in front of his face to shield him from the others, and leaned toward me. "I saw her team coming out of the greenhouse earlier today," he whispered. The man smelled delicious, like vanilla and nutmeg. "Doerr looked ecstatic."

"Like they found something?" I whispered back, my eyes on Fantucci.

"Exactly." He took a sip of champagne and set the glass down. "How about you?"

I leaned away, taking in his Hollywood good looks. "How about me, what?"

"Find anything?" A big toothy smile stretched across his face.

"I can't tell you that."

"Sure, you can," he coaxed, continuing to work his charms on me.

"We're not partners."

"Do you still want to be?"

I glanced over at the associates' table. Zoe was chatting up a storm with Mrs. Fernsby and Billy Jablonsky. She never ceased to amaze me. If a situation required it, the girl could flick a switch and turn on the schmooze. I'd seen her do it too many times. With teachers. Guys. Even my dad, who was virtually unschmoozable. If those people at the table only knew.

"Maybe. I'm gonna have to discuss it with Zoe."

Jimmy appeared surprised. "Really? Aren't you the invited contestant?"

"Why are you suddenly interested in teaming up? Just this morning at breakfast, when I asked you the very same thing, you wanted to give it a few days and then '*reassess*,' I believe was the word you used."

He chuckled lightly. "Indeed, that is exactly what I said. However," he angled toward me. "This contest is *exceptionally* more difficult than I anticipated."

I gave him a coy smile. "Does that mean you made no progress today?"

With a playful smile of his own, he replied, "I wouldn't say that. But I also know, for a half billion dollars, this contest is going to get even harder."

"Really. So, what'd *you* find?"

Brilliant blue eyes flashed his amusement. "Touché." His gaze worked around the table before settling back on me. "This is quite the formidable group. My invitation letter said winning was going to require an extraordinary level of resourcefulness and acumen. At the time, I believed I possessed the skills, intelligence, and wherewithal to win. And win easily. But now…with those people…and after today…Well, I am thoroughly humbled because it is I who has the extreme disadvantage."

"Zoe will be happy to hear you said that. Give me the weekend to think about it and talk with her."

He put out his hand. "Deal."

Karsh Azarian's pretentious voice came from the

end of the table. "It would appear I am now the only courageous one going it alone." He held a glass of red wine aloft in our direction, a smug grin splashed across his stupid goateed face. "As it should be, I suppose. Fair play and what not."

Across from me and next to Olivia Fantucci, Scooter Jablonsky's attention bounced between Karsh, Jimmy, and I. Then he pointed with his half-full drink glass toward Frederick Volkov and Rod Toft, who were seated on our side of the table to Azarian's right. "Hey, Freddie boy, y'all been quiet tonight. Whatsa matter, your contest off like a herd of turtles?"

Volkov fixed his hound-dog eyes on Scooter. "Quite the contrary, Burl. Tell me, have you and Spencer made it out of your rooms yet, or are you still *wrasslin'* with that devilish first clue?" Volkov finished with an amused laugh and clinked glasses with Toft. "Cheers, my friend."

Scooter was about to blow when Spencer Fernsby inserted himself in the conversation. "Frederick, throughout my career, I have seen your kind come and go. Usually to prison for insider trading and fraud, I might add." He raised a water glass to his lips. "My goodness, it would be quite difficult to win the contest from a jail cell, don't you think?"

Volkov jumped to his feet. Even from my vantage point, I could see the blue vein throbbing in his forehead. "Are you threatening me, Fernsby?"

Fernsby smiled warmly, a contrast to his suddenly stone-cold blue-gray eyes. "That certainly wasn't my intention. My respectful apologies."

Jimmy whispered in my ear, "The plot thickens."

Chapter Thirteen

The brainiac?

The next morning after an uneventful breakfast, Zoe and I drove to Finn's office. He agreed to meet on a Saturday for a briefing before we headed off to Tuscaloosa so I could meet Grant for lunch, and Zoe could see her boyfriend, aka my brother, Matt.

I knew it was against the rules, talking to Finn about the contest, but technically I wasn't seeking his help. I was just going to update him. When we pushed through the office door, twenty minutes late courtesy of an especially uncooperative and grumpy Mauz, who now was all too eager to be first inside, Bertie popped out from behind Finn's desk to greet us.

Mauzzy froze, watching Bertie approach from the corner of his eye. Even though I had been working for Finn for seven months, this was Mauzzy's first time to the office. Not because he wasn't allowed to be there, but because I wanted to act professional at work, even if everything about Finn and his office projected something completely opposite.

"Hey, Bertie," I gushed, showing him some loving. "This here is Mauzzy."

The two dachshunds performed the sniffing ritual, all of it, with Mauzzy eventually snorting his approval. Introductions complete, they padded over to the desk, best of friends. Bertie took his usual spot in bed behind Finn's desk, Mauzzy ditching me to join him and nuzzle up into his new buddy. They both sighed, content in their new world.

So much for me.

Typical Sweet Handsome.

Finn sat with his feet up on the desk, beer bottle in hand. "Morning, ladies. Sorry, I started brunch without ya."

Zoe glanced around the crappy office before her gaze settled back on Finn. "Brunch?"

"There's no brunch," I said. "He's *trying* to make a joke."

He pointed the bottle at Zoe and grinned. "This here's my breakfast. Got my lunch cooling in the fridge."

I sat in one of his crappy guest chairs and gestured for Zoe to sit in the other. Addressing her, I said, "Just remember my comment the other day. Despite appearances—"

"He's…the best?" Zoe said as she sat, her questioning tone not matching the words.

Finn took a drink of beer and flashed her a mischievous smile. "Got that right. If I was any better, I'd have to be twins."

I groaned. "Zo, don't even."

"All right, what's goin' on?" Finn asked, draining his beer.

I dug into my backpack and pulled out the contest rules, welcome sheet with the cryptic final paragraph, and both riddles. "First thing you need to know, the prize for winning the contest is five hundred million dollars."

Finn's face scrunched up. "What now?"

I leaned forward and looked into his eyes. "The winner gets a half billion."

He whistled softly.

"That's the minimum," Zoe added. "It could be more. Although half goes back to the contest's founder."

Finn's gaze ping-ponged between us. "A kickback? That don't make no sense. Unless, it ain't his money."

I handed Finn the contest rules and riddles, then took him through the past two days at El Sueño, finishing with last night's fireworks at dinner. As I talked, he studied the papers.

When I finished, he tossed the empty beer bottle into the trash, grabbed his "lunch" from a small refrigerator behind the desk, and twisted off the bottle cap. "Sounds like someone's fixin' to jerk a knot in that Volkov fella's tail."

I shook my head. "Don't think so. Spencer Fernsby seems like such a nice man. He could be my Grandpa Martin."

Finn took a swig, contemplated me, then shrugged. "When I was a cop, I put more than a few granddaddies away who are now doing twenty-five to life."

I stared back. "Are you saying…"

"Just trying to open your eyes to all the possibilities." Finn pulled a notepad from a side drawer and picked up a pen. "Gimme them names again of the competition. Reckon we're gonna need to know who y'all are up against." A pause. "I mean, *really* up against." Another pause. "Can't be too careful when talking 'bout money."

"Hang on," an agitated Zoe said. "What do you

mean by that? Can't be too careful?"

Finn's hand shot out. "Now don't go getting all riled up on me. For the kinda money y'all talking 'bout, folks will do all sorts of things. Just need to get the lay of the land, is all." He looked at me. "Now, gimme them names."

I ticked off the contestants' names, and he jotted them down. Just to be safe, I included Percy Pembarton, Barbara Doll, and Creighton Winston. "Start with Karsh Azarian. There's something about him, other than the fact he's an egotistical slimeball."

"Ain't nothing wrong with that, but you got it. Now lemme write them riddles down."

He scrawled on the notepad, then handed me back the contest rules and riddles.

Zoe scooched her chair forward, elbows on the desk, chin in hands. She peered at Finn, who's head was down studying the riddles. "You find it strange the very first place we're sent to, an art gallery full of Egyptian artifacts, is the very place Sara would know the best?"

Finn glanced up. "How's that?"

Zoe sits back and points to me. "This girl loves Egyptian crap. I mean"—she leaned in—"*loves* it. I don't think it's coincidental the first clue sends us to a place loaded with Egyptian crap, and the combo to the safe holding the next riddle is tied to the same Egyptian crap. Even with her geeking out, it took all day to crack the code."

Finn eyed me, then Zoe. "What's your point?"

"It's odd." She turned to me. "What if this is *all* about you?"

I straightened, head tilted. "What are you talking

about?"

"This contest," Zoe replied. "You think any of those other people are gonna be able to figure out all that wrong dynasty crap anytime soon? They'll never figure it out."

"Don't know," I said. "Karsh is very sophisticated. So is Jimmy, I think. Actually, they're all smart."

"Except for Scooter," Zoe said with a roll of the eyes.

"True, he's an outlier," I said.

"You suggesting this founder *wants* her to win?" Finn asked Zoe.

"I don't know," she replied. "Maybe."

"That's ridiculous," I scoffed.

Zoe arched an eyebrow. "Yeah, I'm not so sure."

"Why?" I asked.

"Maybe you were lured there," Zoe replied. "To El Sueño. But there is no money. It was just the cheese."

"Uh-uh. You know exactly why I went."

"Yeah, and I think you should tell him," Zoe said.

I gave her a quick headshake and stern look.

She replied with an exaggerated smile and nod of the head.

"Tell me 'bout what?" Finn asked, looking at Zoe, then me. "Sara, you holding back on me? This 'bout that second envelope?"

No way I could tell him about the manila envelope. And the doctored photos. The note was crystal clear. As were its implications. Tell no one, or else. I had to trust my instincts. Now was not the time to spill my guts to Finn. Maybe later. But not now. It was way too early in the game and I had no clue who or what I was up against.

I blew out, waving an unconcerned hand. "Pssh, no. It's not important."

Zoe slouched in her chair, arms crossed. "She's lying."

Finn steepled his thick fingers, lips pressed up behind them. His gaze flicked back and forth between Zoe and me. Once. Twice. A third time. With a sharp exhale, he fixed on me. "I'm gonna trust you, Sara, that you're gonna come to me when the time is right." The joking, wisecracking, easygoing Finn was no longer. His tone was serious. Dead serious. The most serious I've ever seen him. "But you best not be late when you do come. And you will come. Until then, I'm gonna dig into this El Sueño and them names you gave me to see what or who is behind this thing. Okay?"

I nodded.

We remained locked on each other for several seconds before he spoke. "Okay, let's talk 'bout this last riddle." He read it out loud.

We can go round and round on this, but trust me, I hold one of civilization's oldest inventions.

"Among the oldest inventions are stone tools," I said. "From like two million years ago."

He took a gulp of beer, studying the notepad. "Mmmm. Not liking it. Irrelevant."

Zoe sat up in her chair. "I said fire. Like maybe it's a fireplace or stove."

Finn shook his head. "Nope. Fire is too old. Besides, I don't consider it an invention."

I turned to Zoe, a sarcastic grin on my face. "Told you."

"That doesn't prove anything," she fired back. "That's just his, and your, lame opinion."

Finn tapped the notepad. "This here riddle says 'one of *civilization's* oldest inventions.' Stone tools and fire weren't invented by a civilization."

I reread the riddle from the paper in my hand. "How'd I miss that?"

"You want me to answer that?" Zoe asked with a smirk.

Ignoring the snarky shrimp, I read the first riddle that led us to the art gallery.

Congratulations. We are just getting warmed up. But be careful with me, lest you get burned. Seek the person who believed in me over all the others.

Other than the initial one-word sentence, everything else in the riddle was pertinent to solving it. The second sentence alluded to heat, which can come from the sun. The third sentence specifically mentions getting burned by something or someone. In this case, the sun. To the ancient Egyptians, known as Aton. And the final sentence refers to Akhenaten, who was a devout worshiper of Aton, the sun's disc, over all other gods. Every single sentence had purpose.

I focused back on the second riddle.

"Whaddya thinking?" Zoe asked, leaning over to peer at the paper in my hand.

"We need to consider the entire riddle. Every word of it. Finn, you're right about civilizations. But we haven't addressed the first part."

"Round and round?" he asked

"Yup."

"A merry-go-round?" Zoe offered.

I gave her a look. "Seriously?"

She appeared genuinely surprised at my response. "What? It goes round and round."

"It's not a merry-go-round," I said flatly.

"It was probably invented in the eighteen hundreds," Finn noted.

"We need to think ancient civilizations," I said. "Egypt. China. Mesopotamia."

With a shake of the head, Zoe chuckled lightly. "Yeah, I'm out. That's not my game."

"Outside the ancient Egyptians, I'm right there with you," I said, taking out my phone. "But we need to search on ancient civilizations' inventions. I'll handle the Middle East. Egypt. Mesopotamia. Sumer. Zo, you look into China and India."

"Sumer," Finn said with a start. "The Sumerians. '*Go round and round.*' They're credited with inventing—the wheel."

Our heads whipped around. Gobsmacked would be an understatement.

His eyes narrowed beneath out-of-control eyebrows. "*What?* I ain't just ruggedly handsome."

"Since when do you know about the Sumerians?" I asked.

"Hey, now, I got depth."

"Try again," I said.

"Since I went to 'Bama." His index finger shot out. "Which is where I got my noted depth."

"Roll Tide," Zoe uttered, head down, fingers working her phone.

He raised his beer in a toasting motion, took a hit, and slammed it on the desk. "Roll Damn Tide."

"You in college was like forever ago," I said, unable to get arms around my boss taking a gargantuan leap up the food chain. "How'd you remember that?"

Finn leaned forward on a forearm, sticking his head

out. "First, that was only twenty-five years ago."

Zoe chuckled, still focused on her phone. "Ha. Only."

"You realize that's longer than we've been alive," I said with a grin.

With a heavy sigh, Finn groaned, "Appreciate that. Really do."

"My pleasure," I sang.

He returned my wiseass smile with one of his own. "Anyway, I minored in history. If I recall, the Sumerians invented the wheel around 3000 BC."

Zoe looked up from her phone, even more astonished than one minute ago. "He's right. They invented the wheel in 3500 BC."

Finn beamed with arms outstretched. "Like I said, ain't just a pretty face. *Depth*."

"You did say he was the best," Zoe said to me. "Didn't expect a brainiac, though."

"Hold your horses," Finn declared, addressing me. "That ain't the first time she's said you been bragging on me." His tired brown eyes were now alive, squinting at me. "You really say that 'bout me? That I'm the best?"

I rubbed my forehead, knowing this was going to be biting me all the way to graduation, whenever that elusive day chose to arrive. And probably beyond. "Maybe."

"She said it more than once," Zoe added, pouring it on, loving every second of my growing misery.

Finn sat back, basking in the glow of himself. "Hey, now, Sara, I appreciate that. I really do."

"I'm sure you do," I grumbled. "Can we get back to the riddle? *Please?*"

"Sure enough," Finn said. "This thing is 'bout a wheel. So, what has a wheel at El Sueño?"

The room fell silent.

"*The garage*," Zoe erupted.

I looked over at my best friend. "What garage? You mean a parking garage?"

She shook her head. "The welcome sheet said El Sueño has a garage. And after getting a load of the mansion, I'll bet the garage is full of all kinds of cars."

"Sounds to me this Monday y'all are visiting the El Sueño garage."

Chapter Fourteen

Together, again?

I picked at the remnants of a crispy taco chicken salad, basically just shards of the taco, since I devoured everything else thirty minutes ago, including Abuela's Casa's fabulous chips and fresh salsa. To the consternation of the waiter, Grant and I had been talking long after we finished lunch.

"I still can't believe you're being transferred to Rome," I said.

Grant pressed his lips tight, his normally vivid blue eyes, muted. Their luster, washed out by the reality of his news. "Yeah, I have mixed feelings, for sure. I mean, it's Rome, so that's awesome. And one of my top priorities is finding Caravaggio's *Nativity*. It was stolen *over fifty years ago* from a Palermo church and is number two on the FBI's stolen artworks list, so if I crack the case, talk about a career boost. And Rome's perfect from an investigative standpoint since so many stolen artifacts are transshipped through the region. But..."

"I know," I said quietly. "But I just can't up and move to Rome after graduation. I have plans."

He forced a smile. "With the cases you've cracked the last couple years, it makes sense to start your own agency. Clients will be beating down the door."

"Hope it's not a mistake."

"You'll be a great PI."

"Thanks." Our eyes locked. A second passed. Then another. "The Universe just seems to have different plans for each of us. With every year, it puts more miles between us."

Grant's short laugh was joyless. Like his eyes. "At this rate, next year I'll be in Beijing."

"Better start learning Mandarin."

He smiled with only his mouth. "I'll get on it."

The most awkward silence we've ever experienced together descended on the table, a heavy shroud of what might've been, and what will be, after we walk out of Abuela's. To our separate cars. And life's deviating paths.

Grant broke the silence, redirecting the uncomfortable conversation back to our earlier discussion of the contest. In a low voice, he said, "You have no idea who this founder might be?"

I shook my head. "Nope."

"Who gives away a half billion dollars? Who can *afford* to give away that kind of money?"

"Zoe doesn't think the money exists. That it's bait to lure us in. She actually said 'me,' but I think it could be all of us. The contestants, I mean."

Grant tapped his lips, his eyes searching mine. "She could be right. It could be you. The other eight sound financially successful. But why? It makes no sense."

"I think all nine of us have a link to the founder. We were each picked for a reason. He needs one of us for something. And the contest is his way of determining the most qualified."

"To do what? And who says it's a 'he?' Did the lawyer give any indication?"

I thought back to the meeting on Wednesday. The one where Creighton Winston read the rules, and had the dustup with Olivia Fantucci. I shook my head slowly. "I don't think so. I guess I just assumed."

His smile was understanding. "The first rule of being an investigator, *never* assume."

I let out a laugh. "Yeah, that's gonna be a tough one for me."

Grant laughed with me. "Don't I know it."

"Well, whomever it is, the person is loaded. El Sueño is amazing. The art gallery is stuffed with what I would consider priceless artifacts. There's even a Stradivarius in the music room."

"*If* that stuff is real. And the place could be leased, not owned."

"But Karsh Azarian, one of the contestants, said it was definitely a Strad. He sure sounded like an expert. And Creighton Winston scolded Jimmy Dougal for playing it."

Grant's gaze briefly drifted past my shoulder, then back to me. "It could all be legit. But it could also be a con. Focus on who owns El Sueño. Then go from there."

"Finn is going to check it out. And all the contestants."

He nodded and reached for the check. "Sounds like you got it handled. We better get going. The waiter has been giving me the stink eye."

As Grant paid at the register, a scratching sound followed by a metallic click and more scratching approached from behind.

It was a familiar sound. I turned around.

Steel-gray eyes stared up at me from a head of soft snow-white curls, wrinkly face, and jowls. Mrs. Majelski broke into a wide grin, her brawny hands gripping a walker with tennis balls on the back legs and a pink-flowered basket strapped to the front. Like she needed a walker. I've seen her run, both on and off the treadmill. The old woman could fly.

"Sara! I thought that was you, dear. Funny meeting you here."

Funny certainly wasn't the word that came to mind. What was she doing here at Abuela's? At the same time, Grant just happened to be in town, having lunch with me. At Abuela's. If Zoe knew they were here together, I'd never hear the end of it. But was she right about them? They do always seem to pop up in the same places at the same time. And I always seemed to run into the old lady away from the gym when things in my life started going sideways. Like now. With those awful photographs. The threatening note. The bizarre contest. And the enigmatic founder. Did she know something? Or was she somehow, someway, *behind* everything? A chill seeped down my spine as my chest tightened. Was I right? Has she been following me around Birmingham and out to El Sueño? It's not like she hasn't done it before. Although, back then, she did it for my protection. At least, that's what she always said. And everything always worked out. Eventually.

I threw the ancient wonder a little wave. "Hi, Mrs. Majelski. I didn't see your truck outside."

"Always the observant one." She hooked a thumb over her shoulder. "Parked out back."

"And I see you're still working the walker," I said

with a raised eyebrow.

With a crooked smile, she replied, "Why not? I'm an old lady, dear."

Grant took his receipt from the cashier and gave Mrs. Majelski a hug. "Sadie. So good to see you again."

Finishing their hug, she patted his back. "And you, too, dear." With a glimmer in her eye, she said, "Congratulations. I hear you're off to the City of Seven Hills."

Grant forced a smile. "You heard correctly. I'd ask how you knew, but…"

Mrs. Majelski cackled, put a gnarly finger to the side of her droopy nose, then pointed at Grant. "Exactly." A wink. "What brings you to—" She caught a glance of me. "Ah, yes. Sorry, dear."

"Yeah, it sucks," I griped.

"Change gets a bad rep. It's called life," she replied matter-of-factly, turning back to Grant. "When you shipping out?"

"A little more than three weeks. Last day in the office is April seventh. But I'll remain in D.C. the following week getting packed out. First official day in Rome is April seventeenth."

"I see. Perhaps we'll run into each other before you leave?" She finished with raised eyebrows.

"You gonna be in D.C.?" he asked.

"Maybe." Mrs. Majelski noticed a couple waiting to pay and maneuvered the walker toward the door. "Let's get out of the way of these nice people."

We moved away from the register, stopping just inside the front door.

"So, who you here with?" I asked her as innocently as I could muster.

"My great-nephew, Billy." She wrinkled into a devilish grin. "You've met him."

Yeah, Officer Rhett Preater, aka Billy, responding to one of my nine-one-one calls a couple years ago was not my finest moment. I frowned. "He still with Tuscaloosa PD?"

She bobbed her head. "He is. Made sergeant a few months ago. He's such a good boy." A puzzled look crossed her face. "Tell me, dear, where have you been this week? I haven't seen you or your cute little friend at the gym."

"Um, I've…we've…been really busy. Spending a lot of time in Birmingham."

She scrutinized me, her steely gaze penetrating my very being. "Birmingham, huh? That's where Finn is. How's he working out for you, dear?"

"Great. I've learned quite a lot from him," I said, laying it on thick. "You were so right about him."

"He finally over that two-timing hairdresser?"

"Says he is."

She slowly shook her head. "He was a first-class cop. And even better instincts. Sharp. Real shame about him getting shot."

"*He got shot?*"

Mrs. Majelksi looked at me, dumbfounded. "I didn't tell you about that?"

"You sure didn't. He really got shot?"

"He did. One of the department's CIs played him, settling an old beef. Finn thought he was getting information on the Black Creek Killer, a sadistic lowlife he'd been chasing for two years. The poor boy let his growing frustration and desire to nail the killer cloud his judgment. He lost his trademark discipline, took a sledgehammer approach to the case, and jumped on the lead instead of crosschecking the CI's intel. Got him one in the hip. Ended his career. And the killer has never been caught."

"He never mentioned any of this to me."

She shrugged. "He was devastated. Then his wife dumped him. Sent him skidding to some dark places."

"That explains a lot."

"Mmmm-hmm. He still got that dog? With the one blue, one brown eye."

"Bertie?"

She nodded.

"Yup. Follows him wherever he goes."

Another nod, followed by a brief glance behind her, then past us to outside. "He's a special pup, that one. Only one who's got Finn's back. Besides me. Some cultures believe mismatched eyes allow people, or in this case, Bertram, the ability to see into both heaven and earth. They call them—ghost eyes."

"Ghost eyes?"

"You heard me."

"So, you know about Bertie?" A beat. "And his...power?"

"I know about a lot of things, dear." A pause. "Tell me, what's really going on in Birmingham." A longer pause. "Besides Finn."

Chapter Fifteen

Crossroads?

After conjuring a story for Mrs. Majelski about helping Finn on a new missing heiress case, I quickly ditched Abuela's and the skeptical antiquity for my cottage. I left with mixed feelings because while I was able to escape further scrutiny from the old lady, I also likely said my final goodbye to Grant.

With a heavy heart, for the rest of the weekend, I kicked around ideas with Zoe and Matt on how to attack the El Sueño garage when we returned, both where the next safe could be hidden and how to uncover its combination. Almost every angle we came up with involved license plates. Unfortunately, there were so many different scenarios, that all we did was frustrate ourselves and drive Matt crazy because he couldn't return with us to help.

When Monday finally got off its butt and decided to show up, and after finishing a riveting morning of mind-numbing business classes, since we were already in Tuscaloosa so why not attend, we sped to El Sueño to get back on the contest. Despite my best friend's frenzied protests and overly dramatic begging for her life, I drove. As we passed through El Sueño's gates, a multitude of flashing police lights reached out to us from the parking lot.

"That doesn't look good," I said, easing the winded hatchback along the driveway.

"If you weren't with me all weekend, I'd say you had something to do with it."

"Good one."

"You make it easy."

The lot was full of luxury cars and SUVs, Rod Toft's obnoxious red racing machine, three police cruisers, two unmarked cop cars, and—a medical examiner's van.

With no available place to park in the crowded lot, I pulled onto the adjacent grass and cut the engine. "You think somebody died?"

"You're gonna make quite the PI," Zoe said, getting out of the car while slinging a backpack over her shoulder.

I jumped out, grabbed my own backpack and a snoring Mauzzy from his milk crate in the back, and leashed up the now piqued pup. We headed toward the mansion, then stopped abruptly. Two men in navy blue windbreakers wheeled a gurney out the front door. On it, a body bag.

"Oh, my God," I whispered to myself. "Someone *did* die."

Percy Pembarton stood in the open doorway, shoulders slumped, face waxen. His usually alert eyes appeared exhausted as they followed the gurney to the back of the medical examiner's van. As the men loaded the body into the vehicle, Percy waved us over.

"Who is that?" I asked the butler in a hushed tone.

He slowly shook his head. "Sadly, Ms. Fantucci."

My mouth popped open. "Olivia? Dead?"

"Afraid so. Quite tragic."

"What happened?" Zoe asked. "She was the picture of health. All Marissa talked about during dinner was how they did yoga and ran ten-K's together."

Percy nodded. "She was indeed fit. Appears to have passed in her sleep. Extraordinary, really."

"Why the police, then?" I asked with a glance at the van, where one of the men slammed the rear doors shut while the other climbed into the driver's side.

"I rang them up," Percy replied, "at the direction of Mr. Winston. He wanted to ensure there was no skullduggery."

Zoe's eyes bugged out. "Skullduggery?"

"Yes, ma'am. Skullduggery."

"You mean murder," I said plainly.

"If you wish."

"Who found her?" I asked.

"Her friend, Ms. Chevalier, upon her return this morning after spending the weekend with family."

"Marissa found her?" Zoe said, astonished. "What are the cops saying?"

"Nothing appears untoward. However, since she was last seen alive Friday at dinner, pending the medical examiner's pronouncement, they are taking statements from everybody who was at El Sueño from Friday night until today when the body was discovered." He fixed on me. "Including you two ladies."

I took a step back. "Wait. What? We weren't even here."

Percy made a clucking noise with his tongue. "From *Friday night* until today. You departed Saturday morning at nine-thirty."

"How do you know that?" I asked.

140

"There is a camera at the front gate, my dear. Now,"—he raised a cautioning finger—"I was instructed by Mr. Winston to remind all contestants and their associates that the NDAs they signed demanding total silence remain in force. You are not to mention anything about the contest to the police. Understood?"

"What if they ask why we're all here?" I hissed, a sudden heaviness in my clenched stomach. "At El Sueño."

"They will not."

"That's all well and good," I retorted, "but what if they do?"

Percy leveled his gaze on me. "Mr. Winston advised the detectives that each of you is here at his personal invitation to reward his firm's very best clients with a fortnight of rest and relaxation at the fabulous El Sueño. As his guests are VVIPs, he stressed to the police the need for discreetness and absolute privacy."

"So, you're asking us to lie," Zoe said with arms crossed, one foot forward, weight on her back leg.

"No, ma'am. You are both here at Mr. Winston's invitation. He is now simply—"

"Like hell it was an invitation," Zoe interjected. "Y'all blackmailed my friend into coming."

Percy straightened, drawing his shoulders back. "Miss Harp, please keep your voice down. I am not privy to any details other than Miss Donovan was invited to El Sueño by Mr. Winston for a two-week stay, and she brought you as her guest. And as I stated, Mr. Winston has already established this fact with the detectives, so they will not be inquiring as to why you are here. Understood?"

Zoe seethed, but said nothing.

Looking at me, Percy said quietly but firmly, "Mr. Winston is simply asking for you and Miss Harp to uphold the terms of the NDAs you signed. Understood?"

I nodded.

"Very well." He retrieved a phone from his inner jacket pocket. "Now if you will excuse me, I must place a call."

We followed Percy into the mansion, who pushed through a murmuring crowd of contestants and their associates, and bolted up one of the twin stairways embracing the domed entranceway, his voice trailing behind. A casually dressed man and woman stood on the far side of the entrance by the arched opening leading into the music room. Both held a small spiral notebook. On their hips, holstered guns, and gold badges. The man was speaking with Rod Toft while the woman listened to a distraught Jessica Doerr.

"It appears the competition has been culled by at least one," Karsh Azarian said with a sly smile.

"My goodness, man," Spencer Fernsby said, aghast. "A person has died."

Jimmy Dougal raised an eyebrow, a suspicious look appearing on his gorgeous face. "Culled? Interesting word choice."

"Perhaps," Karsh replied. He glanced across the entranceway to the two detectives, then back to Jimmy. "And judging by Jessica's reaction over there, we might be in luck and lose a second."

"Enough!" Fernsby snapped. "Show some respect. This is not about the contest."

Karsh flicked a dismissive hand. "As far as I'm concerned, *Spencer*, everything that happens here is about the contest."

My phone chimed. It was Finn. I tugged on Mauzzy's leash and we headed to the front door, stepping outside as I answered the phone. "Hey, you won't believe what's happened."

"Everything okay?"

As I walked toward the parking lot to get away from any prying ears, I filled Finn in on Olivia Fantucci's death, Karsh Azarian's reaction, and Percy's insistence on our silence about the contest.

"I ain't worried 'bout it," Finn drawled. "Folks die in their sleep all the time."

"But she wasn't that old. Maybe early fifties."

"She coulda took something."

"You mean drugs?"

"Wouldn't be the first time."

"Uh-uh. No way. She's all into herself. Runs. Yoga. A real health nut."

"You'd be surprised 'bout them health crackpots. I busted one for possession who ran one of them fancy nature stores."

"Olivia Fantucci was an attorney."

Finn chuckled. "That ain't helping your case."

"I just find her death very suspicious."

"Let the professionals sort it out. With all that dough on the line, you got enough to focus on."

"Yeah, I don't know."

"Look, I already got info coming in on folks from that list of names you gave me, including Fantucci. Until you hear from me, or the cops come up with something, quit your fretting. Okay?"

"You know, she was a real nasty person. I think someone wanted her—"

"*Sara*. Listen up now. That Karsh fella is right. For you, everything should be 'bout the contest. Leave this up to me and the cops."

"What if they ask why I'm here?"

"Honor the NDAs and tell 'em you were invited to El Sueño, which ain't a lie. If they press you, refer 'em to that attorney fella. But whatever you do, *don't lie*, 'cause that'll open you up to obstruction charges if this investigation goes south."

I wasn't going to argue with Finn. He didn't know the whole story, because I chose not to tell him the whole story. If he knew I was coerced into participating in the contest, and that all the contestants were there because they had secrets law enforcement would be interested in, would he still be unconcerned about Olivia Fantucci's death? Was now the time to fill him in on everything? Just two days ago, he warned me not to come to him when it was too late. Had I already reached the crossroads?

"Finn, there's…There's something I…"

I glanced down. Mauzzy stared up at me, his expression urging me to do the right thing. Sure, easy for him to say. He wasn't being framed and blackmailed by someone powerful who knew an awful lot about me. Too much about me.

"You finally coming clean with me?" Finn asked.

I breathed out. "You never said why you called."

"You're right. I didn't."

"And…"

Silence. In the background, Bertie yipped. Finn mumbled something. Another yip. More silence.

"Finn?"

"You best not be late," he warned. "I'm good at

what I do, but I can't work miracles."

"I know. I won't be. Why'd you call?"

He sighed into the phone. "Right. I've been digging into this El Sueño. It's owned by a trust in the Cook Islands."

"Really? That's the same place discussed in the contest rules."

"I saw that."

"What's the name?"

"The One-Eleven Trust. Mean anything?"

"Nope. Whose name is it in?"

"Dunno. One of the advantages of a Cook Islands trust is full anonymity. It's also shielded from creditors and lawsuits."

Full anonymity? That's got to be why the winner is required to establish a trust there to receive the funds. But why the need for anonymity? Unless the money was ill-gotten money. And that's why half goes to the founder. But where does somebody steal a half billion dollars? And if somebody steals that kind of money, why give half of it away? Zoe was wrong. Nobody would go through this kind of charade to lure only me to El Sueño. It was all real. Creighton Winston. The contest. The contestants. The Cook Islands trusts. The money. But why?

"Hello? Sara? Dang it, did we get cut off? Sa—"

"Sorry, Finn, I'm here. I was just thinking."

"Yeah? 'Bout what?"

"When was the place purchased? El Sueño."

"Six years ago. It's heavily mortgaged."

"Through a Cook Islands bank?"

"Nah. But right idea. It's an offshore bank in Palermo, Sicily. Banco di Credito di Sicilia. And get this, they're due a twenty-million-dollar balloon payment on July seventh."

I about dropped the phone. "*Twenty million?*"

"Got that right."

"So, someone has to come up with twenty mil for this bank?"

"Yup. That's less than four months away."

"Or…"

"Or kiss El Sueño goodbye."

"After hearing all this, you still don't think Olivia Fantucci's death is suspicious?"

Finn exhaled. "Didn't say it wasn't suspicious."

"You pretty much did."

"Nah, I didn't. Just trying to open you up to other possibilities. If you're gonna be a private investigator, gotta keep an open mind."

"Ha. Not the first time you've said that to me. And just recently, someone said basically the same thing. That I should never assume."

"Sounds like a smart person."

"So, you *do* find the death suspicious."

"Not yet. Don't have enough details." A beat. Then another. "But I do find it interesting."

"And what will it take to make her death suspicious?"

Finn fell silent again. Only this time, longer. And when he finally spoke, his words slammed into my reeling brain. "Reckon when another body turns up."

Chapter Sixteen

Skullduggery?

Dinner was wrapping up after a long afternoon of questioning by the police, questioning by Creighton Winston, who showed up not long after our arrival at El Sueño, and internal questioning by me if it was wise to continue with the contest. Despite Finn's lack of concern, I couldn't put Olivia Fantucci's death in the "natural causes" column. It made no sense. If it was Spencer Fernsby or Frederick Volkov who died, no problem. Both were well into their sixties and possibly even their seventies. Rod Toft was clearly a druggie, so on any given day I could see him offing himself with the wrong concoction of whatever his drugs du jour might be. And Scooter was just plain unhealthy with his exorbitant belly and matching drinking habits.

But Olivia Fantucci?

Dying in her sleep?

Impossible.

Could Karsh be right, and someone killed her to cull the field? If so, it stood to reason the killer was not going to stop with her. But I couldn't just walk away. It wasn't about the money, if it even existed. It was nailing the person who was framing me, trying to ruin my life. And the only way I could do that was to stay in the contest. Until…

As a waiter cleared the remaining dishes, and Percy delivered after-dinner drinks and "digestifs," as he called them, the ravishing Jimmy Dougal leaned in toward me. "Have you heard any more about…you know."

"Olivia?"

He nodded and took a sip of wine, his beguiling blue eyes working their charm on me.

I shook my head. "That lady detective was more interested in why someone like me was here with people like you."

Jimmy raised an eyebrow. "Really? She said that?"

"Pretty much."

"Interesting. And what did you say?"

"That I was insulted and asked if she wanted me to direct that question to Creighton Winston."

Jimmy's light laugh was genuine. Kind. Sincere. "And?"

"Oh, she was embarrassed. Asked me one more question, gave me her card, and that was it."

He raised his glass in admiration. "Well done."

I nodded my appreciation.

He leaned back in, giving me another delightful whiff of his essence, and whispered, "I overheard the medical examiner saying he suspected carbon monoxide."

I pulled back. "Seriously?"

Jimmy subtly motioned to lower my voice, and put his mouth to my ear. "He said the body's skin color was flushed. Not typical. The autopsy will tell."

Out of one eye, I caught a glimpse of Karsh, who was observing us. Putting a hand over my mouth, I whispered, "What does that mean, carbon monoxide? Is there a problem with the mansion's ventilation?"

Jimmy barely shook his head. "I wouldn't worr—"

"Sara, secrets don't make friends," Karsh called out from his usual position at the head of the table. "Speaking of, Scooter, you were quite the busy bee this afternoon, flitting about the premises as if making up for lost time. Tell me, how was the garage?"

Jessica Doerr looked up, her ice-blue eyes trained on Scooter, who returned her stare with an uneasy smile.

Spencer eyed his flushed partner. "Burl? I thought we agreed out of respect for Ms. Fantucci's passing, we would suspend our endeavors until tomorrow and instead spend the rest of the day in reflection."

"Sorry, buddy," Scooter said, keeping a wary eye on Doerr. "It was during my, uh…reflectin'…that I figured out the clue we been wrasslin' with. Figured you'd wouldn't mind if I got us a jump on tomorrow."

"I would have preferred you spoke with me first."

Scooter hammered home the rest of his bourbon. By my count, the sixth of the evening. "I, uh, didn't wanna bother you. Really didn't think you'd mind."

Spencer Fernsby replied with a warm smile. "I understand. We'll discuss this further at a more appropriate time."

Jimmy stood and straightened his white dinner jacket, which he filled out beautifully. "Before things go any further, I have a proposal. Any interest in everybody going in together on this? That's at least thirty million each, after the founder's cut."

Scooter squinted at Jimmy with one eye closed. "You talking 'bout chopping the pot, Jimbo?"

"I am. Eight equal shares."

Karsh scoffed. "That reeks of desperation. I have no interest in any such proposal."

"Nor should you," came a stern voice from the dining room's entrance, where Creighton Winston stood. He entered the room, stopping at the end of our table opposite Karsh Azarian. "That would be a direct violation of the contest's rules and result in immediate disqualification, loss of your diamond, and very likely, a robust lawsuit from the founder."

Still standing, Jimmy faced the lawyer and put a hand over his heart. "I am at your mercy, sir. All I can offer by way of explanation is it seems one glass too many of your exquisite *Chateau de la Conti* impaired my discretion and resulted in the unfortunate suggestion you just witnessed." He bowed his head. "It shall not happen again."

Winston stared down the contrite Jimmy Dougal. Except for Karsh, who sipped on his white port wine with an amused smile, everyone else at the table was focused on the attorney as he weighed Jimmy Dougal's transgression. Seconds ticked past, the only sound, Karsh Azarian setting his dessert wine glass on the table.

When Creighton Winston finally spoke, his words were measured, the tone, sharp. "You are fortunate, Mr. Dougal, and any of you who were considering his proposal,"—his steely gaze traveled around the table— "that I arrived before anybody agreed to such a blatant transgression of the rules. As such, Mr. Dougal, consider this a reprimand and the issue is hereby closed." He raised a finger. "However, for all of you, also consider this a onetime warning. Any further attempt by anyone to skirt the rules shall be swiftly dealt with by all legal means at my disposal." He took a moment to consider each person at the table. "And take note, disqualification from the contest shall be the *very least* of your worries."

Slow, methodical clapping came from the other end of the table as Karsh stood. "Bravo. Well done growing a spine. Of course, for the *next time* someone breaks the rules. So brave of you."

Winston's face darkened. "Do not push me, Mr. Azarian. Let me remind you of the final rule. Any situation—"

"I am well aware of the rule," Karsh said, waving a flippant hand. "Let's get to the business at hand, shall we? This is the first time you have joined us during dinner. I assume you have news regarding the death?"

Winston breathed in and exhaled through his nose. "Correct. Without getting into specifics, I asked the medical examiner to conduct the autopsy today, and he obliged because he had concerns regarding the cause of death."

"Concerns?" Frederick Volkov asked. "I thought she died in her sleep."

"Preliminary indications from the body at the scene led the medical examiner to suspect carbon monoxide poisoning," Winston said. "During the subsequent autopsy, visual observation of the blood and tissue along with the blood-gas report confirmed Ms. Fantucci died by carbon monoxide poisoning."

Jessica Doerr gasped. "How is that even possible?"

"That is for the police to determine," Winston replied.

"Police?" Volkov asked. "Why the police?"

"Because Ms. Fantucci's death was ruled a

homicide."

Everyone at the table erupted into a frenzy.

"Please." Winston put up his hands, motioning for everybody to quiet down. "Thank you. Be advised, the contest shall continue. We have tested all the suites and there is no evidence of carbon monoxide. However, as a precaution, carbon monoxide monitors have been installed in each. And although the police will be investigating Ms. Fantucci's unfortunate death, I once again must remind you that the requirements of your NDAs shall remain in place."

Chapter Seventeen

The garage

After a restless night following Creighton Winston's unnerving appearance and announcement at dinner, I trudged into our suite's living room with a fuzzy head and downtrodden spirit.

"You going to breakfast?" Zoe asked from the couch, putting her phone down.

I shook my head. "Not hungry. You go, then we'll check out the garage."

"What's going on, girl? You've hardly said a word since dinner, which is so not you. And now you're skipping breakfast and that gruel you swear by?"

"Yogurt, granola, and fresh fruit aren't gruel. They're delicious. And healthy."

Zoe made a gagging sound.

I sat in the leather chair, having sworn off ever again sitting in the precarious red chair, and considered my best friend. "Zo, I'm worried."

"Fantucci's death got you spooked?"

I nodded.

She sighed. "Yeah, me, too."

"I think we need to quit."

Zoe sat up, concern on her pixie-like face. "As much as I *really* hate saying it, bailing is a bad idea."

"Because I'm being framed?"

She stuck her neck out, eyes wide. "Uh, yeah. Someone's trying to take you down. You cut and run now, who knows what they'll do."

"Like pin Olivia's murder on me."

Zoe jumped off the couch and started pacing. "Exactly. What'd that note with the package say, something like *'this is a taste of what I can do?'*"

"Pretty much."

"Your best bet is to stay in the contest and smoke this person out. It's gotta be this mysterious founder, right?"

"Gotta be. But I didn't sign up to get you killed. Or Mauzzy."

On cue, Sweet Handsome came trotting into the room, sat in front of me, and gave me the stare. The "feed me" stare. He wasn't worried in the least bit about his mortality at the hands of the killer. Just starvation.

Zoe stopped her pacing and jabbed a finger at me. "Or yourself. Time to tell Finn what's going on. All of it."

Finn. It was still too early to drag him all the way into this, even with Olivia's death being classified as a homicide. The room of suspects was relatively small. With the kind of life-changing money at stake, it made complete sense the killer was a contestant. Or, considering Olivia's lovely personality, possibly a pissed-off staff member. But most likely a contestant. Starting with the slippery slimy Karsh Azarian. I could see him doing anything to win. Including murder. The big question gnawing at me—was the killer the same person framing me? The fact I knew absolutely nothing about all the contestants made it highly unlikely. It had to be two different people: a killer, and a blackmailer—aka the founder. But, still, I had to consider it. One thing I knew, by staying in the contest, it would keep my adversary at bay while allowing me to keep digging deeper and zero in on the founder's identity. Creighton Winston was at the top of the list, for obvious reasons. Followed by Percy Pembarton, only because he's always around. They could also be partners. But I had no proof. And if either was the killer, even better when I caught him.

Zoe's fingers snapped in front of my face. "Yo, snap out of it. You calling Finn, or am I?"

"Uh…no. Not yet."

Zoe scrunched her face up like she had a brain freeze, hands squeezing the sides of her head. "Are you crazy? Well, of course, you're crazy. But are you *effing* crazy? This is life-and-death crap. *Call Finn.*"

I put out my hands in a silent plea for her to calm down. "You're right about staying in the contest, but I need to be careful how much I pull Finn in on. That note also said for me to tell no one. Finn is already investigating the contestants plus Creighton Winston, Percy, and the chef, Barbara Doll. While he's doing that, we're staying in the contest to see if we can unmask the person setting me up."

"And if that person is also the killer?"

"Then we'll kill two birds with one stone."

"I just hope the killer isn't thinking the same thing, and we're the two birds."

****

I pushed open a solid wood door set in a stacked stone wall and stepped into the garage, followed by Zoe and Mauzzy.

"This is so not a garage," Zoe said, her voice echoing through the cavernous chamber. "What garage has a chandelier?"

The impressive space was split in thirds by wide arched beams of multi-colored stonework supported by matching stone columns. On both end sections, the stone beams framed white coffer ceilings with recessed lighting. The middle section, in which we stood, had a ceiling of four curved white panels from which hung a bronze candelabra chandelier that matched lit sconces on all the columns. Scattered across the immaculate floor of sandstone tiles was a diverse collection of vehicles. Two antique cars, three flashy red sports cars, seven black and gray luxury sedans, a vintage motorcycle with a sidecar, a black SUV, and to the right, on the far end next to the SUV, a black pickup truck.

A monstrous jacked-up truck with expansive bull bars.

A truck that stood in stark contrast to all the other vehicles in the garage.

A truck just like the one driven by Mrs. Majelski. Right down to the fold-down steps retracted beneath the running board.

Zoe pointed to the truck. "Look familiar?"

"It's the right color. And that SUV could've been the one she was driving in D.C. last summer." Unleashing Mauzzy, I walked over to the truck, gripped the chrome grab handle, pulled myself up on the running board, and peered into the cab. "No gun rack, but other than that, this could definitely be hers."

Zoe dashed to the truck's rear and nimbly clambered up over the tailgate into the cargo bed. "She could've easily removed it."

I leaned back to get a better look into the truck's cargo bed, still hanging onto the handle. "What are you doing?"

"I have a hunch," she replied, going straight to the toolbox spanning the width directly behind the cab. "Figures. It's locked. When we came in, I saw a key box by the door."

I jumped down and noted the last three characters of the plate number. "Why the toolbox?"

"We figure there's another safe, right?"

"But in the toolbox?"

"Mrs. M is at it again, following us around Birmingham, and now coincidentally popping up at Abuela's when you're there with Grant, of all people. Why not put the safe in her favorite truck?"

I pointed a finger up at Zoe. "*If* she's involved."

"Ha. She's so involved."

I threw her a "you're crazy" look and headed for the door. Inside the key box, I found a set with a tag matching the truck's plate number. Removing the keys from the hook, I unslung my backpack and dropped it to the floor. I cocked my arm, reared back, took two running hops toward the truck, and fired the keys toward Zoe. They sailed in a perfect arc—right over the truck and Zoe's outstretched hands—and skittered along the floor into the wall.

Mauzzy took off after the rogue keys while Zoe looked at me, open-mouthed. "Since when can you throw like that? I was expecting them to go under the truck. Or behind you. Not over this monstrosity."

"Beats me. All that dodgeball we been playing?"

"Doubtful. You're never in the game long enough

to make a throw."

"Very funny."

"Just speaking the truth."

Throwing the backpack over a shoulder, I chased down Mauzzy, who saw me coming and made a beeline for protective cover. When I dragged him out from under the truck, he was reluctant to give up his newfound toy.

"C'mon, Handsome, give 'em up," I rasped, tugging on the keys.

With great effort, I pried open his mouth, retrieved the keys, and carefully flipped them up to Zoe, who casually snatched them out of the air with one hand.

"Show-off," I groused.

Zoe flashed me an over-the top smile, selected a key, and opened the toolbox. "I was right. *Majelski*."

"Seriously? There's a safe?"

"Come see for yourself."

Refusing to add to Zoe's entertainment at my expense, I unlatched the tailgate and lowered it. No way I was going to try climbing it closed like she did. And instantly I realized this was going to be a problem. Even opened, the thing was higher than my waist.

"C'mon, Sara," Zoe sang. "Whatcha waiting for?"

I set the backpack on the floor and stowed my phone in it. The less weight for this upcoming maneuver, the better. And the last thing I needed was pulverizing my phone in a front pocket while I was embarrassing myself. Pushing my stomach up against the edge of the tailgate, I leaned in, took a breath, and with a little jump and push from my hands, my torso popped up and onto the floor of the cargo bed. Unfortunately, my legs were stuck straight out behind me.

"*Almost*," Zoe called out, thoroughly enjoying my predicament.

With legs kicking and flapping like a beginner swimmer hanging on the wall, I pulled with my arms and wriggled and waggled my body until I was fully sprawled in the back of the truck.

Zoe howled.

Scrambling to my feet, I adjusted my besieged pants. "Thanks for the help."

"Sure thing," she said with a final laugh.

I joined Zoe beside the toolbox. Inside it, the front door of a small safe with an electronic keypad stared up at us. It was about the size of the room's safe. "Well, finding the safe was easy. This one sure won't have a bowling ball."

"Yeah, I don't think anything about this contest is gonna be easy." Zoe counted the vehicles in the garage. "There are fifteen license plates here. And I'm assuming the combo is seven numbers like the other two safes. A standard 'Bama plate has seven alpha-numeric characters. That's one-hundred-five characters. If just half are numbers, we're talking over fifty to pick seven from." She let out a frustrated shriek.

"Maybe it has the same combo as the art gallery safe."

"No way. It's gonna come from these license plates. And it's gotta make sense."

"Like all the numbers in the art gallery came from incorrect dynasties."

Zoe emphatically pointed at me. "Right. That made sense. There's gotta be a story or something to the numbers. A rationale behind them so the contestants can figure it out."

I turned back toward my latest nemesis, the open tailgate. "Only one way to find out."

Zoe vaulted up and out of the cargo bed, landing lightly on her feet way below. I looked over the edge at the grinning sprite. It was at least a six-foot drop. Or four feet too many for me.

I stepped to the tailgate, sat, and with legs dangling off the edge, hopped down. "*Oof.*" I caught a glimpse of Zoe and put up a hand. "Don't even."

"Me? Never," she said with a short laugh.

"Gravity and I are not on the best of terms." I retrieved my phone from the backpack, opened a new note, and took in all the vehicles. "Okay, let's start looking for patterns between the plate numbers."

After plenty of walking back and forth along the line of vehicles, during which time I typed all the plate numbers into my phone, I stopped at a luxury sedan and stared at the plate. "Zo, didn't you say 'Bama plates have seven characters?"

"Yeah."

"This one only has six."

"Then it must be personalized."

I stared at the plate. 21GBE3. "If you're paying extra for a personalized plate, it's gonna have a meaning to you, right?"

"Yeah. So."

I read off the plate number. "How is that a personalized plate? No way it means anything."

"Maybe not to us. Keep looking."

I moved to the next vehicle on my left, another luxury sedan. "Another personalized plate that makes no sense—06RVC9."

"Check the next car," Zoe said.

It was one of the red sports cars. "This has seven characters, like the truck and SUV."

The next vehicle was a sedan. And it also had a strange personalized plate. 17DYZ8.

I stepped back, and as I took in all the vehicles, the pattern revealed itself. "Oh, my God. I can't believe we didn't see it before!"

"See what?" Zoe ran back to the jacked-up truck, and in a second was on the cab's roof, scanning the garage like a captain on the bridge of a ship. "I see it. Seven normal cars." She waved an urgent hand at me. "Keep going. Check out the rest."

I hustled along the line of vehicles. When I was done, only the seven sedans had six-character plates, with each having the same pattern: Two numbers, three letters, then a single number. Since some of the numbers in the first two combos we cracked were double-digits, we focused on the first two numbers in each of the personalized plates.

21. 6. 17. 22. 41. 31. 8.

I returned to the truck and read off the numbers in varying logical sequences, but each time, it ended with Zoe growling or shrieking and giving the toolbox a sharp kick.

I stepped back again and studied the line of vehicles. It had to be something that made sense. The sequence couldn't be random because that would make the number of possibilities beyond impossible to handle, and at the end of the day, the founder wanted somebody to win. The rules even allowed Creighton Winston to take the necessary steps to select a winner if nobody could win the contest outright.

I stared at the numbers in my note until my eyes began to cross.

If there was a pattern, I couldn't see it. I debated calling my math-genius brother but decided against it. Even though I haven't seen any cameras at El Sueño other than the one at the east wing's doors, the risk of getting caught cheating was too great. We were on our own. For now.

Then it struck me.

I looked down the row of vehicles. Then back at my note. When I first typed in the plate numbers, I started at the truck on the far right and worked to my left. Could it really be that simple? Just like the other sequences?

"Zo, I think I got it. We read from left to right. What if we're supposed to enter the numbers starting with the far-left sedan's number when you're standing in the doorway looking out at the vehicles? The plate numbers I typed in my phone started with the vehicles farthest to our *right*."

"Could be." Zoe bent over the safe. "Whenever you're ready."

I read off the numbers, reversing the sedan plates in my note, starting with eight at the bottom of the note, and ending with twenty-one, the first sedan plate I typed in.

"You're a fricking genius," Zoe screeched.

"Score!" I stowed my phone in the backpack, tossed it in the cargo bed, and worked myself up onto the tailgate and into the truck.

Zoe reached into the opened safe and took out four envelopes. She sorted through them, handing me one.

I took the envelope. It had my name in the same

gold-embossed lettering as the one at the art gallery. "Who are the other envelopes for?"

"Volkov and Toft. Dougal. And Doerr and Fantucci."

"Dang it. Karsh and Scooter have already been here. That's what Karsh was alluding to last night at dinner." I tucked the envelope under an arm and retrieved the camera from my backpack. "Anything else in there?"

Zoe turned back to the safe and pulled out a white ballcap. Embroidered across the front in green and red script, *Italia.* "What the heck?"

I took a picture of it, the camera whirring as the photograph slid out from its top. "There's a bank in Palermo holding a mortgage on El Sueño. Maybe there's a connection."

Zoe returned the hat to the safe. "Or maybe not. What's in the envelope?"

I tore it open, took out a half-sheet of ivory paper with two lines of typed text, and read it out loud.

One neighbor doesn't use locks, but has keys. It has a big space people can use, but no room available. And anyone can enter any time, but only one at a time. My other neighbor is a jetsetter, but goes nowhere.

Chapter Eighteen

Checkered and questionable pasts

After taking pics of all the license plates in the garage for Finn to run later, rather than trying to solve the riddle in the garage and risk someone overhearing us, we headed back to our suite to kick around ideas. More like stomp on each other's lame suggestions. For several hours.

"One neighbor is a piano," Zoe insisted from where she sat at the desk, the paper with the riddle laying on the desktop.

"Sure, if you're only considering the first sentence," I shot back from the couch, where Mauzzy lounged by my side.

"That's the genius of it. You ever hear of misdirection?"

"Yeah, and I've also heard that—*you're wrong*."

Mauzzy groaned, jumped down, and disappeared into the bedroom. I'm sure he's known the answer since the garage and was so embarrassed for us, he couldn't take it any longer and needed to take a nap. Or escape our stupidity. His words. Not mine.

"Okay," Zoe said, staring at the riddle. "The second sentence is…a big place with no room." She faced me, eyes wide. "You know, jazz clubs have—"

My phone ringing gave me a reprieve from Zoe's

throwing everything at the wall to see what, if anything, stuck. "Hey, Finn."

He had me on speaker. "Afternoon, Sara. Got a minute?"

"Sure. Why am I on speaker?"

"Need one hand for my beer. The other to write."

I knew Finn. He was up to something. The dude hated using the speaker and hated even more when he was put on speaker. "Who's with you?" I asked warily.

"Nobody here 'cept me and Bertie. Ain't that right, buddy."

Guttural moaning from an ecstatic Bertie came over the phone, clearly loving Finn's ear scratches, the little guy's favorite.

"You in a place no one can hear?" he asked.

I glanced at Zoe, who scribbled on a notepad at the desk. "Sorta. We're back in our suite."

"Sorta?"

"Mmmm-hmm. Go ahead."

Several seconds passed before Finn spoke. "All right then. Starting to get info back on the feelers I been putting out on them names you gave me. Been focusing on Olivia Fantucci and Karsh Azarian, like you asked."

"Lemme guess. Both have checkered pasts."

"Close. Fantucci's is checkered. Azarian's is questionable, at best. The gal was a personal injury lawyer. And if that ain't bad enough, the Alabama Bar has been getting complaints from her clients saying she stole from their settlements. Million-dollar ones. Folks said they only got 'bout ten percent of what they were expecting."

"How much is she accused of taking?"

"Dunno. But based on the number of complaints I

come across, reckon it's for north of twenty or thirty million."

My phone buzzed. It was a text from Zoe. —*Tell him about the manila envelope.*—

I looked at her and shook my head.

She nodded emphatically, her eyes tearing into me.

With all things being equal, Zoe was right. I should tell Finn. He was the perfect person, a former cop, to help me find the blackmailer and put an end to things. But all things weren't equal. Until I had more information, until I fully knew who I was dealing with and what all his capabilities were, it was still too early to get Finn involved. And when the time arrives for me to tell him, it certainly won't be over the phone.

"So that was the founder's leverage on her," I blurted out like an idiot, letting Zoe distract me to the point I forgot an already suspicious Finn was on the other end of the phone.

"Founder's leverage?" Finn asked.

My index finger slashed through the air at Zoe, telling her to cut the crap. She crossed her arms and slowly shook her head, mouthing, "Tell him or I will."

I turned away from Benedict Arnold to focus on Finn. "Um, nothing. What'd you find out about Karsh?"

After a pause, Finn said, "You ain't gonna get me off the scent that easily. We're coming back to that leverage thing. Anyway, this Karsh fella also seems to be up to no good, although he don't have the cops on him. Yet."

"Yet?" I asked.

"He's some big-wig financial asset manager. Runs a billion-dollar hedge fund advertising returns that double the market average."

"Sounds like he knows what he's doing. The guy seems real smart. What's the questionable part?"

Finn let out a scornful half-laugh. "Ain't nobody that good. Not even me. Reckon he's running a Ponzi scheme that just ain't collapsed on him yet." A beat. Then another. "I s'pose if this founder knew what the fella was running, that would be his *leverage* on the rascal. Whaddya think?"

As his words sunk in, the walls inched ever closer together. "I think you're pretty smart, too."

Finn blew out. "Let's cut to the chase. You being blackmailed? 'Cause if you are, I—"

"Not now, Finn."

"What really happened to Olivia—"

"Not. Now. Finn."

His ensuing silence screamed frustration. Apprehension. Concern.

When Finn finally spoke, his voice was soft, but the tone hard. "I ain't liking this, Sara."

Neither was I, but then again, nobody liked being blackmailed. And framed to boot. The words from the manila envelope's threatening note materialized in front of me.

This is just a taste of what I can do. Speak of this to no one. Or else.

My breath started coming in short snatches, cold invisible hands squeezing my throat. Black spots replaced the menacing words floating past my face. Fighting to breathe, my world collapsing, I inexplicably spit out, "Carbon monoxide poisoning. The medical examiner ruled her death a homicide."

Finn exhaled hard. "Dadgum it. Now I *really* ain't liking this. You need to quit and get out of there.

Today."

The anxiety anaconda grabbed hold of my chest as multiple scenarios, worries, fears, and emotions collided in a white-hot explosion of sheer panic. I knew Finn was right. But I also knew the person behind the photographs had a power and reach that could destroy my life and land me in prison, despite my being innocent of all things except occasional bad judgment. Finn could help me, but his involvement could also hurt me. In a big way. Including having Zoe or my family targeted. Even Mauzzy.

With the room spinning and stomach churning, my brain flipped over to autopilot. I heard myself say, "Olivia was a super-nasty person. She obviously pushed somebody the wrong way and got killed for it. But her murder isn't tied to the contest. Maybe it was one of her clients she ripped off."

"Not buying it," Finn said. "Don't reckon you are, neither."

Two sharp barks added an unquestionable exclamation point to Finn's disbelief.

"And 'ole Bertie here's with me. He ain't believing your guff, neither."

Finn was the best PI for a reason. Like Mrs. Majelski said, his instincts were better than first-class. He could read people, even without Bertie's help. It didn't matter if the person was in front of him or over the phone. When he smelled something, he didn't let it go. He pursued all leads, but always ended up circling back to what his gut told him to be true. And when Bertie chimed in, there was no convincing Finn otherwise. They made a formidable team. Because of that, I needed to back him off until I could think more clearly. He wasn't going away, and that was fine, but I wasn't mentally prepared for what he was asking. Not yet. I needed time and space to think through all the repercussions of taking that next possible step.

"Finn, I really need you to focus on those names."

"Uh-uh. You need to focus on getting out of Dodge before you get dead."

"Please, for now, just do what I'm asking. I can't drop—"

My boss about jumped through the phone at me. "*Listen here.* I don't give a rat's ass what you got going on. This is getting serious. Y'all get to the office tomorrow so we can hash this out."

"I can't—"

"*Tomorrow.* Ten o'clock. You best be here or I'll drive out there and yank you out. Got it?"

"Fine. We'll be there." I tapped off, tossed the phone on the couch, and blew out a cleansing breath. Surprisingly, I felt better. It wasn't so much the cleansing action but more the fact that Finn was forcing himself into my situation. And even though it was against all my instincts, for some reason, I felt safe.

"Where we going?" Zoe asked, the mischievous glint in her eye betraying the question. She had ears like Mauzzy.

I narrowed my eyes. "You know exactly where we're going."

"He caught your leverage slip-up, didn't he?"

"Thanks to you."

Zoe threw her hands out in faux disbelief. "What'd I do?"

"Distracted me with your stupid text. He wants to see us in his office tomorrow at ten."

"Good. Never thought I'd be happy about returning to that crappy office. You know you're gonna have to...*Office?*" Zoe spun back to the desk and picked up the paper with the riddle. "It's not a piano."

"Obviously. Or a jazz club."

"It's a computer keyboard," she exclaimed. "Keys with no locks. A big space—bar. And anyone can...enter...but only one at a time." She flipped the paper onto the desk. "*Boom.*"

"A computer is in an office," I said, shooting over to the desk to look at the riddle. "And a jetsetter that goes nowhere has gotta be an inkjet printer."

Zoe pulled out the information guide in the leatherbound notebook and opened it. "El Sueño has an office available to us with a computer, printer, and copier. Whatever is sitting between the computer and printer is our answer."

"Mauzzy," I shouted, picking up my backpack. "Get in here. Time to go."

Chapter Nineteen

Mauzzy to the rescue

We were passing through the domed foyer on our
way to the office when Mr. Dimples, aka Jimmy
Dougal, strolled in from the music room. He looked
elegantly casual, wearing a black sports jacket with a
white-and-red pocket square, dark gray dress shirt
opened at the top, and black slacks. "Hey, Sara," he
said smoothly, "heading to the office?"

"Jimmy. Hi. Um, yeah, I need to use the copier."

His easy laugh washed over me like a cool autumn
breeze. Fresh. Soothing. Enticing. "It's okay. I know
why you're going there."

"You do?"

"Sure. I was there yesterday. Although not for the
copier." A wink.

A warmth seeped into my face. "Oh. I guess…ha-
ha…you do know."

His brilliant white smile put me at ease. "Someone
as smart as you shouldn't have too much difficulty
figuring it out."

"Yeah?"

He nodded. "Trickiest part is finding the safe."

I gave him a playful smile. "Any hints you wanna
throw my way?"

Jimmy chuckled and wagged a finger at me. "Now,

now. Remember. We're competitors."

"Oh, right, I still owe you an answer on teaming up."

"No worries. I figured you were making good enough progress that you weren't interested."

"It wasn't so much that. Yesterday was just so crazy, I totally forgot. I'm not really—"

He put up a hand. "My apologies, but the deal is off. I feel bad for not telling you at dinner, but I made great progress yesterday, so…"

I locked in on his captivating blue eyes. More like, bewitching. "Then why did you make that proposal last night? About everyone going in together."

He flashed me another dazzling smile. "Simple really. A little mentalist trick. I throw out a wild suggestion and read the reactions. It was a safe gambit because I knew not everybody was going to agree to it, like Karsh, and it allowed me to assess everyone's progress."

"You're a mentalist?" Zoe asked, eyeing the Bearded Wonder hard.

"Among other things," he replied, still smiling.

Zoe took stock of the man. "Yeah? So, what am I thinking?"

Jimmy grinned. "It doesn't work that way. Although, you don't trust me."

The petulant peewee leaned in toward the man. "You're right about that. And I don't believe you, either. Guys like you are full of—"

"Sorry," I said, grabbing Zoe's arm. "We need to get going."

He gave her a courteous smile before addressing me. "No problem. I know her type."

"My *type*," Zoe raged, lunging for Jimmy. "Why you—"

I jerked her back. "She gets this way when she doesn't have her nap. See you at dinner."

With a little salute and an amused smile, he said, "Good luck."

Mauzzy and I made our way out of the foyer toward the office with a cursing Zoe firmly in tow. And I mean *firmly*, lest she break my grip, chase Jimmy down, and reduce the competition by one Greek god.

When we got to the office, Zoe had calmed down. A bit. She yanked her arm free of my grasp. "I hate guys who think their good looks entitle them to say whatever they want."

"He wasn't rude, Zoe."

"Not to you."

"Or you."

"Whatever."

"Hey, look at this office," I said, marveling at yet another incredible room at El Sueño.

The expansive office had a light-green oriental rug covering most of a red oak hardwood floor. Lining three walls of the stylish space were mahogany built-ins with lighted bookcases rising from beveled red marble countertops. Books of all colors and sizes filled each shelf. Beneath the countertops were carved mahogany cabinets and drawers with pewter hardware. In the middle of the back wall, surrounded by bookshelves, was a work area with an all-in-one computer, keyboard, and printer. A stack of multicolored paper approximating a half-ream sat next to the printer. Just in front of the work area, a dark wood table with a bowed-out front functioned as the desk. On it, a framed photograph, black desk mat, gold pen, dagger-style letter opener, and a miniature silver telescope and tripod. A dark red leather executive chair and matching guest chairs completed the space.

"Nice office," Zoe said, "but the only thing between the computer and printer is that stack of paper."

Unleashing Mauzzy, I crossed the room to behind the desk, noticing the photograph on it was of a regal chestnut horse. Picking up the paper, I flipped through it. "Everything's blank."

Zoe joined me and took the printer paper, fanning through it. "Why all the different colors? Why no normal paper?"

"It's gotta be tied to the safe's combination. Jimmy said we shouldn't have too much trouble. Let's keep it simple."

Zoe handed me the stack. "Simple would've been having the combination printed on the top page."

I thumbed through the papers. "Is it me, or do the number of sheets vary between the colors?"

"Could be. Except for the red, they all seem pretty even."

I dropped my backpack on the floor, sat in the desk chair, and counted through the pages. "Thirty-eight blue." More counting. "Twenty-seven pink. Twenty-five green."

"Hang on," Zoe said, "there's a reason for the different numbers. Let me in there." She pushed me out of the chair. "I'll count. You keep track in your phone since all our notes are in there."

Taking out my phone, I opened a note and typed in the first three numbers and corresponding colors.

"Okay, ready."

Zoe counted the red sheets, the fourth color from the top. "Sixteen."

I added to the note as Zoe counted the purple.

"Thirty-five," she said, moving on to orange, then finishing with yellow. "That's it."

I read off the numbers and colors. "You think the sequence is the color order in the stack, top to bottom?"

"Good a guess as any." Zoe scanned the office. "Just need to find the safe."

"Which Jimmy said was the tricky part," I said, shoving my phone into a front pocket.

We checked all the cabinets first because they were the easiest place to hide a safe, but with Jimmy's words ringing in my head, I knew we weren't going to find it in any of them. And we didn't.

I slowly turned around, taking in the room. All we had left that could conceivably hide a safe was behind one of the bookcases. "Hate to say it, Zo, but it's gotta be behind one of those sets of books."

"Yeah, I was thinking the same thing. Unfortunately."

Both sides had eight three-shelf bookcases plus the spaces between the countertop and the first shelf holding various knickknacks, framed awards, and photographs. The back wall had four bookcases on each side sandwiching the work area, plus four shelves above it. That meant there were one hundred rear panels to check.

I groaned. "Oh, my God. This is going to take forever, but it fits with what Jimmy said."

"Yeah, well, I can't reach the top two sections so you take all of them and I'll do the bottom two."

"Just be careful with all that stuff on the counters."

"I got it."

"And make sure you put everything back exactly as it was, including the books."

"*Mom,* I said I got it."

Ignoring her sass, I pointed to the far wall of bookcases. "So we don't get in each other's way, you start at that end and I'll start here."

Zoe skipped over to where I was pointing and went to work. We spent the rest of the afternoon and into the early evening pulling off books and keepsakes from each section, feeling around for a latch or lever or button to reveal a hidden compartment, and when finding none, returning everything back to exactly as before. It was tiring. Frustrating. And discouraging.

"That was fun," Zoe groused. "It's almost six-thirty. We gotta get moving or we'll be late to dinner."

I plopped into the desk chair and rolled back up against the work area. "Where the heck could it be? There's no other place."

"Maybe it's not a safe. Maybe it's a secret compartment in the desk."

"Then what are the numbers for?"

"Who says there are any numbers? That colored paper could be a misdirection."

"Like most of the riddle that pointed to this office?" I said with a smirk.

Zoe shrugged. "Just saying."

I slumped in the chair, chin on chest. Closing my eyes, I opened my mind to the possibilities. But there really were no other possibilities. The only places we hadn't checked were the desk and chairs. Could she be right?

Standing, I said with a sigh, "Okay, Zo. You take underneath the desk and I'll check its top and sides."

Pushing me out of the way, she dove under the desk. Five minutes later, we hit another dead-end.

Zoe sat under the desk, her back to the front, legs straight out toward the desk chair still pushed up against the work area. She leaned back on her hands, sucked in a deep breath, and exhaled. "We missed something. Are we even in the right room?"

"Jimmy pretty much said so. And we still have the chairs," I said, stepping around to one of the guest chairs. Finding nothing on the first one, I moved to the other, where I roused a sleeping Mauzzy.

With a huff, Sweet Handsome jumped off the chair and began sniffing the rug around and under the chairs and desk.

"Yeah, well, he's a jerk so I don't place much..." Zoe pulled back. "What the...Mauzzy, you're such a perv."

A snorting Mauzzy pawed maniacally at the rug, cramming his nose between Zoe's butt and the floor.

"All right, now," she said, nudging him out of the way.

Undeterred, he pressed the attack.

"Fine," Zoe said with a giggle and another gentle push of the dogged dachshund. "I'll look. I'll look." Getting on her knees, she felt along the rug beneath the desk, then pushed down hard on it along a line. As Mauzzy supervised, she scrambled out from under the desk, spun around, and shoved her hands underneath the rug as far as she could, ending up on her stomach as her arms disappeared. "We need to move the desk. Clear those chairs out of the way."

Zoe pulled her arms out and jumped up, taking hold of one end of the desk.

I moved the guest chairs to the side, placed the photograph of the horse on its face, and grabbed the other end. "One, two, three."

Mauzzy skipped out of the way as we lifted the desk and moved it forward to where the chairs used to be. Thankfully, it was a table-desk and not some gargantuan double-pedestal monstrosity. For once, the Universe took pity on me.

"We need to pull back the rug," Zoe said, moving to one end of the floor covering.

I stepped to the other end, and together we rolled the edge up until it reached the desk as Mauzzy smugly observed his lackeys from a safe distance. Beneath where the desk used to be, a faint rectangle appeared etched into the hardwood floor. We bent over the spot and realized that what we thought were etched lines were threadlike seams. And in the center of one of the seams, faint pry marks.

Picking up the letter opener from the desk, I slipped its point into the seam at the pry marks and carefully worked it back and forth until the blade's tip disappeared. With one hand gently pressing down on the letter opener, my fingers worked into the growing space until I had a decent grip on the floorboard. When I pulled on it, a series of floorboards rose together as a single panel, revealing—a recessed safe door.

Moving at lightning speed, which was so off-brand for him, Mauzzy was at the edge of the opening, peering in.

Rubbing his ears, I said, "Great job. How'd you know?"

Zoe shrugged. "Beats me. Something didn't feel right when I—"

"I was talking to Sweet Handsome."

"Hey, it was a team effort."

"Sure, it was." Dropping the letter opener, I pulled out my phone and brought up the note with what I prayed was the combination. I studied the numbers for an obvious sequence to use.

38. 27 .25. 16. 35. 47. 41.

Just like the previous combination sets, nothing jumped out at me, so I went with the order from the paper stack, top to bottom.

"All right, let's see if this works," I said. "If it doesn't, we've only got about five minutes before we have to get to dinner."

"Well, then make it good." Zoe got on her knees beside the safe door. I read off the numbers, expecting us to again have the wrong sequence. But when she punched in the last number, a whirring sound indicated we cracked the lock on the first shot.

Zoe opened the safe and took out the familiar stack of envelopes and a black dream catcher with interwoven turquoise beads and dangling turquoise-and-black feathers. She sifted through the envelopes, handing me one. "The only one missing is Jimmy's."

I took the envelope, dug the camera out from my backpack, and snapped a pic of the dreamcatcher. "With where this safe is hidden, that makes sense. We wouldn't have found it without Mauz."

"And me."

"Right." I opened the envelope and extracted the paper with yet another riddle.

Everybody enjoys spending time with me. In fact,

one will always find thirty men and two women around me. Sometimes more. But never less.

Chapter Twenty

A message

A middle-aged, attractive blond man wearing a black vest and bowtie with white gloves met Zoe and me as we entered the grand dining room. "Good evening, Miss Donovan, Miss Harp. Might I get you something to drink before dinner?"

"Good evening," I said, glancing around. "Excuse me, where's Percy?"

"Ah, yes. Mr. Pembarton was called out of town this morning on a family matter."

"Oh, my goodness," I gasped. "Is everything okay?"

"Yes, ma'am. He should be back in a few days. I am acquainted with Miss Harp, but allow me to introduce myself. My name is Reginald DuBois. I will be serving your table this evening."

"Hey, Reggie," Zoe said with an easy smile and flip of the hand. "Moving up to the adult table, huh?"

He returned her smile with an uneasy one. "If you mean the main table, yes, ma'am. Irina Petrova will be filling in my stead at your table."

"You got some big shoes to fill over there," Zoe said. "And a few prima donnas to handle,"—she tilted her head toward me—"like this one."

Reginald cleared his throat. "Anything before

dinner? Champagne, perhaps?"

"That would be wonderful," I said.

"Very good. Miss Harp?"

"I'll have my usual, Reg."

With a sharp nod, DuBois took a step back, spun around, and strode toward the kitchen.

"Your *usual?*" I asked.

Zoe struck a haughty pose. "Indeed. As Reginald would say, water with gas and a twist of lime."

I was about to make a comment when my gaze drifted to inside the room. A stunning Jimmy Dougal, in a white dinner jacket with black bowtie and tuxedo pants, caught me checking him out. He said something to the Jablonsky brothers and Fernsbys, then joined us. "Good evening, ladies," he said, with a slight raising of his champagne flute.

I raised an empty hand in a mock toast. "Good evening. Long time, no see."

"Hey," Zoe mumbled, making her displeasure with the man all too obvious.

"Cutting it close for dinner," Jimmy said with a gleam in his eye. "But I see congratulations are in order."

"Excuse me?" I asked.

He took a sip and saluted me with the half-empty flute. "One step closer. But no surprise here."

Holding his penetrating gaze, I said, "The office?"

"I certainly hope so, unless you've solved another room."

"Um, no, I mean, well—"

Zoe jumped in. "Don't answer him, Sara. He's playing his mentalist BS on you."

Jimmy turned his attention to Zoe, eyebrows

raised. "Ah, you're a believer now."

"Yeah, that you're full of it," Zoe fired back.

Thankfully, Reginald returned with our drinks before she could really go all Zoe on him. He handed me a crystal flute. "Miss Donovan."

"Thank you." I took the champagne and an immediate sip that turned into a swig as Zoe grew increasingly agitated.

"And, Miss Harp," he said, handing her a tumbler of fizzy water with a lime wedge hanging on the rim.

"Thanks, Reg," she said, taking the glass with a fleeting scowl at Jimmy.

"Absolutely," Reginald said, stepping back and addressing the three of us. "If you can make your way to your seats, we will begin the dinner service momentarily."

Zoe gave Jimmy a final look of reproach before leaving for her table while we stepped toward our own.

As we neared the head of the table, Karsh pushed back in his chair and stood directly in front of us. "I'd be careful consorting with her, Dougal."

With a glance at me, Jimmy said, "Whatever do you mean?"

"I make it a point to know who I'm dealing with." Karsh looked down at me with a sneer. "The people she associates with are of a…dubious nature."

With a rare display of self-discipline, I refrained from tossing my champagne on the narcissist and instead glared up at him and snarled, "You should know, you Ponzi scum."

Jimmy stared at me in shock. Either at what Karsh said about me, or my reaction. Or both. He slowly turned back to Karsh. "Such as whom?"

Frederick Volkov, who had been listening intently from his usual spot at the table to Azarian's right, tilted his silver-haired head. The financier's disinterested hound-dog face morphed into a joyous puppy as he waited for Karsh to dish dirt on me.

Karsh waved Jimmy's question off with a slight motion of his hand. "I like you. You're a superb musician. Just know, you've been warned."

Placing his free hand lightly on my back, Jimmy leered at Karsh and pointed toward him with his champagne. "As have you." He guided me to my seat, setting down his champagne to pull out my chair. Easing it in as I sat, he whispered into my ear, "Well played."

****

Entering the combination to our suite's lock after returning from dinner, I said to Zoe, "Man, you were going to town on that shrimp."

"Best appetizer yet. That Cajun grilled shrimp was redonk."

Looking down over my shoulder at her, I said, "So, is a shrimp eating shrimp—a cannibal?"

"Wha…Ha-ha. Very funny."

I pushed open the door where an excited Mauzzy waited, his tiny front paws pitter-pattering on the tile. "Been waiting all night to drop that on you."

Zoe gave me a shove in the back. "Good for you."

We entered the suite where I leashed up Mauzzy and took him out, praying he would cooperate and get on with his business so I could get to bed. I was exhausted and needed a solid night's sleep. Tomorrow was going to be a challenge dealing with Finn. He wanted me to drop out, but I couldn't. Staying in the contest was my best chance at uncovering who was blackmailing me and putting an end to it, although I had not figured out that piece yet. But once I knew who the person was, options would present themselves on how to end things once and for all. Including sending in Finn to handle it. But now seemed too early. Especially after Mrs. Majelski told how he ditched his disciplined approach chasing the Black Creek Killer and ended up getting shot because of it. Plus losing his career. Despite the gruff exterior, Finn liked me. And because of that, my situation was becoming personal to him. If I told him everything and he went off and did the same thing again, things could end badly. For both of us.

Apparently, Mauzzy was also exhausted because he put up no fight and immediately took care of things. When we returned to the suite, Zoe was pacing the living room.

I unleashed Mauzzy, who took off for the bedroom. "Everything okay?"

Zoe pointed to the desk. On it, another manila envelope. "That was on the coffee table. Has your name on it."

"How'd it get here?"

Zoe looked at me like I was an idiot.

"Not good," I uttered.

"You think?"

"What's in it?"

"Didn't open it."

I picked up the envelope and examined it. "Why not?"

"Really? You just asked me that? Last week, you thought an envelope"—she pointed to the one in my hands—"*just like that one* was an effing bomb."

I shrugged. "But it wasn't."

Zoe let out a pained shriek.

"And it was the invitation envelope I thought was a bomb. Not the manila one."

"You're so eff…" Her drawn-out growl swallowed the remaining words.

I gave the envelope another close look. It was sealed, just like the last one, with my name printed on a mailing label. "You know, the last time I opened something like this, it had some very bad pics."

"Well aware. Just open the damn thing."

Puffing up my checks, I blew out, tore open the flap, and peeked in. A fluttery feeling attacked my chest as rubbery legs forced me over to the couch. Through the dizziness, I fought to control my breathing and wild beat of my heart.

Did Finn overreact and already go rogue?

"Sara, you okay?"

I swallowed, sucked in a breath, and let it out slowly. Following another intake of air and a long exhale, I extracted a single eight-by-ten photograph and a printed note.

My dear, forget that nonsense about dropping out. It isn't your *decision to make. I need to know who is the best. Play my game, or suffer the consequences. All of them.*

I dropped the note on the couch and looked at the photograph. When my eyes focused on the image, I froze, as seemingly did time. All I could do was stare at the glossy print in my hand. It was of my dad. In his beloved jeep. Driving out of Fort Meade, where he worked at the NSA.

"Sara?" Zoe sat on the couch next to me, read the

note, and then got a load of the photograph in my hand. "Oh, crap."

I held the pic up close. Other than my dad, the car was empty. I flipped it over, and panic became terror. A strange message was handwritten on the back.

Privet, Sarah. U kazhdogo yest' tsena. Ili tak oni govoryat.

Chapter Twenty-One

Privet, Sarah

Twenty minutes late to our meeting with Finn, courtesy of I-459 construction, Zoe and I trudged up the disgusting stairs to the fifth-floor office. The stairwell reeked of…Well, it just reeked. In a desperate attempt to escape hell's bouquet, Mauzzy had raced ahead and was frantically pawing at the exit door when we finally reached the summit. I bent over, hands on knees, sucking in what I prayed was just compromised oxygen and not a malevolent cloud from the nearby biosafety lab. Zoe brushed past me and opened the door, allowing both a relieved Mauzzy to shoot into the corridor and a burst of stale air to rush into the stairwell, which I gratefully sucked into my burning lungs. Sometimes, you take what you can get. This was one of those times.

Still wheezing, I stumbled into the corridor where the judgmental "hmmm" of fluorescent lights needled me, like I needed any reminders to start working out again. When I got to the door of Finnegan and Associates, where Zoe waited, I stopped to gather myself. All the way here from El Sueño, I ran the gameplan through my head. Let Finn have his say, get his thoughts on the next riddle, and get out of there before Bertie ratted me out. Zoe was going to be the wild card. She and Dad bonded over the summer when they carpooled together during her NSA internship. So, when she saw the photo of him coming out of Fort Meade, we got into it big time over getting Finn fully involved. Although I eventually got her to agree to let me handle it, I also knew Zoe. You could only hold her back for so long. And if someone she cared about was threatened, all bets were off.

With my hand on the doorknob, I looked back at Zoe. "Remember our agreement."

"We're in way over our heads."

"Zoe."

"You're making a mistake."

"Just trust me."

With a dramatic exhale, she signaled with an open hand for me to get moving. I pushed the door open and we filed in, the heavenly aroma of freshly-brewed coffee greeting us. A sudden bombardment of ferocious barks shredded the silence. Bertie darted out from behind Finn's desk and skidded to a stop. Recognizing Mauzzy, he let out two sharp barks and the two pals ran to each other like it had been years, instead of four days, since the last and only time they were together. Playfully bumping and nudging each other, they ran behind Finn's desk and settled into Bertie's bed.

"You're late," Finn fumed, cowboy boots up on the desk next to a stack of folders. He took a slurp from a steaming white mug, annoyance stamped on his rugged face. "It's almost ten-thirty. Didn't think y'all would show." He pointed at Zoe with the mug as she sat in one of the plastic guest chairs. "Reckon Sara's here 'cause of you."

"You reckoned right," Zoe said with an irritated smile. "She wanted to blow you off."

I poured a cup of coffee, dropped my backpack next to the other guest chair, and sat. "Ignore her. We were coming. Just hit traffic."

His eyes narrowed, digging into me. "Mmmm-hmm. And I'm a dang duck." The tone amplified the look on his face. Not good.

"Where's your brunch?" I asked, attempting to lighten the mood.

"I ain't drinking. This is serious business, Sara."

With that warning shot, I knew this was going to be a battle. Racing to drive the conversation before Finn could unload on me, I said with an upbeat note, "Hey, we cracked another room safe and have a new riddle."

He didn't respond, just took another slurp from the mug, eyes trained on me.

"Did you hear me?"

Finn nodded once. His countenance remained hard.

"Wanna see it?" I asked.

"Don't matter none."

Setting my coffee on the edge of Finn's desk, I pulled out the riddle along with my notebook from the backpack. "This was in a floor safe in the office. *Everybody enjoys spending time with me. In fact, one will always find thirty men and two women around me. Sometimes more. But never less.'* What do you think?"

The man just sat there, staring at me. No change in expression. No recognition of the riddle. No hint of anything.

"You thinking?" I asked, peering at him.

He pulled his feet down, setting the mug on the desk. Leaning forward on burly forearms, a timid squeak coming from the chair, his eyes demanded I look at him. "I am. Question is, why ain't you?"

A prickly feeling crawled across my scalp as perspiration gathered at the back of my neck. If this continued for much longer, he wasn't going to need Bertie to expose me. My conscience would take care of that, yet again double-crossed by my gutless body.

"First time I seen you speechless," Finn remarked. His stare worked me over, letting the silence do his dirty work. Finally, he spoke. "You dropping out?"

I drew back. "What?"

"You heard me."

"Like I *tried* telling you yesterday, I can't drop out."

"Why?"

"The NDA I signed won't let me."

A whine, then a groan, floated up from behind the desk.

Damn you, Bertie.

Finn glanced down, then back up at me. "C'mon now, don't let Bertram call you out like that. What's going on?"

A full-blown battle raged inside me. My head screamed to stick to the plan while my heart begged me to pull Finn in and tell him everything.

"Finn, I can't," I whispered.

With lips pressed tight, his gaze shifted to Zoe. "Got anything to say?"

"Stay out of it, Zo," I warned.

"Tell me about this leverage," he said to Zoe. "Can't help if I don't know."

"She's being blackmailed and framed," Zoe confessed. "And now they're threatening her dad." She turned to me. "Sorry, Sara, but he's gotta know."

My head dropped.

"Who's 'they' you talking 'bout?" Finn asked, his eyes on Zoe before focusing on me.

I raised my head and took in Finn. The stone-cold look he'd been wearing melted, revealing the Finn I'd known for the last seven months. "We don't know," I said softly. "But I think it's who the lawyer, Creighton Winston, calls the contest's founder."

"Which could be Mrs. Majelski," Zoe added quickly.

Finn's head whipped around toward Zoe. "Sadie?"

"Maybe," I said cautiously. "She's been following us. And there's a truck like hers in the El Sueño garage."

"You seen her following you?" he asked me, his tone full of skepticism.

"I've seen her truck tailing us all over Birmingham," I replied.

"That ain't what I asked. Have you seen *her* bird-dogging you?"

I shook my head.

"Listen here, her truck ain't nothing special in these parts. And I've known Sadie for years. The 'ole gal is rock-solid. Who else you got?"

"Like I said, whoever is the contest's founder," I answered.

"That the actual word the lawyer used?" Finn asked. "Founder?"

"Uh-huh," I said. "Why?"

"Them ambulance chasers are real slippery with their language. When they start using specific terms, I take notice. Why not say sponsor of the contest? Backer? Guarantor? Why specifically 'founder?' That don't say where the money's coming from. Just says

192

who came up with the contest." He looked at me, then over at Zoe. "This lawyer ever use any other term besides 'founder' for this person?"

Zoe and I both said, "No."

"Y'all positive?"

"Positive," Zoe said.

I nodded in agreement.

"Y'all know who's putting up the cash?"

I turned to Zoe. "Did Winston say anything about that?"

She shook her head. "All I remember is Volkov specifically asking who was funding the contest and Winston said he couldn't get into it, but the source was legit."

Finn picked up his coffee mug, peered in it, and frowned. He worked it around in his thick hands, then set it back on the desk. "The funding source may be legit, but that don't mean the method of getting that dough is." He looked at me with a knowing smile. "Now would be the time to give me that second envelope."

I stared back, refusing to feed his flourishing ego.

He gestured toward the backpack at my feet. "Go on now."

With a scowl tossed in his direction, I dug into the backpack, produced the two manila envelopes, and handed him the one that came with the contest's invitation.

His knowing smiling ripened into a cocky one as he took the envelope. "This the one 'ole Bertram and I caught you lying 'bout?"

"I told you about it," I countered.

"Only after Bertie called you out," he reminded me

with a wiseass grin, extracting the stack of photos and note. After studying the note, he worked through the photographs, briefly stopping on each one before moving to the next, several times with a raised eyebrow. When finished, he set the stack on the desk and motioned with his head toward Zoe. "She said you was being framed. These all fake?"

I winced. "Mmmm, not exactly. Just the last two."

This time, both eyebrows went up. "Really? Even that one of you in the car? Where it appears you're...*That one ain't a fake?*"

I briefly closed my eyes and nodded. "Really."

"Huh." Finn pulled the two phony photos from the bottom of the stack, laid them side by side, and set the others aside. With eyes on the photos, he pointed to one. "That your signature on the bank card?"

I leaned forward to look at the photograph. "Could be mine."

He looked at me through the tops of his eyes. "Is it yours?"

"I know I didn't sign that card."

"That a no?"

I sat back. "I guess so."

"That ain't an answer. You telling me you got no safe-deposit box?"

A nervous laugh escaped me. "I don't have anything valuable."

"You forgetting 'bout that diamond."

I swallowed. "Right. But it's at my place. Hidden."

He grunted, gave the photographs another once-over, looked up and pointed at the second envelope in my lap. "That one 'bout your daddy?"

I handed it to him. "This was in the suite after we

got back from dinner last night."

"How'd it get there?"

"We don't know. Someone obviously has the combo to our door lock."

"It ain't a key lock?"

I shook my head. "Keypad. Seven-digit combo."

With a frown, Finn said, "Hate to tell you, but them smart locks can be hacked."

"*Really?* Is it difficult?" I asked.

"It ain't easy, but it can be done several different ways." He opened the envelope and took out the note and photograph of my dad coming out from Fort Meade. He read the note and looked up, confused. "You been talking 'bout quitting the contest?"

"I mentioned it to Zoe yesterday morning. She talked me out of it even though I—"

"But I told her to tell you everything," Zoe broke in.

His gaze shifted to Zoe, then back to me. "Where were y'all chatting?"

"In our suite. Olivia Fantucci's murder rattled me."

Finn cocked an eyebrow. "As it should. You ain't said nothing 'bout quitting to anybody else or around anybody else?"

I thought back over the last two days and shook my head. "Nope. Just in the suite. Yesterday morning."

"Sounds like your suite's bugged." He examined the photograph, then flipped it over, whistled softly, and studied the writing on the back. "Your daddy a spook?"

I hesitated. "Um…he's a cryptanalyst for the NSA."

Finn nodded, still staring at the writing. "You

know what this says?"

"No clue," I replied. "But I don't think it's a cipher or anything."

"Looks Russian," he said. "Not Cyrillic script, but a transliteration."

"*Russian?*" Zoe and I said together.

"That's what I reckon. Let's see." Finn slid a keyboard over and worked his computer's mouse. With eyes shifting back and forth between the photograph and keyboard, he pecked away at the keys with both index fingers. When finished, he stared at the monitor for a few seconds before turning it around for me to see.

Zoe got out of her chair and together we stared at the words in the "English" box of the English-Russian translation site Finn used.

Hello, Sarah. Everyone has a price. Or so they say.

Chapter Twenty-Two

Finn's pivot

Zoe and I stared at the words on Finn's monitor, as if by doing so, we could change what we were seeing. But nothing changed, sending us back to our seats in stunned silence.

Finn tapped the words on the back of the photograph. "Seems to me this here's implying your daddy's a traitor, spying for the Russians."

"No way," I protested.

With hands up in mock surrender, he said, "Hey, just pointing out the implication. Ain't saying he's guilty."

"Well, he's not," I snapped.

"Fair enough," Finn replied. "Just trying to assess his and your vulnerability, is all. Need to know before I go poking a hornet's nest." He picked up the safe-deposit box photo. "When folks are framed, there's at least a kernel of truth behind it, otherwise it ain't believable. This here"—he showed me the photograph—"is implying you either stole this stuff or were paid with it for doing something illegal."

My gaze jerked to the photo, then back to Finn. "Neither is true."

"I know." Finn dropped the photograph on the desk. "Checked you out after hiring you. But there's—"

"Hold on, hold on," I interjected. "*After* you hired me? You checked me out *after* you hired me?"

Finn shrugged. "Something didn't sit right 'bout you. I know what Sadie said and all, but still, couldn't figure out why a smart capable person like you wanted to work for me."

"I'm still with you, so I guess you figured it out," I said with a hint of pride.

"Reckoned you were desperate. Besides, you're cheap. I'd be crazy as a loon to fire you."

Zoe burst out laughing.

"I'm holding onto the 'smart capable person' part," I grumbled.

Finn snapped his fingers, ending with a wink and finger gun pointed at me. "Getting back to them items in that staged bank box, even though you don't have 'em, you can be linked to 'em. And because of that, even though you did nothing wrong, you felt threatened. Right?"

"Heck, yeah, I did."

"Because somebody put the fear of the unknown in you. If they had all those other photos of you, and they could put *your* signature on a bank card for that box, imagine what else they could do. Even said as much in the note." He held up the photograph of my dad. "Which brings me to this. Know of anything that could link your daddy to the Russians?"

I shook my head.

"He take any overseas trips recently? Don't have to necessarily be to Russia. Could be to Europe. Dubai. Even—"

"*No.*"

"Okay, then." Finn considered me. "He come into

money recently? Maybe buy a new boat or fancy car or something?"

"He's been talking about getting a bigger boat, but that's nothing new," I said.

Finn flipped the photo over and stared at the back, his brow furrowed. With a grimace, he set it back down and addressed me. "I s'pose your daddy's got a high-level clearance. What if someone dropped compelling evidence in the laps of our counterintelligence folks showing him rubbing elbows with the Russians. Evidence they manufactured," he quickly added. "At best, his clearance is suspended while they investigate. But even if he's eventually cleared, it'll hang over him. Might even wreck his career." His impassive gaze fixed on me as he casually tapped his forefinger against his lips, deep in thought. "You were talking 'bout quitting the contest. Somebody clearly don't want you walking away. So, they upped the stakes using your daddy. Got any enemies who wanna do you bad?"

"The only people I can think of are all in prison," I said.

"From them two cases I read 'bout?" Finn asked. "They there because of you?"

I nodded.

"But no connection between 'em? Like a mastermind who got away?"

"None that I know of."

"Okay, in a bit we gonna circle back to why someone wants you staying in this contest." Finn pulled a file from the pile on the desk, sat back in his chair, and opened it. He read the first page, sifted through the folder, and brought another page to the top. "I got more info after we talked yesterday. Appears this Spencer

199

Fernsby rascal has key investors who are quietly threatening to sue him for two hundred million."

"Two hundred *million*?" I repeated in shock.

His eyes widened. "Big number, ain't it?"

I slowly shook my head. "He's such a sweet old man."

"Yeah, well, remember me saying I put a lot of fellas like that away for a long time?" Finn said. "Appears these investors think your sweet old granddaddy falsified company assets, among other accounting hijinks, to increase private capital placements in his company. Money he then used to fuel growth by buying up other companies. Apparently, his company ain't worth close to what the financials show. Either he makes them folks whole, or they gonna be filing a lawsuit."

"Which is why he's participating in the contest," Zoe said. "He wins, he pays everybody off, and his problems are solved."

Finn wiggled a hand. "So long as the feds don't start snooping around." He held up a sheet of paper. "And this here is a recent article in a business journal detailing Frederick Volkov's impressive string of investment successes. Specifically, 'bout his corporate takeovers and large stock acquisitions occurring right before megamergers. What they call his 'prescient' investing raises a big 'ole red flag called possible insider trading. I reckon the SEC is gonna start sniffing around him soon, if they haven't already started. That means, right now, I got four of eight contestants who at best are no-good snakes in the grass." He counted off on his fingers. "Fantucci. Azarian. Fernsby. Volkov. All crooked. One's dead, and the other three might be lawyering up real soon."

A statement during the opening meeting popped in my head. "Um, there's something Creighton Winston said during the opening meeting I forgot to tell you."

Finn leaned forward, a suspicious look on his face. "Yeah? Something else you ain't been telling me?"

I swallowed. "No, something I *forgot* to tell you. He said all the contestants were selected by the founder because each had a secret that law enforcement would be interested in."

"He said that?" Finn asked. "Law enforcement?"

"The lawyer called them lucky secrets," Zoe added.

"Why lucky?" Finn asked. "Sounds like everyone is being blackmailed."

"Because the winner will be rich," I said.

Finn picked up the note that came with the photograph of my dad and gave it a long look. "Yeah, something ain't right. There are plenty of other contestants who could win, so why does someone not want *you* to walk away?"

Pointing to the note in his hand, I said, "That note is clear. The founder is looking for the best of the contestants. Since the contest seems to be about solving riddles, I think we were selected for our problem-solving skills."

"Problem-solving?" Finn asked. "For what?"

"To steal the half billion dollars," I replied. "Nobody gives away that kind of money. You even touched on it. Although the source of the money might be legit, the method to obtain it might not be. Maybe the founder is a banker with inside information but needs someone to take it and develop a master plan to steal the money. In exchange, that person gets to keep half."

Finn looked past us for several seconds, then focused on me. "You might be onto something. Although, ain't many places you can steal that kind of scratch from. It's gotta be some kind of bank or investment fraud scheme. I read 'bout a group who stole just shy of a billion dollars in three days from three Moldovan banks using a revolving series of layered bank loans. It was highly sophisticated and involved multiple banks and shell companies. Same kinda thing almost happened with the Bangladesh national bank."

"Most of the contestants have backgrounds in finance or investing," Zoe noted.

"Except me," I said, "and Scooter and Jimmy."

"And Fantucci," Zoe added. "But she's dead."

Finn scratched his goatee peeking out from a scrabble of whiskers. "The first note you got said the person's been watching you closely for some time. That person probably read your press clippings and reckons you can pull off whatever this is all 'bout."

That got a cynical laugh out of me. "And obviously *not* read my FBI file."

"Don't sell yourself short," Finn said, leveling his gaze on me. "If I was looking for someone to plan a scam, I'd consider you."

With those words hanging in the air, Zoe broke the silence. "If we're gonna catch whoever is blackmailing Sara, we need to win the contest so the person reveals him or herself, right? I mean, they gotta give her the information in order to plan the scheme."

A pained expression came over Finn's face as he struggled with Zoe's statement. With a sharp exhale, he said, "I don't like it, but she's right. Y'all gotta stay in the contest and win it so we can figure out who's behind this. As long as you keep making progress in the contest, you're protected. Hopefully, we can nail the person before then, but if not, winning the contest will flush 'em out in the open. Then we get the authorities involved. If we go too soon, we risk getting blown and Sara and her daddy being fed to the cops. Besides, there's no hard evidence. But no worries. I'm an ex-cop and licensed PI. If things go sideways, I can straighten it out with folks."

"What about Fantucci's killer?" Zoe asked. "If it's one of the contestants, we're at risk."

Finn puffed up his cheeks, letting the air out slowly. "Ain't no way around it. Y'all just gonna have to be careful. That means focus exclusively on the contest and leave everything else to me." He pointed an accusing finger at me. "Look, I know you. Whatever you do, *don't* try to unmask the founder because if you get caught, the person will go rabbit on us and then all bets are off. In the meantime, I'll run down info on the other four contestants plus that Winston fella, see if I can start drawing a bead on someone. And take Bertie with you. He'll help cut through any hogwash and maybe get some intel you can feed me."

"Will do," I said. "Hey, I'm going to send you pics of license plates from all the cars in the garage. Maybe they're registered to an actual person instead of the One-Eleven Trust."

"It's worth a shot," Finn said. "Although whoever owns El Sueño has been careful 'bout hiding ownership, so I reckon we'll find them vehicles are registered to an entity. But hey, you never know, crooks make mistakes, too."

"Cool beans." I turned to Zoe. "As for taking Bertie, looks like this contest has been giving you anxiety attacks and your doctor recommends an emotional support dog. Everybody will easily buy it."

Zoe threw me an exaggerated smile. "Funny."

"I'm also gonna need y'all to call me every morning before breakfast and every night before hitting the hay." Finn dug around in a desk drawer and pulled out a small black box with a knob on one end. Handing it to me, he said, "When you call me, turn this on and keep your voice low. It's an audio jammer that generates white noise. Always carry it with you and use it when y'all talk 'bout the contest." He stuck out a finger. "And don't forget to call, 'cause if I don't hear from you, I'm gonna start kicking up a ruckus."

"Yes, dad," I said with a face.

"Don't worry," Zoe said, shooting me a look. "I'll set reminders for us to call."

"Good," Finn said with an approving smile. "And now that y'all got a contest to win, hit me with that riddle."

I read it to him again. *Everybody enjoys spending time with me. In fact, one will always find thirty men and two women around me. Sometimes more. But never less.*

Finn placed his elbows on the desk and steepled his fingers. He closed his eyes for a few seconds, then opened them with a broad smile, his eyes alive. "There a game room at El Sueño?"

Chapter Twenty-Three

The game room

By noon we were back from visiting Finn and stood in the doorway leading to the game room. A magnificently elegant game room. Three black walnut beams arched across a gleaming red oak hardwood floor. Between the beams, light-gray ceiling panels curved upward into domes with walnut ribs meeting in the center of each dome. The beams sprang from square mahogany columns with carved lions' heads filling the upper panels and accent lighting projecting up from atop the columns. The beams and columns combined to separate the room into thirds, accented by sweeping silver curtains and thick tie-backs matching the rich fabric. A poker table, chess table, and backgammon table populated the left section, and a stylish bar with high-backed chairs and pub tables filled the right. In front of us, in the center section, sat a red-felted antique pool table on a blue oriental rug beneath two crystal chandeliers. On the table, billiard balls were racked and ready.

We unleashed Mauzzy and Bertie, who immediately followed their noses to the bar area while Zoe shot to the game section, stopping at the chess table.

"That's not it," I called to her. "You've gotta read

the whole riddle."

"I know it's about the room, but there might be a clue here," she said, examining underneath the table.

"We first need to find the safe."

"If there is one," she said, feeling along the edges of the table.

I wandered over to check out the chess game's setup. Since a chessboard was numbered, if the chess pieces were placed in an unusual layout, they could reveal a clue. Possibly the combination to the game room's safe. The oversized set was impressive, with three-inch pawns and kings twice that height. But there was nothing unusual about the setup. The pieces were arranged on the pale-green board in their starting positions.

"This set looks expensive. You think it's jade?" I asked.

Zoe picked up a black rook, turning it around as she inspected if from all angles. "Could be, but I didn't know jade came in black and white."

"Me neither," I said, lifting a pawn, pushing on the square it came from, then scanning the room as I listened and watched for any telltale signs of a hidden space revealing itself. With no success, I returned the pawn and repeated the action with the next one.

Zoe replaced the rook and watched as I moved on to a third pawn. "What are you looking for?"

"A button or sensor that might release a hidden panel or door."

"Brilliant," Zoe said, picking the rook back up and checking its square.

We quickly worked through the rest of the game pieces, with the same result each time. Nothing.

"With that riddle, I really thought this chess table was gonna have something," Zoe griped, moving over to the backgammon table, and beginning a new search.

"Make sure you check all the pieces, then do the poker table. I'll check the pool table," I said, walking back toward the room's middle section.

I ran my hands over the table's edges and poked around in each of the empty pockets. Finding nothing, I got on the floor, eased under the table, and continued the examination. Seeing me on my back, Mauzzy ran over from the bar area and mauled my face with kisses.

"Thank you, Handsome," I said, pushing him away, only to be attacked with more kisses from another angle. "Okay, okay. Love you, too," I said with a laugh, rolling out from under the table and pushing to stand.

Crack.

After taking a few seconds to gather my senses, and unfortunately allow the pain to fully register with my scrambled brain, I crawled a little further out to *fully* clear the table and stood, rubbing the crown of my head. With a quick glance across the room to see if Zoe heard the latest transgression against myself—she had—I leaned against the table, lowered my head, and closed my eyes, waiting for the throbbing to subside.

A far-to-close and overly exuberant voice rattled my befuddled senses. "Off the top of your head, any thoughts where to search next?"

Angling my head toward the obnoxious disturbance, I cracked an eye open to see a beaming Zoe. "Hilarious."

She chuckled. "I thought so. Witty, too."

"Should've let you check it. You could've walked

under the dang thing." I gently felt around on my head, fingers grazing a way-too-familiar growing bump.

Mauzzy padded over to Bertie, who was sniffing around a pub table positioned against one of the mahogany columns by the bar area. As Bertie worked around the table, Mauzzy investigated the base of the column.

Following Mauzzy's lead, I pushed off the table, walked over to another column, and began examining it. "There might be a safe hidden behind one of these panels. Like in the art gallery."

Zoe bopped over to a third column, her little hands roaming over its surface. Quickly finished with the flat lower panel, she raised up on tiptoes, arm extended high, fingers stretching for the carved lion head on the upper panel.

"Don't worry about that," I called over to her. "You just focus on the lower parts. I'll take of everything *out of your reach*."

She scowled at me from under her arm. "Amazon."

I grinned back at her. "Payback, shorty."

We quietly searched the six columns, high and low, but found no hidden compartments holding a safe. The bar area was the only place left to be searched. I retreated to a pub table where Zoe sat perched on a chair and stared at the bar spanning the width of the room beneath classic pendant light fixtures. Behind the counter, tall walnut cabinets and backlit mirrored shelving loaded with glasses and mugs flanked a large flat-panel television. The safe had to be back there. Somewhere.

"You start beneath the bar and then help me with the cabinets and shelving," I said.

"And if we don't find anything?"

"We'll start knocking on every inch of the floor."

Zoe groaned. "You really think they're that stupid to put another safe in the floor?"

"No, but we're running out of options. And I don't think Mauzzy will get lucky twice."

Obviously hearing his name mentioned, Sweet Handsome trotted out from behind the bar, followed by Bertie. They sat in front of me and stared up. Hopeful.

I glanced at my watch. "Guys, it's not dinnertime."

With that word uttered, *the* word, Mauzzy's ears perked up, his front paws trembling. Bertie maintained his cool, not budging, eyes locked on me.

"Let's find that safe," I said, standing and heading to the bar, Mauzzy and Bertie dancing around my feet, eyes glued to me the entire time. Behind the bar, the beautiful hardwood floor gave way to sandstone tiles. "We only have a few hours before…" I glanced down at the dancing dachshunds. "Um…we eat, and we still gotta figure out the combo once we find it."

Searching the bar was a painstaking and time-consuming task because of all the glasses, bottles, decanters, dishes, and accoutrements we had to remove before we could search behind a shelf or cabinet. And then said glasses, bottles, decanters, dishes, and accoutrements had to be placed back before we could move on to the next area to be searched. Two fricking hours of remove, search, replace, repeat. A fruitless test of patience.

When we were done with the bar, cabinets, and shelving, and after our rising hopes were dashed when the television didn't budge, Zoe let loose. "No effing way I'm crawling all over this place pounding on the floor."

I moved out from behind the bar, pulled out a barstool, and sat. With a dramatic sigh, I said, "Then what do you suggest?"

She threw up her hands. "How the hell do I know, but we keep looking."

"*Where?*"

The perturbed pixie glanced around the game room, her shoulders dropping when she came to the realization nothing was left but checking the floor. With a deep-throated moan, she surrendered to the inevitable. "I'll start over by the game tables, you can have fun with the stone crap here."

Mauzzy came out from behind the bar, sat at my feet, and hit me with another unwavering "feed me" stare. But this time, without Bertie.

"Sorry, Mauz, but you're gonna have to wait," I said, climbing down off the stool.

Mauzzy yipped and disappeared behind the bar. When I rounded the counter, he and Bertie were waiting for me beside a recessed fridge, expectant looks on their mugs. I stepped past the famished friends to the far end of the bar and with a grunt, got on my hands and knees and began knocking on the tiles. The *stone* tiles. In the distance, Zoe energetically echoed my frustration as we crawled along the floor searching for the phantom safe. I worked my way backward toward the open end of the bar, rapping fast-bruising knuckles as I went.

"Sorry, guys," I said, my feet bumping into the pups as I slid back over the floor. I looked over my shoulder. They didn't move. "Guys, c'mon now, I need to get past. There's no food in there for you."

They refused to budge.

I nudged Mauzzy with my foot, but all he did was climb over it and reposition himself with his butt right up against the refrigerator, beseeching hazel eyes on me. "Handsome, let me finish this and then I'll feed you."

Bertie let a sharp bark fly and set himself directly beside Mauzzy, his one-brown-one-blue pair of eyes laser-focused. Together the little guys offered up a silent shout-out for their newfound best buddy in the world, the resplendent refrigerator. That depository of deliciousness. The trustee of treats. The glorious giver of—

The refrigerator?

I eased Mauzzy and Bertie out of the way and opened the refrigerator. It was stocked with beer, sodas, and water. After I emptied the bottom shelf, I gave the back of the fridge a shove, but the only thing that moved was the entire unit.

Backward.

A good number of inches.

I stood, gripped the top front edge, and tugged forward. The refrigerator fought back, like a leashed Mauzzy refusing to step outside in the rain. "Zoe, get over here and help." With considerable effort, I walked the unit forward until it was protruding halfway out from the cabinets.

When Zoe got there, she pushed me to the side, grabbed the open door and the top edge, and slid the fridge out of the space and onto the floor. "No problem."

"Seriously?"

"I keep telling you to work on hand strength."

"And I keep telling you, those squeezy things are

211

impossible." A pause. "And dangerous." I peered behind the fridge. Staring back at me from within the dark space, the ghostly image of a safe. "We found it."

Chapter Twenty-Four

The brainiac–part two

Zoe shoved me, and then the refrigerator, out of the way and stuck her head into the open space. "I guess I'm gonna be the one crawling back there to open the thing. No way you can fit in here."

"Agreed. Just need to figure out the combo."

Zoe pulled her head back and stood. "I got an idea. It was something I noticed after you split your skull."

"Don't start," I cautioned.

She grinned and ran out from behind the bar, stopping at the pool table. "Check it out."

I walked over and stood beside her. "What?"

"Notice anything?"

"About what? The balls?"

"Yeah. See how they're racked?"

I assessed the colorful triangle of orbs. Everything seemed normal. "I don't see it."

"What's the most popular pool game?"

"Eight ball?"

Zoe's face lit up. "Impressive. And how do you set the rack for eight ball?"

I shrugged. "Put all the balls except the white one in that triangle thingy."

"The balls go in that 'triangle thingy' in a certain way. They alternate between solid and stripes along the

213

outside, and the eight ball goes in the center of the third row." She pointed to the rack on the table. "Now look again."

$$2$$
$$9—3$$
$$5—7—14$$
$$1—6—15—12$$
$$10—8—11—4—13$$

"The eight ball is in the back row." I glanced up at Zoe. "And there are no alternating solids and stripes on the outside."

Her brilliant white smile was triumphant. "Exactly. In fact, those balls are not set up for any game. At least not one I know about."

"Maybe somebody just threw them into the rack," I suggested.

"That's a possibility, but maybe there's a specific reason for their positioning."

I looked at the configuration of balls. If Zoe was right, finding a safe combination in the alignment was going to be difficult bordering on pure hit-and-miss. "Assuming the combination is like the first four, we need seven numbers, but there are fifteen balls in five rows. So, it would have to be some combination of balls for at least part of the numbers."

"What if we combine the numbers from each set of two adjacent balls?" Zoe suggested. "Like the two-ball in the first row and the three to the right of it in the second would be twenty-three. And we just work around the rack."

"I like the idea, but a couple problems right off the bat. The outer double-digit ones make it impossible. The combined numbers would then be in the thousands or hundreds, and all the combination numbers have been either one or two digits. Plus, what about the three balls in the middle?" I slipped out my phone, snapped off a pic of the rack, and walked over to the safe. "Let's try using the sum of each row for a number."

Following behind me, Zoe said, "But that only gets us five numbers."

I stopped at the empty refrigerator space, motioning for Zoe to climb in. "And then we use the middle ball, seven, as the sixth number and take the sum of the other two interior balls for the seventh."

"Sounds screwy, but okay." With an exhale, she worked her way into the narrow space and following a few choice words, called back, "Give me the numbers."

"Two. Twelve. Twenty-six. Thirty-four. Forty-six. Seven. And twenty-one."

"Nope."

I called out several more number sets, trying different approaches as I switched and swapped balls, but each time it ended with an increasingly more frustrated "nope" from Zoe.

I studied the pic. Just like the other safes, the methodology for discovering the combination had to make sense. Pure randomness would greatly increase the chance no winner would be found, which wasn't the point of the contest. But finding a logical order with just fifteen balls didn't seem possible.

After some grumbling, banging around, and another salty word or two, Zoe poked her head out. "Can we just call the brainiac?" she whispered, wisely aware of possible listening devices like in our suite. "I can't stay in here forever."

"Matt?"

"You know any other brainiac?"

"Mauzzy. Obviously."

"Call him," she snarled.

I sent the pic to my brother with a message to find a set of seven one or two-digit numbers using a logical approach, and advised we would be calling in five minutes.

"Let's go outside, Zo."

I helped her out and we navigated our way outside to an interior courtyard that excited Mauzzy and Bertie to no end.

As they sniffed every tree and bush, I called Matt and put him on speaker. "Any ideas?"

"This for another safe combination?"

"Yep. We're on our fourth room," I replied.

"That's progress. The other three also seven-number combos?"

"Yep," I said. "Comprised of single and double-digit numbers."

"Same for our suite's safe that started this whole thing," Zoe added.

"Okay, got it." A pause. "Huh. That's interesting."

Zoe looked at me, then at the phone. "What's interesting?"

"The middle ball in the rack is the seven."

"So," I said.

"All your safe combinations are seven numbers," he replied. "Typically, electronic safe combinations range from three to six numbers. I've never heard of seven."

"And your point?" Zoe asked.

"In numerology, the number seven is very powerful. It describes intellectuals, deep thinkers, philosophers, people considered visionary with a unique way of thinking. Because they spend so much time thinking and absorbing knowledge, they tend to be reclusive and have difficulty making friends. And—"

Zoe jumped in, repeating her question with added emphasis. "And your point?"

"Um, you've been trying to find the contest's…founder…I think is what you called him."

With a quick glance at me, Zoe said, "Not anymore. Finn is working that angle while we stay focused on the contest."

"Oh. Then tell Finn the person he's hunting for might consider himself a seven. It would explain the preponderance of sevens you're coming across."

"Hey, the object in the first safe was a seven-pound bowling ball," I said.

"It fits," Matt said. "You're looking for a seven."

"Seriously? Somebody considers themselves a frigging *number?*" Zoe asked, her eyes popping out of her head.

"Considering the totality of the evidence, yeah, pretty sure," Matt replied.

Zoe took a step away from the phone, then spun and leaned back in toward it. "You realize if that's the case, we're dealing with someone certifiable, which doesn't fit *anybody* associated with the contest. Except maybe a crazy chef."

I considered what my brother was suggesting. As a gifted mathematician, he looked at the world through numbers, which definitely helped us last summer unravel the whole Carlton affair. Could he now be onto something with numerology being involved somehow? Again?

"Thanks for the insight, Matt," I said. "We'll pass it on to Finn. But right now, can we focus on the pool table?"

Zoe's shake of the head and rolling of eyes screamed she wasn't buying it, even if he was her boyfriend.

"Sure. What have you tried so far?" Matt asked.

We explained Zoe's idea, the immediate problems it raised, my failed attempts, and the need for the solution to be logic-based.

"You're overcomplicating it," Matt said.

"What'd you expect from your sister."

There was a pause. "Valid point. Have you tried using Occam's razor?"

"What, for our legs?" I quipped.

"No, sis, for your approach," he said in a matter-of-fact tone.

"A fricking razor?" an increasingly exasperated Zoe barked.

"It's not an actual razor. It's a problem-solving theory. Basically, the simplest explanation is usually the best and most preferable one."

Zoe looked at me, then shook a fist at the phone. "Which is…*what?*"

"In the rack, there are twelve exterior balls and three interior ones. Six numbers come from the exterior and one from the interior."

"How?" I asked.

"By adding the exterior balls two at a time, starting with the two-ball in the first position and going counterclockwise for a total of six numbers, and then simply add the three interior balls for the seventh number."

Zoe put her hands on hips, as if Matt were there, and let it rip into the phone. "The obvious, most *simple* way, Mr. Occam, is to move *clockwise*." She finished with a smug smile and wink at me.

"Um, sure, you can try that first." Another pause, only this time, the longest yet for the call. "It's just that counterclockwise is considered positive. You know, from a torque perspective. So, that's where I would start."

"Of course, positive torque," Zoe said, sticking a finger in her mouth and making a gag noise.

"Okay, we'll try it," I said, exchanging a look with Zoe. "Any other ideas?"

"Nah, pretty sure that'll work," Matt replied.

"It better," Zoe advised, "because your girlfriend here has to squeeze into a dark, cramped space to enter the combo and she will be pretty fricking annoyed if it's the wrong number."

"It'll work," my poor brother said, his voice cracking.

"Thanks, Matt, we'll let you know." I tapped off and looked at Zoe. "Why he's with you…"

She grinned. "He knows I'm kidding."

"Uh-huh. Sounded like it. Let's go give it a shot."

We rounded up a reluctant Mauzzy and Bertie, who were playing an exciting game of find-the-petrified-chipmunk, and returned to the game room.

Zoe crawled into the space with the safe. "Fire away."

I read off the numbers using Matt's counterclockwise suggestion. "Eleven. Six. Eighteen. Fifteen. Twenty-five. Seventeen. And twenty-eight."

"He's *such* a brainiac," Zoe sang. "I love him."

"It opened?"

She banged around some before coming out with a familiar-looking envelope and a gold pen.

I took the items from her and helped her stand. "Any other envelopes in there?"

"All of them," she said with a smile. "We're the first here. Open yours up."

I ripped it open and took out a single sheet of typed paper.

Well done on making it this far. But if you haven't noticed, I've been watching from the shadows. Even though everybody has fun around me, I'm kept out of sight.

Chapter Twenty-Five

An epiphany? Or a big mistake?

Instead of focusing on the next riddle, all I could think about was the founder being an intellectual who couldn't make friends. When I told Finn during last night's end-of-day phone call about my brother's hunch the person was a numerologist focused on the number seven, he laughed it off and chalked it up to Matt "just being another Donovan." Despite Finn's skepticism, Matt was a genius who didn't think like normal people. So, when he says he's pretty sure about something, I listen. And when I woke up this morning, after an incredibly crappy sleep, I had an epiphany.

Even before my first coffee.

Every time I cycled through the list of possibilities, one name kept coming back to me. Finn wasn't going to like it. At all. And neither was Zoe. But I knew what needed to be done. What *had* to be done.

Cozying up to Karsh Azarian.

Going against my whole "put-it-off-until-you-can't" philosophy, and without discussing it with Zoe for obvious reasons, I decided to approach him this morning. Better to ruin today's breakfast than tonight's dinner when Chef Doll was in the kitchen serving up five-star creations. And the occasional outburst. Or two.

"Mind if we join you?" I asked Karsh, stopping

abruptly at the middle table where he sat by himself reading the newspaper.

A startled Zoe bumped into me, followed by a sharp knuckle into the small of my back, and a single cough.

Karsh closed his paper, folded it in half, then again in half, and set it on the table beside a plate of plain wheat toast. Taking a sip of tea, he considered me, expressionless. "Why?"

And so, it begins.

"Excuse me?" I asked.

Gesturing with his head but keeping his eyes on me, he said, "There are plenty of empty chairs elsewhere. Why do you wish to sit here? With me?"

"I dunno. We've never really talked. Thought I'd get to know you better."

I glanced back at Zoe. Her eyes were locked on me, chiseled emerald daggers warning me to shut up and move on.

He tilted his head of impeccably-styled dark-brown hair. "Really? After calling me, what was it,"—he waved a hand through the air, like a master of ceremonies regaling an expectant audience—"ah yes, Ponzi scum." He finished with a condescending smile.

Dang it. Forgot about that altercation at dinner. Not how I envisioned this whole cozying-up thing. This was going to take some finesse. "Sorry about that, but you questioned the integrity of my friends. That makes me say things I don't necessarily mean."

He raised the teacup, pausing it in midair. "Well, I meant every word." With a devastatingly charming smile unleashed on Zoe, he pointed at her with the teacup. "Present company excluded, of course."

I peeked over my shoulder at her. The girl's jaw was set, eyes hard, fists clenched. Even though the man had her by almost two feet, his physical well-being was in serious jeopardy. Or it could be mine, considering she was watching me do the very thing Finn adamantly warned against.

Karsh returned his attention to me. "Although, if you recall, I was not referring to your friends but rather your associates."

I saw my opening and grabbed it. "You're right. And you know what they say, you can choose your friends but not your associates."

Another disdainful smile. "Mmmm, not how it goes."

Fighting back the urge to disintegrate the guy, and praying Zoe held it together and not blow everything up, I gave him a pleasant smile. "The real reason I wanted to sit with you, Karsh, was to better understand your investment strategies, since when I win, I'm going to need a financial adviser. And from what I hear, you're the best. So, can we join you?"

Another cough from Zoe, this time louder and ending with a sharp grunt.

Suddenly smiling like a wolf, he gestured to a seat across the vacant table from him. "Please, by all means."

We sat and Reginald DuBois hurried over to take our order. When he left, an incredulous Karsh addressed Zoe. "Sounds like breakfast is your big meal of the day."

I jumped in before Zoe could eviscerate the man. "She considers it her most important meal."

"Evidently." Karsh tore off a piece of toast and

delicately put it in his mouth. Keeping his eyes on me, he finished chewing, took a sip of tea, set the teacup down, and dabbed his lips with a linen napkin. "So, you think you can win?"

"Sure. Why else would I be here?"

With an amused smile, he said, "Yes, why indeed." He surveyed the room, then Zoe, then me. "It is a lot of money, isn't it."

"Which is why I wanted to talk with you."

The amused smile disappeared, replaced by the wolfish one. "Francois-Marie Arouet, whom you might know by his *nom de plume*, Voltaire, wrote in a letter to Madam d'Epinal, *'Quand il s'agit d'argent, tout le monde est de la même religion.'* In other words, you have stirred my interest. What is it you would like to know?"

"For starters, what you just said," I replied.

With a disparaging chuckle, Karsh said, "Ah, you don't speak French. No surprise. Allow me to translate. *'When it is a question of money, everyone is of the same religion.'* Better?"

Reginald returned with a large glass of orange juice, a coffee cup, a silver French-press, and an insulated carafe. He set the juice in front of Zoe, then slowly pressed the plunger down, filled the cup, and poured the remaining coffee into the carafe. He set the filled cup in front of me saying, "Would you care for your yogurt and fruit now? Miss Harp's breakfast will take a bit longer to…assemble." He turned to Zoe. "Or I can bring your toast, biscuits, gravy, and grits now while everything else is being prepared."

"That's okay," Zoe said with a tense smile. "I can wait."

"Miss Donovan?" he asked.

"Thank you, but I can wait for Zoe's."

Reginald nodded once and moved to the next table where the Volkov twins talked in hushed tones with Rod Toft while his indifferent girlfriend messed with her phone.

Karsh extended an open hand toward me. "Your question is…"

Okay, Sara, time to suck up to the jerk. Good thing it's on an empty stomach.

I casually knocked back a couple hits of coffee, trying to appear the opposite of what I was feeling. "Right. My question. I'm a poor college student with zero money-management skills. So, if I win the money, what do you recommend? Like, what should be my first step? Open an investment account? Get a lawyer? An accountant? Or do all three? And should I keep all the money in the Cook Islands trust account? Or just half, and move the rest to an investment account? I just don't have a clue."

He popped another piece of toast in his mouth, followed by a sip of tea. "My dear, I am surprised by your myriad questions."

I exchanged a glance with Zoe. "Why? It's a ton of money."

He calmly returned the teacup to its saucer, the cup touching down without a sound. "It is. But so is a half million dollars to a *poor* college student."

I froze in horror at the slow-motion train wreck I just created. The man was toying with me, like a cat with a cornered mouse. The Carlton Museum's reward money was never announced. And Zoe, Matt, and I honored our agreement to keep the payments secret.

Yet Karsh knew. But how?

I eyed Zoe, who appeared ready to throttle me. Having been called out, no sense feigning ignorance. "You know about my reward money," I said evenly.

"Among other things," he said, his lips curling up into a smirk. "Your clumsy dissembling is as amusing as it is telling. As the strategic genius Sun Tzu wrote in his timeless *The Art of War*, 'If you know the enemy and know yourself, you need not fear the result of a hundred battles.' I know myself very well. And I know you even better."

"That reward money was supposed to be a secret," I bristled.

A snide chuckle. "So are a lot of things, I suppose."

I considered the man. He quotes Voltaire, in French no less, and Sun Tzu. Like an intellectual. He knows about the reward money. He says he knows me better than... The photo of dad driving out of Fort Meade flashed in my head, followed by the bogus safe-deposit box.

A cold realization settled into my very core, although at some level, I already knew.

I was sitting with the founder.

I glared at the pompous jerk. "I know who you are."

He raised his eyebrows. "Do you?"

"I do. The question is, how well did you know Olivia Fantucci?"

The same annoying amused look appeared back on his face. "Are you the police?"

"No, but if you supposedly know about me, then you know I've worked with them."

"Really?" he said with a short, mocking laugh. "I

didn't realize getting arrested was considered working with the police."

"I was never arrested. And later, both times the FBI called me a supersleuth with an uncanny knack for solving crimes."

Another sardonic chuckle at my expense. "I believe the news accounts said 'an amateur with an extremely unorthodox knack for *somehow* solving crimes.' Nice try, my dear." He picked up his paper, snapped it open, and began reading it. Without looking up, he said dismissively, "Run along now."

Chapter Twenty-Six

Detective Lilley

I opened the door to our suite and pushed in past an excited Mauzzy and Bertie, who danced around me as I raced to put distance between me and a close-following Zoe.

She caught up to me before I could make it to the safety of the bathroom, grabbed my arm, and spun me around. "What the frick were you—"

Putting a finger to my lips, I whispered, "Shhhh," and dug into my purse. I took the audio jammer out, turned it on, and cranked the volume. "Keep it down."

We moved to the living room and sat on the couch. Mauzzy and Bertie snagged the cushion between us, so I set the hissing jammer on the coffee table.

Zoe unloaded in a harsh whisper. "What the *frick* was that all about at breakfast? You couldn't even go twenty-four hours before doing the one thing, the one fricking thing, Finn warned you about doing? Now you've alerted that jackwagon Azarian that you know he's the founder."

I took a breath, more to deescalate Zoe than calm me. "You're missing the point. Now we know who's been blackmailing me."

Zoe's finger shot out at me. "No, *you're* missing the point. As usual. What if he's the effing killer, too?

228

He dodged your question about Fantucci. You just put us on his list. If you—"

Two sharp knocks at the door rescued me and set Mauzzy and Bertie barking as they launched off the couch to investigate and intimidate.

I looked at Zoe, surprised.

"What're you looking at me for? It's probably your new buddy coming to whack us. He knows it's the only way to shut you up."

I turned off the jammer and tossed it in the desk drawer on the way to the door. Amid the canine commotion at my feet, I cracked the door open and peeked out. Percy Pembarton stared back, looking more grim than usual. Standing behind him, the woman detective who interviewed me the day Olivia Fantucci's body was discovered. Not good.

"Welcome back, Percy," I said through the opening. "Everything work out with your family matter?"

"Thank you, yes. Mother is recuperating at home. Miss Don—"

Bertie's barking abruptly shifted to a loud tortuous whine, drowning out Mauzzy's high-pitched yapping. I looked down. Bertie lay prone on the floor, paws over his eyes.

"*Miss Donovan*," Percy said over the ear-splitting noise as he leaned in, eyes focused at my feet.

Bending down, I gently cradled the chin of each pup in a hand and shushed them. "Guys. Enough. Stop. Thank you."

Surprisingly, Mauzzy and Bertie quieted down. Not because of my dog-whispering capabilities but more likely due to their lack of conditioning. Yeah, they were winded. Something I could commiserate with, after spending the last seven months scaling the stairs in Finn's crappy office building.

"Miss Donovan," Percy said with an irritated huff. "What is that dog doing here?"

I straightened. "Mauzzy? He's my emotional support dog. You said he could stay."

With a quick shake of the head, he shoved his hand through the opening and pointed at Bertie. "That one."

"Oh, this is Bertie. He's Zoe's emotional support dog."

Bertie let loose with a drawn-out whine.

Seriously?

With a quick glance down at the narc, who pawed at his eyes, I continued. "Her doctor recommended she get one to help calm her because of—"

A low escalating moan, ending in a high-pitched yelp.

Percy held up a hand. "Fully understand. Makes perfect sense, really. Good for her getting help." He snapped his hand closed, dropped it to his side, and pulled his shoulders back. "Miss Donovan, Detective Lilley here wishes to speak with you. And Miss Harp."

"Sure. Here, okay?"

The detective leaned around the butler and smiled politely. "Good morning. Yes, that would be fine."

Stepping back, I held the dogs with a foot and fully opened the door. "Come on in."

Percy stepped to the side to let the detective pass. "Detective Lilley, when you are through, please ring Security and someone will show you out." To me, he forced a smile, followed by a quick glance down and a sniff. "Have a pleasant morning, Miss Donovan."

Detective Lilley followed me into the living room, my inquisitive K-9 team on her heels. "I appreciate your time this morning. Missed you yesterday when I was out here."

My stomach tightened. It's never good when the Law *wants* to see you. "Oh? I didn't know you were looking for me."

"Not a problem." She sat effortlessly in the fiendish red chair. Of course, it cooperated with her and didn't even wobble, let alone become the whirling dervish it's proven to be. Apparently, just with me. "Nice chair. Comfortable."

Bertie and Mauzzy stopped in front of the cop, sizing her up. Actually, Mauzzy was coolly sizing her up. Bertie was the opposite of cool, his butt and tail wiging and wagging so much he might need doggie traction for a slipped disc.

The detective leaned down to pet the pups but stopped abruptly when Bertie reared up and attacked her face with kisses. "Oh, my," she said with a surprised laugh, containing him with ear and head scratches. "He's so *cute* with the blue and brown eyes."

Mauzzy snorted his embarrassment for his fawning junior partner and jumped on the couch, settling back down on the middle cushion, attentive eyes on the stranger.

With one final ear scratch, Detective Lilley eased Bertie down and focused on me. "This shouldn't take too long. I just need to follow up on a few things."

I returned to the couch where Zoe had remained sitting, as did Bertie, who tucked himself into the watchful Mauz. "Making progress?"

"Sorry, it's an ongoing investigation."

B.T. Polcari

"If you haven't already, you might want to focus on Karsh Azarian," I suggested. "When I asked him—"

"How about I focus on you?"

I swallowed. "Me?"

With a restrained smile, she leaned to the side and pulled a small notebook out from a back pocket of her jeans. Even with her movement, the chair remained steady as a rock. Flipping the notebook open, she thumbed through several pages before addressing us. "You left here together at nine-thirty-three on Saturday morning for Tuscaloosa and returned Monday after the body was discovered. We confirmed most of your timeframes for Tuscaloosa, but where were you between when you left here and noon Saturday?"

An explosion of adrenaline hit me, arms and legs on fire, stomach clenched. She really *is* focused on me. But I didn't do anything. Well, I didn't kill Olivia. But I did tell Finn about the...

"Um, besides driving time, we were in Tuscaloosa, like we already told you," I said, fighting to act natural.

Bertie sighed loudly and covered his eyes.

Unbelievable.

Before the little fink got out of control, I added, "But on our way there, we stopped where I work in Birmingham to see my boss about something."

"Where?"

Crap.

"Yeah, you wouldn't know the place."

"Try me."

Crap. Crap. Crap.

"Second Avenue South."

She winced. "What'd you go *there* for?"

Why does she care where we went? All that should

232

matter is we weren't at El Sueño where the murder happened. Or was she after something else? I couldn't let on I went to brief Finn on the contest. What I did was against the rules and if Detective Lilley inadvertently mentioned it to the wrong person during her investigation, I could be out of the contest. And worse. Much worse. With Bertie laying there eavesdropping, this called for some of my best subtle deception.

"My boss asked me to drop by to discuss a big case he just picked up. I do all his research."

Bertie let fly a long, miserable moan.

Why can't that *dang* dog save it for the perps? We're on the same team.

"Something wrong with Bertie?" the cop asked, concern in her voice.

"Um, just a sour stomach," I said. "He ate the other one's breakfast when I had my back turned. He's our little food whore."

Bertie looked up at me, yipped, then went back to his traitorous bellyaching.

"The poor thing sounds absolutely miserable," she said sympathetically.

I scratched the snitch's ears, then his stomach. "Yeah, well, he gets what he deserves. He'll be fine. Not the first time this has happened."

Thankfully, Bertie shut his yap, a belly rub the price for fleeting loyalty.

The detective redirected her concerned gaze away from Bertie and back on me, her gentle smile vanishing as our eyes met. "What's your supervisor's name?"

"Is that important?"

"I need to confirm your statement for my report.

Just a formality, really."

"Oh, sure, that makes sense. His name is Melvin Finnegan."

She cocked her head. "Finn Finnegan?"

"Yes, ma'am."

"Huh. I'll be darn. Haven't seen him since he left the force. How's he doing?"

"I've only worked for him for seven months, but he's doing great."

I waited for Bertie to rat me out, but he remained quiet. He knew better than to out the man who's filled his food bowl since he was a pup.

"I'll give him a call," she said. "During your time here, have either of you seen anybody carrying an exercise ball?"

"The big rubber ones?" Zoe asked.

"Yes," the detective answered. "Specifically, green or blue."

We shook our heads.

"They could have also been deflated?" she prodded.

I thought about it but nothing popped in my head. "Nope."

"Same here," Zoe said.

"How about gas cylinders?" she asked, her eyes studying us.

"Gas cylinders?" Zoe asked. "Like what?"

"The type used for oxygen or helium. Any size."

"No, ma'am," Zoe said.

I shook my head. "Sorry."

She stood, tucking the notebook away in a back pocket. "Okay, thanks for your time. If you remember anything later, you have my card from Monday." She stepped to the desk and called Security.

As she spoke on the phone, I stood and moved to the front door. No way I was going to allow her to linger around the suite while Security took their sweet time getting here. When she hung up, with a polite smile plastered on my face, I held the door open.

"I'll wait outside. Have a good day," she said, walking past me and stepping out into the hall.

"You, too," I said, closing the door behind her and turning to face Zoe. "Did you hear that?"

"Sure did," Zoe replied. "Winston said Fantucci died of carbon monoxide poisoning. Sounds like someone filled her exercise balls with the stuff and put a little hole in each."

"Ingenious. Who do we know around here who comes off that way?"

"The dude you just tipped off at breakfast."

Chapter Twenty-Seven

A savior? Or threat.

After Detective Lilley left, we spent the better part of the morning going over the latest riddle.

Well done on making it this far. But if you haven't noticed, I've been watching from the shadows. Even though everybody has fun around me, I'm kept out of sight.

With nothing obvious, we considered the four photos of objects from the safes, hoping they would clue us in to the riddle's answer. A seven-pound orange bowling ball, black dream catcher with turquoise beads, a white ballcap with *Italia* in green and red script, and a gold pen. But no matter how we laid them out, strung together letters from their descriptions, interchanged the words, combined the colors, and even crazier ideas, nothing worked.

"It's gotta just be the riddle's last sentence," I said, studying the page. "The first sentence is a throwaway. And the second—"

"The second one says somebody is watching us, girl. Karsh all but said the same thing."

I shook my head, refusing to consider Zoe's interpretation. If we were being watched, then everybody was being watched. This was bigger than just me. "The riddle's answer could be a hidden camera. It fits."

"Uh-uh. No way. Who loves to be around a hidden camera? Nobody, unless you're a perv. I'm telling you, he's using that second sentence to screw with us." She pointed at me. "With you."

"If he is, we can't let it bother us. He probably put it there to unnerve us."

Zoe bounced up from the couch, startling the snoozing pups, and began pacing. "Yeah, well, it's working. Don't know about you, but I don't appreciate a killer watching me."

"I seriously doubt he's the killer."

She stopped and glared at me. "What's changed your mind over the last three hours?"

"I've been rolling it around in my head. It's in his best interest to keep everyone in the contest. He needs to find the best person to plan the heist or scam or whatever he's up to. He even said so."

"Maybe seeing who's best at staying alive is part of the deal?"

"It's illogical."

Zoe let out a sarcastic laugh and resumed her pacing. "If your brother said something's illogical, I'd buy it. Coming from you, not a chance."

"You'll see."

"Hopefully, and not before someone other than Karsh is about to slit my throat."

I waved her over to the couch. "C'mon and sit down. Your pacing is making me nervous."

For once, she listened to me and dropped onto the couch.

"I'm going to read the first part of the last sentence," I said. "Don't think about it, just go with what pops in your head, and I'll write it down. Ready?"

Zoe nodded.

"Close your eyes."

She did.

"What does everybody have fun around?"

"Me."

I gave the smiling wiseass a look through the tops of my eyes. "*What*, not who."

"Just being spontaneous."

"Let's try it again. Clear your mind. That shouldn't be too hard for you."

"Funny."

"*Just being spontaneous*." I winked. "Now relax. Ready?"

She closed her eyes, breathed out, and nodded.

"What does everybody have fun around?"

"A buffet. The kitchen. The TV. A firepit. The pool. The...mmmm...the..." She opened her eyes. "That's all I got."

I looked at the list, then the riddle. "Okay, any of those five kept out of sight?"

"A kitchen?"

"Agreed." I picked up the El Sueño information guide from the coffee table and consulted it. "This map shows an indoor/outdoor pool. You think an indoor pool is something considered kept out of sight?"

Zoe took the binder and studied the map. "I dunno. Could be, I guess. This also shows stables and a shooting range. Those would be out of sight, right?"

"True, but not everybody has fun around those things."

Her eyes widened. "The shooting range? Are you kidding me?"

I gave her a look. "It's not the shooting range."

"Says you."

"You know I hate guns."

"Then I say we hit the pool."

"Really? You like it over the kitchen?"

"No, but the last thing I wanna do is get anywhere near that crazy chef. Especially in her kitchen."

I pictured Barbara Doll with searing black eyes shoving her wooden spoon up under Karsh Azarian's chin. "The pool it is!"

****

We stood inside the doors of the indoor pool, marveling at yet another incredible area of the mansion. The best hotels on the planet would kill for this pool. I sucked in the gloriously intoxicating smell of sanitization. Indoor pools rocked the best smells ever. Chlorine and bleach. The rock stars of clean.

"Holy crap, this is so not what I expected," Zoe said.

I stared in awe, mesmerized by the world we stepped into. "I've never seen anything like it."

A series of curved floor-to-ceiling tinted-glass panels towered on the far end of a free-form stone pool deck meandering to the outside. The textured interior walls were alabaster-and-wheat-colored plaster with intermittently-spaced sconces. Exotic plants including Ficus trees, potted palms, and broadleaf greenery were strategically placed along the walls and curvatures of the decking. Arched paned double-doors flanked both sides of the glass wall, with one slightly ajar. Outside, lush foliage amid elevated rock outcroppings embraced the pool as majestic waterfalls tumbled into sparkling blue water. The two center panels of the glass wall were retracted to each side, resulting in an opening to the outside that allowed swimmers to pass between the two sections of the pool. Teak chaise lounge chairs and side tables dotted both the indoor and outdoor areas.

Mauzzy trotted up to the pool's edge, hung his head near the water, sniffed, then sneezed so violently his little body jolted back. With a startled shake of the head, he pawed at his nose, and sneezed again. Bertie shot past the distraught Sweet Handsome, squeezed between the open door leading outside, and began exploring a new frontier of smells. Recognizing the pool wasn't his thing, Mauzzy took off for the door, leaving us to find the safe on our own.

"This place is redonk. We should've brought our suits," Zoe complained

I strolled around the deck. "And that's exactly why we didn't. C'mon, start looking."

Zoe stepped to the edge of the deck and peered into the water. "You think it's down there?"

"Doubt it. I've never heard of an underwater safe."

"Dang it. I'd love to hit that pool."

"Give it up. Besides, you didn't bring a suit."

She grinned. "Never stopped me before."

I shook my head and continued searching. Even though the pool deck was rough-hewn stone with subtle ridges and depressions, I saw no evidence of any seams or indications of where it might have been cut to accommodate a safe.

Zoe examined the space's walls. "You're gonna have to take the upper half of these things, Stretch."

"I'll check what I can, but even I'm not tall enough to reach all the way up. Although no way someone's putting a safe up that high."

Zoe positioned herself beneath a sconce and jumped straight up, arm outstretched. Her fingers barely reached the base of the unit. "Too high. Check if any of these are levers."

I walked over to the sconce, reached up and gently tugged down on it. "Nope, but good idea." Following behind Zoe as she checked the lower portion of the walls, I probed as high as I could reach and checked all the sconces. But again, nothing.

After we looked unsuccessfully behind and under all the plants, except for the massive palms which were impossible to move, I took in the yawning cave-like pool area. "Not many places to hide a safe in here, and nothing comes close to resembling a set of numbers."

Zoe's gaze traveled along the deck to outside the glass wall. "You think out-of-sight could mean in those rocks out there?"

I considered the outdoor pool. "Yeah, why not. That whole area is secluded."

"One of them could be fake, like where people hide a second set of housekeys."

"In this place, anything is—"

The interior entrance door opened and in strolled a tall wiry guy around our age wearing a short-sleeve denim work shirt, *nicely*-fitted jeans, and swept-back blond hair. He acknowledged us, and even from a distance, his crystal-blue eyes transcended the rippling water between us. Slipping along the back wall, he opened a door in the corner and disappeared. Sadly. A motorized humming sound escaped into the pool area before quickly being swallowed by the silence as the door quietly closed behind the Tall Glass of Water.

I faced Zoe, brimming with excitement.

She pulled her head back, a pointed look on her face. "Dang, girl, reel it in."

"That's not it. Well, not entirely it. *But right?* Anyway, did you see where he went?"

"You're not going after him. He's working, and you don't want any more stalking accusations, do you?"

I frowned. Leave it to Zoe to dash the moment by bringing up unpleasant memories from my not-too-distant past. "Both times I was fully exonerated," I countered.

"Eventually."

"Still."

Her hand arced through the air toward the back door. "Then by all means, go for the trifecta and see what happens."

"I'm not chasing after him, although we're going into that mechanical room." I thought back to those rude stalking accusations. "*After* he leaves."

Zoe scrunched up her cute little face. "Why would we…" Her mouth fell open. "Everyone has fun around a pool, *but the mechanical crap is kept hidden*."

"Yep. That mechanical room is out of sight."

"I'll get the dogs."

"I'll keep an eye out."

She flashed me a sly knowing smile like only Zoe could. "Just stay put and no talking. If he approaches you, keep your hands to yourself."

I put my hands up, palms out. "Not even a handshake."

Zoe contemplated me before turning and hurrying toward the door leading outside. "Don't go anywhere," she called back to me.

I did as I was told and stayed put. Outside, Zoe

chased Bertie and Mauzzy around pool furniture, over rocks, and through ornamental grasses. Before she could corral the romping rascals, the door opened and out walked the pool guy.

Doing as Zoe instructed, I didn't move. Not an inch. But, *boy*, did I stare.

He glanced over at me, puzzled.

I threw him a casual wave and big smile. "Hey, there."

He responded with a nervous flip of the hand and escaped through the door into the hallway.

With the fantabulous show over before I could even think of screwing things up, I walked to the outside door and hollered for Bertie and Mauzzy to get inside. They immediately stopped messing with Zoe and zipped past me, not stopping until they were at the door leading to the hallway.

Zoe stomped up to me, breathing hard. "What the eff is with those dogs?"

"You're fresh meat. Mauzzy knows better than trying that crap with me."

She pushed past. "Ha. Right. You keep believing that."

"Breathing a little hard, are we?" I crowed.

Marching along the pool deck toward the mechanical room, and without turning back, she threw up two middle fingers.

Chuckling to myself, I hurried to catch up with my feisty friend. As I passed Mauzzy and Bertie, I said, "Let's go, guys."

The best buds fell in line trotting proudly alongside me, but noticeably keeping their distance from Zoe. They may have had their fun with her outside, but they were smart boys. Real smart.

I pushed open the door and we entered the mechanical room, the wonderful scent of chlorine hitting me anew as the equipment droned a steady beat of monotony. Black pipes rose from the concrete floor, extended from a white cinderblock wall, and crisscrossed between and into a large beige tank. Next to it, two blue kettle-shaped tanks sat on black pedestals with side latches holding the tops in place. More black pipes ran to and from one of the blue tanks, but nothing was attached to the other.

Approaching the unattached tank, I said, "This seems too easy."

Zoe joined me at the tank and together we undid the latches, hefted the lid off, and set it on the ground. Mauzzy and Bertie pounced, immediately commencing their investigation.

When we looked inside the tank, a safe resting on its back greeted us.

"This has gotta be a decoy," Zoe said, leaning in to get a closer look at the safe. "It was way too easy."

"Or maybe we're getting good at finding the safes."

She pulled her head out and gave me a questioning look. "It's a decoy."

I reached into the tank and tried to move the safe. "It's bolted down or something. If it's a decoy, would you go through the trouble of attaching it to this thing?"

"Sure would. Anything to screw with people like you." She finished with an inflated smile.

With a rueful shake of the head, I said, "Why'd I ask."

"Why do you do a lot of questionable things?

Because you're Sara Donovan. It's your brand."

"Okay, you wanna prove me wrong? Find the combination numbers in here that *don't* open that safe."

We split up but after fifteen minutes of searching, and clearing out more than a few disgusting spiderwebs with my face, it became clear there were no numbers in the room other than a digital readout on what I assumed to be the pool's water heater.

"There's nothing here. Let's go check outside," I said, walking toward the door.

"Like I suggested earlier?" Zoe sang as she, Mauzzy, and Bertie bounded past and out the door. No doubt Mauzzy was eager to have more fun at the expense of his latest foil, and he's dragged poor innocent Bertie into his scheme. At least it wasn't me. For once.

"You suggested looking for the *safe* outside," I shouted to the fast-moving Zoe. "Not for the combination."

Just as I passed through the doorway to the indoor pool area, I stopped and poked my head back into the mechanical room. Something caught my eye. A clipboard holding a thick stack of paperwork hung on a hook beside the doorframe. On the top page—

I turned back to my racing cohorts and yelled, "Hold up."

Already on the far side of the pool and making tracks for the exterior door, all three stopped and spun around. "*What?*" Zoe shouted, clearly impatient to get outside and prove me wrong.

"I found a stack of daily checklists with all kinds of water test numbers."

Zoe let her annoyance be heard and made her way

back to me. Mauzzy and Bertie didn't hesitate. They turned and headed back outside, the reaction screaming volumes about their confidence in my investigative abilities.

While waiting for Zoe, I scanned the top sheet. Under the "water test results" grid of the checklist were five categories: four chemical levels like chlorine and alkalinity, and the water temperature. Excluding decimals, the chemical readings included single digits for chlorine, two to three digits for hardness and alkalinity, and two digits for pH and water temperature. The numbers were all over the place. Consistent within each category, but collectively, all over the place.

Hmm.

Maybe I shouldn't have yelled for her to come back.

When Zoe reached me, she grabbed the clipboard before I could dig deeper into the stack, studied the first checklist, then the next several pages. With a cutting laugh, she handed it back. "Are you kidding me? How you getting any usable numbers from that crap?"

I thumbed through the papers, quickly searching each page before moving on to the next.

"You're wasting your time," Zoe said. "I'm going to look outside."

Without looking up, I said, "Just remember, in twenty minutes, we have to get ready for dinner."

"Fine, but you're getting the dogs."

Zoe left as I worked through the next page. And then the next. And the next. The numbers were all in the same ranges as the previous pages. Until—

My pulse quickened.

The water temperature on the page I was looking at

wasn't in the typical range of eighty-four to eighty-eight. The reading someone wrote for March seventh was forty-nine. No way that was right. I checked March sixth. The reading was eight. If that was truly the correct water temp, people were ice-skating on the pool that day. I checked March fifth. Twenty-nine. With adrenaline coursing through me, I kept flipping back. Fifteen. Thirty-six. Ten. Thirty-two. It wasn't until I hit February twenty-eighth that the readings went back to the mid-eighty range where they should have been all along. Seven straight numbers well below the proper temperature range.

Seven numbers?

I thought about calling Zoe back, again, but quickly ruled it out. The girl was my best friend and like a sister, but at times, I could only take so much crap from her at my expense. This was one of those times. I stepped over to the tank with the safe and keyed in the numbers from the clipboard, starting with March seventh and working back. But when I entered the last number, thirty-two, nothing happened. Remembering Matt's razor thingy about simplicity, I simply reversed the order, starting with the March first reading and finishing with March seventh's forty-nine.

A familiar electronic whirring sounded.

Twisting the handle, I opened the safe door. Inside it were only two envelopes and a compass. I took the envelopes out. One was addressed to me and the other for Jessica Doerr. After taking a pic of the compass, I returned it and the Doerr envelope to the safe and opened mine. As I read the typed words, my throat tightened.

I am many things throughout this game. A savior to

one. A threat to the rest. For this game, some might associate me with a word that has three consecutive double letters, but that would be wrong.

Chapter Twenty-Eight

Rule Five

"Thank you, Percy," I said, taking a flute of bubbling champagne.

The butler nodded, handing Zoe a glass of sparkling water, a lime wedge hanging on the rim. "Miss Harp."

"Thanks, Percy," she said, taking the water and immediately squeezing the lime into the glass before dunking the rind.

"You're welcome, ma'am. The dinner service will begin soon so please make your way to the associates' dining table." He snapped the service tray under an arm and slipped away.

"Every time he says that, I feel like a second-class person," Zoe muttered under her breath.

"Don't worry about it," I said. "I really appreciate you being here."

Jessica Doerr was off by herself, uncharacteristically drinking a martini instead of wine. Her frail mother, Virginia, was nowhere to be seen. Jessica gulped down the martini and signaled Percy for another. Something was off. Her actions showed anxiety, but her face appeared relaxed. Relieved, even. It was an odd dichotomy.

To my right, Karsh, Spenser Fernsby, Scooter,

Frederick Volkov, and Jimmy were in an intense discussion. Across the room, Ivan Volkov and Billy Jablonsky stood silently with a hand-wringing Mrs. Fernsby, their eyes glued on the group of men. As he spoke, an animated Scooter brandished his drink in Karsh's face like a menacing saber. Just as he reacted to Barbara Doll's vicious wooden spoon, Karsh showed no emotion and relinquished no ground to the much shorter but burlier man. However, Frederick Volkov's normal dispassionate demeanor was anything but, his heavy-lidded eyes wide and active, shifting repeatedly between Karsh and Scooter.

"Whatcha thinking?" Zoe asked, observing me observing them.

"Something's happened. Volkov is losing it."

Zoe glanced over at the group of men. "Dude looks like he's tripping. My bet is the jackwagon set him off."

"I'm going over there. Alone."

"Not sure that's a good idea."

"Why? I can handle myself."

"Not doubting that. I just think a good rule to *live* by is staying away from killers whenever possible."

"He's not going to do anything here," I said with a dash of derision. "And I'm not convinced Karsh is the killer. He could be the founder, but not the killer. He's too arrogant to think he needs to resort to killing to get what he wants."

"Just don't say anything," she hissed. "They could all be in cahoots."

"Cahoots?" I whispered back. "Over what?"

"Dunno. The murder? The contest? Both?"

I threw her a little headshake. "Spencer and Jimmy are not murderers, and both hate Karsh."

"Who doesn't? Just be careful."

"Don't worry," I said, turning toward the men.

Behind me, Zoe growled, "If I only had a dollar…"

Approaching the group, I held up my champagne. "Hi, guys. Happy one-week-aversary."

Jimmy stepped to the side and beckoned me into the circle between him and Spencer. "Hi, Sara. It's been quite the eventful week, that's for sure. We were just discussing Olivia Fantucci's murder."

Scooter knocked back his drink, held up the glass, and wiggled it in the direction of Percy, who stood between the tables waiting for us to get seated. "Another bourbon." He turned to me. Beads of sweat glistened on his shiny pate. "Cops pay you another visit, too?"

"Yes, Detective Lilley spoke with me this morning," I replied.

"About Rod?" Scooter asked.

I drew my head back. "No. About exercise balls and gas cylinders." The realization of Scooter's question slammed into me. A quick glance around revealed Rod Toft and his girlfriend, Ashley Tennison, were missing. "Did *Rod* do it?"

"Most certainly not," Volkov snapped, shooting a look at Scooter and Karsh.

"He ain't here tonight, is he?" Scooter fired back. "The fella and his gal hightailed it outta here after them cops showed up yesterday. He saw 'em getting close so they skedaddled."

I watched Karsh. He was in full control of himself, as impassive as Scooter and Volkov were not.

"Nobody has seen Mr. Toft or Ms. Tennison since dinner last night," Spencer confided in me. He appeared as unfazed as Karsh.

"Cameras recorded Rod's car leaving just after midnight," Jimmy added. "But all their personal items are still in his suite."

"How do you know that?" I asked.

"I asked Security to check on him when he didn't show up for breakfast or answer his phone or door," Volkov said.

"Was Rod driving the car?" I asked.

Judging by the reactions to my question, it was something nobody considered.

I tried another angle. "If Ashely is missing, too, do we know if there were two people in the car?"

More puzzled looks.

"Frederick, did Rod mention *anything* to you?" I asked. "Like maybe he was considering quitting?"

"He did not. In fact, he was very upbeat yesterday evening before dinner."

I regarded the men, letting my gaze linger on each before moving on to the next. "Did anybody see him or Ashley leave the mansion after dinner?"

A variety of questioning and suspicious looks bounced among the group, but nobody responded.

Jimmy broke the uneasy quiet. "What are you suggesting?"

"Maybe it wasn't him in that car," I replied. "Maybe something's happened to him. And possibly Ashely. Here at El Sueño."

"*And* Ashley?" Volkov asked incredulously.

Spencer appeared shocked, his calm demeanor no longer. "More murders?"

"That doesn't explain the car," Jimmy said. "Why would someone take his car? Especially one so recognizable."

"Maybe somebody got rid of them and at the same time framed Rod for Olivia's murder," I suggested. "Make it look like he's on the run with Ashley."

"He ain't being framed. He did it," Scooter said. "He's some computer whiz. That's how he got past her suite's lock."

Volkov bristled at Scooter. "There's no motive. We were close to…" His gaze flicked to Karsh, then back to Scooter.

Karsh raised an eyebrow. "Cat got your tongue, Frederick?"

Volkov gulped down his wine and turned for the main table. "We should get seated."

Scooter grabbed his arm with a powerful hand. "Your boy is gonna be dq'ed in about thirty seconds, and I'm gonna see to it you're kicked out, too."

Surprisingly, the slender Volkov shook free from Scooter's grip. "You have no grounds, but touch me again and I shall sue you for assault and see to it *you* are disqualified."

Scooter jabbed a finger in the arbitrageur's face. "No grounds, my butt. I heard you on the phone going on 'bout the contest. And it sure weren't no—"

Spencer Fernsby put an arm between the warring men, gave Scooter a brief but blistering look, then addressed Volkov with the piety of a priest. "I sincerely apologize for my partner's inappropriate actions and threats. It is not indicative of our approach to the contest or our competition."

"This is not the end of it," Volkov spat as he walked away.

Kathleen Fernsby wandered over to the associates'

table where Zoe sat by herself, followed by Ivan Volkov and Billy Jablonsky. Over the past week, the numbers at the table dwindled from seven to four. And there was still one week left in the contest.

"That was fun. I guess the show is over," Jimmy said with a cheerful smile. "Shall we sit for dinner?"

Our group broke apart as everybody took their seats at the main table, while Percy stood at the empty end opposite Karsh. A waiter appeared carrying a loaded serving tray and folding stand. He set the tray on the stand, quietly placed an appetizer in front of each of us, grabbed the tray stand, and disappeared into the kitchen.

"Depending on what you ordered yesterday, tonight's appetizer shall be either squid sashimi with avocado, Kobe beef with burrata cheese, or lobster with confit vegetables. Bon appétit."

As Percy left, Creighton Winston entered the room and stood at the same end of the table. "It is seven o'clock and the dinner service has commenced. It is hereby noted that Mr. Rodney 'Rod' Toft is not present and therefore per Rule Five, he is disqualified from the contest. Mr. Volkov, as Mr. Toft is your partner in a duly-registered alliance, you are hereby notified that while you may continue, you are not entitled to select a new partner per Rule Two. Are there any questions?"

I watched Scooter and Volkov. Both sat poker-faced, staring at Creighton Winston, giving away nothing. It was as if what I witnessed less than five minutes ago never happened. And now the contest was down to seven of us.

"Very well," the lawyer said. "As tonight marks the midway point of the contest, and there has yet to be a winner declared, I wish each of you the very best of luck over the coming six days. Good evening."

Chapter Twenty-Nine

The letter

The next morning after breakfast, Zoe and I worked on the pool mechanical room's riddle. It was difficult to concentrate because Rod Toft and Ashley Tennison remained missing, and Jessica Doerr dropped a bombshell after dinner that she was dropping out after mortgage and wire fraud charges were filed against her. Today she was turning herself in to the FBI, saying it was time to move on with her life and get this behind her instead of living under a constant cloud of threats and suspicion. And judging by her face and demeanor, I believed her. She seemed relieved, like a tremendous burden was lifted off her. While not going into any details, but staring directly at Karsh as she spoke, Jessica said she wasn't surprised charges were filed and in a funny way, she was grateful.

"What's wrong?" Zoe asked. "You still thinking about Jessica bailing?"

I swallowed hard, my head buzzing like the hissing audio jammer on the coffee table as all kinds of thoughts tore through it. "How could I not? In less than one week, one contestant is murdered. Another disappears along with his girlfriend. And now a third drops out after federal charges are filed against her. Who's next? And how are they gonna be knocked out?

What if it's me? Us? It's obvious the founder is a rich, powerful person with a long reach. What if he's behind all this?"

Zoe trained her eyes on me. In a steady, reassuring voice, she said, "Listen, you heard Finn last night and again this morning. You need to let him handle all that. The best thing we can do is keep solving riddles. Like Finn said, 'Progress protects us.' Okay?"

"Unless the person knocking out contestants is a contestant, in which case progress will get us—"

"*Sara!* Leave it up to Finn."

I stared at my best friend. Zoe knew me better than anybody else in the world, always trying to protect me from myself. She was the more conservative one, and here she is emphatic that I stay in the contest and leave everything else to Finn. Although not always, many times in the past when I got myself into situations, I ended up regretting not listening to her. Something told me this could be one of those times and to pay attention.

I sucked in a deep breath, held it, then exhaled hard. After a second exhale, I said, "Thanks. I'm better."

"Good." Zoe picked up the riddle and read it out loud. "*'I am many things throughout this game. A savior to one. A threat to the rest. For this game, some might associate me with a word that has three consecutive double letters, but that would be wrong.'* You know, this is like part statement, part riddle."

"I agree. And the first part fits Karsh perfectly. Only that scuzz would refer to himself as a 'savior.' The dude is such a narcissist."

She dropped the paper on the coffee table. "So,

you're still thinking he's the founder?"

"Everything fits. But we need proof."

Zoe screwed her face up. "Then why is he a contestant in his own contest?"

I shrugged. "Maybe to keep an eye on everybody? You know, at dinner and stuff."

"Like Percy does every night?"

Zoe's words smashed into me, pounding my skull like a hammer on an anvil. After breakfast yesterday with Karsh, I came away convinced he was the founder. But one possibility I never seriously considered was Percy Pembarton. A man who put forth such an air of refinement, it wouldn't be a stretch for him to be an intellectual. A man always at dinner, watching us. A man always around El Sueño. Also watching us?

Bertie and Mauzzy casually strolled into the room, jumped on the couch, and tucked themselves into the corner behind me. The fact neither one acknowledged us set off alarm bells in my head. And a bit of panic. Mauz was nothing if not crafty, and now that he had a partner in crime, I could only imagine the schemes he had in various stages of development. I made a mental note to conduct a thorough inspection before we left the suite today. It wasn't Bertie I was worried about, although I've noticed he's been falling under Sweet Handsome's manipulative spell, so I guess Bertie might also—

Bertie?

A thought tripped a breaker in my brain.

At the time, there was so much commotion going on, I totally missed it.

But yesterday morning, when Percy brought the detective to my suite, Bertie caught him in a lie. When I asked Percy if everything worked out with his family matter, he said his mother was recuperating at home. And right after that, Bertie whined and covered his eyes, a clear indicator Percy lied about his reason for being gone that day. But why? Was he simply hiding something from his employer, like maybe he just wanted a day off? Or was he hiding something else? From the contestants?

My thoughts traveled back to three days ago. It was the only day Percy was not at El Sueño. And that night, I received the threatening photo of my dad. Could he have gone up to Annapolis that day or the night before, snapped the pic when my dad left work, and made it back in time to put it in my suite? It was possible. I know there are direct flights between Birmingham and BWI airport because I've taken them to go home on spring break. And Percy gave me the info packet that included the door combo when we first checked in. Was I wrong about Karsh, and Percy was the founder, with all the sinister connotations? It was easy seeing Karsh in that role. But Percy?

"Yo, Sara. You in there?"

My eyes focused on Zoe waving a hand in front of me. "Yeah, sorry."

"What's going on? I mention Percy and you space..." Zoe slumped into the couch. "Ah, man, now you think Percy is the founder."

"Maybe." I took her through my thought process, ending with Percy lying to me.

Zoe slowly shook her head. "I don't know. He's stuck up and all, but he doesn't seem like a conniving slimeball."

"Well, I know this, we need to be careful around

him."

"Yeah, and you need to tell Finn."

"I will tonight. Let's get back to the riddle."

"Okay, the first part is the founder's statement, so focus on the second half of it."

Nodding, I picked up my phone and searched on words with three consecutive double letters. "Hey, it's an old riddle. The answer is 'bookkeeper.' But—" I leaned over and studied the riddle on the coffee table. "—associating it with the answer to our riddle would be wrong."

I picked up the information guide and took out the map of El Sueño.

Zoe leaned over to get a look at the map. "What are you looking for?"

My eyes scanned over the estate's layout. "Dunno. Anything that might tie back to a bookkeeper."

"Bookkeepers work in offices. Maybe we go back to the office?"

"No, the contest wouldn't include the same place twice," I said, studying the map. "And associating a bookkeeper with an office isn't wrong."

"True. It can't be right. It needs to be wrong." She squeezed her head and groaned. "This is so effed up."

"That's strange." I looked up. "This shows stables and a shooting range."

"Yeah, I mentioned that yesterday. Besides proving that you never listen to me, what's your point?"

"I listen to you, but something's not right here." With the map in one hand, I consulted the letter addressed to me at the front of the information guide. The one describing the amenities at El Sueño. "How come this welcome letter doesn't mention them?"

"Huh?"

I handed the binder to Zoe. "It lists the recreational amenities but not horseback riding or the shooting range. Why?"

Zoe studied the map, then read the letter. "There's also miniature golf, bowling lanes, and a theater. Plus, the stables and shooting range. But the letter only mentions the game room, pool and hot tub, library, and music room. I recognize it says 'some of the estate's amenities,' but why mention a stupid music room and not the fun stuff like bowling or miniature golf." A pause. "Or the shooting range." She looked at me, eyes narrowed. "Why not mention all that other stuff?"

I took the binder back and read the entire letter, starting with 'Welcome, Miss Donovan.' When I finished, something nagged at me. I couldn't place it, but it felt like the answer was buried in the letter. I read it again. And again. And on the third pass, I found myself holding my breath as my stomach tightened and head swam.

A pattern had revealed itself.

Chapter Thirty

Serendipity?

It was so obvious, I couldn't believe we hadn't seen it earlier. I lowered the information guide and looked up at Zoe. "A library."

"What?"

"That's the answer to the riddle. It's a library."

Zoe grabbed the paper with the riddle. "Some might associate me with a"—she raised a finger for emphasis—"*bookkeeper*, but that would be wrong." Zoe's jaw dropped. "Oh, my God. That's it. A library is a keeper of books, but it's not a bookkeeper. How'd you…"

I tapped the welcome letter. "It's all in here."

She took the binder from me and studied the page.

"You see it?" I asked.

"Uh-uh. It mentions the library, but other stuff, too."

"Read it again, but this time, look for a pattern. Keep in mind, the letter says it's listing only *some* of the amenities available."

Zoe focused back on the letter, mumbling to herself as she read and reread the letter. She glanced up. "You got the order of the places we been to for the contest?"

I grinned and took out my notebook from the backpack sitting at my feet. As I flipped through and read from my notes, Zoe turned back to the letter. "Art gallery. Garage. Office. Game room. Pool area."

She looked up at me, stunned. "Library is next on the list of amenities."

"It sure is," I sang. "It's our personal roadmap for the contest."

Zoe smacked her forehead. "And it's been there the whole time." She glanced at the letter, then back at me. "Hey, according to this, we've only got one more place after the library."

"Yep, we're almost there. We're on the sixth level of seven."

She exploded from the couch, startling the sleeping pups. "Tomorrow's Saturday. Let's get cracking and win this thing before the place shuts down for the weekend."

Fifteen minutes later, we walked into yet another lavish room at El Sueño. The library was a two-floor circular open space finished in rich cedar panels with a ribbed dome ceiling above a wide opening to the second floor. Built-ins filled with books lined the walls of both floors. An elegant spiral staircase with a carved banister led to a wood balcony ringing the upper floor that looked back down on an oversized red-and-cream oriental rug holding two leather armchairs and ottomans. Bright sunlight spilled into the space on both levels through floor-to-ceiling panes of glass on both sides of the room.

"This is a library?" Zoe said, her eyes wide.

Ever the strategist, Mauzzy shot up the stairs for the high ground, followed closely by Bertie. At the top, he stuck his head through the balcony's balustrade and stared down at us, proud of his tactical advantage.

"Heck, yeah, it is," I said, slowly turning around. "If I lived here, you'd never get me out of this room."

"I feel like calling it a room is an insult."

My shoulders dropped. "Now I feel dirty."

Zoe let out a giggle. After all that happened yesterday, hearing her was refreshing. That little laugh represented a link to our carefree lives less than two weeks ago, before everything changed with that damn package. And this contest. A contest with profound implications, win or lose. If we win, although handsomely rewarded, I suspect we'll be railroaded into doing something illegal. If we lose, the prospect of being blackmailed again will hang over me. And if I go to the cops, forgetting about me, the founder will see to it my dad is destroyed.

I pushed the negative thoughts out of my head and focused on what Finn said. Progress is protection. Win and we flush out the founder.

And then Finn will take care of him.

I took in the area, hoping to find an obvious location for the safe like what happened in the mechanical room. While the wall panels and built-ins presented opportunities, a crushing realization hit me.

"This is gonna be a tough one, Zo."

"Finding the safe?"

I shook my head. "The safe's combination."

A puzzled look crossed her face but was quickly displaced when the same realization hit her. "Ah, crap. There's like a gazillion numbers in all these books."

A spark of positivity picked me up. "Although, we had the same possibility with the office and all its books, but the combo was tied to the different colored paper. Maybe there's something like that here, too."

"Doesn't look good. All I see are books. And more books."

"That's why it's called a library." My gaze traveled around the lower floor, then the upper. "Because there's so many books, you go over them for anything that could clue us in to the numbers. I'll search for the safe."

"Sure, give me the hard job."

"What?" I said defensively.

"How am I gonna find seven crappy numbers buried in all these books?"

"Don't worry about page numbers. Focus on the titles."

"That makes it *so* much easier. Like what?"

I shrugged. "Not sure."

"Thanks for the help," Zoe deadpanned.

"Listen, Matt says this guy considers himself a seven, which represents intellectuals, deep thinkers, philosophers. So, look for books on numerology, philosophy, the arts. Stuff like that."

"Highbrow crap?"

"Exactly."

"In other words—boring—which is your thing. Why don't I look for the safe and you look for the numbers?"

"Because you can't reach the top bookshelves. You gotta be able to look behind them."

She waved a dismissive hand. "I can easily climb those things."

I chuckled. "I'm sure, but these aren't the stacks at 'Bama."

Zoe pulled her head back in mock surprise. "You don't want me climbing them?"

"Pretty sure Percy would frown upon it."

As soon as I said his name, the brief levity of the moment evaporated, replaced by the reality we were up against. A reality augmented by the very real possibility Percy was the founder.

We stared at each other, recognizing the changed situation, and the implication. Without a word, we split up to begin searching for a safe and its combination.

Remembering where the office safe was hidden, the first thing I did after dropping my backpack was move the furniture off the rug and roll it back. Getting on my hands and knees, I called up to the second level. "Mauzzy. Bertie. Get down here and help."

A flurry of pitter-patters preceded the dynamic duo charging down the stairs, followed by scratching nails and crazed yips as they hit the ground floor and searched for traction while making the turn toward me. With paws working furiously, they made headway and soon slid to a stop where I was feeling along the floor.

"Not here, guys. Look over there," I said, gesturing to the other end of the rolled-back rug.

They put their noses to the ground and zigzagged across the floor, working their way over to where I pointed. Despite a cacophony of snorting and sniffing from my K-9 team, and my own crawling over the grody floor, we found nothing. While I checked the first-floor sconces to see if one was a lever, the pups went back upstairs, hopefully to continue searching. I wasn't optimistic, though.

After checking the sconces and wall panels, I was going over the built-ins when Zoe let out a frustrated shriek. "I'm going upstairs."

"Hang in there. At least we know we're in the right place."

Stomping up the stairs, Zoe grumbled, "Big effing deal. We can be in this place for a week and not find the combination."

As Zoe blew off steam from above, I continued searching for the safe on the ground floor. Unsuccessfully. There were only a few hours left before dinner when I finished up downstairs, and we had found squat.

With my head down, I hoisted my backpack over a shoulder and trudged up the stairs to start the search on the second level. "How you coming?"

"What do you think?" came Zoe's snarky response, followed by a string of colorful observations. She obviously had more steam to let loose.

I sighed, walking to a sconce. "Yeah, me, too."

We pressed on. Zoe pored over the titles, stepping back and craning her neck for the top shelves. Occasionally, after I scolded her for climbing the shelving, she requested my help when she couldn't read a title up high. Albeit, each "request" came with plenty of attitude. In between helping Zoe out, I hit all the sconces, then turned to each built-in, my fingers running over the surfaces searching for a recessed latch or button. As I finished checking one built-in, I noticed an untitled black leatherbound book on the end of the middle shelf. Instead of any lettering on the two-inch spine, five red horizontal lines created four distinct black blocks on the leather. In the top one was an embossed gold dagger pointing downward. Like dripping blood, gold droplets ran from it down the length of the spine.

I pulled the book from the shelf. It was lighter than its appearance, had no title on the front cover, and thick gold-edged pages. When I went to open it, the cover didn't budge. Like it was glued shut. Gripping the cover, I gave it a tug. After a moment of resistance, it gave way and opened, revealing a cavity holding a silver metal disc with a black knob in its center.

"Found something." I held the book and object high for Zoe to see. "How'd you miss this book? It has no title."

She glanced over at me from across the opening to the lower level. "Haven't gotten there yet, you skank. Whatcha got?"

I studied the object. "Looks like a magnet."

"A magnet? For what?"

"Something important. Otherwise, why hide…"

It hit me. People hide keys.

I ran the magnet along the right inner side of the shelf where the book was stored. Nothing. I tried the sides above and below it. Nope.

Zoe was up on her tiptoes, staring across the space. "What're you doing over there?"

I worked the left side of the unit, hoping to hear a lock being released, but nothing happened. "I think it's a key for one of these built-ins."

"To a secret compartment?"

"That's what I'm hoping," I replied, moving to the next set of shelving.

"I'm coming over there."

"No, keep doing your thing. There's only one key."

The left side of the next unit was another miss. But when I ran the key along the right side of the middle shelf, a metallic click sounded. Gripping the bookcase, I gave it wiggle, then pulled on it. The entire shelving unit swung out toward me, revealing a safe sitting on a pedestal.

"Found it," I yelled.

Zoe let out a triumphant squeal. "Me, too. Maybe."

"Maybe?"

"I found a book with the number seven in the title."

"Yeah? What's it called?"

"*The Serendipitous Seven.*"

Chapter Thirty-One

The book

The title struck me.
The Serendipitous Seven.
Serendipity. Another word for good luck. *Unexpected* good luck. With lucky number seven?

Creighton Winston's words rang in my head. *'Everyone is here because of a potentially lucky secret.'* Two days ago, Matt zeroed in on sevens popping up throughout the contest, and suggested the founder considered himself a seven. Was it possible *The Serendipitous Seven* alluded to both the key for winning the contest, and the founder's self-identity as a seven?

"Zo, lemme see that book."

She shot around the balcony and handed me a thin book. "I haven't looked in it, yet."

The book, written by Laszlo Nagy, was a mere seventy-seven pages. The spine was so narrow there was barely enough room for the title. More like a pamphlet with a hardcover than a book. The plain cover was rust-brown with the title and author name in a colorful blend of orange-yellow print.

I pulled out my phone and snapped a pic of the book. "How'd you even find this?"

Zoe gave me a proud, toothy smile. "Serendipity."

That got a laugh out of me. I opened the cover. "Interesting. No copyright info. No publisher. Just a basic title page, table of contents showing seven chapters, and then the prose starts."

"Self-published?"

"Probably."

"What's it about?"

I scanned the first few pages. "How the number seven fits in numerology. Kinda along the lines of what Matt said. It's more focused on intellectual and logical approaches to life than emotional."

"Blah blah blah. It's gotta have the combo in it. Somewhere."

I fanned through the book, stopping at the beginning of each chapter to do a quick check for clues. "Huh. That's strange."

Zoe looked at the page I stopped on. "Chapter thirty-seven? I thought it had seven."

"It does. This is the last chapter. All three pages of it. The chapter number jumping to thirty-seven tells me this chapter is special."

"Maybe it's one of the numbers." She pointed to the text. "Look, 'had' is bolded."

"Sure is." I turned to the next two pages. "Two more bolded words. One on each page. 'It' and 'right.' Why?"

"Typos?"

"Doubt it. Not three times with bolding."

"Even if those three words somehow convert to numbers, plus the chapter number, that only gives us four. We need seven."

I flipped to the chapter's first page, then back to the last two. "Maybe the words are converted by taking the number of letters in each. Three, two, and five."

"How about the chapter's page numbers? There's three of them and we're looking for three more numbers."

I shook my head. "All the previous combinations haven't had a number out of the forties, let alone in the seventies."

We stared at the last two pages of the chapter.

Zoe looked up from the book, her face alive. "Maybe we only need four?"

I pressed my lips tight. "Love the whole thinking-out-of-the-box thing, but it doesn't fit the contest's logic."

"Logic? Oh, my God. You sound like your brother."

Ignoring her comment, I flipped back and forth between the chapter's pages. One chapter number and three words we could convert to numbers. Leaving us to find three more numbers. From three pages. But nothing else was bolded. We had three bolded words, in three different paragraphs. Three different—

"What if the paragraphs were numbered?" I exclaimed. "Then the corresponding number for each paragraph containing a bolded word becomes one of our numbers."

Zoe took the book from me, stared at the chapter's first page while counting to herself, then turned the page. "So, the second, twelfth, and…twenty-seventh paragraphs."

I took out my phone and typed the numbers into a note, labeling them as paragraphs. "Right. Along with thirty-seven and the length of the three bolded words."

"Three, two, and five."

As I typed in the last set of numbers for the word lengths, I immediately realized something was wrong. "I don't think we can have two twos. None of the other combinations had repeated numbers. Either the numbered-paragraphs angle or using the length of the bolded words is wrong."

We thought about the situation for a moment before Zoe spoke up. "You mentioned the contest using logic. If the numbered-paragraphs approach is correct, maybe the words in each paragraph are also numbered, and their length is irrelevant."

"Works for me. What are the words' numbers?"

Zoe turned back to the book. "The second paragraph's word is the...fourteenth." She turned the page. "The next is the third. And the last is the fourth. You got it? Fourteen, three, and four."

I deleted the last three numbers from the note, typed in the ones Zoe called out, and thought about the sequence. "Let's try going front to back, starting with the chapter number, then the first paragraph and its word, and so on."

"Go for it."

I turned to the safe and punched in the numbers. Nothing happened. Keeping thirty-seven as the first number, I reversed the sequence of the paragraph and word numbers. It didn't work. I tried thirty-seven, then the paragraph numbers front to back, followed by the word numbers. Another failed attempt. When I reversed that sequence, it also failed.

I turned to Zoe. "Any thoughts? I could move thirty-seven to the last spot, but I really think it's the first number."

"Let's think about it *logically*. The sequences

we've tried have been first-to-last or last-to-first. Keeping thirty-seven as the first number, for the next two, let's take the *middle* paragraph and word numbers, then the first paragraph and word numbers, then the last? And if that doesn't work, then middle, last, first?"

"I like it. Kinda like the art gallery when it went low-high-low." I handed Zoe my phone and faced the safe. "Call 'em out."

"Thirty-seven. Twelve. Three. Two. Fourteen. Twenty-seven. And four."

A mechanical whirring sounded. I looked back at Zoe. "Matt will be proud of your logic."

Inside were envelopes for everybody except Karsh, and a pair of red eyeglasses. I fished out my envelope and handed it to Zoe, then tried on the glasses. Everything became blurred.

"Anything?" Zoe asked.

"Nope, can't see a dang thing. Maybe there's a hidden message in my envelope and these glasses act as a filter to bring it out?"

Zoe opened the envelope, extracted the now-familiar ivory paper, and handed it to me.

Keeping the glasses on, I looked at both sides of the paper. "These things are useless." I took them off and read the riddle.

Well played. One to go, but time is ticking. Although the box you seek holds keys that open no locks, it provides the framework you need to open everything.

And return my book where you found it.

Chapter Thirty-Two

What?

With the contest's middle weekend forcing us to leave El Sueño before we could solve the final room, Zoe and I stopped in to see Finn on our way to Tuscaloosa. As I pushed open the door to Finnegan and Associates, an exuberant Bertie rushed past me into the crappy office. Right behind him, Mauzzy shot between my legs in a desperate attempt to either get out of the foul-smelling corridor or away from me. I'm going with the stench.

Finn jumped up from his wobbly chair and came around the desk, arms outstretched. "Bertie!"

The longhaired dachshund let out an earsplitting high-pitched bark and scampered across the dingy floor. Finn knelt, scooped him up, and gave the wiggling pup vigorous ear and chin scratches as Bertie smothered him with kisses. You'd think it had been a year instead of three days since the two last saw each other. And putting on his typical don't-forget-about-me act, Mauzzy danced all around the big man's feet, staring up expectantly at his latest most-favorite human.

"Has she been taking care of you, buddy?" Finn crooned as he nuzzled his partner.

"Of course," I said, sitting in a guest chair. "If I didn't, he'd rat me out for sure."

Finn set Bertie down, gave Mauzzy a couple of ear scratches, then returned to his chair. Both faux attention-starved dachshunds settled in at his feet. "Got that right. Bertram help out any?"

"He did," I said, explaining about Percy lying when he brought Detective Lilley to the suite.

"By the way," Finn said, "forgot to mention to you last night on the phone, she called me yesterday."

I nodded. "She said she was going to call you."

"We had a real nice chat."

"She mention they're looking at exercise balls filled with carbon monoxide?" I asked.

Finn's eyebrows went up. "She tell you that?"

"No, but she was asking if we'd seen anybody with exercise balls or gas cylinders, so…"

"You put two and two together," he said with a thin smile.

I shifted in the chair. "Wouldn't you? Seems obvious to me. The suite's bedroom is real small, too, so it wouldn't take much gas."

"Seems diabolically resourceful to me," Finn replied. "And out there."

"Which makes it a perfect murder weapon," I countered.

Finn corrected me. "If it's true, *almost* perfect."

"It's true," I said.

"You know," he said, eyeing me closely. "Lil's liking you for it."

"Liking me? For what?"

"The murder."

In a flash I was standing, my heart coming through my chest. "*What?*"

He let out a long, dramatic sigh. "You heard me.

276

She said other folks overheard you badmouthing the victim. Sara, it don't look good. I tried to tell her—"

"Oh, *come on*. Olivia Fantucci was a bitch. *Nobody* liked her."

Finn put out a hand, telling me to calm down. "Just passing on what she said."

I glanced back at Zoe, who stared back in disbelief. "You hearing this?"

"There's gotta be a mistake," Zoe said.

"I can give you a lawyer, if you want," Finn offered, his tone grim.

My head whipped around. "A—lawyer? Are you kidding me?"

"I am."

"You're what?"

"Kidding you."

Seconds passed as I first processed the information, then considered killing the man and looking for that lawyer's card on the desk since I was going to need a good one.

Finn broke out laughing. "You swallowed that like a large-mouth on a crankbait."

"You realize with my law enforcement love-hate relationship, that's not funny," I fumed.

He stopped mid-laugh, his face turning serious. "Hey, now, sorry 'bout that. Just having a little fun, is all. Didn't mean to upset you."

I sat and slumped into the chair, the last ten seconds washing over me. With an exhale, I said, "Apology accepted."

"Appreciate it." He snapped his fingers and pointed at me. "But I got you good."

I forced a smile. "You did. Let's move on."

Straightening, I said, "What do you make of Percy lying to me?"

Finn stroked his beard, the biweekly goatee performing its latest disappearing act. "He may be helping the founder, like going off and snapping that picture of your daddy, but he ain't the founder."

"You sound pretty sure," I said.

"That's 'cause I am. Although I ain't buying your brother's numerologist malarky, he told you the founder is some fancy-pants thinker whose nose is stuck up in the air. If he's right, and from what I've seen I reckon he is, nobody like that is gonna pretend to be a butler and serve folks. Just not gonna happen."

I pulled up a photo on my phone and handed it to Finn. "Speaking of numerology, we got the combo to the library safe from this book."

"*The Serendipitous Seven*." He leaned back in the chair and considered me. "Seven again, huh?"

"Yep."

He held my phone up. "And I s'pose you telling me this here means your baby brother is right about the founder being some quack jacked up over the number seven."

"I never said Matt thought the person was nuts."

"Matt said the guy considered himself a seven," Zoe blurted, making a crazy sign with her index finger. "The dude thinks he's a fricking number."

"Sounds crazier'n a road-runnin' lizard, if you ask me."

"Regardless of the guy's mental state, that book has seventy-seven pages," I said, pointing at the phone in Finn's hand.

He glanced at the phone. "Sounds like your brother

could be right." A beat. "Huh. Not even gonna try pronouncing it, but that author has a strange name, don't he?"

"Hungarian or something," Zoe said.

"You don't think that's the founder's name, do you?" I asked. "I mean, why would he put his real name on the book when he's clearly trying to hide his identity?"

"Ain't no shrink, but I reckon someone who fancies himself a number is gonna put his real name on a book he wrote—'bout his favorite number. 'Specially if he's as stuck up as your brother says." Finn wrote the name down and handed me my phone. "I'll look into this Nagy fella."

"Who else could it be?" Zoe asked.

"Don't know," Finn replied with a shrug. "But based on more info I got in, I know who it probably ain't."

I inched forward in my chair. "Who?"

"Several. For one, this Creighton Winston fella. He's 'bout as slimy as lawyers come, representing politicians and other lowlifes, but it don't make sense he's the founder. Why would he require a one percent fee from the founder if he *was* the founder? Just don't make no sense. Besides, he's got zero debt, owns a place in Mountain Brook with his own private park, and ain't never got crosswise with the law. Not even a parking ticket. And that crazy chef, Barbara Doll? The gal is harmless. All bark, no teeth. Best I can tell, she's a sucker for pups, and don't suffer fools lightly. But she also ain't in debt. Not desperate 'bout nothing. And got no life outside cooking. No way she's the founder."

"What about Jimmy Dougal?" Zoe asked.

I faced Zoe. "Jimmy? No way."

Finn stood, ambled over to the coffee pot, poured himself a mug, and returned to his chair. "Now he's an interesting one. Can't find much on him. Good looking fella, for sure. Don't look the part of an evil mastermind, but also don't have much of a footprint. He ain't active on social media, and his website says he's a realtor for high-end custom homes, but it don't have no listings." He took a sip of coffee, eyeing me over the mug. "I find that kinda strange."

I shook my head. "He's a nice guy. Not full of himself like Karsh."

"I'll keep digging," Finn said.

"Suit yourself, but you're wasting your time," I replied.

"Maybe Spencer Fernsby?" Zoe offered.

"No way," I protested. "He doesn't—"

Zoe put out a hand. "Just hear me out. Finn said the guy's facing a huge lawsuit from his investors. And he's a big-time CEO. That gives him access to all kinds of corporate information he could leverage into a financial scheme to get him out of his predicament. He's sophisticated enough to pull this contest off, is all I'm saying."

"Valid point," Finn said. "He stays on my list."

"It's not him," I said with a huff.

Zoe scowled, then turned to Finn. "I know I've said it before, but what about Mrs. Majelski?"

"*Zoe*," I exclaimed.

"What? I don't trust her."

"Nah, we already been over this," Finn said. "Sadie Majelski might be a lot of things to a lot of different folks, but she ain't no crook. I'll stake my reputation on it."

Zoe glanced around the shoddy office with, at best, secondhand furnishings and frowned. "Wow, really putting yourself out there."

He gave Zoe a knowing wink. "Also got my doubts 'bout Scooter Jablonsky. He's just a good 'ole boy with a salesman's talent but don't got the sense God gave a goose. Big lifestyle. Bigger spender. Been stealing from his employees' 401(k) funds and not paying their payroll taxes. Also been borrowing from family based on all kinds of bogus promises. The fella is the posterchild of desperate equals stupid. He sure don't fit the founder's profile."

"Makes sense," Zoe said. "I've been wondering why he's even in the contest."

"He certainly isn't like the others," I said with a short laugh.

Finn leaned forward, forearms on the desk, paws clasped. "Now I've been giving this a think. If I was running a closed contest to find the best person to help me...*steal*...a half billion dollars, I'd damn well make sure I was around them folks to identify that person and make sure he or she won."

"What are you suggesting?" I asked.

"That the founder might be one of the contestants," Finn said.

"We've talked about that, but if that's the case, we're running out of suspects," I said. "Olivia's dead. Rod's missing. Jessica dropped out. That leaves us with just five."

"Wait, why couldn't it be Rod or Jessica?" Zoe asked. "Maybe they were there at the beginning to scope everybody out, make sure the contest got started right, and once they figured out who was best for the scheme they cooked up, disappeared to watch from a distance."

Finn considered Zoe before shaking his head. "Nah, this rascal's got an ego the size of Texas. He's gonna make dang sure to stick around and watch all the fun he stirred up."

"I still think it's Karsh," I said. "He fits the profile."

"He *is* an arrogant asshole," Zoe said.

"And an intellectual," I added. "The guy knows Voltaire's real name and quotes him in French."

"Right? Like, who does that?" Zoe said.

"So, we got five left, huh?" Finn fingered the coffee mug, his attention on the desk. He looked up, eyes narrowed. "But there were eight plus you, right?"

I nodded. "At the start."

"Y'all remember when I called that diamond place to check out that rock you got? International Institute of Gems or something. They said yours was one of eight they received together for grading and certification."

"Okay," I said. "What does that…" I froze, mouth open.

A broad smile crossed Finn's face.

"There were nine contestants including me. But only eight diamonds."

Finn's hand smacked the desk with a resounding thud. "I'm right. The founder is the ninth contestant. And one of the remaining five."

Chapter Thirty-Three

Septem

After we left Finn's office, I drove to my cottage
with a white-knuckling Zoe and snoring Mauzzy. Bertie
stayed behind to spend the weekend with Finn while he
did a deeper dive on the author of *The Serendipitous
Seven*, Laszlo Nagy, and also El Sueño in hopes of
finding the real ownership, not just the Cook Islands
One-Eleven Trust. When I pressed him on exactly what
he meant by a "deeper dive," he blew me off with a
charming "just trust me" and a wink. Considering that
every time I used that very same line, it came with the
unsettling fact I had no fricking clue what I meant,
Finn's bold confidence did nothing to alleviate my
growing concern. But I had no choice. We were
entering the final days of the contest and I needed to
know the identity of the arrogant puppeteer threatening
me and my family. Because if I lost…

"There's only five left?" Matt asked, slouched on
the couch, Zoe leaning into him.

"Five plus me," I said from a crappy folding chair
at the card table pulling double duty as my crafting
station and kitchen table. "Although, Finn is convinced
one of the contestants is the founder, which means there
are only five real contestants left."

"And he's still okay with you participating?" Matt

asked, eyes wide. "Even with someone getting murdered and another disappearing?"

"Don't worry," Zoe said, "we're on the very last level. And we know the room location."

"And the answer to the riddle," I said proudly.

"Hopefully on Monday we can get in there and end this thing," Zoe added.

"Hopefully?" Matt looked over at me, then Zoe. "Sounds like you haven't checked it out. You sure about the answer?"

"Positive," I said. "It fits perfectly with the last room in the welcome letter."

"You wanna try guessing it, brainiac?" Zoe teased with a nudge to his ribs.

"Guessing is not part of the equation," Matt said. "It's like I tell you with your number puzzles. You never guess. You solve."

Zoe sat up and turned her body to face Matt, legs crossed on the couch. "So, you wanna try *solving* it?"

"Sure."

I took the library envelope out of my backpack. "Here you go. '*Although the box you seek holds keys that open no locks, it provides—*'"

"A piano," Matt said.

"'*—the framework you need to open everything.*' Seriously?" I tossed the paper onto the table. "You couldn't even wait for me to finish?"

Zoe punched Matt in the arm. "Cheater."

Matt rubbed his arm and shrugged. "Kinda obvious."

I let out a groan. "Obvious? How's a piano a box?"

"It's just a giant music box," he replied, "with keys that don't go to locks. Like I said. Obvious."

I dug out photos of the six objects from my backpack and spread them out on the card table. "Okay, try finding the *obvious* connection between these pics."

Matt pulled himself up out of the couch and stood over the table. "These came from the safes?"

I nodded. "Yep."

Minutes passed as he studied the photos, periodically rearranging them, his brow furrowed the entire time.

"Anything?" Zoe asked as she joined us at the table.

Matt slowly shook his head. He picked up a piece of yellow construction paper from my crafting supplies and a pen, sat at the table, and began scribbling away. "Bowling ball. Baseball hat. Dreamcatcher. Pen. Compass. Glasses." He analyzed the words, tapping his lips with an index finger as he mumbled to himself. After several minutes, he leaned back and ran his fingers through his hair. "This is impossible. Too many variables."

"At least we know it's not just us," I said.

Zoe gently placed a hand on my brother's shoulder. "Maybe you can try again later."

He sucked in a breath, held it, then exhaled. "Maybe, but doubtful I'll see anything." He squinted at me. "You sure these play a role?"

"I guess. Why else would they be in the safes?"

"And us being given a camera to take pictures of the things?" Zoe added.

"Diversionary purposes," Matt suggested.

"Diversionary? In what way?" I asked.

"Dunno," he said. "Maybe only one is relevant." He stared at the yellow paper with his scribblings, then looked up at us. "You sure those glasses didn't reveal a hidden message somewhere? Maybe in your suite?"

"First, we can't remove the objects from the rooms," I said. "And second, the lenses were so thick you could barely see through them."

Matt scrutinized each photo, rearranged them yet again, then shook his head. "Let's see what the final object is, but I really think these are all red herrings. They have nothing to do with the contest other than to throw you off."

"Throw us off from what?" I asked.

"Beats me," Matt said. "From figuring out how to win? It's forcing you to waste finite bandwidth on a meaningless exercise."

"I don't think so," Zoe said. "Those objects will come into play after we open the last safe. Somehow."

Matt stood and returned to the couch. "I'd like to see how. They're so disparate."

My ringing phone kept me from making a crack about my brother's vocabulary. "Hey, Finn. What's up?"

"Just came across some interesting info on Nagy."

I put him on speaker. "I've got you on speaker. Zoe and Matt are here." To them I said, "Finn has some info on Laszlo Nagy. Matt, that's the author of the book we used to crack the library safe."

Matt nodded knowingly. "He's the seven, isn't he."

Finn spoke up. "After what I found, very possible. I'll say this, with a name like that, it made searching a whole lot easier. Appears to be some kinda computer fella. Twenty years ago, he bought an IT company in California for cheap when the tech bubble burst. Changed the name, took it private, then sold it ten years later to a whiz kid who kept the company name but moved it to Birmingham and got into the lottery business."

Matt got off the couch and returned to the table. "By any chance, was it building random-number-generator machines?"

"Bingo. Came up with some fancy software to spit out unpredictable numbers. They called it infallible. Their machines are used by lotteries all over the world."

"They probably measure some kind of indeterminate environmental indicator or system to determine the seed," Matt said.

"How's that?" Finn's incredulity at my brother burst through the speaker. Just the latest in a long line of people initially stunned by my brother's disgusting genius.

"I'll keep it simple and not get into the details. Basically, the machine would rely on an external variable impossible to predict. For example, it might use a Geiger counter to measure the radioactive decay of a designated isotope. Say, Americium-241. The micro-sievert reading is then converted into numerical code, known as the seed, and embedded into a pseudorandom number generator—the algorithm. The seed gives the algorithm the randomness it needs to generate the winning lottery numbers."

Seconds passed. The only sound in the room was Mauzzy snoring from his recliner.

I leaned in toward the phone. "Finn, you there?"

"Yeah, I'm here." A beat. Then another. "That's keeping it simple, Junior?"

"It is for him," I said. "So, Nagy sold his company ten years ago. What's he been doing since then?"

"Stayed on as the company's security director and senior coder. He left the company in the last year."

"What's the company's name?" Zoe asked.

"Septem Global LLC."

Matt startled, then stared at the phone. "*Septem?*"

"Yeah," Finn replied. "You heard of 'em."

"No, but 'septem' is Latin—for seven."

My eyes locked onto my brother. "Like the number?"

"Like the founder," Matt said.

"Son of a gun," Finn said quietly. "We're on the scent."

"Where'd he go?" I asked.

The clicking of a computer keyboard came through the phone. "Your guess is as good as mine. Can't find nothing after he left Septem."

"Got a picture?" Zoe asked.

"Nah, but I'll hit a DMV buddy up on Monday. He owes me."

I eyed Zoe. "Finn, didn't you say during one of our calls that El Sueño was last purchased six or seven years ago?"

More keyboard clicking. "I did. Six years ago. By the One-Eleven Trust."

"Which was after Septem Global was sold by Laszlo Nagy," I added. "Who presumably moved here since he stayed on with the company. How much did he sell it for?"

"Dunno. It was a private transaction. I'm on their website but don't see nothing in its newsfeed 'bout the sale."

"Could it have been enough to purchase El Sueño?" I asked.

"Hard saying not knowing. But, there's a twenty-mil mortgage on it, so if he sold Septem for five million or so, he could afford the down payment."

"Did you say a trust called One-Eleven owns the property?" Matt asked.

"The One-Eleven Trust," Finn confirmed. "In the Cook Islands."

Matt held my gaze, his typical pale narrow face, flushed.

"It means something, doesn't it," I said.

"It does to a computer person," he replied, smiling broadly. "Like Laszlo Nagy."

Zoe let out a soft groan. "Just spit it out."

"In binary, three consecutive ones is the number seven."

"*One-eleven*." Finn's intake of air was audible. "Or, the Seven Trust to a computer geek."

"We got him!" Zoe shrieked. "We effing got that narcissist a-hole!"

"We ain't got *him*," Finn cautioned. "We got his name. Still gotta run him to ground."

"Since we're looking for a guy, and even though she's gone, that rules out Jessica Doerr," I said.

"And that crazy chef, too," Zoe added.

"Hang on, y'all," Finn said. "Might have something here."

"What?" I asked.

Silence.

"*Finn?*"

"Dadgum, Sara, gimme a second. I'm reading."

Seconds slipped away. The three of us stared at the phone, waiting.

"You think he's there?" Zoe finally asked.

I put up my hands, palms out. "Not asking."

"I'm here," Finn growled. "Y'all ever hear of the Billionaire's Bonanza?"

Zoe's green eyes opened wide. "It's a huge fricking lottery. My dad's been playing it every month. Mom hates it because it's something like ten bucks a ticket."

"That's right," Finn said. "Couple years back, Congress approved this one-of-a-kind national lottery to bail out the United States Postal Service. It has a monthly drawing with the top prize *each month* being a minimum of one billion dollars, but could be higher depending on participation. Ticket sales open on the first of each month and run for twenty-eight days, with the drawing being the night of the twenty-eighth day. It's what's called a roll-down lottery, so if nobody hits the jackpot at the end of the month, the payout rolls down and is divvied up among winners who matched the next most numbers, and so on. Guess how many numbers are drawn?"

"Seven," we said in unison.

"Correct." A pause. "And the *seventh* monthly drawing is this Wednesday night at nine."

"The same day the contest ends," I noted.

"Interesting, right?" Finn said. "And guess who won the contract to build the specially-designed drawing room and outfit it with the number-generating machine?"

We stared at each other, mouths agape.

The words "Septem Global" crackled through the phone, filling the stunned silence.

Chapter Thirty-Four

Narcissism at its best

We spent the rest of a mostly fruitless weekend scouring the Internet for Laszlo Nagy, Septem Global, or anything with One-Eleven in the name. Finn confirmed Nagy was working for Septem when they won the Billionaire's Bonanza contract, adding to the possibility he rigged the lottery. Finn was convinced if Nagy rigged that lottery, he also rigged other lotteries prior to it, possibly providing him the money to buy, furnish, and operate El Sueño. So, he investigated lotteries that used Septem machines, while Matt focused on *how* Nagy could have done it and slipped his code past gaming regulators, since their approval of the algorithm was required.

All Saturday night and Sunday, my brother talked in gibberish. It took Matt-speak to a whole new level. Coding languages, translators, logical tests, conditional and unconditional crap, and so many acronyms he sounded like a crazed government bureaucrat. Unfortunately, he couldn't figure out how to get around the whole random-seed thingy without writing so much code it would have inflated the file size to a point that regulators would have easily spotted it. When Monday rolled around, we were no further along on where Nagy went after he left Septem, or how he rigged the

291

Billionaire's Bonanza. If he even did it.

On our way back to El Sueño, Zoe and I dropped by Finn's office to pick up Bertie. When we entered Finnegan and Associates, the aromatic glory of all that is coffee greeted us, the tantalizing bouquet masking the pervasive stuffiness of the place. Mauzzy and Bertie danced and pranced around each other before trotting side-by-side to behind Finn's desk, settling down in the bed at his feet.

"Morning," a rough-looking Finn grunted, his eyes glued to the computer monitor.

"Hey," we replied in unison.

"Grab some coffee. I found something."

I poured myself a mug while Zoe plopped into a guest chair, the plastic crap issuing a screeching complaint as it jerked back on the scarred linoleum. Thankfully, the girl despised coffee. The thought of a caffeinated Zoe was terrifying. Like rogue-nation-with-a-nuke terrifying.

I settled into the other guest chair and took a couple slurps. After all, first things first. It was a Monday morning. "Geez, Finn, you look like hell."

"Rougher'n a cob." He pulled his attention away from the computer. Fatigue stared back at me, deep bags reaching down and kissing the fast-disappearing goatee or ever-burgeoning beard. "Been here all night."

"Looks it," I said. "Why?"

"Fell into a rabbit hole. Next thing I knew, the sun was coming up."

"What'd you find?" Zoe asked.

"That my suspicion was spot-on," Finn replied, a proud smile juxtaposed on his haggard face. "This Laszlo Nagy rascal been cheating lotteries for at least

292

the last three years, though I'm expecting to find more earlier than that."

"How'd you figure it out?" I asked. "The last time we talked yesterday, you were, how shall I say it—frustrated?"

"Got that right. I was getting nowhere fast. Was fixin' to head outta here when"—he picked up a piece of paper—"these contest rules of yours going on 'bout Cook Islands trusts caught my eye. Got me thinking. If this is all 'bout cheating the Billionaire's Bonanza and stashing the money in a Cook Islands trust, what if he already did it with other lotteries Septem was supporting?"

"You mean like a test run?" Zoe asked.

Finn shook his head. "Nah, I mean like for his livelihood. A way to support his extravagant lifestyle at El Sueño. I reckon after he bought that place, he realized it cost a pretty penny to maintain. Just the annual property taxes gotta be well north of a hundred grand. So, he cooked up a scheme to win jackpots."

I cocked my head and eyed Finn. "How? Even my genius brother can't figure out how to do it."

Finn gave a little shrug. "Dunno. Ain't no genius. But I damn sure know he's been ripping off lotteries. Just can't prove it one-hundred-percent. I searched for Septem-supported games that allowed winners to stay anonymous. Then working back, I searched them for payouts to Cook Islands trusts and found five ranging from five-hundred-thousand to two-and-a-half million."

Zoe let out a soft whistle. "How much total?"

"Little over six million." He leaned forward on his forearms, thick neck stuck out, eyes wide. "Five jackpots going to Cook Islands trusts in the last three years? That ain't no coincidence."

"But how?" I pressed.

"The fella obviously knows the numbers to play." He threw up a quick hand. "*Don't* ask me how. I don't know. But I know he's been doing it, using them lotteries as a big 'ole ATM, and I know he's gonna do it again. 'Cept this time, he's gonna cash in the *big* score and disappear. For good."

"So, this proves the contest isn't about a financial scam—" I reasoned.

"It's a lottery scam," Finn finished. "And the winner of the contest is gonna buy the winning ticket, since the Billionaire's Bonanza don't allow anonymity."

"Why would he do that?" Zoe asked. "Give away a half billion. Why not just buy the ticket himself?"

Finn shrugged. "Probably can't since he worked for the company supplying the machine, and all them places selling tickets got cameras. You know, gas stations, liquor stores, minimarts, and what not. For the kinda money we're talking 'bout, I reckon the lottery folks are watching *real* close. Maybe even piggybacked on the ticket sellers' camera feeds to run some kinda facial recognition to search for past and current Septem and lottery employees."

"Which forces him to find someone to buy the ticket for him," I said. "Someone who couldn't be traced back to him."

"And someone he knew wouldn't—couldn't—say no," Finn added. "If he approached a random person, and that person said no, it would risk the entire scheme. Something he couldn't afford with his once-in-a-lifetime score in the balance."

I was mid-sip when it hit me. Burning the roof of my mouth as I forced the scalding coffee down, I burst out, "*That's* the reason for the contest. It allows him to anonymously select his accomplice without giving anything away."

"And he can control the losers through blackmail," Zoe said. "Because each has a secret the cops would love to hear about."

I raised my hand. "Except me."

"Except you," Zoe confirmed.

Leaning on an elbow, chin resting in hand, Finn studied me. "You know...If this contest is just 'bout finding someone to buy his lottery ticket, then we been wrong 'bout why *you* were drug into it."

"Because she's not a *total* lowlife like the others?" Zoe asked.

I glanced over at my supposed best friend. "Appreciate the vote of confidence, Zo."

"Nah, because she's the opposite," Finn said, sitting up, his tired face awakening. "Zoe even said it over the weekend."

"She says a lot of things." I threw her an exaggerated smile.

Zoe flicked me the bird before turning to Finn. "What brilliance did I impart?"

"You called the founder a narcissist a-hole."

"Because he is," Zoe responded.

"Well, I'll do ya one better. He's a *supreme* narcissist a-hole who's out to prove a point." Finn looked at Sara. "He's already said he's been closely watching you for a while, probably reading all 'bout your exploits." He paused, exchanging a glance with Zoe. "Maybe even been the mastermind behind them capers you solved."

I shook my head. "Impossible. They caught everybody."

Finn raised an eyebrow. "Sure 'bout that? I mean *the* mastermind."

For some reason, an image of Mrs. Majelski popped into my head. Was it possible? She's always been hanging around on the fringe. Always been...I rattled my head, shoving the crazy notion back where it came from. "They caught everybody."

His wry smile told me he thought otherwise.

"It's true," I insisted.

Another quick glance toward Zoe, then back to me. "He also told you he needed to know who was the best, back when you were talking 'bout quitting. Remember?"

I nodded.

"We thought he was saying he needed to find the best mind to plan his scam, that he had some inside info but needed help cashing in on it." Finn wagged a finger. "But now we know he's already got his scheme laid out and in motion. Which makes sense. A turd like that ain't gonna ask nobody for help planning nothing. Nah, what he was saying is, he needs to know who's better. Him"—he pointed at me—"*or you.*"

I angled my head toward him. "What? Me?"

"Got that right. The man's been pitting his self-anointed brilliance up against you, the supposed great up-and-coming investigator. He could've arm-twisted any one of them contestants to buy the ticket, but where's the fun in that? Nah, he devised this whole contest for the great Sara Donovan. To prove a point. To you."

"Like what?"

"That you are what he already knows you to be. An unsophisticated college kid who stepped in it a few times, yet always came out smelling like a rose. That you're no sleuth but just damn lucky. In other words, a sham."

"*Hey.*"

Finn's hands flew up in a defensive posture. "I ain't calling you a sham. I know your capabilities. I'm just figuring that's what Nagy thinks. All your news coverage the last couple years been like a pebble in his boot, so when he came up with his lottery scheme, he saw an opportunity to put you in your place while retiring with a career-defining score. Win-win for him. And by having all the other contestants be high-functioning greedy crooks, one of Nagy's own will also win big while he gets his narcissist jollies watching everyone go at each other's throats. It was his own high-falutin' cage match."

"But what if she wins?" Zoe asked. "We're real close."

Finn blew out, then scratched his beard. "Hard saying not knowing. He's been guzzling so much of his own bathwater, I reckon he might not have considered the possibility."

"So...like...where does that leave us?" I asked cautiously.

His gaze settled on me. "Until we find Nagy, watching each other's back."

The last two years of my life crashed down on me, a cacophony of sound ripping through my head. Breathing became a conscious effort as my chest constricted, crushing lungs and heart. I fought the panic, squeezing my eyes shut as I slowed my breathing, a single thought making it through the noise.

Who is Laszlo Nagy?

Chapter Thirty-Five

Music to my ears

As we entered the grand foyer Monday afternoon, an incredibly sad melody drifted out from the music room. Some tortured soul was pouring their very essence into the piano. Despair pushed through the air with every note. Heavy, mournful, despair.

I stopped to listen. "Oh my gosh, it's so beautiful."

"Depressing as hell, if you ask me," Zoe mumbled, stopping beside me.

A low chord sounded, followed by silence. Then three more muted chords in deliberate succession, the last ending in a somber, sustained, echo of sadness that faded away to nothingness.

"Holy crap, someone is having a really bad day," Zoe said.

With Mauzzy and Bertie out front, we started back up, walking beneath the dome toward the wide arched opening leading into the music room. When we neared the entrance, the piano began playing, the music just as heavyhearted. I stopped and put an arm out, signaling Zoe to do the same.

"Let's listen," I mouthed to her, peering into the room.

Jimmy Dougal sat at the grand piano, its top propped open, his back to us. The man's beautiful head of wavy, black hair rode the haunting music as his hands floated over the keys, caressing each chord and note with a respectful dignity and expressive purpose. The music was so exquisitely played, I found myself being moved to tears.

Zoe's smack to my arm snapped me out of it. "Buck up," she whispered.

I nodded, breathed in through my nose, and pushed away a tear. "Wait 'til he stops," I whispered back.

The music built in intensity, each successive note ringing sharper and clearer before sliding into a series of rising and fading notes. Suddenly, Jimmy's fingers hammered the keys, the heavy resonance of the chords obliterating the sadness, revealing anger. A dark, foreboding anger. Bordering on...

Vengeance.

I glanced over at Zoe. Her mouth was parted, unblinking eyes fixed on the man demanding the piano to speak.

As quickly as the tone became angry, it abruptly shifted again, back to sadness. But strangely, not the same heavy sadness as at the beginning. More like...resignation. Then, with a final dramatically-rolled lower chord followed by a similar higher one, it was over.

I stepped into the room. "Absolutely beautiful. And touching."

Jimmy half-turned toward me. "Ah, Sara. How long have you been there?"

I approached the blue-eyed wonder, Zoe trailing behind. "A few minutes. All of the last piece and some of the one before it."

A dazzling white smile crossed his beautiful face.

"Two of my very favorites. Both were played at Chopin's funeral, by far my favorite composer."

"They certainly fit a funeral," I said.

"Indeed. 'Prelude in E Minor' is considered Chopin's most mournful prelude, and of course everybody is familiar with Mozart's 'Lacrimosa' from his fabulous *Requiem*. A wickedly sad piece riding the emotions of a man coming to terms with his pending death." He put a hand to his chest. "At least, that's my humble interpretation."

"Man, I know it's a Monday and all..." Zoe quipped.

Jimmy chuckled lightly. "Guess I should have played some ragtime, although that would have been doing"—he gently patted the piano—"this exquisite concert grand a terrible disservice. Tell me, what brings you to the music room?"

"We were just passing by and heard you playing," I lied.

Bertie laid down, whined, and covered his eyes.

Jimmy glanced down. "Everything okay with him?"

I waved a dismissive hand. "Yeah, he got into the treats back in our suite. He'll be fine."

The whining morphed into low-pitched groaning.

Can't he give it a rest? Ever?

He bent down and rubbed Bertie's head. "I love dogs. Poor little guy. Sounds miserable."

"Ignore him, he did it to himself," I said. "Have a good weekend?"

Jimmy stood. "I did, thank you. Fit in an open house for a listing I picked up a few weeks back. Had a very good turnout. You?"

Bertie's protests grew louder.

"It was okay. Got some studying in. Finals will be here before you know it."

Jimmy's electric-blue eyes grew wide. "Ah, right. You're still in school. Sometimes I forget that with how you carry yourself."

So much bellyaching was coming from Bertie, a concerned Mauzzy nuzzled his pal and began licking his ears.

I nodded my appreciation.

Jimmy's eyes locked on mine, one side of his mouth curling up into a smile. "I guess I should attend to the contest. Something tells me I have some catching up to do."

A low, dismal wail enveloped us. You'd think he really did get into the treats.

Jimmy glanced down at Bertie, then back up to me. With an easy smile, he said, "I'll leave you to do your thing in here." A wink, and before I could respond, he strode out into the foyer and was gone.

I bent down and scratched Bertie under the chin. "What was that all about, bud?"

Zoe huffed. "That whole conversation was one big effing lie, that's what. Something's up with your boyfriend."

"Yeah, he's closer to winning then he lets on."

"That, too."

I stood and walked over to the piano. Picking up sheet music from the music rack, I flipped through it. Seven pages. All one piece. "He was playing that stuff from his head. This isn't the same music."

"Seriously?" Zoe bopped over, taking the music from me. "Oh, my God, musicians are so full of it."

Pomposity infused her tone as she read the title. "Ladies and gentlemen, I have here Chopin's 'Etude in C Sharp Minor Opus Ten, Number Four.' *Gag*."

I took the music back. "This is the piece Jimmy played the very first day. When he got in trouble with Creighton Winston for playing the violin. I remember the key. C-sharp minor."

"You're such a band dork."

"Got me out of PE." I returned the music to the rack and took the riddle for the music room out of my backpack. "This says the piano 'provides the framework you need to open everything.' That tells me the combination is somewhere on or in the piano."

"I agree." Zoe took in the magnificent room with the spectacularly-tiered crystal chandelier dropping down from the gaping opening to the upper level. "Still gotta find the safe."

"I'll take the piano. You look for the safe." I studied the elegant room. The walls were a good fifteen feet high, with the bottom two-thirds comprised of rich deep-red wood with four rows of carved panels. The upper third was a flat ivory-colored surface set off with intricate gold bordering. "Start with the wall panels."

"There's gotta be over a hundred of 'em, and I can't reach half," Zoe complained.

"If there's a safe behind one of those, it won't be higher than six feet off the ground."

Zoe stood back, her arm sweeping up and down along her body. "Uh, hello? Five feet, sister."

"Don't worry. I'll get the third row. The fourth is too high for a safe."

"Effing tall people," Zoe groused as she headed for a wall.

I checked the piano's bench, hoping to get lucky. Since this was the final room, I had a suspicion finding and cracking the safe wasn't going to be easy, but a girl could try. Unfortunately, it was clean. Not even a single page of music stored inside it. I ran my hands all over the instrument's lacquered turquoise-colored surface, searching for a button or latch or lever hidden by the flamboyant gold-marbled patterning. Nothing. With a wary eye on the stick holding up the lid, I stuck my head inside the piano. The last thing I needed was a Marie-Antoinette incident.

On cue, Zoe called out. "Hey, hey, watch it over there."

I oh so carefully pulled my head out and looked over to a smirking Zoe. "You *trying* to get me killed?"

She giggled. "It'd definitely be a new one in the *Book of Sara Donovan.*"

"Very funny. I'm going back in." I stuck an index finger out. "No loud noises, yells, or anything else distracting."

Zoe put her hands up. "You won't hear anything from me. Unless, of course, I find the safe." She grinned. "Then, no guarantees."

I narrowed my eyes, gave an emphatic warning with my still-extended finger, and turned back to the piano. Like a mechanic tending to a stricken car, I stuck my head and right hand into the piano, checking each of the pins holding the strings in place. No amount of wiggling, twisting, or pushing budged any of them. I scanned the golden interior for numbers, but found nothing. Not even a serial number. My fingers flicked the hammers forward, hoping one would release a latch. I worked my way along the…

"*Found it!*"

I jerked up. The force of my skull slamming into the lid raised it up enough to dislodge the prop arm, sending it into the piano with a bang. Somehow, someway, my left arm instinctively shot up and caught the heavy lid before it crushed me.

"*Aaagh.*"

As I fought to keep the lid up, my right hand fumbled around inside the piano in a panicked search for the fallen prop arm. Suddenly, the weight lessened.

"I got it. I got it." Zoe was by my side, holding up the lid, allowing me to escape my disappointed executioner.

I raised the prop arm and reinserted it into the notch as Zoe eased the lid down, returning it to its open position. I took a step back and confronted my rescuer. "What the hell, Zo. I mean. What. The. Hell."

She stuck her neck out, a big smile stretched across her cute face. "You're welcome."

"For almost killing me?"

"Please. It wouldn't have killed you. Just given you a headache."

"Thanks," I grumbled.

With arms outstretched, she said, "Hey, I said no guarantees."

I summoned my fierce look and let Zoe have it.

Obviously, it still needed work because all she did was laugh at me. "Yeah, girl, you gotta come up with something better than that because it looks like you got gas."

"Nailed it."

"Not even."

"After all that, I sure hope you found the safe and

not religion."

"It's behind a panel on the first row."

"Hey, for once your lack of height came in handy."

Zoe gave me a sarcastic smile. "It butts up against the floor, wiseass."

"Let's put it to good use again. Crawl under the piano and look for a serial number or something."

She scowled at me, then shot under the piano like a toddler scooting under the kitchen table. Seconds later. "Found it."

"Are there seven numbers?"

"Nope. Six plus the letter 'D' is all I see."

"Nothing else? Any hidden buttons or levers?"

Zoe quickly ran her hands along the underside. "Nope."

"Dang it, it's gotta be here somewhere."

She scrambled out and stood. "What about the music?"

"What about it?"

"It's got numbers. And the clue says the piano provides the framework that opens everything. The framework is the music sitting on the piano."

I snatched the pages from the music rack and studied it. "Tempo markings. Measure numbers. Page numbers. Chopin's birth and death dates. Opus number. Number of sharps. Number of flats." I lowered the music. "There are eighty-two measures alone. This is gonna take some time."

"Okay, I'll close the panel to the safe. Let's take the music back to the suite and call Matt."

"I don't know if we're allowed to. Like with the objects. We could get disqualified."

"I haven't seen anything saying we couldn't."

"But the objects," I protested.

"Which this isn't. The objects are *in* the safes. That"—she pointed to the music in my hands—"was *on* the piano. Not in a safe. C'mon, let's take it."

"How about if I take pictures of the pages?"

Zoe shook her head. "We might miss something. Like, maybe the numbers are written in invisible ink."

I stared down at her through the tops of my eyes. "Really? Invisible ink?"

"Hey, you never know. We're so close, why risk missing something?"

As much as I hated to admit it, Zoe had a point. Why risk it?

I took a quick look around the room. All clear. So, against my better judgment, I stuffed the music in my backpack and threw it over a shoulder. "Let's get outta here before we get caught."

Out in the foyer, Zoe's phone rang. "Hey, babe. What's up?"

Babe? I gave her a "seriously?" look.

Zoe returned it with a mischievous smile while listening to my brother. "You figured it out? Okay, hang on, hang on. I got your sister here." She put the phone on speaker. "Okay, Matt. Say it again."

"Hey, Sara. I figured out how he did it."

"Who did what?" I asked.

Matt's excitement poured through the phone. "How Nagy rigged the random-number-generator machine and got around the gaming regulators. He used a root kit. All he—"

"Not here," I whispered into the phone. "We're headed back to our suite. I'll call you from there. We need to patch Finn in, too."

When we got back to the suite, I turned on the jammer and got them on a group call. "Finn, my brother figured out how Nagy rigged the lottery. Go ahead, Matt."

Finn interjected before Matt could get rolling. "Keep it simple, Junior. *And my kinda simple.* Not yours."

Matt took a deep breath. "I'll try. So, he used what's called a rootkit. It's malicious software that can be installed on a computer with a flash drive that allows the person to remotely take control of the computer. He must have done this when he was still working for Septem and before the RNG machine was delivered to the lottery. Nagy kept the rootkit disguised, buried in the code, until he was ready to activate it this month to specify the winning numbers prior to the drawing. Immediately after, he has the rootkit delete itself, leaving no trace it ever existed."

Nobody said anything, obviously trying to grasp what Matt just laid out, before Finn finally spoke up. "That sounds too Hollywood. You sure 'bout this, that self-destructing gizmo?"

"It's the only way I can think for him to do it without tipping off the regulators and later covering his tracks. And that's assuming he had access to the RNG before it shipped."

More silence.

"How sure are you?" Finn asked.

"It's how I would do it," Matt replied.

"Good enough for me," Finn said. "Okay, we know how he did it. Now we gotta get the proof. The drawing is Wednesday night at nine. That gives us two days to flush him out. By the way, got some bad news. My

308

DMV buddy ain't gonna be back 'til Thursday. Off fishing."

"The contest ends Wednesday," I said. "Why don't you call Detective Lilley for a favor? You two are friends, right? She can get us the photo."

A beat. "Yeah, don't know 'bout that."

I looked at Zoe and winked. "Work your magic. I can tell she really likes you."

Finn grunted. "Right. My magic."

"Just don't give away our suspicions," I cautioned. "We don't want the cops coming down on Nagy until we're one-hundred percent sure about him."

"If they can even find the fella," Finn said. "Sara, listen up. Instead of asking Lil for a favor, why don't I just tell her what's going on? It'd be easier."

"Not yet. Scar tissue."

"You mean your little FBI run-ins?"

"Like I said. Scar tissue."

"Tell you what, I'm gonna wait on my buddy before I go possibly stirring things up by chatting with Lil. Nagy ain't going nowhere."

"Your call. Hey, Matt," I said. "Find Chopin's 'Etude in C Sharp Minor Opus Ten, Number Four' online and download it."

"Sure, but why?"

"I think the next safe's combination is embedded in it. Break it down from a mathematical standpoint. See what seven-number combinations you can develop. We'll take a crack at it, too, and get back together later."

"Sounds good."

Chapter Thirty-Six

Occam 2.0

We spent the rest of Monday on repeated video calls with Matt, but none us of could figure out how a safe combination could be hidden in seven pages of flamboyant notes. Late last night after Zoe completely lost it, we agreed to get a decent night's sleep and start over semi-fresh in the morning. Unfortunately, we needed more than a few hours' sleep, because by Tuesday afternoon it was painfully obvious, we needed a fricking miracle. The contest ended tomorrow evening at seven, and as each hour slipped by without even a hint of the solution to finding the combination, the ever-increasing pressure and tension made it near impossible to concentrate as my life slid closer to Laszlo Nagy's well-constructed abyss.

With hands clasped behind my head, I took in a deep breath, and blew out the hours of frustration. "Okay. Let's just start over. The numbers gotta be in that music. We're just missing something."

Zoe flipped through the pages of music and groaned. "Yeah, because every line starts with a flipping number. Going up to eighty. How the heck we gonna do this?"

"I already told you, those are measure numbers. And there's eighty-two."

"Whatever. Doesn't answer the question, dork."

"Just trying to enlighten you."

Zoe rolled her eyes. "Save me your BS."

"You'll thank me later."

"Doubt it."

I returned her snarky grin with one of my own. "To answer your question, let's break the measures down into numerical patterns and see what we come up with."

Zoe hung her head. "Oh, my God, I'm living my worst nightmare."

We proceeded to spend hours on the couch, poring over seven fricking pages of music besieged with sweeping and swooping runs of heavy black notes. As we worked, it became clear that even if we could zero in on the seven correct numbers, the sequence was going to be near impossible to figure out. As logical an approach Matt was likely utilizing, ours was the exact opposite. We pulled from all kinds of crazy ideas, with the simplest being focusing on the measure numbering. We wrote down every seventh measure's number. Might work, we agreed. Now, let's try every fifth, we thought. Okay. How about every fourth? Third. How about adding every three? Every four. Every…

Pages filled with numbers as we spiraled ever deeper into our conundrum.

Then we *really* got into it. Deep. Some of our more exotic ideas, or in Zoe's words—dorkiest—included focusing on Chopin's use of two-bar and four-bar alternations between the two hands to arrive at numbers by stringing or adding them together.

Exactly.

And despite mining the brilliant depths of our—my—musical virtuosity for developing a combination to the safe that made sense, I liked none of the haphazard results.

After releasing a pained cry of frustration, Zoe popped off the couch and faced me. "Let's channel Matt's razor crap again. It worked with the game room."

I tilted my head back, sucked in a breath, and let it out. "Occam's razor?"

She brightened. "Yeah, that's it. Occam's razor. A brainiac's version of the KISS principle."

"Go for it." I sighed.

Zoe plopped back onto the couch. "Okay. There's a ten and four in the title. That's gotta be two of them."

My mouth fell open. "How'd we not think of that before?"

Zoe smirked. "Because *one* of us chose to overcomplicate things right out of the gate. As usual."

"Touché," I said, writing the numbers down. "And keeping it *simple*, beneath Chopin's name, his birth and death years are 1810 and 1849. So, let's consider eighteen, ten, and forty-nine."

"There you go. See? You *can* dumb things down when you want."

I wrote the numbers on my notepad. "How about seven? For the seven pages?"

"Seems to be the magic number in this whole thing."

"We need one more."

Zoe stuck a finger out. "I know what you're thinking, and we're not messing with any measurements."

"Measures."

"Sure."

I picked up the music and scanned each page. Even though the key changed several times through the piece, and ignoring all the measure numbers, one thing struck me as incredibly consistent. "Zo, I think it's the notes themselves." I handed her the music. "Take a look. What do you see?"

She folded her arms and leaned away from my outstretched hand like I was giving her a rabid rat, refusing to take the music. "*Enlighten* me, maestro. But you better keep it simple."

"Gladly." I set the music down between us and tapped the top page once. "This is all about stacked sixteenth notes. They're in every measure except the very last one. And not just one or two notes per measure. They're continuous. Either in the treble or bass clef. Sometimes both. But it's all about the sixteenth note."

Zoe squeezed her head. "My brain hurts."

"But it works, right? The number sixteen?"

She exhaled hard and waved a hand in surrender. "Just saying, you're back to overcomplicating crap."

I wrote down sixteen as the final number in the set and returned to the music, scrutinizing it for what seemed like the thousandth time.

My phone signaled a video call was coming in. It was Matt. "Hey, bro."

"*Please* tell us you got something brilliant," Zoe pleaded. "*Anything.*"

"Maybe. Although I wouldn't call it brilliant. How about you guys?"

I took him through all the methodologies we tried since yesterday, finishing with Zoe's Occam's razor approach. "Whaddya think?"

He grimaced. "Not feeling it entirely, although I think you're on the right track with Zoe's approach."

She pointed emphatically at the phone and beamed at me. "Occam, baby!"

I gave her a little headshake and glanced at the ceiling.

Matt smiled awkwardly. "Uh, definitely try that last set of numbers, but I have another angle to try. It's similar to Zoe's."

"I already love it," Zoe crowed.

"Let him talk," I scolded. "Go ahead, Matt."

After a brief pause, Matt spoke. "Okay. The riddle talks about the piano providing the framework to opening everything."

"Right, the sheet music I took from the piano," I said. "One of the contestants played the heck out of this right before the contest's opening meeting started."

"Mmmm, not sure the physical sheet music is primarily it," Matt said. "The riddle specifically uses the word 'framework.' That's not a typical word. For that reason, I believe it's the *key* word."

"Why wouldn't it be the sheet music?" I asked.

"I don't consider pages of music to be part of a generic framework, per se. To me, the framework referenced in the clue is all the basic *elements* that describe the piece you took off the piano. Sorta like an outline."

Zoe slapped her forehead. "Oh, God, please don't tell me you're talking about all those measures."

"More basic than that," Matt said. "If somebody were to give a brief description of the composition, it would include the title. So, for our purposes, ten and four come into play. Composer, which is immaterial for this exercise. Date composed, or 1830, which I had to look up. Date published, or 1833, which I also had to look up. And any defining characteristic behind the piece. Number of measures aren't defining. Those are more like the number of pages in a book. Nobody cares. But something I noticed that is def—"

"Chopin's heavy use of alternating runs of sixteenth notes," I spit out.

A knowing smile crossed my brother's face. "You saw it, too."

"So obvious," I said with a flip of the hand.

"Please," Zoe choked.

Matt continued. "Therefore, assuming only one of the eighteens from the dates is used, my theory gives us ten, four, eighteen, thirty, thirty-three, and sixteen."

"That's only six," Zoe said.

He raised a finger. "And that's why I said pages of music aren't part of a *generic* framework for a composition. The number of pages in a piece of music are dependent on each publisher's use of various fonts and sizes. However, when considering our current situation with a gamemaster who views himself a seven, it is highly significant that the number of pages we have for this *specific* sheet music is seven. It is also extremely relevant that this is the last safe combination you are seeking, so why wouldn't he include the number upon which he has based the entire contest? And apparently, his life. Seven."

I sucked in. "I like it."

"Way better than our complicated crap," Zoe added with a sidelong glance at me.

Matt nodded. "Me, too. Now the sequence."

"This is gonna be brutal," I warned.

"Not necessarily," Matt said. "Up to now, this guy has been logical in his approach. Nothing has been asymmetrical. Run by me the methods used for determining the number sequencing for the other combinations."

I looked at Zoe. "Okay…High to low. Low to high then back to low. Um…"

"Left to right, in the garage," Zoe said. "For the car positions."

"Good, forgot about that," I said. "Top to bottom, for the paper stack in the office."

"Right," Zoe said, bobbing her head. "Counterclockwise, as my brilliant boyfriend figured out for the game room. Because it's considered positive."

Even on the phone's small screen, Matt's instantly ruddy complexion shone through. "Um, from a torque perspective."

"Right," Zoe said with admiration in her voice and a coy smile for my brother.

I visualized the clipboard in the pool's mechanical room. And the daily checklists it held. "Order of appearance, for the pool water temps. And for Nagy's book…How'd it go? Chapter number first, then…I know next was the middle paragraph and word numbers."

Zoe jumped in. "Then the first paragraph and word numbers, then the last."

"That's it," I agreed. "Chapter number, middle para and word, then first para and word, then last."

Matt held an index finger to his lips like a teacher silencing the class. "So, every sequence has been logical in its construct, although that last one is a bit odd, but definitely not random. No reason to believe this one is any different. My first choice is the exact sequence we came up with when determining the numbers."

"You mean the sequence *you* came up with," Zoe corrected Matt with a wink at me.

"Um, uh, yeah, I guess," Matt conceded.

I jotted the numbers down and stuffed the music into my backpack. "Thanks, Matt. We gotta get going before anybody finds out this music is missing."

"Call me if you need me."

I ended the call and leashed up Mauzzy while Zoe took care of Bertie. Throwing the backpack over a shoulder, I hurried to the front door and yanked it open.

Waiting for me with a dark face and extended hand was…

Chapter Thirty-Seven

The end of the line? Or a new beginning?

Percy Pembarton.

I took a step back. "Hey, there. What's up?"

"Good afternoon, Miss Donovan. Please hand it over." His tone was hard, the words sharp enough to cut paper.

I gave the bristling butler a little headshake. "Hand what over?"

He pulled his shoulders back, chin raised. "Are we going to play this game, hmm?"

Gently nudging Bertie behind me with my foot, I replied in a hushed tone. "What are you talking about?"

He cocked his head, eyes narrowed. "Why the whispering?"

"Don't want to disturb anyone."

"It's four-thirty in the afternoon."

"Someone could be napping. So…"

Percy emphasized his stuck-out hand. "Please. The music."

I briefly dropped my head in resignation, then produced the sheet music from my backpack and handed it to Percy. "We were on our way to return it."

He sniffed. "I'm sure you were. It should have never been taken. Unfortunately for you, I will have to report this transgression to Mr. Winston."

"Why?"

"The contest rules strictly forbid the removal of anything from any room at El Sueño."

Zoe appeared by my side, shoving a piece of paper at Percy. "The rules say nothing about it."

Percy took the paper, scanned it, then handed it back to Zoe. "Very well. However, I was instructed by Mr. Winston prior to commencement of the contest that nothing could be removed from any room or structure on the estate and I was to report any instance of such removal as it would be grounds for that contestant's disqualification."

Zoe stepped in front of me and invaded Percy's personal space, her finger poised just under his chin. "That's a bunch of bull and you know it. And—"

He took a step back. "I do not—"

She moved right back into his space, neck craned, finger deployed. The wee girl was fearless. "*And*, if you report us, we'll report *you*."

Percy drew back. "Excuse me, *you* will report *me*? For what, may I ask?"

"You didn't have a family emergency last week," she sneered. "I don't know where you disappeared to, but it sure wasn't to take care of your dear 'ole mum. And I'm sure the cops would be interested in knowing you took off the day after they showed up to investigate Olivia Fantucci's death. And that you lied about where you went."

"I did no such thing," Percy huffed with exaggerated indignation. "There was a family emergency I needed to address. My mother was taken to hospital. She was quite ill."

A deep guttural moan came from behind me.

Zoe glanced back at Bertie. His eyes were covered, head on the ground. She whipped her head back around toward Percy. "You're full of it, pal. And while you were missing for two days, Rod Toft and Ashely Tennison also disappeared. I'll leave it up to Detective Lilley to decide if that's a coincidence."

Percy glared down at the pugnacious pixie, who returned his angry stare with a stone-cold one of her own. *I've never been prouder of my best friend. The girl was fierce. And beyond scary.*

Seconds passed as the two traded venomous looks. Eventually, Percy broke eye contact, his gaze shifting to me. He took two steps back, straightened, and cleared his throat. "My apologies, Miss Donovan. I clearly misunderstood Mr. Winston's instructions." He held up the sheet music. "I shall return the music for you, and nothing shall be spoken about this,"—a quick glance at Zoe—"*any of this*, to anyone."

She made no acknowledgement, her death stare still locked on the man.

"Thank you, Percy," I said.

The beaten butler inhaled through his nose. "You're quite welcome." He tossed a parting scowl at Zoe, pivoted, and marched sharply down the hall, heels echoing his resounding defeat.

Zoe turned to me, her eyes, blazing green beacons of triumph. "Schooled."

I punched the air. "So schooled. You were amazing."

Her smile widened as she folded and stuffed the contest rules in the back pocket of her jeans. "I was, wasn't I."

"Heck, yeah, you were."

Zoe scooped up Bertie and cuddled him, who reciprocated with excited kisses and nuzzles, his tail wagging furiously. "This little guy is something else."

"Great call by Finn having us take him."

"Sure was."

A sharp bark rang out, but it wasn't from Bertie. I picked up a perturbed Mauzzy and gave him some loving, too. Unlike Bertie, the peeved pup didn't reciprocate. "I know, Sweet Handsome, you've helped us find at least two safes. You're something else, too."

Mauzzy smiled and gave my cheek a single lick. All was forgiven.

For now.

Hopefully.

I set Handsome down. "Let's get to the music room and win this thing."

Zoe gave Bertie one last kiss and hug, then set him down. The four of us hustled out of the suite and down the hall on our way to winning the contest, a half billion dollars, and putting an end to Laslo Nagy's hold over me.

When we arrived at the music room, the sheet music was back on the piano's music rack and the place was empty. Zoe shot over to the panel hiding the safe. She got on her knees and ran her fingers over the panel next to it until she found a slight indentation in the bottom-left corner of a carved design. With a soft hiss, the adjacent panel slid up and disappeared behind the one above it, revealing the seventh and final safe.

I slung the backpack off my shoulder, dug out the notepad and, fighting to keep my voice low and slow, read off the numbers in the sequence we developed with Matt. "Ten. Four. Eighteen. Thirty. Thirty-three.

Sixteen. And seven."

Zoe slammed the safe with the base of her palm. "Maybe I entered it wrong. Read it again."

I did, and she hit the safe again. "Any ideas?"

I studied the notepad. No way any of the hundreds of number sets Zoe and I came up with were correct. My brother was all over it, as usual. He cracked an uncrackable cipher last summer. A hundred-fifty-year-old cipher the experts couldn't solve. This was just a seven-number combination. Child's play for him.

"I believe in my brother. He's the smartest person I know. The numbers are right. We just need to use logic and come up with the sequence."

"I believe in him, too." She looked back up at me. "What if we start with seven?"

"Just move it from the last number to the first?"

Zoe nodded. "Why not? It's the dude's favorite number, right? And he's all full of himself. Maybe for the last safe, the big one for all the marbles, he put *his* number in the first position."

"Because he considers himself above everybody."

"Yup. First among everybody with no peers."

"Let's give it a shot." I read from the notepad. "Seven. Ten. Four. Eighteen. Thirty. Thirty-Three. Sixteen."

The familiar whirring sound didn't happen. My body sagged. Hammering heart, silenced. Hopeful anticipation, crushed. Taking a deep breath, I consulted the notepad.

"We did it," Zoe said quietly.

I continued to study the numbers, looking for a logical sequence. "Did what?"

"Cracked the safe, idiot."

My gaze traveled from the notepad down to where a beaming Zoe sat next to the open safe.

The open safe?

"Oh, my gosh. We did it," I exclaimed.

"Yeah, we did," Zoe sang.

"What's in it?"

Zoe peered in the safe. "What the eff? There are five envelopes." She took out a familiar ivory envelope and a computer mouse. "I thought this was the last safe."

"It still might be. You could be holding the winning ticket's numbers."

Zoe stood and handed me the envelope. "You have the honor."

I took the envelope, opened it, and extracted a single piece of paper. "No numbers."

"Seriously?"

I handed her the paper. "See for yourself."

Zoe read it and looked up, her mouth open. "Now what?"

Congratulations! You have conquered the seventh and final level. It's all in your hands now. Just remember, a light can shine dark, and be revealing all the same.

Chapter Thirty-Eight

Dark times

Zoe handed me back the paper, glancing around the music room. "We're close, right? I mean, the effing thing is congratulating us for beating the final level."

"Yet we still have one last step," I said, taking the note.

"Which makes no sense if we beat the last level. The dude isn't playing fair."

I studied the message. "The 'it's all in your hands now' is telling us this is it. No more riddles. The last sentence is the final clue. We solve it, we win."

"You think it's another room?"

"It's gotta be, right? Up 'til now, it's been seven levels, seven rooms."

Zoe stood beside me, staring at the paper. With a smack on my arm, she cried out, "*A darkroom*. It's a fricking darkroom."

I rubbed my upper arm. The girl could pack a punch. "I don't remember seeing a darkroom on the El Sueño map. And it wasn't mentioned in the welcome letter."

Zoe waved me off. "C'mon, a darkroom's red light isn't bright, but allows enough light to see while developing film."

"Like it shines dark." My eyes widened. "To allow

photos to *reveal* themselves."

"*We got it.*" Zoe grabbed the backpack at my feet, dug out the map, and studied it. "This place has everything."

"A darkroom?"

Her index finger touched a spot on the map. "Bam."

I took a pic of the computer mouse, returned it to the safe, and closed the door. "We've got a couple hours before dinner. Let's get moving."

Zoe ran her fingers over the panel adjacent to the safe, and the recessed panel slid back into place, the safe disappearing behind it.

Ten minutes later, we stood in the doorway to the darkroom, which was—dark. There were two light switches inside the door, one labeled "white" and the other "red." I flicked the "white" switch, illuminating the room in normal white light. The space was small with a counter lining the far wall. On it were four large trays and bottles and jugs of various sizes, presumably holding whatever chemicals were used for developing film. Strung above our heads and the counter between the side walls were wires with black clips for holding recently developed photographs, but nothing was hanging. A counter ran along the left wall on which sat several pieces of odd-looking equipment. On the right wall, another counter loaded with supplies, utensils, and small tools.

We roamed around the space, looking for anything out of place. Although this was our first darkroom, everything appeared normal. But we're talking blind leading the blind here.

"Let's try the red light," I said. "Maybe it will

show something we can't see in the normal light."

Zoe walked over to the light switches and closed the door leading out to the hall. "Ready?"

I nodded.

She flicked the switch labeled "red." The white lights cut out as the room became bathed in an eerie red light.

"Cool," Zoe muttered from the door.

We again searched every corner of the room. Every inch of space on the counters and walls. Every surface of every bottle, jug, box, and package. We even managed to turn on each piece of equipment without blinding ourselves or blowing the place up. But no hidden message appeared in the soft red light.

"What a waste of two hours," Zoe huffed.

"I really thought this was it," I complained, glancing at my phone. "Geez, we gotta get going or we're gonna be late to dinner."

We hightailed it out of the darkroom back to our suite. After feeding Bertie and Mauzzy, and a quick change into our ridiculous business-casual dinner clothes, we headed out for the grand dining room. At the end of the long hall where our suite was located, a very short, squat lady slowly pushed a cleaning cart. A cleaning lady with snow-white hair. A cleaning lady about the height of—

"Mrs. Majelski?" I called out, running toward the old lady.

She didn't acknowledge me. Just picked up her pace, looking to the right as she scooted around a corner on the left, effectively shielding her face from me.

Zoe tore past me and disappeared around the same

corner.

When I finally rounded the corner, halfway down the hall the cart stood abandoned outside a door. I raced to it, and just as I got there, Zoe appeared from the inside.

"Whoever it was is gone," she said matter-of-factly. You'd never know the girl just finished sprinting down two long hallways.

Sucking air into my lungs, I stepped into the room. It was another suite, furnished identical to ours. "How'd…" Deep breath. "…you get in?"

"The door was ajar."

I bent over, hands on knees, head hanging down.

"Good job remembering hands on knees. Just breathe in through your nose."

After a few seconds, my jackhammering heart downshifted and breathing slowed enough for me to talk. I angled my head up at Zoe. "Get a good look?"

She shook her head. "That person can flat-out run."

I stood and blew out. "That was Mrs. Majelski."

Zoe's eyes bugged out. "No effing way. I'm telling you, that person was *fast*. Somebody was made up to look like her."

"I'm telling you it was her. I've seen her run. And not just on the treadmill. She's quick. Her walker is just a ruse."

"Pretty sure I can run down an eighty-year-old lady. Even in these stupid clogs."

I let out a short laugh. "Not her. How'd she get out?"

Zoe motioned with her head toward one of the windows in the living room. "Open window."

"Anybody in the bedroom?"

"Nope. Doesn't look like anybody's been staying here, either."

I walked over to the ground-floor window—its glass pane slid wide open. The view was of the grounds and parking area in front of the mansion. I poked my head outside and glanced around. Far down the entranceway, sitting outside the closed gates, a multitude of flashing red and blue lights.

I pulled my head back in and rushed toward the front door. "Cops are coming."

"Cops?"

"We gotta get to dinner."

Minutes later, we were met by Percy as we entered the dining room. Everybody was already seated. "Just in time, ladies. Dinner shall be served shortly. Champagne?"

"Please," I said.

Zoe glared at the man.

Percy raised his chin, staring down at her through the bottom of his eyes. "Miss Harp, I shall do nothing untoward with your food or drink."

"Zo," I hissed. "Act cool."

"Sparkling water with lime," she said, the words fighting their way out past a fake smile.

With a quick nod of the head, Percy turned and marched for the kitchen.

I made my way to the main table as Zoe took her seat at the shortened associates' table with Kathleen Fernsby, Billy Jablonsky, and Ivan Volkov. Over the weekend, two leaves had been removed from the table so it appeared less cold and desolate than last Friday night.

We were being served our appetizer when

Detective Lilley, her partner, and two uniformed police officers swept into the room. The next few seconds were filled with gasps, turning of heads, and open mouths of surprise. The foursome trooped up to our table, stopping behind a sweating Scooter Jablonsky and a calm Spencer Fernsby.

"Burl Jablonsky?" Detective Lilley said.

"Yes, ma'am," Scooter replied warily as he twisted around, color rushing into his blotchy round face.

"Sir, I have a warrant for your arrest for the murder of Olivia Fantucci."

"What?" he exploded. "*What?* That's impossible."

"Sir, please stand and step away from the table," she said.

"I ain't done nothing," he protested.

"Sir, please," she persisted.

Billy Jablonsky jumped up and started toward the main table. "Hey, now, he said he didn't do nothing. You just can't—"

Detective Lilley's hand shot out in the direction of the fast-approaching Billy. "*Stop right there, sir.*"

The detective's partner took two steps toward the brother.

Billy froze in his tracks. "Ma'am, he's been—"

"Return to your seat, sir," she commanded, then addressed Scooter as Billy retreated to his table. "Mr. Jablonsky?"

"But I ain't done nothing," Scooter pleaded.

Spencer put a hand on Scooter's arm. "It's best you do as she says. We'll get this sorted out."

Scooter gulped down his bourbon, slammed the glass on the table, stood, and faced Detective Lilley.

"Please turn around, sir," she said. "Hands behind

your back."

A red-faced Scooter raised his hands. "Lady, ma'am, you're making a big mistake. I wasn't even here when—"

"Turn around. Hands behind your back," she repeated, her tone no longer polite.

The two uniformed officers took a step toward Scooter.

"But—"

"*Now*," Detective Lilley commanded.

The flustered car magnate swallowed his words, turned, and put his thick hands behind his back. His face went from red to crimson. I half-expected him to have a stroke. Detective Lilley cuffed him, repeated why he was being arrested, and recited his Miranda rights.

One of the officers took the distraught man by the arm and gently pulled on him to go, but Scooter resisted, calling over to his brother, who was back sitting beside Zoe. "Billy, call Bobby. Tell him I ain't done nothing and to call Buster. Tell him—"

"*Let's go, sir.*" The officer tugged on Scooter and dragged him toward the door, followed by the other cops.

"Spencer," Scooter called back over his shoulder. "I ain't done this. I ain't done this. That damn Volkov done…"

His protestations faded away as the entourage exited the room and moved down the hallway.

Karsh broke the stunned silence. "I didn't think he was smart enough to come up with such a clever plan."

Volkov raised a wineglass to his lips, a wicked smile stretched across his face. "The fact he was caught says it wasn't clever at all."

"I beg to differ," Karsh said. "The plan was exceedingly clever. Apparently, the execution, not so much."

"Point taken," Volkov said, taking a sip of wine and setting the glass down. His gaze shifted to an ashen Spencer Fernsby. "Looks like someone lost their partner," he scoffed. "Everybody is on their own now."

Spencer's face flushed, his blue-gray eyes staring hard at Volkov. "So, it would seem."

Volkov smirked. "My goodness, it will certainly be difficult for Scooter to win the contest from a jail cell, don't you think, Spencer?"

"If you had anything to do with this, I'll..." Spencer set his jaw.

Volkov arched an eyebrow. "You'll what? Have me jailed?" A hollow laugh followed. "I believe you already threatened that and yet, I'm still here." A beat. "And Scooter is not."

"We'll see about that," Spencer snarled, the grandfatherly persona obliterated.

"Spectacular," Karsh intoned, his eyes alive. He lifted his wineglass in Jimmy's and my direction. "One day left. And only five of us. I wonder who's next." He took a sip of wine, keeping his eyes trained on Jimmy and I, then quietly set the glass down. A dark smile spread across his face. "Should be a fun finish."

Chapter Thirty-Nine

Tick. Tock.

Despite the unnerving events at dinner, I went to bed determined to get a good night's sleep. I needed to be sharp if we were going to have any chance at solving the last riddle and winning. However, all night too much crap was rattling around in my head. Mrs. Majelski's appearance. Scooter's arrest. Our failed darkroom theory. Karsh's kinda-veiled threat. Not to mention, tomorrow was the last day of the contest. And we had to win. For my dad's protection. And mine.

Yeah, I slept like crap.

A blast of sunlight crashed into me, jolting my body awake and sending Mauzzy under the covers.

"Let's go," Zoe called to me. "We're gonna miss breakfast."

A hungry Zoe Harp, especially in the morning, was not someone you wanted to antagonize. She was almost as bad as Mauzzy. Almost.

I rolled over. "Go. Just grab me a chocolate chip bagel. I'm gonna need the sugar."

"Fine, but you need to call Finn for your morning check-in before he freaks out."

"It's the last day. He's fine." I put up a hand and threw her a half-wave. "Bye."

Something hard slammed into my upper back,

sharp pain registering in my exhausted brain.

"I'm not leaving until you call him."

I rolled back over toward Zoe. My phone, which I keep on the bedside table, lay next to me on the bed. "Seriously, that hurt."

"I'm starving. Call him."

Still reclined, I picked up the phone and placed the call. "Hey, Finn. I'm alive."

Zoe grabbed the phone from me. "Finn?"

"Yeah."

"Just making sure it was you. Here's Sara." She handed me back the phone with an over-the-top smile. "See ya."

Zoe bolted out of the room as I got back on the phone. "Sorry about that."

"What was that all 'bout?"

Zoe returned to the room with the jammer. She set it on the bedside table, turned it on, then shot back out of the room, the sound of the front door slamming reaching back into the bedroom.

"She's hungry. And I'm tired."

"Ain't gonna ask."

"Don't." I thought about yesterday evening. "Finn, did you send Mrs. Majelski out here to check on us?"

"How's that?"

I repeated the question.

A second stretched into two, then three. "Why would I do that?"

"You're worried about me. About this contest. And it coming to an end."

"She been out there?"

"Yesterday."

"What'd she say?"

"Got away before we could talk with her."

Finn chuckled lightly. "I ain't asked her to do nothing, but it don't surprise me with that 'ole gal."

"I don't know what to do with that."

"Be thankful. Hey, been thinking 'bout that clue y'all got from the music room. It could be a black light."

I scrambled to sit up. An energy infused me. A black light?

"Hey, whatcha thinking?" Finn asked.

I jumped out of bed, grabbed the hissing jammer, and ran into the living room. Setting the jammer on the couch, I picked up the clue from the coffee table.

It's all in your hands now. Just remember, a light can shine dark, and be revealing all the same.

"Oh, my God. You're right. It's a tricking black light."

"Dunno what you do with it though."

"We use it to *reveal* a secret message. Like lottery ticket numbers. Written on the paper with the last clue."

Finn didn't sound convinced. "Mmmm, this Laszlo Nagy is a clever rascal. Seems to me, putting them winning numbers in writing leaves direct evidence to the lottery scam. Nah, it's something else."

"Like what?"

"Beats me. A phone number to call to get the numbers. Or a place to meet with him. But it just ain't gonna be the ticket numbers appearing and you're done."

"Only one way to find out," I said. "I gotta go buy a black light."

I ended the call, threw on yesterday's clothes, and raced out the door, but not before leaving a note for Zoe to feed Mauzzy and Bertie. The last thing I needed was a pissed-off Mauzzy when I returned.

An hour later, Mauzzy and Bertie greeted me as I entered the suite with excited pitter-pattering and yips of glee.

Zoe, on the other hand, greeted me from the couch by winging a bagel at me, bouncing it off my shoulder. "There's your breakfast. I fed them."

Mauzzy and I raced each other for the bagel, me snatching it off the carpet right before he chomped down on it. I wasn't racing him because it was my breakfast. The thing touched the floor. It was no longer edible. I just didn't want the food whore chowing down on it with the chocolate chips and later ending up at the pet hospital having his stomach pumped.

I closed the curtains, turned off the lights from a wall switch at the desk, and sat on the couch. Flipping the bagel to Zoe, I said, "Enjoy."

Zoe caught it and tore off a piece. "You and your germs. It was on the floor like a second."

I pulled a black light out of a superstore bag and switched on the jammer. "Where all kinds of things walk. And—crawl."

"That's a black light? Looks like a flashlight."

I picked up the final clue. "It is. Ready?"

Munching on a piece of bagel, Zoe leaned over toward me. "Hit it."

I positioned the flashlight over the paper and snapped it on, a dark purple beam shooting out.

"What the hell?" Zoe said.

"A website?" I flipped the paper over and aimed the light on the back. "Huh. That's all there is."

Zoe typed and swiped on her phone, then showed

me. The website had a black background with two empty login fields. Nothing else. "We need an ID and password."

"Figures. I assume the ID is my name, but for the password, no telling how many characters."

"Bet it's seven."

"All numbers?"

She screwed her face up. "That'd be my first guess."

I pulled up a note on my phone. "Okay, I've kept all the combinations we've used, including the one for the room safe." I set the phone on the cushion between us, silence descending on the room as we scrutinized the rows of numbers.

48. 40. 39. 31. 19. 13. 10.
1. 2. 4. 42. 30. 26. 25.
8. 31. 41. 22. 17. 6. 21.
38. 27. 25. 16. 35. 47. 41.
11. 6. 18. 15. 25. 17. 28.
32. 10. 36. 15. 29. 8. 49.
37. 12. 3. 2. 14. 27. 4.
7. 10. 4. 18. 30. 33. 16.

"First thing that jumps out is we have eight combos," I said.

"From a dude who loves seven."

"You think any one of these is the password?"

Zoe shrugged. "Who knows? I'll put in the first one from the room safe and see what happens."

"Use 'Sara Donovan' for the ID."

"Okay." Zoe's eyes flicked between my phone and hers as she entered the first combination. "Incorrect user ID or password."

"Crap," I said under my breath.

"At least we know the password could be one of the combos because the field took all the numbers."

"Yea, us," I said with a weak fist pump. "But we don't know if the ID is wrong or the password."

"Or both," Zoe added.

"Let's minimize the variables. Assume the password is one of the combinations. We'll just come up with possible user IDs and try them with each combo."

Zoe looked at me like I was an idiot. "A user ID can be anything."

"Got any better ideas?"

"Not at the moment."

"Then let's get started. We have less than ten hours to crack this thing."

Time slipped away as we cycled through user IDs based on my name. Upper and lower case. All upper case. All lowercase. No space between Sara and Donovan. First initial and last name. First name and first initial of last name. And more. Yet again, and again, and *fricking* again, we got the same error message: *Incorrect user ID or password.*

At some point, after numerous calls to Matt went to voicemail, we assumed one of the many user IDs we came up with had to be correct, so we began recycling through them to focus on cracking the password. We worked through the rows of numbers by taking the first number from every row except for the last row. Then except for the second-to-last row. And so on. Then…Then…Then…

Around four in the afternoon, Zoe's phone went flying across the room into the far wall. She retrieved it from the cratered drywall and on we went, the phone's protective case proving once again to be a wise purchase decision.

Two hours later, we were frazzled, frustrated, and near defeat.

"Where in the hell is Matt?" Zoe raged, pacing the room, arms flailing. "We have less than an hour."

I picked up my phone. "I'll try him again."

Matt answered. "Hey, Sara. What's up?"

"*Where have you been?*"

Zoe stopped mid-step, an icy stare on her face.

"Sorry. Phone crapped out. Guess you been trying to reach me."

"Good guess," I snapped. "Didn't you get any of my voicemails?"

"Hadn't checked yet. Just got back from the phone store."

I quickly brought him up to speed on the situation. "I'm going to send you a note with the safe combinations. Call me back."

Ten minutes later, Matt called me on a video chat. "I don't see any obvious patterns. You've tried all the number sets?"

"And then some," I replied.

Matt's eyebrows raised. "Really? I would have thought the seventh set of numbers would work."

"We've tried all the obvious crap," Zoe barked at the phone, dropping onto the couch. "We've been at it for hours. C'mon, put that genius brain to work."

"Okay," Matt said slowly. "There's gotta be a logical methodology behind determining the password. Presumably, a methodology we're expected to know."

"Yeah, well how come we don't know it?" Zoe fired back.

"Just give me a second," Matt said calmly.

I sent the video to background to focus on the phone note. Nobody spoke as we examined the numbers. In the back of my head, I could hear time draining away.

Matt broke the minutes-long silence. "Now that's interesting."

Chapter Forty

Hiding in plain sight?

Zoe about jumped headfirst into the phone. "*What? What's interesting?*"

"The first set of numbers has no multiples of seven. The other seven each have one."

My eyes worked across the numbers in each row. "The first was our room safe's combination that started the contest. The other seven were to the safes with the objects and riddles."

"The objects," Zoe exclaimed. "You think they're the link to figuring out the password? Like maybe it isn't numbers but letters?"

"Not likely, but run them by me," Matt said.

"Hang on," I said, pulling up another note that I kept for all the objects. "I'm sending you the list. But you gotta go fast. We're inside a half-hour."

Bowling ball, seven pounds, orange.

Ballcap, white with Italia embroidered in green and red script.

Dream catcher, black with turquoise beads and turquoise-and-black feathers.

Pen, gold.

Compass.

Prescription eyeglasses, red.

Computer mouse.

More silence.

"Yeah, I still think those objects are red herrings," Matt said. "The earlier list was before you solved the last room. At the time, I was hoping the last object might shed some light on this angle, but the computer mouse is another one-off object. I don't see a single connection between any two of them, let alone all seven."

"So, giving us that camera and putting the objects in the safes was all BS?" Zoe asked, her tone boiling over with attitude.

"Yep, that's what I think," Matt said.

"That's something Karsh would do, for sure," Zoe snarled. "What an a-hole."

"Sara, read me that last clue again. The part about the hands."

I picked up the paper. "You mean, 'It's all in your hands now. Just remember, a light can shine dark, and be revealing all the same.' That part?"

"That's it. I assume you tried the black light on all the other clues?"

"Huh?" I uttered.

"Since the clue says it's *all* in your hands," Matt explained, "maybe 'all' means all the clues *in your hands* have a hidden number."

My jaw dropped.

"How'd we miss that?" Zoe exploded.

I pulled the clues from my backpack and shined the light on the first one, from the art gallery. Despite the light in the room, the number thirteen glowed faintly on the paper.

"Uh, Matt, there's a thirteen on one of the clues," Zoe said.

"The next one has thirty-one," I said, fanning out the papers on the couch and running the purple beam across each. "They all have a number."

"Call them out," Matt said. "In the order you found the clues."

I made sure the clues were in the proper order. "Thirteen. Thirty-one. Nineteen. Forty-one. Seventeen. Forty-seven. And eleven."

"All prime numbers," Matt said.

"Prime can mean the best or top choice," I said. "Could that mean those numbers are the ones?"

"It's possible," Matt replied. "But it's an interesting choice putting thirteen in the first position."

I stared into the phone. "Really? The whole thirteen-is-bad-luck crap? That's a thing?"

"It has long been considered unlucky in Western civilizations. And in *Tarot*, the Death card is numbered thirteen."

Zoe glanced at me, then the phone, her eyes wide. "Are you seriously suggesting just because the first number is a thirteen, that the whole black-light number set is unlucky? It means death?"

"I don't think it's coincidental."

Zoe threw her hands in the air. I've seen this before with her. Going all the way back to middle school. The girl was amping up fast.

"So, what do we do?" I asked the phone with a wary eye on my agitated best friend.

"Even though I find it interesting they're all prime, looking at the evidence *in toto*, we need to consider the possibility those black-light numbers are like the objects from the safe," Matt reasoned. "I am positing they're all red herrings."

Zoe teetered on the edge, color rushing into her face. "*In toto? Positing? What the*—"

I motioned for her to calm down. "Matt, why hide the numbers if they're bogus? If you're leaving red herrings, don't you want them found?"

"You do. He knew if you figured out the black light and found the hidden website, you'd also find those numbers," Matt explained. "Hiding them, but making sure you found them, was his attempt to manipulate you into believing they were important. Like for the website's password."

I glanced up at a darkening Zoe, then back to the phone. "But what's the point, if they're wrong?"

"To waste your time," Matt said. "There are thousands of permutations for a seven number set. I believe he made the first combination, the one to your room's safe, also without any seven multiples to get you to waste more time."

"Which we're doing right now like effing idiots," Zoe growled. She let out a shriek. "I *hate* that guy."

"Hang on," Matt said evenly. "It's so obvious. It's right there in front of us."

"What?" we asked together.

"The password. It's gotta be it."

"What?" we yelled at the phone.

"For someone who considers himself a seven, built this contest around the number seven, it would seem fitting that the password to the winning numbers is comprised of sevens."

Zoe and I exchanged a confused look.

"All sevens?" I said into the phone.

"Uh-uh," came the reply. "All *multiples* of seven. From the last seven combinations in your list."

Zoe and I about cracked our heads together as we focused on my phone's list.

"In what sequence?" Zoe asked.

Matt blew out. "That's the problem. I could argue several different ones."

"You better pick one," Zoe barked. "We've got less than ten minutes."

"The last one, to the safe in the music room, started with the number seven. Maybe this one does the same?" I offered.

"Possible," Matt said. "But I'm gonna think like a megalomaniac for a second, which is clearly Laszlo Nagy."

"A second is about all you got," Zoe warned harshly.

An unperturbed Matt continued. "In his warped self-concept, he is a seven. Someone like that will want the very last number to be the key number. His number. Because when you put that last number in, seven, he's staring back at you. He's the last thing you see before hitting enter and opening the website, revealing the winning numbers."

"*Meaning?*" Zoe shouted.

"Meaning the sequence starts with the first seven multiple, forty-two, and goes in order, ending with seven."

"The same order we solved the riddles in?" I asked.

"The same," Matt confirmed.

Zoe picked up her phone. "What ID we going with?"

"Use the most logical one. Sara Donovan," Matt said.

"Got it." Zoe's index finger hovered over her

phone. "Read me the numbers."

She typed as I read off the numbers. "Forty-two. Twenty-one. Thirty-five. Twenty-eight. Forty-nine. Fourteen. Seven."

"Damn it!" Zoe raised her phone, arm cocked.

"Zo," I cautioned.

She slowly lowered her arm. "We got a couple minutes. Matt, need our best guess."

"Nagy is a megalomaniac with an unhealthy affinity for the number seven. Therefore, it stands to reason the password to the website is based on the number seven. It's logical. Those are the numbers. We just have the wrong sequence."

"Maybe the black-light numbers are the ones?" Zoe threw out.

Seconds passed.

With a watchful eye on Zoe, I said, "Matt?"

"Negative. In addition to my thirteen-positional theory, none of those are seven multiples. That conspicuous absence along with the same from the first set of numbers juxtaposed with the seven multiples embedded in the other safe combos is glaring."

Zoe stuck her face over the phone. "*Glaring?* What the *eff* are you talking about?"

"They're too obvious."

Another shriek of frustration.

I considered a frazzled Zoe and winced. "I'm afraid to ask, but what do you think?"

She sucked in deep, puffed her cheeks up, and blew out hard. And just like that, her stress disappeared. "It's obvious the black-light numbers are super important." A beat. Then another. "And that's why I believe Matt. It's too obvious."

All my life, snap judgments almost always ended badly for me. Everything was riding on this one decision. We were about out of time, but I wasn't going to blow it again by making a rash decision. I ran everything through my head. Matt's logical conclusions. How the contest was structured. The design of the clues. The harmonic rhythm of the number seven throughout.

I let out a cleansing breath. "My inclination would be using the black-light numbers as the password. So, let's use the seven multiples. We just need to come up with another seque—"

A possibility so preposterous, yet so perfect, slammed into me. It couldn't be, could it? Something so utterly stupid, something I've dealt with my entire life, is the answer? The mistake I'm constantly correcting people on is now…correct?

"Sara?" Zoe asked.

"Exactly," I said with a broad smile.

Zoe gave a little headshake. "What?"

I pointed to Zoe's phone. "Type in this user ID. *'Sarah Donovan.'*"

Her eyes narrowed. "That's what we've been using. You okay?"

"It's not what we've been using. You've been spelling my name correctly. Try Sara with an *'H.'* I think Mr. Perfect Seven spelled my name wrong."

Zoe's eyes widened as she typed into her phone.

"Ready for the numbers, Zo?" I asked.

"Fire away, Sara with an H."

"Forty-two. Twenty-one. Thirty-five. Twenty-eight. Forty-nine. Fourteen. Seven."

"You Donovans are effing geniuses," Zoe

screamed as she handed me her phone.

Regrettably, congratulations. You are the unanticipated winner. Despite my obvious and profound disappointment, I shall abide by the rules. Stand by.

Chapter Forty-One

The Universe

I read aloud the website's message on Zoe's phone. "Stand by?"

My phone signaled an incoming call. It was from an unknown number. I tossed Zoe's phone on the couch and picked up mine. "Matt, I gotta hang up."

"Why? Sounds like you—"

I dropped the call with my brother and tapped on the incoming one. "Hello?"

"Take me off speaker," a distorted voice commanded.

I did what it said, holding the phone up to my ear. "Okay."

"You just made it. In one minute, Creighton Winston was set to invoke Rule Four, and my dear, you were *certainly not* going to be selected as the winner. In case you didn't realize, tonight you shall be purchasing a single Billionaire's Bonanza lottery ticket. Write this down. Twenty-two. Ten. Fou—"

"Hold on, hold on." I snatched a pen off the coffee table and flipped over one of the clues to write on the back. "Okay. Twenty-two. Ten…"

"Fourteen. Eight. Forty-six. Three. Would you venture a guess at the Bonanza Ball?"

"Seven," I seethed. "I know who you are, Laszlo

Nagy."

Even through the distortion, the voice's laugh was contemptuous. Maniacal. Spine-chilling. "Very good, my dear."

"I'm going to—"

"Don't waste your time. Read the numbers back."

Fuming, I complied.

"Very good. You have one hour to get that ticket purchased. Buy it and continue to comply with the contest rules, and upon receipt of the money in my account, I shall call us even and you will never hear from me again. On this you have my word. However, failure on your part shall be..." A short, malignant laugh. "Well, you can just imagine."

I snarled into the phone. "*If you so much as*—"

The line went dead. I looked at the phone. The caller was gone. My heart thundered. Muscles quivered. Stomach tightened.

Zoe's gaze shifted from me to her phone on the couch. She looked up, eyes bulging. "It's gone."

I sucked in deep and blew out hard. "What's gone?"

"The website. It's like it deleted itself."

"The message is gone?" I asked, sucking in another breath before letting it go.

"Gone."

One more cleansing breath. "You get a screenshot?"

She shook her head. "Didn't think of it."

"Me either, until just now. Let's get Matt back on." I called my brother back via video and set the phone on the couch.

"Everything okay?" he asked, his forehead

furrowed.

"Yeah," I said. "Had a call from Nagy to give us the ticket numbers."

Matt's narrow, pale face brightened. "We did it?"

"Sure did. You're effing brilliant," Zoe gushed as she leaned down and planted a kiss on my phone's screen.

Grimacing, I made a mental note to clean my phone later. I loved the girl like a sister, but germs love no one.

I folded the paper with the numbers and tucked it in a back pocket. "Okay, what time tonight do they stop selling Billionaire's Bonanza tickets?"

Zoe typed, swiped, and scrolled on her phone. "Says here cutoff time is eight o'clock. Drawing is at nine."

"We have less than an hour," I said. "Matt, we gotta go. Call Finn and let him know what's going on. I'll send you his info. And give him this phone number." I read him the unknown number off my phone. "Tell him Nagy called on it to give me the numbers."

"Will do. Good luck, Sis."

I tapped off and shared Finn's contact info with my brother. "Zo, where's the closest place selling tickets?"

"Out in these boonies, who knows?" More typing and scrolling. "Looks like…nineteen miles. A general store."

"Cool. That's only fifteen minutes away."

Zoe lowered her phone with a sarcastic huff. "Not on these winding roads. Even with your crazy driving. Closer to forty."

"We'll see about that," I said, scooping up Mauzzy

from the corner of the couch where he and Bertie had been snoozing.

Zoe moved to get a dazed Bertie. "God help me," she said under her breath.

With the pups tucked under our arms, we ran out of the suite and through the mansion for the parking area. At my crappy hatchback, I gently placed Mauzzy, and then Bertie, in the back seat's milk crate, tucking them in with Mauzzy's favorite pink blankets.

Jumping into the driver's seat, I fired up the engine and slammed the car into reverse.

The passenger door flew forward as Zoe lunged for it from her seat. "Cripes, girl. Can you let me close it first?"

I hit the brakes, shoved the gearshift into drive, and glanced over at Zoe. "You ready?"

She yanked the door closed, twisted around, and reached for the shoulder restraint. "Just—"

I mashed the accelerator and cranked the wheel, the car's rear violently swinging out as the tires scrambled to find traction on the pavers.

"Wha—" Zoe pitched into the door, her face connecting with a thud. "*Oof.*"

With a screeching squeal, the tires found their footing, sending the car blasting forward toward the long entranceway.

Zoe went from being plastered into the door to being thrown into the back of her seat. "Aaagh."

"Aren't you buckled up?"

"If I…wasn't…pulling…ten G's, I'd…effing *clock you.*"

We rocketed down the drive, the closed gates fast approaching. I hit the brakes, the car skidding to a stop just out of reach of the inward-opening gates.

Zoe exhaled dramatically and got buckled up.

"Ow," I cried out, grabbing my right arm.

"That's for face-planting me."

"I asked if you were ready."

"Next time wait for the answer," she snarled. "And let's get there in one pieee—"

I crushed the accelerator to the floor, aiming the car through the ever-widening space between the two gates.

Her hands flew to her head. "Oh, my God. Watch out for—"

The car shot through the still-moving gates, easily clearing them by a couple inches.

As we tore down the drive for the road, I looked over to a wide-eyed, open-mouthed Zoe. "Where we headed?"

"To our deaths if you don't…Slow. The eff. Down!"

I eyed the clock on the dash. "We're fine. Got forty minutes."

"*Then slow down.*"

We neared the end of the drive. "Right or left?"

Zoe checked her phone, activating the navigating app. "Right."

I tugged hard on the wheel, the right-side tires bouncing over something, a ginormous lighted stone pillar fast approaching.

Zoe cringed. "*Eeeeeeeeeeee…*"

The car bounced out onto the road, and after recovering its balance, leaped forward into the fast-darkening night.

"That was a little close," I remarked.

Zoe responded with a quiet whimper. "One piece. Please."

I maneuvered my charging steed into a sharp curve, heaving Zoe into the door. "No worries."

For the next twenty minutes, we drove in silence, except for the occasional gasp or "Oh, my God" from the passenger seat. In the back, Mauzzy and Bertie snored.

According to the app, we had four miles left on this one *very* country road, then another half-mile and we would be at the general store.

Something flashed in the headlights.

A loud clunk sounded from under the front of the car, followed by a *bang* and violent veer to the right.

"What the hell?" Zoe yelled, grabbing for the handle above her door.

I fought the swerving hatchback, a horrific scraping sound beneath us. "Might've hit a raccoon."

"*Oh, God.*"

I got control and pulled over, the car straddling the tarmac and grass. I went to put it in park so I could check for damage, but the gearshift just slid without any tension. "Hmm." I pushed and pulled on the shift. It slid effortlessly back and forth. "Uh-oh."

"Problem?"

I set the emergency brake. "It's not going into park. Actually, any gear."

"That's a problem."

I turned the flashers on and checked the backseat. Bertie and Mauzzy had their heads up, searching outside. "I'm gonna check the front."

Zoe glanced around. It was almost dark. "Be careful."

Turning on my phone's flashlight, I climbed out of the car and walked to the front. The plastic panel beneath the license plate was broken and touching the ground, like something had ripped through it. I bent down and shined the light underneath the car. I wasn't a mechanic, but even I knew what a growing puddle of oil looked like.

I returned to inside the car and checked the gearshift. It still slid effortlessly. "Big puddle of oil under there, and it won't go into gear. We need a tow."

"Damn."

I slammed the steering wheel. "Fricking Universe."

Zoe checked her phone. "I got one bar."

"Me, too. Try and call a tow truck. We have fifteen minutes. I gotta get hold of Finn."

"I'll call my roadside assistance company."

While Zoe placed her call, I pulled the paper with the ticket numbers out of my pocket, stepped out of the car, and called Finn. "Hey, we got a problem."

"Y'all okay?"

"Yeah, we're fine. Broken down. I hit something."

Finn exhaled into the phone. "Anybody hurt?"

"No, just my car."

Another exhale. "Thank the good Lord for that. You buy the ticket?"

"No. That's why I'm calling. Can you buy it?"

"I can try. Hang on." He set the phone down, and when he came back on, I was on speaker. "Gimme the numbers."

I turned the phone's flashlight on, put him on speaker, and read the numbers.

"Got it. Twenty-two. Ten. Fourteen. Eight. Forty-six. Three. Bonanza Ball is seven."

"Correct."

"I'll let you know. Y'all got a tow?"

"Zoe's working it."

"Have 'em take your car to Big Mike's Garage here in Birmingham. He's a friend of mine. He'll get you sorted out tomorrow. Gimme a holler when you get there and I'll pick y'all up. Just in case, send me your location. And keep the car locked. I'll call you in a bit."

I got back in the car, brought up our location on my phone's navigation app, and sent it to Finn.

"We'll have a truck here within an hour," Zoe said.

I hit the car's locks. "Finn's gonna try and buy the ticket."

Zoe looked at me, a weak smile on her face. "So, tell me about your hopes and dreams."

Waiting for Finn's call was excruciating. Our attempt at small talk did nothing to make the time go any faster. Zoe even commented this was the first time she could remember when I found it difficult to make conversation. Something about a silent Sara Donovan and a herd of unicorns.

Eight o'clock came and went.

"It's ten after," I said. "Why isn't he calling?"

"I'm sure everything's okay. He'll call."

At eight-twelve, my phone rang. "Finn, did you get it?"

He sighed. "No."

Panic tore through me, my insides fluttering. "*What?*"

A concerned Zoe leaned over to listen.

"Missed it by two minutes. Tried to get the fella to sell me one anyway. He couldn't do it."

"Why not?" I protested. "It's two lousy minutes."

"Easy now. He woulda if he coulda. But the lottery's terminal shuts off at eight. I'm sorry, Sara."

"Thanks for trying," I said, fighting back tears.

"Easy now, we'll get it sorted. Remember, call me when y'all get to Big Mike's."

Sitting in my dark broken car in the middle of fricking nowhere, with eyes welling, the anxiety monster squeezed until I could no longer breathe. Laszlo Nagy's final distorted words echoed in my head.

Chapter Forty-Two

Blind good luck

"Now don't you worry," Finn reassured me as I climbed down from his beat-up pickup with Mauzzy under an arm. "We'll figure it out in the morning."

Zoe clambered down after me, Bertie moving over to reclaim his passenger seat. She turned and rubbed the perceptive pup around his ears. "Thanks for all the help, Bertie."

He smiled and let out a low groan, turning his head to make sure Zoe didn't miss a spot. This time he wasn't ratting anybody out. The little guy just appreciated the loving.

I poked my head back into the cab. "What's Nagy going to do?"

"Nothing, if he knows what's good for him."

"But I didn't buy the ticket. I'd been better off losing and keeping my mouth shut instead of winning and then not buying the dang thing."

Finn leveled his gaze on me. "Ain't nothing gonna happen tonight. Tomorrow sometime I'm gonna have that DMV photo, and then I'll run him to ground." He paused, rubbed the back of his neck, and let out a breath. "Wasn't gonna tell you this 'til tomorrow, but seeing how you're feeling, I called Lil earlier tonight. Gave her a heads-up."

The anxiety monster roared back with fangs bared. "*Heads-up?* What'd you tell her? Oh, my God. Finn, I didn't buy the ticket. He's out almost a billion dollars. And my dad. What'd you say—"

Finn quietly shushed me. "Hey now. Easy. Easy. Just told her I might have somebody she's gonna wanna chat with, that she might need to get the feds involved, but first I gotta confirm something. That's all. Really."

"*The feds?* You know I don't—"

"I know, I know. But you didn't do nothing wrong. And getting them involved will protect you. And your daddy. Trust me."

I stared at him, slowly shaking my head. My body was jittery. Heart thudding. Head ringing. Chest beyond tight.

Mauzzy reached up and gave me a single kiss, followed by Bertie leaning over and doing the same. They both were there for me, and I knew Finn had my back, too. But the feds?

The big man gave me a quiet smile. "Just need to ID him tomorrow, then I'll sic Lil on him. Now y'all go on in, get a good night's sleep, and I'll be back in the morning."

I returned his smile the best I could. "Thanks, Finn. For tonight. And everything."

"You got it. Now get on in."

As rattled as I was about the coming wrath of Laszlo Nagy, my sheer mental exhaustion made for a night of comatose sleep. When my blaring phone woke me, it was almost nine in the morning. Zoe wasn't in her bed.

I fumbled for the phone on the bedside table. It was Finn. "Hey," I mumbled.

"Morning, Sara. Everything okay?"

I rubbed my eyes. "Mmmm, yeah. Just woke me up."

"Sorry 'bout that. But this is important."

I sat up. "You got it?"

"Don't say nothing 'til you turn the jammer on."

With phone in hand, I crawled out of bed and walked into the living room where the jammer sat on the coffee table. "Okay. It's on. Did you get it?"

Zoe entered the suite and tossed me a bagel. "Hey, look who's up. You missed breakfast."

"On the phone with Finn," I said, putting the call on speaker.

"Hey, Finn."

"Morning, Zoe," Finn said. "I was fixing to tell Sara, I'm gonna be out there to pick y'all up in 'bout an hour. After I swing by to get the photo from my DMV buddy."

"Why doesn't he just send it to you?" I asked.

A beat. "He ain't s'posed to be doing it, that's why."

"Oh," I said softly.

"Okay. Y'all get packed and stay put. I gotta call Lil, then I'll be out there."

Zoe addressed me. "Actually, Sara, Percy announced at breakfast that all contestants need to be in the music room for a nine o'clock meeting with Creighton Winston."

A chill ran through me. "A meeting? Now?"

Zoe nodded. "Uh-huh. But just the contestants."

"He say what it's about?" I asked nervously.

"Nope. But I bet it's about what's all over social media and the news today. You see it, Finn?"

"Nah. Been busy pulling a file together on this Nagy rascal to give Lil. Why?"

"There was one jackpot winner." Zoe paused. "And the ticket was bought in Alabama."

Silence.

Zoe bent toward the phone. "Finn, you hear me?"

"Yeah, I gotcha. They say where in 'Bama?"

"Nope."

I stared at Zoe, my jaw slack. "That's impossible."

"Apparently it's not," she said. "Somebody hit it."

"You think he bought a ticket?" I asked Finn.

"Nah, I don't s'pose. Too much risk for him, and ain't no way he coulda known you didn't buy it. Someone just had some blind good luck."

"They're saying this is the first time someone hit the jackpot picking all seven numbers," Zoe added. "The odds of hitting it were almost one in seven hundred million. For the first six drawings, two had rolled down to six numbers and four times it went to five."

"Them are some big-time long odds," Finn remarked. "And quite the coincidence the winning ticket was bought in 'Bama. Could one of them other contestants have gotten the numbers?"

I shook my head at the phone. "I don't think so. The lawyer, Creighton Winston, said at the beginning there could only be one winner."

"The very first rule said it was an all-or-nothing contest with only one winner," Zoe confirmed.

"Well, considering the snake behind the contest, that don't mean much to me. But then again, if this is a random lucky winner, this works to our advantage," Finn reasoned. "Long as the lottery don't announce who the winner is or where in 'Bama the ticket was bought, we can leverage that to have Nagy think Sara bought the ticket. Ought to buy us some time to find him."

"What if Creighton Winston talks to me today about establishing the Cook Islands trust?" I asked. "What do I do?"

"You do whatever he wants," Finn replied.

"Just like that?" I asked. "I don't have the ticket to show him."

"If he asks to see it, you tell him it's with a friend for safekeeping. If he pushes you, tell him it's with me."

"But you don't have the ticket," I protested. "*We* don't have the ticket."

"Look, the only folks who know you didn't buy it are on this call. Let's keep it that way 'til we can roll Nagy up."

"What about my brother?"

Finn paused. "Don't recommend it."

"I can't tell him? Seriously?"

"Too risky. Look, you best get to that meeting. Just play along like you got the ticket and if the lawyer asks you for it, you gave it to me for safekeeping. I'll be out there by ten-thirty at the latest. You got this, Sara."

I ended the call and scrambled to make myself halfway presentable in the three minutes I had before the meeting started. Thank God for scrunchies and messy buns.

As I ran out the front door, I called back to Zoe, "Take care of Mauzzy?"

"You got it. Good luck."

I hustled down the hallway and made tracks for the

music room. When I got there, everybody was waiting. Karsh Azarian sat ramrod-straight in the same armchair he used for every meeting. Surprisingly, Spencer Fernsby and Frederick Volkov shared one couch. Volkov appeared ready to chew nails while Fernsby was a picture of calm. On the other couch, Jimmy Dougal sat with legs crossed and hands clasped in his lap. Could one of these four men have possibly purchased the ticket? And which one was Laszlo Nagy? Anger and angst battled for control of my body and emotions.

Creighton Winston, who stood at the open end of the furniture arrangement, turned toward me as I rushed across the floor. His usual dour lawyer-face lit up when he saw me. "Ah, perfect timing." He motioned to the couch where Jimmy sat. "Please take a seat."

I sat on the end opposite Jimmy and gave him a polite smile. "Morning."

His return smile was warm, gentle even. "Good morning. Sleep well?"

I nodded. "Like a rock."

"Wonderful," he said with another smile and twinkle in his eye.

Creighton Winston cleared his throat. "I shall be brief. The purpose of this meeting is to advise that we have a winner in the contest. And fortunately, I didn't need to invoke Rule Four and select a winner. Somebody in this room won the contest outright."

Everybody glanced around the room at each other. Volkov and Karsh were ready to explode. Spencer briefly raised his hands and sighed, "Oh, well." Jimmy, who continued to smile, seemed relieved. I was the opposite of relieved. My insides were a jittering juddering mess.

"Well, I'm glad it's over," Jimmy said. "At least I can get back to my life."

"Yes, it will be good to see the grandchildren," Spencer said wistfully. "Little Lucy has a birthday coming up."

"And I have finals coming fast," I choked out.

Volkov glared at me, a vein throbbing at his temple.

"I wish to lodge a complaint," Karsh growled at the lawyer. "Your contest had a technical malfunction yesterday evening that cost me the win. I was logging into the website when it just disappeared."

"Sir, it was not a malfunction," Winston explained. "The founder advised me that the website was specifically designed to lock everyone else out and delete itself soon after the first person solved the login and entered it."

Karsh tensed, his neck cording, face growing red. "Who?"

"I am not at liberty to say," Winston replied. "But I will be contacting the winner later today to go over the necessary paperwork. To everyone, I wish to remind you that the NDAs you signed before the contest commenced remain valid and in full force, as do the ones signed by your associates. Your complete and total silence regarding the contest is required in perpetuity and anything by any of you or your associates to the contrary shall be immediately dealt with in accordance with the terms of the NDA." He raised a cautioning finger. "And remember, you are fully responsible for your associate's conduct. As a final note, you must be checked out of El Sueño by noon today. When you are ready to leave, please call Percy so he can inspect your suite. Are there any questions?"

"Why can't you tell us who won?" Karsh fumed. "That wasn't in the rules."

"Well, at least we know one person who didn't win," Jimmy said with a broad, toothy smile.

Spencer Fernsby's laugh belied his quiet grandfatherly persona. "Indeed, we do."

Chapter Forty-Three

Him

Two hours after the meeting with Creighton Winston, a loud double-knock sent Mauzzy flying off the couch and charging for the suite's front door, a barrage of frantic barks warning whomever was on the other side of the door to back off.

I walked to the door, where my oversized suitcases and Mauzzy's travel bag sat, and opened it. "Hi, Percy."

"Miss Donovan, fitting you are the final check-out."

Not knowing how to respond, I just smiled politely and stepped aside to allow the butler to enter.

He roamed around the space like a drill sergeant inspecting the barracks. He checked closets, the bathroom, TV, even under the beds, before returning to the front door. "Everything appears to be in order."

"Really?" I asked, my gaze inadvertently flicking to the obvious scar in the living room wall from Zoe's flying phone yesterday.

Percy's eyes followed mine to the caved drywall, then snapped back to me. "Miss Harp's doing, I presume?"

I nodded, stealing a look at the sullen guilty party standing next to me.

He sniffed. "Yes, I thought as much. I shall not hold you responsible for her ill-advised actions as we all have that one friend…" Another sniff. "Well, yes. No worries. I will take care of it." He motioned to the suitcases. "That's quite a bit of luggage. Do you require assistance?"

I waved him off. "That's okay. They're rollies."

He stuck out a hand. "Very well, then. Miss Donovan, the pleasure has been all mine."

I took his hand. "Thanks for everything, Percy."

He gave me a thin smile, then addressed Zoe with a quick nod. "Miss Harp."

Zoe narrowed her eyes. "Percy."

The butler returned her glare, pivoted, and exited into the hallway, the clicking of his heels slowly fading away.

I leashed up Mauzzy and extended the handles on my suitcases. "Let's get outta here before Winston tracks me down."

In front of the mansion, Finn waited with Bertie in his truck. When he saw us come out, he climbed out of the cab and came around, taking my luggage and unceremoniously chucking each in the cargo bed. After doing the same with Zoe's carry-on-sized bag, we all climbed into the cab, the wee feisty one in the middle with Bertie, Sweet Handsome curled on my lap in the passenger seat.

"Somebody got all cleaned up," I noted.

Finn rubbed his reemerged goatee. "It was getting shabby."

I laughed. "Sure was. I guess those sideburns needed raising and trimming, too? And your ponytail is nice and tight."

Finn grunted.

I leaned around Zoe and flashed a lecherous grin. "Someone got a date tonight?"

Finn ignored me and started the truck. "Got some good news. Got some bad news. Spoke with Big Mike on the way over 'bout your car. Busted oil pan and broken shifter cable. Lucky for you that piece of junk has been one of the more popular vehicles over the years. Was able to get the parts no problem. We can pick it up on the way to the office."

I braced for the news. "How much?"

Finn exited the parking area and we headed down the driveway for the gates. "He owes me a favor. Only gonna charge for parts. Couple hundred. I'll cover you and take it from your pay."

"I guess it could be worse. Thanks, Finn. Now, what's the good news?"

He glanced over at me, brown eyes wide. "That *was* the good news."

"It was?"

"Yep."

I cringed. "Then what's the bad?"

He stopped the truck and while waiting for the gates to open, leaned over and popped the glovebox. "It's in there. White envelope."

"You got it?" I asked.

Finn gave me a dead man's stare. "Yes and no."

I stared back at him for a moment, then took the envelope out and opened it. Inside was a folded piece of white paper. I pulled the paper out, unfolded it, and stared at the DMV mug shot of Laszlo Nagy. Or what was supposed to be a mug shot. Instead, staring back at me was the headshot of a clown. With a big smile. And an extended middle finger.

My shoulders slumped as despair washed over me. Our best and only shot at identifying my blackmailer and ending this nightmare was gone, replaced by the mocking pic rubbing my face in his total victory. And when he realizes there is no money coming his way, his retribution will be... A chill ran through me as his arrogant voice and maniacal laugh echoed in my head. Nagy was smart. Resourceful. Ruthless. And judging by yesterday's call, unbalanced. Capable of anything. The man will become unhinged when he finds out I didn't buy the ticket.

Zoe leaned over and whistled softly. "Seriously?"

"There was a DMV hack couple months back," Finn said. "Folks reckoned it was to steal socials and DL numbers. For identity-fraud scams." He pointed his head toward the paper in my hand. "But with that there, now I ain't so sure. He deleted all his personal data 'cept his name and replaced his photo with that clown."

"He's making a fricking point," I fumed, staring at the mocking smile on the paper.

"Sure enough is," Finn said. "Calling us all clowns."

"Fits the a-hole," Zoe said with a huff.

"Got that right." Finn drove the truck through the open gates. "I also took a run at Septem, figuring they might have an ID photo in their badging system."

"Did they?" I asked hopefully.

Finn glanced over and shook his head. "They did once, but it's all gone. His HR hard file is missing and the digital was erased."

I let out a long sigh. "Of course it's all gone. He's always one step ahead. So now what?"

"We go into protection mode 'cause when he finds out you ain't the winner, he's gonna come for you. Hard."

"Protection mode?" I asked in disbelief, my heart racing. "You mean witness protection?"

"Nah, time to get out in front of this with the cops." He turned onto the road, took out his phone, and placed a call. "Hey, Lil. Yeah, I got her." He gave me a sidelong glance. "Right. Like we discussed. Uh-huh. Used a burner? Bounced it all around? Right. Rascal's slicker'n owl..." Another quick glance my way. "Right. Can do. Let's meet at my office. Great. Gotta pick up her car, so gimme an hour. See y'all then." He tapped off and looked over at me. "That call you got from him, when he gave you them numbers?"

"I heard. They couldn't trace the phone."

"Yep. Went out of his way to make it impossible. The fella knows what he's doing, I'll give him that."

"Why are you meeting Detective Lilley at your office?" I asked. "She's investigating Fantucci's murder."

He looked over at me. "*We're* meeting with Lil at my office."

"We?"

"We."

"Terrific," I said.

"And she's bringing a couple agents."

"Just terrific."

Chapter Forty-Four

The feds

It's been three days since my FBI interview at Finn's office when I told them everything, except for the diamond I got at the beginning of this whole fricking mess, including my belief that Karsh Azarian was both the founder and the killer. Finn insisted it wasn't a question of *if* but *when* Nagy came after me or Dad and strongly suggested they assign protective details to us. The lead agent contacted the U.S. Marshals, who agreed to provide security until the FBI could determine the extent of the risk, and one currently sat in his car outside my cottage. Dad wasn't happy to hear from me about the photo of him and its implications, and the "circumstances" surrounding it, but he was appreciative the feds were on the case and said he would advise his bosses and security investigation people of the issue. Then we had the same "talk" I've been hearing my whole life about judgment, decision-making, and how my "choices" affect everybody around me.

Loads of fun.

My cottage was quiet except for Mauzzy's light snoring as he snoozed blissfully in his recliner. Matt napped on the couch while I sat at the card table trying to push Nagy's impending retribution out of my mind and *finally* focus on studying for my fast-approaching finals. I was running through notes and flashcards on my Fraud-Risk Management class when the phone erupted, causing me to jerk into the table and knock over a full water bottle I just cracked open. My survival instincts, well-honed over the past few years from similar incidents, kicked in. With one hand I stood the gushing bottle back up as the other swept everything else, including the phone, off the table in one life-saving motion.

I jumped up to track down the blaring phone, my body slamming into the table, sending the water bottle over. Again. After righting the now quarter-full bottle, I searched for the waylaid phone. Spotting it halfway under the fridge, I shot over to it just as the ringing stopped. I tapped on the missed call and brought the phone to my ear.

"Finn?"

"Hey, catch you at a bad time?"

"No, sorry about that. I was studying and the phone...Never mind. What's up?"

"Just letting you know we're on McFarland so we'll be there soon."

My stomach tightened. Even though I knew they were on the way, the thought of allowing feds into my living space set the perspiration machine into overdrive. "We'll be here," I croaked.

After several seconds of dead air, Finn asked, "You okay?"

"Not really, but what choice do I have?"

"Ah, it'll be fine. You met 'em. They're the good guys."

"Still."

"How's Matt? He still nervous about this?"

I looked over at my unconscious brother. "Yeah, he's over it."

"Great. See y'all in a bit."

I tapped off, grabbed a scorched oven mitt from the counter, and launched it toward the couch. Not surprising, the mitt missed the mark, clipping the water bottle on the card table, and finishing the job I started only seconds earlier.

With a sigh, I pulled another water from the fridge, picked up a dishtowel, and returned to the flooded card table. Mopping up the water, I yelled, "Matt, wake up. They're almost here." When he didn't move, I retrieved the mitt, stood over the couch, and slammed it into his back. "*Matt.*"

He shot up and twisted around, unruly hair going every direction, brown eyes wide until he focused on me. "What the…Oh, it's you."

"They're gonna be here in a minute. Fix yourself up."

He squinted at me. "Wha?"

"Hello? The FBI? They wanna talk about your lottery-rigging theory?"

"Oh, yeah, right. Now?"

"*Now*. Comb your hair."

He fumbled with his hair, fingers flattening and reining in rebellious brown locks.

A knock on the front door yanked Mauzzy from his slumber and propelled him toward the intrusion, a fusillade of crazed barks warning the world: *Enter at your own risk.*

I stepped to the door, scooped up my guard dog, and peeked out the side window. On the front deck stood Finn with the two agents from the other day and a short skinny dude who could be an older version of my brother in ten years. Agent Johnny Bragg was a tall attractive man dressed in a navy-blue suit with short dark hair and square jaw. Agent Martha Swift, with shoulder-length blonde hair and just a few inches shorter than Bragg, wore a black business suit and a serious expression.

I grasped the doorknob, took a breath, and opened the door. "Hey, welcome to Tuscaloosa. C'mon in."

With a mumble of thanks and hellos, the group filed past me into the tiny living space. I closed the door and released Mauzzy, who immediately made his presence known, sniffing and dancing around everyone's feet.

"Mauz, leave them alone," I scolded.

Agent Swift bent and gave him a scratch. "Good to see you again, Mauzzy."

Finn strode across the room in three steps and stopped at the card table, surveying the notebooks and index cards strewn across the floor and the soaked dishtowel on the table beside the empty water bottle. He turned back toward me with an amused grin. "Interesting studying methods. Times have changed since I was in school."

I brushed past him and pulled two folding chairs out from the table for the agents. "Yeah, like five presidents and the Internet."

Finn grabbed the other two chairs and lined them up next to the ones I placed, forming a semicircle facing the couch. "You forgot the six football championships we added. God love Nick Saban."

"Roll Tide," I droned, motioning for Finn and the

feds to sit in the folding chairs. For once, the chairs' crappiness came in handy. Never let The Man get too comfortable in your own place. I plopped onto the couch next to my brother.

When everyone was seated, Johnny spoke. "We appreciate your time, Matt. I'm Special Agent Johnny Bragg. This is Special Agent Martha Swift and"— his arm extended toward the scrawny dude— "he is Digital Forensic Examiner Aiden Parker. But before we get started"—his gaze settled on me— "we're going to need that diamond. It's potential evidence."

I pulled my head back and gave a little headshake. "Diamond?"

Agent Bragg nodded.

My eyes cut to Finn, who winced. "Sorry, Sara. After your interview, I realized you *forgot* to tell them about the diamond, so I called Johnny and filled him in." He finished with a subtle nod.

I let out an embarrassed laugh. "Oh, *that* diamond. Right. Totally slipped my mind." I turned to Agent Bragg. "I thought you were talking about the Star of Midnight, which, uh, well, you know all about that, I'm sure."

Agent Bragg smiled evenly. "Of course. Is it here?"

I stood, walked over to the kitchen, and took the red-velveteen jewelry box from the oven. Returning to my seat, I handed the box to Agent Bragg.

He opened the box, examined the stone, then snapped the box closed and put it in his jacket pocket. "Nice hiding place."

"It's the only thing it's good for," I replied with a shrug. "More importantly, did you find Laszlo Nagy?"

With a quick headshake, Agent Bragg said, "Finn warned us about this guy. It's like he just vanished."

I exchanged a concerned look with Finn, then focused back on the G-man. "If he's still out there, what about mine and Dad's protective details?"

"They'll remain for the next several weeks until we sort things out," Agent Bragg replied. "We're still searching for him as a person of interest, but we've confirmed he had no ties to the Billionaire's Bonanza winner. Although I can't divulge her identity as she wishes to remain anonymous for obvious reasons until she claims her prize at the lottery's headquarters, she's an eighty-two-year-old great-grandma who bought the ticket as soon as that month's sales opened, or two weeks before your contest began. She has zero ties to Nagy or any of the people associated with the contest."

A white-haired image with a droopy nose and steely eyes popped into my head, but I immediately pushed it out. No fricking way it was Mrs. Majelski. Right?

"The lottery announced the winner was from Mobile," I said. "That's why Creighton Winston never contacted me to complete the contest winner's paperwork. No way I could've made that drive in the time I had left."

Agent Swift spoke up. "Speaking of Winston, he's refusing to cooperate, citing attorney-client privilege. Although, he was quick to point out that everything he's done has been above board and he knows nothing about *any* lottery scam, including the Billionaire's Bonanza."

"What a surprise," I quipped.

"Okay," Agent Bragg said, "let's talk about

Septem's random-number-generating machine. Aiden conducted a forensics analysis of the machine and the algorithm used for the Billionaire's Bonanza drawing. He—"

"Um, excuse me, sir," Aiden said, his voice cracking, "but we also examined the five machines used for those other lotteries Mr. Finnegan found where payouts went to Cook Islands trusts." He paused. "I had Simmons and Goldberg examine the other five."

Agent Bragg pressed his lips tight. "Fine. Why don't you tell Matt what you found."

Aiden turned to Matt. "That's just it. I didn't find anything unusual on the Bonanza machine. Everything appeared normal. The seed was determined from a Geiger counter measuring for Americium-241."

Matt nodded. "What algo was used? Mersenne Twister?"

Aiden shook his head. "Negative. Something I've never seen before."

"Not a Frankenstein one?"

"Negative. There is nothing in it taken from existing pseudorandom number generators. At least, none that I'm aware of."

My brother's eyes narrowed. "Is it secure?"

Aiden nodded. "Appears to be. No exploitable bias or patterns."

Matt rubbed the back of his neck. "What about someone predicting output bits?"

My brother and the FBI geek went back and forth with that techno-crap for what seemed like hours, but was probably only ten minutes.

I was being put to sleep when Matt raised his theory. "Any evidence of a rootkit?"

"None," Aiden responded, "but if it was placed by the person who developed this algo, I certainly wouldn't expect to find it."

Matt nodded. "Makes sense. Probability of a self-deleting one?"

"Medium to high. Although, with the sophistication of this algo, a malicious code could have been buried in it and we wouldn't know what to look for. I suppose it could be found, but it could take months or years, and we still might not identify it."

After another ten minutes of paint-drying tech talk between the two brainiacs, Aiden asked Matt, "Any other ideas?"

Matt pinched his lips, scratched his head, and squinted at Aiden. "Nope. Nothing on those other lottery machines?"

"Negative. All the same."

"Yeah, then I got nothing."

Agent Bragg looked at Matt. "Would it help if we gave you access to the algorithm?"

Aiden tensed as his eyes locked onto Matt.

My brother twisted his face up. "Mmmm, doubt it. Sounds like Aiden has it covered. I can review it if you want, but probably would be a waste of time. Like he said, I could spend months going over it and still might not find it because I wouldn't know what to look for."

As Matt spoke, I noticed a subtle relaxing of Aiden's jaw and body.

Agent Bragg exchanged a look with his partner before focusing back on my brother. "So, what's your assessment?"

"Of what?" Matt asked.

Aiden tensed again.

"Was the lottery rigged?" Agent Bragg asked.

"Obviously," I interjected. "I had the winning numbers."

Agent Swift addressed me. "Everyone we've talked to, including the BB lottery director, said it's impossible to rig the lottery. That the machine they use is infallible and secured in a room that rivals a Top Secret SCIF. If we can't determine how it was rigged, we have no case, despite you having the winning numbers."

"So, Matt, was it rigged?" Agent Bragg asked again. "And if so, how?"

"Definitely. But you'll never be able to prove it."

The G-man pulled his head back. "Why?"

"Based on everything Aiden said, you're dealing with a highly-intelligent person who seems to have taken every precaution not to be caught. Or at least, not prosecuted."

"Not prosecuted?" Agent Bragg repeated. "Explain."

Matt shrugged. "If somebody is going to make the concerted effort to develop a new PRNG algo instead of using existing robust ones such as Mersenne's or a variant of it, or come up with a Frankenstein combo of what's out there, that tells me the person left nothing to chance." He addressed Aiden. "Based on your analysis, can you *prove* any of those lotteries were rigged?"

Aiden shook his head. "That's why we're here talking with you."

Matt turned back to Agent Bragg. "Pretty obvious to me. Short of a confession, you're out of luck."

Finn's phone rang. He stood and stepped into the kitchen, like that was going to give him any privacy in my palatial cottage. "Lil, what's up? How's that? *He's out?* I'll be damned. Nah, Dougal and Toft are both in the wind. Can't find either one. Dunno. Right. Is he cooperating? Yeah, 'bout what I'd expect. What're you gonna do?" He exhaled. "Yeah, he's probably long gone but you gotta try. Maybe y'all will have better luck than me. I'll let you know. Right. Thanks for the call."

He tapped off and took a step toward us. "Scooter Jablonsky got all charges dropped."

"*What?*" I exclaimed.

"The cops arrested him based on evidence they found on his computer. Emails to and from gas distributors, invoices for carbon monoxide cylinders, and articles on an anesthesiologist in Hong Kong who filled leaking yoga balls with carbon monoxide that killed his wife and kid. Jablonsky's defense team had a forensics analysis conducted on that computer. They found malware that allowed someone to take control of his laptop."

"Like Matt's rootkit thingy on the lottery computers?" I asked.

Johnny jumped in to correct me. "That hasn't been established."

"Allegedly," I added, throwing him a look.

"Beats me," Finn said, gesturing toward Aiden. "You'd have to ask those guys. But the point is, Jablonsky downloaded the malware through an email that allowed the killer to later plant emails and documents leading the cops to him. When his lawyers presented the evidence to the prosecutor, she dropped the charges."

"So now what?" I asked Finn.

"Lil has an arrest warrant out on Rod Toft for the murder of Olivia Fantucci."

"What?" I exclaimed. "Rod?"

Finn nodded. "Yup. They raided his office and found evidence on one of his laptops proving he created the malware used against Jablonsky. Plus, he had the opportunity and motive, knocking out a contestant. They've got his contest partner, Volkov, cooperating. Albeit, reluctantly."

I shook my head. "Doesn't make sense. Rod doesn't fit our profile of a seven. An intellectual. A deep thinker. Someone refined. Rod Toft is *far* from all that, unlike Karsh Azarian."

Finn put out a cautioning hand. "Hang on now, you're talking 'bout the contest founder's profile. I ain't so sure the founder is also the killer. No apparent motive for him to kill one of his own contestants. Seems to me you're confusing the two cases. Lil is investigating the murder. The FBI here is working the lottery scam."

"I can see Azarian being both," I said defensively.

Matt sat up and twisted toward me. "Hey, Sis. Remember that sheet music with the embedded safe combination? I believe it was Chopin's 'Etude in C Sharp Minor Opus Ten, Number Four.' You said somebody played the heck out of it?"

"Uh-huh. He was amazing."

"Who was it?" Matt asked.

I gave him a little headshake. "Jimmy Dougal. Why?"

Matt looked over to Finn. "That the same guy you can't find?"

"One of 'em," Finn replied.

"No way it's Jimmy," I protested. "He's nothing like an intellectual. He's a dang real estate agent."

"Yeah, 'bout that," Finn said. "With Dougal, it ain't just I can't find him."

I cocked my head toward Finn. "What do you mean?"

"I can't find no evidence of him. Anywhere. Like he don't exist. Even that real estate website of his I found earlier? The one with no listings? It's gone, too."

Chapter Forty-Five

Who are you?

A voice blasted from the Gorgas Library PA that about caused...Let's just say I was immersed in my studying, had multiple bottles of water in me, and it *really* got my attention. It was the Friday night before Finals Week started, after which next Saturday I will be attending graduation at Coleman Coliseum. Hopefully, as a relieved but proud participant sitting on the floor. Not as Zoe's guest in the audience.

It was hard to believe a little over six weeks ago I convinced myself that skipping two weeks of classes to participate in the contest, including GBA480, the destroyer of dreams, was no biggie. That I could handle it. After all, I was on pace to graduate *cum laude*. It was only four measly classes per course, and I could get the lecture slides from my professors. So, I bet on myself, which at the time, made perfect sense. But right now, as I struggled to absorb the missed lectures, that bet was looking shaky. The odds of passing GBA480 were looking grimmer and grimmer with each passing day, and all I got out of the contest was a pissed-off founder looking to get revenge for me not buying that dang ticket. Like Finn said to the feds, it wasn't a question of if. It was when.

I gathered my notebooks and flashcards, stuffed

them in my backpack, and plodded out into the heavy night air. It was midnight and low dark clouds obliterated any natural light, setting a somber stage as I took the path exiting the Quad toward Capstone Drive where I could catch a campus bus to my parked car. As I approached the gleaming-white Round House, a pre-Civil War former guardhouse, a quick movement in the shadows between it and Gorgas Library caught my attention. I continued on the path, but kept a watchful eye on the narrow space between the buildings.

When I reached the turreted structure, a shadowy figure stepped out from behind it. "*Pssst*. Over here, dear."

I stopped and peered into the darkness. "Mrs. Majelski?" I whispered.

The figure took a step toward me, a head of soft white curls catching a hint of light from Gorgas. "No names. Get over here."

I glanced around, then scurried off the path toward the old lady as she slipped back into the darkness between the Round House and Gorgas. When I reached her, she was deep in the narrow recess between the two buildings. "What are you doing here?"

She put a gnarled finger to her lips. "Shhhh. Keep your voice down. We need to talk."

"Now? Here? I'm exhausted. How about tomorrow? At your place."

"No time, dear. I'm leaving tomorrow."

"Leaving? Where to?"

"Overseas."

"Overseas? Where?"

"Around." A wink. "You know, here and there."

I stared down at the ancient lady. The last time I

had seen her, or thought I'd seen her, was at El Sueño in the hall outside my suite. "Why did you run from me at El Sueño? And why were you even there?"

"Pish posh. I'm always looking out for you. You know that."

"But why did you run?"

"You know why."

I gave her a little headshake. "No, I don't."

"It's why I'm here now. I won't be able to protect you while I'm gone."

The more I talked with this enigma, the more confused I got. "Okay, whatever, forget about why you ran. You said you can't protect me. From who?"

"Him. It's far from over, dear."

"You know about Laszlo Nagy?"

She chuckled lightly. "Of course. Although not much to know. I just got back from California. I can't find anything about him before twenty years ago when he bought that IT company out there. Just appeared out of thin air. That's why I'm leaving tomorrow."

"I don't understand."

"The best way for me to find him is to follow his trail when he was Nagy. We know he left California and came to Birmingham about ten years ago. While there, he—"

"*We?* Who's we?"

Mrs. Majelski waved a burly hand at me. "Watch your voice." She stared back through the narrow space we were in toward Capstone, then around me out into the Quad, then back up at me. "You and I. *We.*"

I studied her wizened face. Even in the dark, there was a hardness to it, despite the fleshy jowls and droopy nose. "I don't believe you."

She shrugged. "Okay."

The more I stared, the steelier her eyes became. "You're going to the Cook Islands, aren't you?"

Her eyes stayed locked on mine. "Perhaps."

What I earlier thought was a coincidence quickly faded during the last few minutes. "Did you buy that ticket?"

With brows knitted, she asked, "What ticket?"

"You know what ticket," I hissed.

Her face wrinkled into a sly grin. "The jackpot-winning one?"

I leaned down toward her. "Versus what?"

She didn't budge, just stretched her neck upward. "I don't play games of chance, dear, but I do enjoy playing with you."

I pulled my head back. "Just what does that mean?"

Mrs. Majelski cackled quietly, her eyes lighting up as her demeanor relaxed. "You're cute, that's why I like you. Of course I didn't buy that ticket. But you're correct, I *am* going to the Cook Islands. Part of my skip-tracing process."

"For Nagy?"

She nodded firmly. "Or whoever he is."

"You don't think that's his real name?"

With a shake of the head and another glance around, she said, "Not a chance."

"Why don't you just let the FBI track him down?"

She let out a hoarse chuckle that ended with a choked cough. "You know why. They can't find him. Neither can Finn."

I considered her. It was time to pop the question. The one that has been nagging at me ever since

385

freshman year. "Who are you working for? Homeland? The FBI? CIA?" I lowered my head. "*Mossad?*"

The super-senior was unfazed. "Does it matter?"

"Yeah, it kinda does."

She looked off, pausing for a moment, then back up at me. "In life, dear, there are some questions one should never ask." A beat. And another. Then a third. Her gray eyes bored into me as she raised a finger. "Just always remember, no matter what you hear, what anybody says, I'm one of the good guys. And I will always protect you. As best I can."

With those words, my head exploded. A thousand thoughts tore through my mind, from the very worst to the very best. Ever since I met the lady three years ago at the gym, Mrs. Majelski remained an ever-shifting dynamic I could never fully get my arms around. From that first day, when she embarrassed me with her treadmill and iron-pumping feats, every time my life took a turn, she appeared out of nowhere with a helpful hand. Or a hidden compartment in her truck. Or a deftly-wielded blowtorch. Or words of sage advice. Or sinister warnings. And after each, she would disappear. Until the next sharp turn. But she always seemed to be there, hiding in the shadows, like we were now.

"Who are you?" I asked. "Really."

She gave me a thin smile and slow shake of the head. "You didn't hear a word I said, dear."

I crossed my arms and stuck my neck out. "Oh, I heard. Who are you? *What* are you? And, why me?"

For a brief second, I saw emotion in her, like I hurt her. But as quick as it came, it went. Her resolve hardened. "Has it ever occurred to you that your actions two years ago crossed somebody, a person of considerable means and resources, and that made you a target ever since?"

"What are you talking about?"

"Somebody with a very long reach."

A shiver ran through me as I considered the old lady. She appeared dead serious. "Two years ago? What the heck are you talking about? *Who* are you talking about?"

"I don't know. That's why I'm leaving tomorrow. To find out."

"You mean Nagy?"

"Or whoever he is, yes."

I could feel myself starting to freak out. "You're scaring me, Mrs.—"

"*No names.*" She studied the Quad behind me, then put a hand on my arm. "You need to get going, dear. We've been here too long."

I grabbed her wrist. "I believe you. I think. You've never done anything to hurt me. I think. So, if you're leaving, and I've made someone angry, who's going to protect me?"

She patted my arm with her other hand. "Stick close to Finn. He's a good guy."

"Does he know what you know?"

"I briefed him. He knows enough."

Just when things couldn't get more confusing, she drops that little line on me?

"Like what?" I asked.

"That over the last two years, your stumbling and bumbling and independent curiosity has cost someone a *lot* of money." She stared hard at me. Even in the dark, there was a fire in her eyes. "And that person isn't going to stop until you've been destroyed."

I swallowed hard as I held her gaze, my mind racing back over the past two years. "You mean…"

She nodded slowly. "This entire time, there's been an overall mastermind you've been dealing with, only you never knew. Until right now."

"That's impossible," I said, taking a step back. "I mean, the whole Carlton affair? If what you're saying is true, that would be such a random coincidence that…" I rattled my head. "It's just too bizarre."

"Occasionally, dear, bizarre coincidences occur in this world. People's paths cross multiple times for no apparent reason." She shrugged. "Makes things more difficult to sort out sometimes." A pause. "Or impossible."

"But Dad always says there's no such thing as coincidence."

"He's wrong. It's rarer than people think, but it does happen. Believe me."

"And that's why you're leaving. To catch this mastermind."

"It has to end. I won't live forever, dear."

That thought hammered me. Mrs. Majelski's mortality never occurred to me. The ancient relic was vitality itself. I couldn't imagine her…Well, it just was impossible to consider. I shoved it out of my mind.

"Where are you really going?"

"I told you. Cook Islands. From there, we'll see. Maybe Palermo."

"Palermo? Doesn't a bank there hold the El Sueño mortgage?"

She nodded. "I'm also interested in the olive groves there. Fake extra-virgin olive oil is big business."

"Nagy is into that, too?"

"It's possible. Great way for him to launder his money."

"From the lotteries he scammed?"

Another nod. "Among other schemes."

"Like antiquity smuggling?"

She put a finger alongside her nose, then pointed at me. "You need to go."

"How long will you be gone?"

She shrugged. "As long as it takes."

"Like a month?"

"Or months." A pause. "Could be years."

"That long to catch him?"

Mrs. Majelski pushed on me to leave. "You really need to go."

I stood firm. "That long to catch him?"

The little old lady stared up at me, set her jaw, and shook her head. "That long to *end* him. And all of this."

I stepped out of the shadows, but when I turned back to say goodbye, she was gone.

Who was this lady?

Chapter Forty-Six

Nice shoes?

This was it.
Or was it?
I was sitting in a sea of black on the floor of the University's Coleman Coliseum, wearing sparkly high-top tennis shoes I specifically bought for the occasion. My heart was racing as the perspiration machine cranked things up. Finals Week didn't exactly end as I envisioned with me sailing through my exams and going out celebrating the night before my graduation as an esteemed business major. Instead, during my GBA480 final at Bidgood Hall, which was the last one on the University's exam schedule, I locked up. When I read the exam's first essay scenario, Mrs. Majelski's words last week behind the Round House came crashing down on me, shoving any remnants of studying out of my brain and obliterating my ability to recall anything. Up until that point, I had done a good job not thinking about what she told me. But for some reason, with graduation dangling in the balance, that haunting moment came flooding back. It took me a good thirty minutes before I could focus enough to gather my thoughts and start writing. But when I left the classroom, I knew it was over. No way I was graduating the next day.

For whatever reason, the University schedules commencement the day after finals end, so there were always a few prospective graduates swinging in the wind. Like me. I left Bidgood yesterday afternoon considering my options. Become an English major. Forget about ever graduating and work full-time for Finn. Or open my own detective agency.

I tried logging into the University computer late last night to check if my GBA480 grade was posted. Of course, the website was down for unscheduled maintenance. And this morning before I had to leave for Coleman, it was still down. Just one more parting shot by the Universe.

The University president continued to drone on about something, but nobody was paying attention. Do any of these mind-numbing speakers realize none of us listen to them? All around me, soon-to-be graduates whispered among themselves. Undoubtedly about me.

Pssst. Did you hear? Sara Donovan isn't walking today.

I know, right? I hear she bombed her last final.

I've heard of this happening. How embarrassing. Can you just imagine?

Hey, dude, what're you doin' tonight? Goin' to that kegger?

Within ten minutes of me sitting in my rock-hard folding chair, I was a squirming, fidgeting mess. No matter how much I tried, there was no waking my butt. And while it blissfully snoozed, my besieged brain couldn't concentrate on anything. *GBA480* kept pulsating through my terrified body, making it difficult to breathe. For all I knew, the University president was informing the entire gathering of my status.

Ladies and gentlemen. Before we begin today's joyous ceremony, please be advised that Sara Donovan, who we thought was one of our better students and on her way to graduating cum laude, unfortunately failed her very last final. Therefore, she will not be graduating today. Thank you, parents, grandparents, and friends of Sara Donovan, for coming to see your daughter, granddaughter, or friend fail spectacularly in a public and humiliating fashion. Security, please escort Sara Donovan from the premises. Parents, grandparents, and friends of Sara Donovan, please feel free to stay.

I spotted Mom, Dad, and Matt in the crowd and waved, just as my phone buzzed. It was Zoe.

—*Turn around you idiot.*— her text said.

I discreetly twisted in my seat, making sure I didn't lose the stupid cap stuck to my head. And I mean *stuck*. Mom said she just used a few bobby pins, but I swear she stapled the crap out of it directly to my scalp. And who came up with these getups anyway? I looked like a dysmorphic blob of black polyester with a dang board stapled to my head.

Five rows back, little Zoe stood on her chair with an exaggerated smile, waving wildly at me, the new crimson streaks in her hair blazing from beneath her cap. I flipped her a brief wave and smile before turning back to face forward.

—*You're crazy.*— I texted back.

—*Right? Relax, girl, ur gonna b fine.*—

—*IDK. So screwed.*—

The row in front stood and filed out toward the stage. Right after I put the phone away in a pocket that stopped somewhere down around my knees, it buzzed. I took it back out and saw it was a text from Finn, who earlier in the day surprised me by showing up at my cottage clean-shaven and freshly shorn, the ponytail no longer. He brought Bertie to see Mauzzy and a wide gap-toothed grin for me. When I asked why he came, he said with a hearty laugh and wink, "Wouldn't miss it for the world, 'cause seeing is believing."

I read the text.

—Just wanna be the first to say Congratulations to my best employee. Look to your left.—

I turned.

The phone buzzed again.

—Your other left.—

Fricking GBA480 and Laszlo Nagy. I shifted my gaze to the left. Finn was standing and swinging his arms back and forth over his head like a castaway signaling a passing rescue plane. We made eye contact, and he started jumping up and down, his arms still flapping. This was my boss? It was by far the most animated, and crazily uninhibited, I'd ever seen him. I can't believe he's allowed to carry a gun.

Finn's antics forced a giggle out of me before I faced front and noticed our row was about to stand and march me to my doom.

I fired off a text to Zoe before I had to put my phone away. *—It's been great—*

Crap.

The phone tumbled out of my hand and onto the floor beneath the chair in front of me. I bent down for it and—*crack*—my forehead smacked the edge of the front chair's seat. As my head rebounded upward, one of the corners of my unfashionable headwear caught the underneath of the chair's back, ripping the cap forward off my head along with I'm sure half my hair and scalp.

The left side of my row had already exited and fallen into the procession line. The students to my other left were standing there, turned, waiting to file out. Waiting for me. I fumbled with the cap, trying to straighten it back on my balding head. With it halfway secured, I angled my body and crouched back down, reaching cautiously for the phone. Grabbing it, I slipped it back into the cavernous pocket, and got ready to file out. I swung to my left, smack-dab into a glaring girl whose own cap was precariously perched atop way out-of-control frizzy hair.

I gave her a look that said, '*I understand you're annoyed at me holding up the line, and the Alabama humidity totally blowing up your hair, but at least you're graduating. Be grateful.*'

Yeah, it was a multi-level killer stare.

I casually eased around to my other left and filed out of the row and on to my public demise. Within one minute, I was standing at the base of the steps leading up onto the stage. At the top of the steps and standing behind a lectern, the cool linguistics professor continued to read off each name. Every year the dude was the rock star of the ceremony. His pronunciation of every name was so perfect he never stumbled to get a name right. And some names looked like word jumbles from hell. Each time he flawlessly announced a name and any honors, the named student climbed four stairs and walked across the stage amid applause, whistles, and shouts from the stands. After shaking hands with the president and dean and posing for a photograph while receiving his or her coveted diploma, the graduate exited the stage at the far end, taking maybe six or seven seconds. Then the next name was called and the ritual repeated itself. It was an exercise of precision and cadence. One that was going to be disrupted when my name wasn't called and I had to slip across in *front* of the stage while the murmurs rippled through the crowd.

That's her.

Did you hear what happened?

I've heard about this happening before. How awful.

The dude in front of me climbed the stairs and worked his way across the stage, garnering all the accolades and applause I'm sure he so richly deserved. Probably an English major.

"Sara Maria Donovan, *cum laude*."

Over my shoulder, I gave one last b-slap glare at the girl, whose hair impossibly seemed to have frizzed up even more in the last minute, before I sidestepped around the stairs to cross in front of the stage. A man cleared his throat from atop the stage. I stopped and looked up. The cool linguistics professor was staring at me over his reading glasses. What was his fricking problem? I was leaving as fast as possible. Deal with it, dude.

"Sara Maria Donovan, *cum laude*."

I eyed him and pointed tentatively to myself. He nodded back with a faint smile and motioned to me with his eyes to get moving *up* the stairs. Not *around* them.

The realization slammed into me. Oh, my God. I passed. Somehow, someway, I passed fricking GBA480.

I smoothly sidestepped back, whipped around, and

smiled ever so sweetly at Frizzy Hair. Before the dean or my professor could change their minds, I ran up the stairs to receive the accolades and applause that I, Sara Donovan, *cum laude*, so richly deserved. How, I had no idea, but mine was not to question. They obviously knew what they were doing.

I smiled broadly to the cool linguistics professor as I cleared the top of the stairs and advanced smartly toward the outstretched hand of the president.

"Congratulations, Sara" the president said, shaking my hand. "We're *very* proud of you."

"Thank you. *Thank you*."

I took three more steps and shook hands with the dean as she handed me my diploma case. "Congratulations, Sara," she said with a slight head bob and professional smile.

"Thank you, dean." My excitement was so high I almost choked saying the words. We posed for a photograph, and I turned to leave the stage.

I was now a graduate of the University of Alabama. The Capstone. The stage was miles beneath my flying feet. As I floated toward the exit stairs, I peeked inside the diploma case. Just to make sure.

A shot of adrenaline jolted me like a double espresso.

There was no diploma.

Ah, but there was a note saying I would get my diploma after I turned in my cap and gown. That was a trade I would gladly make.

I arrived at the top of the stairs and stopped.

Holding the diploma case high in the direction of Mom and Dad, I lit up the coliseum with my profound elation. Fueled by equally profound shock. Gathering myself, I reined in the flowing robe and prepared to enter my new world as a college graduate. Starting down the first step, I made a snap decision. Laying head back and thrusting the diploma case toward the rafters, I closed my eyes in pure unbridled ecstasy and hollered at the top of my lungs, "*Roll Fricking Tide!*"

Not missing a beat, the crowd murmured, "Roll Tide."

With my arm, head, and eyes lifted upward exulting the heavens, the rest of my body forgot what it was supposed to be doing. The result? My left foot missed the next step and I went tumbling down the stairs. At the bottom was just a black heap of polyester—and a 'Bama diploma case. "Roll Tide," I repeated peacefully from the floor.

That was clearly a bad snap decision. As most of mine were. But I didn't care. I was a new business graduate of the University of Alabama. Ready to kick butt and take the business and PI worlds by storm.

As I lay there, reveling in my unexpected success, I remembered seeing a second note tucked in one of the upper corner ribbons. I cracked open the diploma case. A small square of white paper stared back at me. On it were neatly printed words.

You have cost me dearly. I do not believe in violence, but do believe in vengeance. And I shall have mine. Until we meet again, my dear. By the way, love the shoes.

I jumped up and scanned the crowd in the stands. Perched at the end of a row by a concourse exit, a large pair of binoculars beneath a low-slung red ballcap looked directly down at me, the face obscured by the lens and hands. But as I stared at the person, the binoculars slowly came down, and vibrant blue eyes locked onto my widening ones. A gleaming white smile crossed Jimmy Dougal's beautiful shaven face as he wagged a finger at me. I turned to signal Finn that Nagy—Jimmy—was here, but my crazy boss was gone. And when I looked back to Nagy, he was gone, too.

Deep in the concourse, a flash of white hair shot past the section opening.

At that very moment, I realized, my new reality was just beginning.

****

Back at my packed-out cottage, no doubt Mauzzy was sharing his recliner with his best bud in the whole world, Bertie the Narc. Together, they made a formidable team.

They waited. And not just for dinner.

They watched. Also, not just for dinner.

Bertie listened, ready to call out the next unsuspecting dupe's deceptions and lies.

And Mauzzy, he contemplated life after graduation. His future. My future. Our future.

He was my Sweet Handsome.

And I loved him.

Acknowledgements

Writing a book is extremely difficult and takes the input and assistance from so many people to eventually transform a "what if" idea into an actual book available in virtual and brick-and-mortar bookstores. This is my attempt to put arms around all of you who helped me get *Lucky Secrets* out of my spinning head and into a book.

First and foremost, my humblest thanks, appreciation, and copious amounts of love to my amazing wife, Mary, for all that you have done to support me. Throughout the writing process for the book, you have been a cheerleader, beta reader, editor, psychologist, sounding board, listener, cover consultant, (did I mention psychologist?), and most important of all—a partner. Plus, incredibly understanding and patient. And when this book hits the market, add chief marketing rep and salesperson to your titles—"Hey, you, buy my husband's book!" Words can never express my gratitude, thanks, appreciation, and love, so this lame paragraph will have to do—until the next book when hopefully I can do better.

A gazillion thank-you's to my brilliant and very well-read daughter, Maria, for continually getting me out of my head (a very scary place to be, trust me) and back on track during my in-depth plotting process. Like your mother, add psychologist to your resume for the countless hours you sat with me at the outset as we talked things through, during which you poked, prodded, and repeatedly questioned me until the plot eventually crawled out and presented itself. Only to do it *all over again* after I was halfway into writing the sixth chapter when I decided the plot was too soon in Sara's development and I set the entire project aside after two months of building out the story (this will become the fourth book in the series). Like a pro, you listened to my reasoning, gave me a paper bag, instructed me to breathe into it, and then got to work pulling yet another plot out of my muddled brain. Without you and your spreadsheet (wink), this plot would have been the proverbial Swiss cheese of plots.

Speaking of Swiss cheese plots, a massive thank-you to Giselle Palmer for sucking it up and agreeing to read the manuscript and provide input after I thought it was ready to send off to my editor. Boy, was I wrong. Giselle, you saved me too many times to mention with your insight and tremendous attention to detail, politely pointing out plot holes, areas that didn't make sense, and places that needed improvement—like the ending! I am extremely grateful for your time and willingness to help. The book is so much better because of you. BTW, my offer stands to come in and talk with your students. If I can encourage just one child to aspire to becoming an author, then it's time well spent. Plus, it gets me out of the office where I spend the days banging my head against the desk searching for the perfect plot angle, the perfect sentence, the perfect word, the perfect… Sigh.

To my developmental editor, Jeni Chappelle, and Lea Schizas, editor with The Wild Rose Press, your encouragement and guidance continue to be priceless. Thank you for wading through my jumble of words and helping me see the forest, then guiding me through said forest. Editing a mystery is complicated because so many elements are tied together, and when one starts pulling on that thread, bad things can happen—like an unraveling plot. And author. Because of your herculean efforts, not only did the plot and I not unravel, it and I became unfathomably better. It is said a good editor is worth his/her weight in gold, but for both of you, it is platinum. Or better yet, palladium.

Barbara Doll, a good friend and lover of my Italian cooking, thank you for allowing me to include you in the book and take a little poetic license with your character. After all, you're not a chef. Insert sly smile. Although, if pressed, I suppose you could wield a wooden spoon "like a crazed ninja in a knife fight." It was loads of fun writing you into some scenes, so many thanks.

Emily Lilley, co-owner of the wonderful Book and Cover bookstore and co-host of the Thursday Murder Book Club, thank you for your support, kindness, enthusiasm, and willingness to allow me to include Bertram, aka Bertie, in the book. I thoroughly enjoyed writing him into the plot, and am excited to include him in the list of ongoing characters for the series. Mauzzy is also appreciative.

And speaking of the Book and Cover's Thursday Murder Book Club, thank you to all the "murder folks" in the club for allowing me to soak up and process all your insightful thoughts on what works, and more importantly, what doesn't, in mystery novels. Every month it's fascinating to listen to astute readers share their thoughts on characters they like or dislike and why; a story's strengths and weaknesses, and gasp, plot holes; and the infamous 0-5 rating segment at the end of the meeting with all the reasons given for each rating. You're my unwitting focus group that I hold near and dear, and your lively input has made me a much better writer.

A big thank you to The Wild Rose Press and co-founders Rhonda Penders and RJ Morris for believing in me and my stories. Getting a book through the editing gauntlet to the release date can be difficult, frustrating, and more, like a trip-to-the-dentist more, yet you make it as painless as possible. That speaks volumes about your leadership, vision, and management, and all the great people at The Wild Rose Press.

To my mother, Ida Lou, thank you for your support and encouragement going *all the way* back to when I was a wide-eyed fifth grader expressing an interest in being an author. It may have taken a "few" decades, but now I have three books out and more to come. Every time I write a book, it reemphasizes you were right all those years ago—that I can truly do anything if I put my mind to it. Thank you, Mom.

A huge thank you to Mauzzy for all your antics, your personality, and your gift of life to my family. I am proud to be able to immortalize you in my books. You deserve it. Rest in peace, my man.

Finally, the biggest thank you of all to you, the reader, for choosing my book out of the millions that are published each year. I hope you enjoyed the read, had a chuckle or three, and couldn't solve any of my riddles and puzzles. Wink. Keep reading and remember to smile at least once per day. And if you can laugh each day, even better.

Praise for B.T. Polcari

Against My Better Judgment

2021 Eric Hoffer Awards—Honorable Mention, Mystery/Crime category; Grand Prize Finalist; First Horizon Award Finalist

2022 Readers' Favorite Awards, Silver Medalist

2022 American Fiction Awards, Category Finalist

"Polcari's debut novel…the first book in a series, is a winner.…spot-on dialogue and characters…laugh-out-loud funny…a mystery of plot twists and adventure. Readers of all ages will find much to like in this page-turning offering, keeping them reading into the wee hours."

—Recommended, The US Review of Books

Fire and Ice

2022 American Fiction Awards, Category Finalist

2023 Eric Hoffer Awards—Mystery/Crime Category Finalist

"Both young and adult readers will quickly be charmed by this standalone sequel to *Against My Better Judgment*, the first book in Polcari's award-winning A Mauzzy & Me Mystery Series. …a well-researched crime-busting adventure that takes on ever-deeper meaning and mystery with every page.

—Recommended, The US Review of Books

A word about the author...

B.T. Polcari is a graduate of Rutgers College of Rutgers University, an award-winning mystery author, and a proud father of two wonderful children. He's a champion of rescue pups, craves watching football and basketball, and, of course, loves reading mysteries. Among his favorite authors are D.P. Lyle, Robert B. Parker, and Michael Connelly. He is also an unapologetic fantasy football addict. He lives with his wife in scenic Chattanooga, Tennessee.

www.btpolcari.com